I0670369

To request permissions, contact the publisher at
ScharaReevesPress@gmail.com

Paperback: 978-1-7362987-5-6

First paperback edition August 2023.

Edited by Alyson Montione
Proofread by ScribeCat (ScribeCat.ca)
Cover art by Jake Bartok

Schara Reeves Press

ScharaReevesPress.com

ACKNOWLEDGEMENTS

Editor:

Alyson Montione

Proofreader:

ScribeCat (ScribeCat.ca)

Cover Art:

Image by Jake Bartok

Text by Ashley Harris (The Modern Jane)

General Support:

Jesus Christ

Family

Friends

Schoharie Library Writing Club

NYTHRIL

PRONUNCIATIONS

Aelor Ven (AY•lor vehn)

Allonbrais (al•on•BRAZE)

Ameri (uh•MAYR•ee)

Ascriot (AS•kree•ot)

Asher (ASH•er)

Astra (AS•trah)

Azxi (AHZ•she)

Baeno (BAE•no)

Bandilarian (ban•duh•LAYR•ee•un)

Bandon (BAN•dun)

Baradeen (bare•uh•DEEN)

Cederyc (SAID•rick)

Cerdris (SIR•driss)

Cithan (SIGH•than)

Coryn (COR•in)

Cyl (SILL)

Dannsair (Dan•SAYR)

Delnor (DEHL•nor)

Destrin (DES•trin)

Dia (DYA)

Drogan (DROH•gan)

Eatris (EE•tris)

Entrais (ENT•rays)

Ethian (EE•thee•uhn)

Farian (FAIR•ee•un)

Gavin (GAH•vin)

Graece (GRACE)

Grenedil (GREN•uh•dill)

Havirax (HAVE•uh•racks)

Ithynian Gasper (eye•THIN•ee•un GAS•pur)

Itso (IT•so

Ivinon (IHV•ih•nohn)

Jahng (J pronounced like ge in beige: JAHNG)

Julyn (JOO•lin)

Kaeden (KAY•den)

Kassander (CAS•and•dur)

Kayliene (kay•lee•EN)

Keeshiff (KEE•shiff)

Killyan (KILL•ee•an)

Kryso (CRY•so)

Kythdexlentu-Orsha (KITH•de•len•ta-OR•shah)

Laosim (LAOW•simm)

Lieris (LEER•ys)

Litash (lih•TASH)

Louko (LOO•co)

Lucian (LOO•shee•un)

Macridean (MACK•rih•dee•un)

Mariah (mah•RY•uh)

Matthes (MATH•es)

Melye (MEL•yay)

Merimeethia (mer•eh•MEETH•ee•ah)

Merym (MER•im)

Miadoris (mee•ah•DOR•is)

Mil-Seo (mill•SEOW)

Mitheau (MITH•eeyou)

Nythril (NITH•ril)

Omath (OH•math)

Ovok (OH•vok)

Ravyen (rah•VEE•en)

Ren Dhag (REN DAHG)

Rhioa (rye•OH•uh)

Rhumir (rue•MEER)

Rufio (ROO•fee•oh)

Rusie (ROO•see)

Silbyr (SILL•beer)

Soletuph (SOUL•tuff)

Tahrin (TAW•rinn)

Takarast (ta•ka•RAST)

Tallaman (TAW•lah•mahn)

Tehng (TENG)

Thikao (TEH•KOW)

Therune (theh•RUNE)

Tirzah (TEER•zah)

Tuloi (TOO•loi)

Tyron (TIE•ron)

Tzaro (TSAH•row)

Verzaer (Ver•ZAYR)

Xianti (SHAHN•tee)

Xyrilcylduin (zy•rill•SILL•doo•inn)

Zhahn (ZAHN)

A SUMMARY OF THE EXILED: A GAME OF WITS

They'd reached Nythril at last, but at a cost. Before crossing the border, Astra was captured by Tyron and Louko pursued to try and save her. When weeks pass with no word from either, Keeshiff takes some of his men to go after his brother and Astra. They find the two in dire condition with Astra near death and Louko deeply traumatized. Managing the treacherous journey back to Nythril and to the manor of Louko's uncle, Aelor Ven, Astra finds she is anything but safe when Tyron sends her a set of TetraChess and a note saying, *Your move.*

Before Astra can regain her health, she and Louko are summoned to the capital of Nythril by the ruler Dia Tzaro. The king arrests Keeshiff's men and uses them as collateral to force Astra into a quest to bring back an escaped prisoner. Along the way, more notes from Tyron appear, predicting each turn of events through moves on the TetraChess boards.

Dia Tzaro's escaped prisoner turns out to be a young Drogan—otherwise known as Myrandi—named Mitheau. Unwilling to turn her in, Astra, Louko, and Keeshiff decide to break the knights out instead of fulfilling Dia Tzaro's deal, but they're captured by Dia Tzaro's niece, the Drogan Hunter named Jahng, before they can do so. Astra and Keeshiff are imprisoned with the knights, while Louko is given back to the custody of his uncle.

With Astra deathly ill once more, they are out of time. Louko, his uncle, and the newly repentant niece of Dia Tzaro work together to stage a coup against Dia Tzaro himself. But they can't break Keeshiff and his men out first—the group survives a multi-day siege from within their prison cell. Meanwhile, Mitheau flies Louko and the barely conscious Astra back to Litash and to Astra's brother Entrais, getting her the help she needs just in time. But they are not as safe in Litash as they thought they'd be. Right as Astra is beginning to recover, Mariah arrives with the next note in Tyron's Game.

To Mira, the colorful personality behind
Dannsair, my wonderful childhood friend,
and the best dog a girl could ask for.

You will be missed.

THE EXILED:

BATTLE FOR THE BLACK QUEEN

A DAUGHTER'S RANSOM: BOOK V

BY NIAMH SCHMID

AND REBECCA SCHMID

CHAPTER I

Astra:

Twenty-three days since Astra had returned to Silbyr, and Astra wanted to find herself anywhere other than standing in front of the Court of Litash, clad in red-bronze chains. This seemed very familiar. Maybe except for the curtains...they must have redone those back when Astra had nearly toppled the place.

"So, you are telling us that Tyron returned from the dead, disguised himself as a Merimeethian dignitary, murdered their king, framed their princes, captured you, experimented on you, and left you so close to death that you had to come here for healing?" Lady Therune, Astra's elected prosecutor, stood poised as she asked the question. "Or did I miss something?"

Astra did not grace the question with an answer. Why bother?

The sound of fingers drumming against wood echoed from where Ent sat upon his throne, overlooking the crowded hall with deep displeasure.

Lady Therune turned back to the Court and continued her long speech. Honestly, Astra wasn't even listening anymore. This was the third day of the trial and it was just as much of a sham as the first day had been. The Court had already decided to indict her, whether they would say so or not, and now they just wanted to decide how to punish her. She hadn't realized how little power Ent had until she had been caught. He hadn't even been able to stop her from being thrown in the dungeon.

1

Granted, it was a very comfortable dungeon…but that had not seemed to cool Ent's open rage at the fact. Or Louko's panic, for that matter.

Astra wondered where Louko was in the crowd. No one would have expected the Merimeethian prince to be all the way in Litash, and few among the citizenry would know Louko enough to recognize him even if they did know he was here. So he'd slipped into the court hall and was somewhere listening. But Astra was in no position to search the crowd, nor did she want to bring any possible attention upon her friend. Instead, she looked back at Ent. Rarely had he borne such a dark countenance even in the days of The War, and it appeared that the nobles in the Court were a little anxious at his demeanor. Astra knew he was doing that on purpose. Funny how someone who had little power over the proceedings was yet able to have such a powerful presence.

"And will you still not say who it was that treated you?" Lady Therune's voice broke through Astra's wayward thoughts.

Not for the first time, Astra replied, "I will not." Even as much of a pain as her uncle was, she had no plans to reveal Tallaman's involvement to the Court. If they had proof that he—or any of the others—had known of her presence and never reported it, the Court would have the grounds to stir up further trouble. Bringing the Elves into this would only deepen the mess.

"Then how can you prove you were even injured in the first place?" the lady challenged. "You seem in well enough health to me."

Astra remembered her ragged reflection and decided to take that as a compliment. "I cannot prove it," she stated calmly.

"Might I suggest, then, the possibility that the Princess Astra was never in any danger, and returned to the capital for other reasons?" Lady Therune turned to the Court as she put the idea forward.

Many of the Court nodded. Others glanced at Ent, whose drumming fingers had increased their speed.

"Why, then, did you return, Princess?" The lady walked back towards Astra, regarding her with a certain cunning that left a sour taste in the girl's mouth.

"Do not ask me any question you have already asked and expect any answer different from the one you have already received. Neither should you bother to ask any question when you do not plan to take the reply seriously," Astra's answer was cold. "Investigate me as you wish, but I will not play any of your games." She'd had enough of games for a lifetime.

"Well, Princess, I might ask the same courtesies in return." Lady Therune smoothed her skirts as she spoke. "You continue to tell us Tyron is alive, and yet you have not given us any proof to back up that statement."

"But I have given you several pieces of information that would be simple enough to verify if you would but put in the effort to do so," Astra said, not bothering with frustration. That's exactly what this woman wanted.

"What you have suggested is that we walk up to Merimeethia—who we only have a tentative treaty with, mind you—and tell their steward that our exiled princess thinks he's a dead man walking." Her tone was haughty but calculated. "I trust you can see the complications of us taking such action."

Ent's fingers drummed even louder, if that was possible, and Astra saw him shift in his seat. She could feel his Gifting pulse with his anger.

"And didn't Kaedan serve under Omath *during* the time Tyron was in Alarune?" Therune asked.

"Kaedan was often known to disappear for months at a time. He told the king that it was for diplomatic purposes, but it would have been easy enough to travel back and forth between Alarune under that guise," Astra explained, hoping that someone listening would put the information to good use. "Another indication worth noting is that there is no record of Kaedan in Merimeethia until after Tyron's exile."

"She has a point." Whichever delegate spoke up sounded more moved by boredom than by Astra's case.

"A point? Perhaps," Therune turned to the panel, cocking her head and tossing her pale blond hair. "But still nothing more than vague conspiracies that she cannot prove. And certainly nothing which could constitute a threat to Litash—the *only* reason she might be pardoned for violating her exile, might I remind you. Besides, we all know that Nythril would say anything to give itself the excuse to attack Merimeethia. Why should we trust the word of a country that has only ever been hostile to our Merimeethian allies?"

And so the trial dragged on and on, Astra feeling more annoyed and restless than anything else. Finally, right when Astra thought she could have gotten up and screamed at the lot of them, the trial adjourned for the day. With this, Astra's numerous guards guided her through a back passageway and down a tunnel leading to the dungeon beneath the Proceedings Hall. This was one of the few spaces in Litash where neither the king nor the Ethian Council had any say.

The guards returned Astra to her cell and double checked the red-bronze shackles around her wrists. These were then attached to a longer chain that bound her to the stone wall. Yet this was done gently and with no shortage of apologies, for they were all former soldiers who had either fought under her brother or alongside Astra during The War. She did not hold their duties against them.

"Your friend was already waiting for you when we brought you down," one of the older guards said. "May we let him in?"

With Astra's nod, he motioned to one of the other soldiers who opened the door. In walked Louko, looking a combination of annoyed, deeply worried, and amused.

"That went well," he said as he plopped onto the stone bench beside her, setting the book he was carrying down on his lap.

"As ever," Astra commented in return. She tried not to sigh.

"How are you holding up?"

Astra looked at him for a moment. Here he was, forced out of his home and into a foreign country, not knowing if his brother or uncle was alive, putting up with a sister who had betrayed him, hunted by a man who had hurt him beyond belief...and he was asking about her. It didn't surprise her anymore—she knew Louko too well for that. And yet, that did not diminish the weight of it.

"Just tired, I think," Astra finally replied. "But I'm alright. How about you?"

Louko ran his hand through his hair. "I wish Keeshiff would get here."

Wanting to provide some form of comfort, Astra put a hand on his arm. The effect was somewhat lessened by her chains scraping over the stone. "Knowing him, he likely decided to come himself instead of sending word. It would take him some time to come all the way from Nythril."

"Yeah," He did not sound convinced. "I'm sure that's it."

They sat on the bench in silence until even the soft sputtering of the nearby torch seemed loud. What did Astra dare say? She didn't want to bring up Mariah, or Tyron's last note, or the Court....

"How, um, how is Ent doing?" she finally managed.

Louko shifted uncomfortably. "He's...doing well. I think?"

That was the worst thing about being in the jail below the Proceedings Hall. It was the jurisdiction of the Court—not the Council of Ethians. As such, they dictated all the terms of Astra's imprisonment. Ent was not even allowed to visit.

The sound of keys in the cell door startled them both and Astra looked up as one of the guards entered. She tried to recall his name. Riff, perhaps?

"Sorry for the interruption, but you have another visitor."

Astra straightened. "Did they give a name?"

"I thought I'd give it to you myself," came the familiar voice.

Louko jumped up—his book falling to the floor in the process. "Keeshiff!"

The guard stepped aside and let the visitor in. He was mud-splattered, half-soaked, in need of a shave and a bath, but it was definitely Keeshiff.

The elder prince's eyes widened as he realized too late Louko had ignored the grime and gone in for a hug.

"Oh—you—are stronger—than I thought—" Keeshiff wheezed, struggling to breathe in his brother's fierce embrace.

Louko let go awkwardly. "Oh, sorry. Just—er—glad you're alive," he said.

Astra watched them, unable to hide her smile. "We'd been worried when no one could get any news from Nythril."

Now Keeshiff's eyes lit up and, returning Astra's smile, exclaimed, "Astra! You look so much better." Then he paused, grin turning sheepish as he opened his arms. "While I'm making a fool of myself...do you mind?"

Er, well.... "Not at all."

He apparently needed no further encouragement, wrapping her in a giant hug that was somehow not suffocating. It was a little bit like hugging Ent. A much shorter Ent.

"Okay so this...*this* is a little awkward." Louko butted into the moment.

A second more and Keeshiff released his hold, stepping back and rubbing the back of his head as he turned to his brother. "What? She's like a little sister. It's not weird."

"But then that would mean she's my sister too...and that would be weird." Louko's face scrunched in disgust.

Astra...was a little lost. "Why would that be so bad?"

Keeshiff and Louko stared at each other, a grin forming once more on Keeshiff's face even as Louko's went beet red.

But just as Keeshiff was opening his mouth to say something Louko growled, "Shut up."

Astra had no idea what was going on. But she decided not to ask. "Speaking of sisters, perhaps we should tell him of who else has arrived."

The mood died almost instantly.

"Right," Louko's tone lost all its humor. "Mariah's here."

Keeshiff went rigid. "*What?*"

"Yeah. Showed up while Astra was recovering. Had Astra's broken bow and a note from Tyron. She claims she stole the note from his desk and ran off after she found out what was really going on," Louko explained. He'd voiced his doubt countless times to Astra.

"What a *convenient* change of heart," Keeshiff muttered in a low voice. "I hope they're keeping her in a cell like this one."

Astra stepped in. "My brother has her in a guest room within the palace. She is kept under a close watch."

"I will happily take you to see her whenever you wish. But perhaps you should...bathe, first. You look like a Merimeethian mud pit," Louko said with a smirk.

"I—" Keeshiff broke off whatever argument he was about to begin when he looked down at himself. Then he looked back at his brother and narrowed his eyes. "Fine. But I'd like nothing more than to throw *her* in a mud pit."

Louko raised an eyebrow. "Duly noted."

After Louko had scooped his fallen book from the floor, the brothers turned back to the door. Louko knocked to signal the guards.

"Let me know how it goes," Astra said. She sat back down on her bench before adding, "And be careful."

<u>Louko:</u>

"So how is she, really?" Keeshiff asked in Merimeethian as soon as they were out of the cell and away from any guards.

"Really much better," Louko replied, thinking back to just a few weeks ago when she'd been so close to death. That being said.... "She isn't sleeping much, though." He sighed. "I don't blame her. I just...yeah. Stuck in chains, again." Was there ever a time she wasn't?

Keeshiff had his hands jammed in his pockets. "Can't Entrais do anything about it? I mean, he's the king of Litash, isn't he?"

"I...things seem a bit more...complicated than I thought. Entrais seems to have almost no power over the Court," Louko tried his best to explain, frowning. "The Court and the Ethian Council seem to be two separate entities, and the king is only head of the Council."

"But isn't the Ethian Council supposed to have more ruling power than the Court?" Keeshiff asked. "Surely they can do *something.*"

Louko shrugged. "Things have changed, I guess." What he didn't dare say aloud was that most of the Court was apparently made up of the same people who had ruled during Euracia's bloody reign. One of the Ethians had said something about the Court using the chaos to seize more power when Euracia fell, meaning that the Ethian Council was little more than glorified bodyguards while the Court ran Litash however they wanted.

9

Safe to say, it was a far cry from the balanced system of ruling councilors and legislative courtiers that Tyron had once taught him about.

"I…see…" Keeshiff replied in a way that clearly showed he didn't quite understand, but he seemed to think better about asking for details as they came out into one of the many courtyards on the palace grounds.

"What about you?" he asked at last, seeming to understand that the topic of politics was too sensitive to talk about openly. "How are you doing with all this…" He gestured loosely with one hand. "…mess?"

"I've been worse." Right?

Louko felt more than saw Keeshiff's sideways glance. There was a pause, as if his brother was trying to figure out what to say. "We'll figure this out. I mean, we've made it this far and everyone's still alive."

Louko's laugh was a nervous one. "Yeah. That has to count for something. So…then everyone's okay?" He'd been loath to bring it up and terrified of what would be said when he did. But now even before Keeshiff replied, relief began spreading through him. No one had died?

"Your uncle is still incurably irritable and was solidifying his rule over Nythril, but the rest of us are fine," Keeshiff replied as they entered the palace through a small side door. "Nothing more than a few cuts and scratches, and Grandfather Asher patched those right up."

"I am glad to hear that," Louko replied, not hiding the sincerity behind it. Then he gingerly shouldered his brother in attempted playfulness. "Because I really didn't want my last memory of you to be me trying not to blubber like a fool." *Idiot*. That was awkward. Why had he brought that up? Forget *that*—what if he'd shouldered Keeshiff too hard? Or somewhere one of those 'cuts and scratches' had been?

Keeshiff laughed, a deep, warm sound that echoed more in Louko's mind than reality. "That's alright. I did my share of blubbering—just ask Astra." He shook his head and chuckled again. "I think she just does that to people."

Louko smiled against his will. "Yeah. She does."

They reached the other side of the courtyard at last and entered into yet another set of corridors leading to the guest wing.

Keeshiff looked at him again, this time with a weird kind of mischief in his expression. "Have you, uh, you know, talked with her yet?"

Brow furrowing, Louko stopped in his tracks. "Uh. Like...five minutes ago. You were there...."

"No, I meant," Keeshiff stopped, too, hands back in his pockets. "Like, *talked* with her."

Louko blinked. "Uh." Why was Keeshiff being so weird? "Oh look. We're at your room. What a shame," he said as they arrived at an empty guest room that had been prepared in anticipation of Keeshiff's possible arrival.

Grumbling something along the lines of, "Right, of course," Keeshiff stopped at the door.

"If you need anything, just let me know. My door is on the right. There are a few others here—Mitheau's down on the left and...Mariah is all the way at the end of the hall. Guarded by an Ethian, so don't worry. But if you need anything and I'm not around, feel free to ask one of them." He hated bringing up Mariah again. Even more, he hated telling Keeshiff where she was. They didn't need another murder in the family.

"Okay." Keeshiff dipped his head. He had one hand on the door latch, but still hesitated. "You know, this is kind of weird. Every time we've parted ways in the last few months, we weren't sure we'd see each other again. So, I guess I've forgotten how to say goodbye like a normal person." He chuckled, looking nearly sheepish.

Louko ran his hand through his hair and made an effort not to look embarrassed. "Yeah well, that's true. Should I just run down the hall? Close your eyes and count to three?" That was dumb.

"Those, uh, those actually sound more awkward than just going in my room," Keeshiff said, finally opening the door. "I guess I'll see you soon."

Now Louko grinned. "Hey, it worked. See you soon," he replied. He had no idea what in Eatris possessed him, but he brought his fist up and gave Keeshiff's shoulder a nudge like he'd seen some of the knights do playfully. Then halfway through the action he lost courage and just sort of brought up his hand to his hair and ran through it again, pretending nothing had happened.

Keeshiff looked at him, blinked, then made a face like someone trying to hold back a cough. He ducked into the room and closed the door behind himself. But it wasn't *quite* thick enough to muffle the sound of his laughter.

"I...I can still hear you...." Louko endeavored to remain serious.

The laughter inside only doubled.

"Um, what are you doing?" Louko spun around to find Mitheau staring at him.

"I, uh...hi. How long have you been—uh—standing there?" He swallowed the nervous chuckle threatening to find its way up.

Mitheau tugged on a strand of white hair. "Less than a minute, but I'm not sure that context would have made any of this clearer."

"Yeah...probably wouldn't." He rubbed the back of his head, realized that was something Keeshiff usually did, and somehow that devolved into him just looking at his hand awkwardly. With a cough he looked back at Mitheau. "Anyway.... Was there something you needed?"

"I was actually just going to ask how Astra was doing," Mitheau replied, but now her eyes wandered towards Keeshiff's door. "Did your brother bring any news about Grenedil?"

Oh. Right. "Everyone is alive and safe, from what I gathered." He swallowed the awkwardness still residing in the air, beginning to walk back down the hallway so that he wasn't standing outside his brother's door.

Mitheau's shoulders dropped slightly in relief as she fell in step with Louko. "That's good." But there was a measure of disappointment, too— disappointment that Grenedil had not come with Keeshiff, and honestly, Louko realized it was a bit odd. Why had Mitheau's friend stayed in Nythril?

"Astra is back in court tomorrow, correct?" Mitheau's next question broke his train of thought.

"Yes. Unfortunately." He sighed.

"Could I go with you?" Mitheau asked. "I mean, you always go to watch, right?"

Louko raised an eyebrow. "I mean...sure but I'm not doing anything important. Are you *that* bored?"

Mitheau scuffed the floor with one shoe as they walked—a very odd behavior for someone who was *apparently* sixty-three. "When you put it that way, yes. I'm tired of sitting on my hands and being useless."

"Well, you won't be much use in there either, I'm afraid." Louko couldn't say he didn't relate to her sentiment. "But you are welcome to join me if you want."

Sighing as if this confirmed some doubt, Mitheau still nodded. "Alright. Thank you."

Louko hated how crowded it was. On the one hand, it was good; it meant the common people were invested in this mockery of a trial and perhaps would put pressure on the Court. It also meant it was easier for him to blend in—not that people would recognize him anyway, unlike Keeshiff who had been forced to stay behind. But on the other hand...he hated crowds. And people. And being short.

"I can't see anything," Mitheau grumbled from next to him, elbowing a stranger that was trying to press between her and Louko. The man scowled and sidled around them.

"Join the club," Louko replied, craning as usual to try and see over the sea of heads.

He was distracted by the distant droning of Lady Therune, probably going on some new diatribe about how dangerous Astra was.

Then Mitheau prodded him in the ribs. "Hey, maybe we could actually see if we get up on those." She was pointing to a set of wooden crates stacked against the wall.

"Uh, I don't think…."

But Louko was too late; Mitheau was already pushing her way through the irritated bystanders.

So much for that. If only to keep her from getting into some unfathomable trouble, Louko went after her, constantly apologizing on Mitheau's behalf as he passed by the victims of her shoving.

Apparently, manners weren't a natural Drogan trait.

Mitheau clambered up onto one of the crates, peering towards the front of the hall. "I see her," she announced.

Louko was at a loss as to why seeing her mattered. He wasn't even completely confident who *her* was. The unpleasant Lady Therune or Astra all chained up and paraded in front of everyone? Either was an unflattering view.

Before he could clarify, however, Mitheau ducked and scrambled back down from her makeshift perch. Without warning, she grabbed Louko's arm and started pulling him towards the double doors in the back, whispering, "We need to get out of here."

"Uh…." Louko had been in enough absurd and time sensitive positions to know better than to fight against her grip, and yet it didn't stop his anxiety from rising to the roof even as his confusion rose with it. Was Astra in danger? What was happening? The crowd was suddenly even more suffocating than it had been before, and the room seemed to spin around him as Mitheau dragged him far away. He wanted to go back. What had spooked the girl? What about Astra?!

They slipped out the back doors, but Mitheau didn't stop. She pulled him at a run all the way across the courtyard and into the first wing of the palace.

Enough was enough. They were clearly out of danger *now*—if they'd even been in danger in the first place—and Louko was not going any further until he knew what was so terrifying. Digging his heels into the ground as he forced himself to keep his breathing steady, he practically yelled, "Would you stop just for a minute?"

Mitheau finally released her death grip on his arm. Her whole face was nearly as white as her hair, even after all the exertion of running across the courtyard.

"That's it, I'm going back in there." Panic tightened around his chest. What if Astra really *was* in danger?

"Wait," Mitheau panted. "I don't know if she saw me—she might have recognized me."

Having no self-discipline left, Louko grabbed hold of both her shoulders and shook her. "Mitheau, *who?!* What's going on?"

"Astra's prosecutor, she-she's," Mitheau was still stammering. "She's Myrandi, too."

Somehow this was...very anticlimactic. "Okay and *that* warranted you dragging me halfway across the court grounds in a panic? This is *Litash*; they have shifters literally running the country, Mitheau!" Of course, Mitheau wouldn't have been the only one to have the idea of hiding out in Litash. What exactly did this change?

Mitheau started shaking her head wildly. "You don't understand—her name is Tirzah. She's one of Ovok's daughters."

16

Louko went deathly still. "Wait. As in...she's Tyron's sister-in-law?"

"Yes." Mitheau's reply was nearly exasperated.

"Oh great, he's in The Court—we need to tell Entrais." Who, of *course*, was inside the hall at the moment, presiding over the trial. He ran his hand through his hair. Tyron was here. He knew they'd come here from the start. This was still part of his twisted plan. What did he want?! What was this stupid Game for? And... "So why does it matter if she recognizes you?" Louko suddenly turned his attention back to the still shaken Mitheau. Clearly, Tyron already knew where they were, and obviously Mitheau was one of the Drogans—er—Myrandi. Why would this be a problem?

"Because I don't know which side she works for anymore." Mitheau's voice dropped back to a near whisper. "When-when Ovok forced my people to leave, she was the one who kept us safe. When she couldn't do that anymore, she split us up to try and keep us safe. But if she's here—and under an alias—then she might be doing Ovok's bidding again."

"So...you're afraid she'd keep you safe?" Louko's head hurt.

Mitheau shuddered. "I'm afraid she'd bring me back. If Ovok has returned...." She trailed off and started shaking her head again.

Flustered, heart refusing to acknowledge the false alarm, and patience drained, Louko once more ran his hand through his hair and gave a gruff, "Fine then, stay out here. I'm going back in to try and see what this Tirzah wants with Astra and how it plays into Tyron's stupid Game. I don't have time for—" He stopped, flailing his arms. "—This. Whatever this is. I don't...." Realizing he was coming off a bit harsh,

Louko almost instantly deflated, adding, "Sorry, I am just...don't scare me like that. Stay out here and wait for the session to finish and then we can tell Entrais and figure out what's going on...because apparently things like being complicated."

Finally calmer, Mitheau gave a hesitant nod. She didn't say anything else as she took a seat on a nearby bench. Sixty-three or not, she really just looked like a kid when she was sitting there and swinging her legs.

Reluctantly, Louko turned and trotted back towards the Proceedings Hall, heart hammering unbearably as he tried not to think about the fact that Tyron's sister-in-law was trying to condemn his friend.

CHAPTER II

Entrais:

The clamoring of the Court hearing was still ringing in Ent's ears as the doors to his throne room shut behind him. He hadn't slept in days...or was it weeks? He was losing count. If not for the nightmares, he wouldn't even remember ever falling asleep. But now they didn't appear to *wait* for his eyes to shut. Everywhere there seemed to be spies, lurking and listening for him to make a mistake. And oh, he made plenty. He had played right into Tyron's twisted hand, sending Astra to Merimeethia with no one to protect her. He had left her to a repeat of what had happened in The War; the memories of which Ent still couldn't shake. How could she have survived that twice? As Ent shoved his scarred wrists into his pockets, he tried not to think of it.

But that was not something he was apparently good at. No. So many things crowded his paranoid mind, and yet the searing of knives and the echoes of chains against stone still floated to the surface, stealing the breath from his lungs.

This was all falling to pieces. He'd tried so hard to keep Astra safe—to get her out of the country so no one could touch her. Yet here she was, standing like some shackled prize as she was ridiculed and harassed hardly three weeks after she'd shown up in the middle of the night *dying*. And what could Ent do? Nothing. Absolutely nothing. The Court had its hands around nearly everything now, and as hard as he'd fought to keep control, it was slipping through his incompetent grasp.

He was letting Astra down. Again. He couldn't let it cost her life.

"Ent?" The voice called quietly from a little ways away, but even with the gentleness in the tone, it did little to stave off the clutch of panic that rippled through Ent's body. He reached for the sword at his side, swiveling around to find Jade.

She'd been waiting for him. Of course. Because she was always here. They were in this together; stuck going down with the ship just like they inevitably did every time.

"How did it go?" she asked.

Ent forced himself to release the hilt of his blade and remain calm, even as he wanted nothing more than to throw his hands up in the air and scream. "About as well as we expected. Probably a bit worse. It doesn't matter what the people believe because the Court has decided what *they're* going to do, and I can't do anything about it. I can't do anything but let it happen because I can't figure out what in Eatris Therune could want—except for maybe sending Astra back to—" His lungs squeezed, desperate for air as Ent suffocated under the idea of what Therune wanted. Was it really to send Astra back to Tyron?

"Then perhaps it's time to start exploring other options." Jade's voice drew him back to his surroundings. Very tentatively, she reached for his hand.

He jerked away at first, then muttered an apology. Stupid reflexes. "What other options? We've been exploring other options since she was found, Jade. I can't...I can't." He took a deep breath. *Get a grip. Calm down*. He needed to stop letting his mind go there. He couldn't leave her to Tyron again. He couldn't watch that happen.

Jade took his hands firmly now. "We know that she has others who are willing to protect her. Perhaps if we could get her back to Nythril, we could buy some time to get the Court back under control. I've already caught Soletuph up on what has happened." Her brother had returned with Keeshiff.

"I can't even get in to see her. How are we supposed to get her to Nythril?" Litashian prisons were literally *built* for those with Gifting. It was impossible to break her out—they had shape-shifter inhibitors and checkpoints everywhere. Ent had already made and discarded about a dozen plans.

"We will find something," Jade replied, ever persistent. "There are enough guards that are still loyal. And if we can't find a way to smuggle her out, then maybe there's a way to leverage her Elvish title without actually involving Cithan."

Cithan; the Elvish city. Ent's entire body tensed even further, if that was possible. He'd tried so hard to keep his parents out of this; to keep them safe. All he'd done instead was make Astra think she'd been abandoned. "Yes. We'll figure it out," he whispered the words, wishing he believed them.

A steady knock on the doors behind him nearly startled Ent out of his skin. He turned around just as Ascriot slipped in.

"Oh, um," The Ethian looked uncertain. "Are you alright? Is this a bad time?"

Inhaling sharply, Ent shook his head. "No. I'm fine, just...digesting everything from the hearing. What is the matter?" Was it Astra? Lady Therune? Had something happened?

Ascriot scratched the side of his head. "Well, um, your mother and father are here. And I think they caught all of today's hearing."

Jade squeezed Ent's hand a little harder.

As if things couldn't get worse. "Let them in."

With a dip of his head, the Ethian slipped out the door, but not before leaving Ent with a reluctant, "Good luck."

Ent was pretty sure he'd run out of that a long time ago. "This is going to be bad." Really bad. And the last thing they needed was a war between the Court and Cithan.

"Then we'll face it together," Jade murmured back.

But Ent's fears were only confirmed when *both* doors opened and his mother strode in. Her face was a shade of red that nearly rivaled her hair. "What in the *world*, Entrais?! We hear nothing from you in months— *months!*—and then we show up to find your sister in chains? On trial for *treason?!*"

"Ameri," came the much quieter voice from behind her as Ent's father walked in behind her.

Ent released Jade's hand and shoved both his own into his pockets. He had to keep it together. This wasn't the time. "I'm attempting to do...damage control. I'm sorry." Sorry wasn't good enough, he knew it. But what was the point in explaining any of it? They were right: He'd let Astra down. He'd let everyone down.

"Damage control?" his mother echoed, only more irate. "How did it even get this far? For goodness' sake, she's not even an adult! She should never have been put in this situation in the first place!"

"*Ameri*," his father, Destrin, cut in with more force, though not raising his voice. He put one hand on Ameri's arm and she clamped her mouth shut. Then he turned to Ent. "Sorry for the abrupt entrance. We left as soon as we received your letter, so there wasn't time to send word. Are you alright?"

"Yes, I'm fine—Astra's better but she's being held by the Court and not me so...I don't know if you will even be allowed to visit. It's very...complicated."

At the mention of Astra being alright, Destrin's shoulders sagged in relief.

"Complicated," Ameri grumbled. "She is our *daughter*. They have no right to keep her from us."

"Yes, complicated. There is more going on than can be explained, and we aren't at war anymore. We can't just go pulling out swords and causing anarchy, Ameri," Jade interjected despite Ent's silent plea not to. He'd seen the way her cheeks had reddened at his mother's tirade.

"I don't care how complicated it is. I'm seeing my daughter *now*." Ameri's eyes shone with the edges of rage. A rage Ent did not want to test. A rage he understood.

Destrin kept a hand on Ameri's arm. "Is there any way that we could rephrase it politically? Astra is still of rank in Cithan and Ameri is the appointed governor there. Doesn't the Court have to honor that?"

"I'll see what I can do," Ent rasped. "But please. Don't try anything...unofficial. Things are tense and we cannot risk jeopardizing Cithan when it's only just getting back on its feet."

His mother looked ready to burst, but his father nodded. "We understand," he said. Then he let out a deep breath. "So what exactly are they trying her for? And what do they stand to gain?"

"For violating her exile and endangering Litash. I...I am not sure what they want." Ent had several hunches, none of which were flattering. One included trying to get him to do something stupid that would get him deposed. Stupid politics. This was exactly why Ent had never wanted to be king. He hazarded a look at Jade, who was the only one he'd shared all those fears with. She met his eyes with that same quiet steadiness, and no matter how much he loathed eye contact, he was always able to find comfort in hers.

"How did they even *find* her?" Ameri's tone wobbled, a tell-tale sign that she was struggling to keep it at a reasonable level.

Here came the next wave. Ent took a deep breath to prepare for the hurricane of fury that would follow what he was about to say.

Only Jade beat him to it. "Tyron is alive and currently running Merimeethia under the guise of Kaeden. We don't know what he wants but we had suspicions he was in the Court for a long time. While he is not *personally* in their midst, he has spies. They are undoubtedly who leaked her whereabouts."

Ent had thought at the time sending Astra far away to Merimeethia was the safest place for her. That it was away from Tyron. Instead, he'd served her up to him on a silver platter. How could he ever forgive himself?

Destrin cut in before Ameri could. "*Tyron?* Are you sure?"

"Unfortunately," Ent murmured, not daring to look either of his parents in the eyes and instead looking out to one of the full-length windows off to the side. "He's likely been poisoning The Court's opinions for a while now."

Ameri went back to grumbling while Destrin frowned in confusion. "But, even if he has been alive all this time, what would he care? I thought he only ever wanted to get rid of Euracia—and you ended up doing that for him."

"I don't know," Ent replied, trying to ignore the dread growing at each passing moment. "I've been trying to figure it out and it doesn't make sense. He never seemed out for power and I didn't think he could be so ridiculously obsessed with Astra, but here we are and here we will stay."

Jade came a little closer. Why was Ent so weak? He felt like she was the one holding him up when they'd agreed to be there for each other. But they weren't cleaning up her mistakes; they were cleaning up his.

"Obsessed with Astra?" Ameri asked, her confusion bursting Ent's spiraling thoughts.

"That's what it seems." Ent's hands turned to fists from behind his back. There wasn't time for this. He needed to consult the Ethians and check in with Louko and get up to speed after the last hearing. It had been a firestorm, as usual. Explaining the mess out loud only made it feel worse. "He's messing with her with some stupid chess game and I don't know why. Apparently, he was running some form of experiments in Merimeethia and that's what almost got her killed."

Ent looked backed out the window. He didn't want to see the horror on their faces. But even then, he couldn't escape the sound of it in their voices. "Did you say *experiments?*"

"Yes. That's what almost killed her." There was no way to put this in a softer light and he was too exhausted to break it gently. He didn't care how angry they got, at this point. It couldn't be nearly as much as he was at himself.

Somehow it was even worse that neither got mad. They both stood in stricken silence until Destrin cleared his throat. "So, how are we going to get her out?"

"I am...working on it." *And failing miserably.*

Once more, Jade stepped in. "But this is *not* the place to be discussing things, and honestly, we've already said too much. Why don't you get settled and I can keep you updated if anything changes—"

She was interrupted by the door opening once again, and none other than Louko came hurriedly into the room. "So things are getting complica..." he trailed off, eyes widening as he noticed Ameri and Destrin. "Oh. Uh. Hi."

"...Louko?" It was Ent's father that seemed baffled. "What are you doing here?"

"Uh...I just...going wherever Astra goes, I guess." Louko looked over to Ent.

"It's...complicated." Ent wanted to just scream. *Everything* was complicated. Just...there was too much going on. Sitting around explaining it to everyone repeatedly did nothing but waste time.

Louko gave an awkward cough. "Speaking of...er...complicated things. There is some new information."

Ent's head was throbbing and he had to remind himself not to put a hand to it. "Then now is a good time to go somewhere more private. Mother, Father, please: Get settled and then meet me in my study. Louko—why don't we go there now." *Breathe. Just breathe.* He felt like his whole body was trembling with stress, making it incredibly difficult to think straight.

Whatever Ameri was going to say was cut off by Destrin taking her arm. "That sounds like a good plan," he said. "We'll be up soon."

Jade put a hand on Ent's shoulder before showing them out, but not even their exit from the room could completely hush his mother's disapproving grumblings.

"So...study? Then we can panic?" Louko's comment was far from helpful, and it was all Ent could do to remain composed as he struggled to breathe evenly.

"Yes," Ent replied, and without another word, led him through the shortcut to his study, where the Ethians, Faedrian and Tilera, were guarding the door. No one said a word as both Ent and Louko slipped inside.

"Alright." Ent began as he made his way around his desk and sat down—if only to avoid pacing. "So what has gone wrong, now?"

Louko sat down stiffly on the chair across from him, legs twitching as if he might spring back up again. "Well, not wrong, per se, but, uh, Mitheau said she recognized Lady Therune. Said she was a Drogan named Tirzah and, er," He ran a hand through his hair. "That she is Tyron's sister-in-law."

Ent sighed. At least it was none of his worst-case scenarios. Granted the situation as a whole was bordering one…. "I suppose it just confirms what we suspected. Tyron is trying to seize control. Does your friend know anything more that might help us with dealing with this Tirzah?"

Louko's shrug was taut. "I'm not sure. She was pretty freaked out about it; kept saying that she couldn't let Tirzah see her."

"Wait. Why?"

"Honestly, I'm not quite sure." Louko was back to running a hand through his hair. "Something about Tirzah's father? He's a Drogan lord named Ovok and I guess he was pretty bad. I think I'm more worried about her connection to Tyron."

Ent didn't like this. He felt so torn in every direction that he wasn't quite sure what needed more of his attention. What if he focused on the wrong thing, missed it, and caused Astra's death? He'd already done that so many times. He'd thought Tyron was here in Litash and not Merimeethia, and look what it had cost Astra.

"Alright. Well. Where is this Drogan lord, all the same?" The last thing he needed was for yet another face to show up and mess things up.

"Remember what I told you about that man Grenedil we met and how he kept talking about other worlds?" Louko paused, only continuing after Ent nodded. "Well, I guess he's on one of those other worlds. Mitheau seemed scared that Tirzah might somehow still be working for him."

"And didn't you say something about Tyron trying to get *off* world?" Ent managed to ask. Was that what the connection was?

Louko sighed. "I—yes, Grenedil mentioned that, too. I guess it's possible that that's who Tyron is trying to get to."

"Great, this is all connected." And all of this connecting didn't help much if they couldn't even figure out what on Eatris Tyron wanted! If it was even him pulling the strings. For all they knew, it could be Ovok who was the bigger worry. "And we still have no idea *why* Tyron wants off-world for sure? Does Astra have any other theories?" His throat caught on the name of his sister, and he again suppressed the urge to ask how she was. Horrible. She was probably doing horrible. How good could one be when wallowing in a dungeon?

"She isn't sure. She, um, she did mention some things from various memories and from, uh, when we were in there." Louko's tapping foot went still. "She thinks he's looking for someone, but didn't seem to be confident in the Ovok theory."

'There.' Neither Louko nor Astra ever referenced their capture directly. Ent couldn't blame them. "I see." At this point, it wasn't as if they could really do much about any of it. The most they could do was try and get Astra out. But with the Court now confirmed to be in Tyron's grasp, what exactly was their next plan?

Astra:

The next day, Astra was escorted from her cell before Louko could make it down to visit. Four guards walked behind her, four before, and one on either side—the usual arrangement. Between that and the

29

constant clatter of her chains, a dramatic entrance was inevitable. Astra and her entourage reached the corridor that led to the Proceedings Hall and already she could hear the cacophony of voices. It built higher and higher until they reached the entrance and the sound hit her like a wave.

Astra could pick out individual voices now. Calls of, "Look—there she is!" or "Look how many guards she has!" abounded. She even caught someone asking, "Is that really her? I thought she'd be taller."

As her guards led her to her place on the stand, she preoccupied herself by listening to the mixed opinions of the crowd. No one could decide on her, it seemed. Apparently, such mystery attracted further attention; she was certain that her audience grew larger with each session. She wondered where amongst them Louko was. Keeshiff had the good sense to stay hidden—unlike Louko, he was too recognizable.

A hush fell over the crowd and Astra looked up to see the door behind the thrones swing open. First came Soletuph, dressed in the dark leather armor of the Ethian Guard. He stopped, scanned the room, then stepped aside. A tall figure in purple came forward as a herald announced:

"All kneel for King Entrais, Hero of the Great War, Head of the Court of Litash, Unifier of the Elves, and Wielder of Fiondyn's Blade."

Unable to kneel, Astra bowed her head and thought again of how much her brother likely despised this part. She looked up in time to see him sitting down on his throne, gesturing for the crowd to rise. Only then did Ent meet her gaze, and for a tortured moment, Astra saw his stifled panic.

Then, as quickly as he had locked eyes, he looked away, motioning to Lady Therune to take the floor.

"May I continue the questioning, my liege?" the blond lady asked as she rose from her seat among the courtiers. The silken skirt of her gown rippled as she descended the few steps to the marble floor.

Ent looked so tired, but maintained an even voice as he replied, "You may proceed."

Lady Therune turned to Astra, cold elegance in every move. "Princess Astra, why are you here?" The way she asked seemed as if she was addressing the Court more than Astra. "Is it to see your brother? Is it to get something you need, perhaps?" There was something dangerous in the way she spoke.

Astra proceeded with the caution she knew her brother needed from her, but she did not play along. "If you would truly like to hear the story I have given you five times already, I will tell it again. Otherwise, please get to whatever point it is that you are trying to make."

"Princess Astra, you are *obsessed*," the lady said with a great sweeping gesture. "It is understandable. You have spent all your life trying to put an end to Tyron's injustices. You endured indescribable things at his hands. When he was gone, you just couldn't believe it; your life goal was finished at only fifteen. No child should have had to do what you did, Princess. And with the power you have, one could see how this could affect the mind."

Therune kept doing this. She kept sprinkling in references of the days Astra and Ent had spent in captivity, as if to rile Ent. If she wasn't doing that, she was constantly insinuating that Astra's power made her unstable. Which seemed, unfortunately, too true to prove otherwise.

"Lady Therune, if anyone is obsessed, it's you, and you're beginning to sound like a parrot," It was Ent, cutting through with sharp, angry tones. "Perhaps your life goal of serving Euracia and Tyron was completed at the end of The War, and you all just couldn't figure out what else to do with yourselves." The suddenness with which he turned on the rest of the Court was startling. "But apparently you have nothing better to do with your pathetic existences other than to threaten and harass the life out of the person that saved your necks. Can no one see the fresh scars? Princess Astra; where did you get them?"

Astra was slow to recover, taken too off guard by her brother's reaction. Ent hadn't said more than the required formalities since the case had started. But now he was looking right at her, eyes blazing as he waited for her reply.

"I was held captive by Tyron for one month in Merimeethia," she stated, not for the first time.

"Oh, but he's dead." Scorn dripped as he turned on Therune, "She must be imagining the fresh *scar* on her face and the new manacle marks, and the fact she's half starved to death. I don't recall any of those being there when we shipped her off to Merimeethia. She must also be imagining that the new king of Nythril is more than happy to call witnesses to her defense if you would only accept their testimony. Let's forget that, because we know what's really happening here, don't we?" Astra could tell; the Elvish fury was alight in her brother's eyes, and that was a dangerous thing indeed. "This trial is as real as my sway over this Court, and if you're not going to listen to anything Astra has to say, stop

32

bothering with the pretense of civility. She's not a trophy to be paraded about a room—and you're more a rat than a bird of prey."

This was bad. And worse, Astra had no idea what to do. Her brother had not even reacted this badly in private—much less before the Court and half of Litash.

To top it off, Lady Therune didn't even have the decency to look frightened. She feigned surprise and then concern. "My king, this is all very sudden; are you sure that you are well? Should we send for a physician?"

The swiftness with which Entrais stood was frightening to Astra, if no one else. As was the near murderous look he gave Therune. The entire hall seemed to hold its breath.

Someone coughed in the outer part of the court, and it appeared to break Ent from his spell enough to say, "We are adjourning for the day. I advise *all* to rethink their lives and come back when they feel less inclined to degrade the person who is the sole reason you have the freedom to insult her."

With that, Ent spun around and stalked out, followed closely by Soletuph.

The crowd began to murmur as Lady Therune retreated to rejoin the other courtiers. By the time Astra's guards had taken up their formation, the conversations had resumed their tumultuous pitch. But they weren't talking about her anymore: They were talking about Ent.

Astra had never been so anxious as she left the trial. As her guards locked her back in her cell, her stomach was tied in knots. What had just happened? And what was going to happen because of it? Why had Ent reacted so strongly? Had something happened with Jade? Or their parents back in Cithan?

The sound of keys in the door cut off any further questioning, and soon Louko and Keeshiff entered the cell—Louko with his usual book tucked under his arm.

"That was...lively," he said with a cough.

"*That* was not good," Astra added with a murmur. "Did something happen? Ent is not one to lose his temper like that."

Louko winced. "I'm not really sure. He's...." The sentence remained unfinished.

"Well, you don't look too much better." Keeshiff cleared his throat. "Do you actually sleep, or are you spending all night on this stupid thing?" He gestured to the chessboards on their rickety table.

Astra sat down on her stone bench. "In my defense, manacles don't make for the most comfortable sleeping arrangement," she grumbled. But she didn't miss Louko's stricken expression, no matter how quickly he hid it. So she added, "At least they keep the memories away."

"Yeah, I suppose that is something," came Louko's hollow response as he sat down beside her.

Keeshiff gave a strange cough and Astra looked over to find him fighting some sort of amusement. Did she miss something? She looked between the two brothers, but Louko seemed purposefully intent on the book he'd brought.

So Astra moved on. "How is Mitheau doing? Any word from Grenedil yet?"

"Grenedil...well, he disappeared after Aelor Ven got us out of the tower. There was this whole political mess and Grenedil said he needed to go find that Cyl guy and figure out what was going on with one of those other...planets...I guess...and so. He, uh, just sort of left, saying something about a portal site." Keeshiff shifted uncomfortably as he explained.

"Yeah. And then Mitheau is rather in a panic at the moment, actually..." Louko then proceeded to catch Astra up on what had happened with the young Drogan in court. "So I guess this is just getting worse every minute. At least we know who Tyron's spy is?" The last remark was hardly confident.

Wait. Lady Therune...that was Tirzah? Rhioa's *sister?* Astra winced, recalling flashes of Rhioa smiling, or dancing, or falling.... "One of them, anyway," she heard herself reply. She let her head droop onto Louko's shoulder.

A noise came from outside; the sound of keys jingling and being placed in the lock. But even more audible was the bickering...Astra recognized her uncle's irritated tenor easily, but more confusing was the higher-pitched voice that could belong to none other than....

"Please, Ameri, you're going to do nothing but make this worse!" Tallaman growled as he barged into the room first, followed by....

"Mother? Father?" Astra bolted upright, looking to Louko with wide eyes. No one had told her that her parents were here!

"Astra!" Ameri flew past Tallaman and up to Astra, stopping just short and looking as if she'd only barely stopped herself from embracing Astra. "Are you alright? How are they getting away with chaining you like an animal?!" Her eyes traveled wildly up and down Astra, ending their inspection at the chains around Astra's hands.

"Um," Astra fought the urge to put her hands behind her back. "I'm alright—really. It's just red-bronze." She saw her father enter the cell behind everyone else. "When did you both arrive in Silbyr?"

"Yesterday. So in time to see that circus up top," her father replied as he came beside Ameri, putting a gentle hand on her shoulder.

Astra heard her uncle grumble, "Just in time to make a worse mess of things," even as he pushed between the two and came beside Astra for his usual inspection.

Louko moved a little further down the bench to make room as Tallaman felt for Astra's pulse and temperature. Keeshiff looked uncomfortable, edging to the back of the cell. At least she wasn't the only one feeling overwhelmed.

"Is there anything we can do?" Destrin asked quietly.

Astra held out her wrists as Tallaman cleaned the raw skin beneath her manacles. "I'm really alright down here. There's not much for me to do." She glanced towards Louko, still sitting with the book in his hands. "But Ent—Ent needs your help. He's already carrying too much and this has only made it worse."

Destrin and Ameri shared an uneasy look.

"How is she, Tallaman?" Ameri asked at last as Tallaman finished his usual rounds.

"Out of danger," he grunted in reply. "But the red-bronze isn't good for her. Especially not so soon after."

Astra's hand itched to go to her wrist in nervous habit.

Ameri's shoulders sagged in some semblance of relief. "That's good, at least."

Meanwhile, Destrin had been watching Astra, quietly, gentle eyes holding worry. "Have you even been able to see Ent?"

"Only during the trial proceedings," she replied, trying to let out her pent-up breath. "I...I'm worried for him."

"Surely there is some way he can come see you? It's *his* city, after all?" Astra's mother sounded distressed.

Astra shook her head as her defensiveness grew. "I'm in The Court's custody—not his. Exile is under their jurisdiction so he has no say. And they've declared that, since he is part of the judicial process, he is barred from visiting me just like all the courtiers."

Ameri's fists clenched, and Astra's elvish ears heard her murmur, "What in Eatris."

"So then...how can we be of service, Astra?" Destrin asked, ignoring the glares Tallaman was now throwing his way.

Again, Astra looked to Louko, who's tight-lipped expression gave away a hesitance to get involved. He was regarding her parents almost guardedly. What had she missed?

"I don't know," she finally admitted. "I'm afraid that I'm quite useless down here." Her focus shifted to the chessboards then down to her feet. "If the Court can't be won over, then we will have to find some other way. I don't know what that would be."

"So you need an exit strategy?" Destrin asked. "I suppose the hardest thing would be getting you out of here. You'd be safe in Cithan. The Elves all love you there—even him." Her father gave a cheeky smile as he pointed in Tallaman's direction.

Her uncle rolled her eyes.

And for that very brief moment, Astra was confused. Her uncle absolutely despised his brother-in-law. In fact, it was Tallaman trying to kill Destrin that had caused Ameri to renounce her title and leave Cithan all those years ago. But was that…was that humor that had just passed between them?

"I can't." At the nearly hurt expression on her mother's face, Astra hurried to explain, "I have to go back to Nythril. I am needed there." After Tyron's last note—brought by Mariah, of all people—Astra knew The Game wasn't over.

"Then we'll come with you," Ameri's insistence betrayed her anxiety.

Astra saw Louko stiffen.

"But who would run Cithan? Ent needs as many allies as he can get *here*." Astra scrambled for a way to put this without seeming unkind. "I'll be safe in Nythril, but much bigger things are at play than my safety."

"We'll talk with Ent," Destrin answered. Astra noticed another wince from Louko, but then her father went on. "But you can't keep doing this alone. This is out of hand already and if you and Ent don't start asking for help, I'm afraid it will be the death of you both."

Astra took a deep breath. "I have help." She looked purposefully at Louko, then to Keeshiff still making himself inconspicuous in the back. "But Ent, he…I don't think he remembers that he *can* ask." Or perhaps he did not know who he could trust enough to do so.

Destrin's face drew back in a grim expression, but he said quietly, "We will talk with him."

"But for now you should leave. You've been here long enough and Astra has plenty of eyes on her as it is," Tallaman scolded as he stood up, brushing himself off and glaring at his sister and her husband. "Let's give her some room to breathe; she's been bombarded enough already."

Ameri cast one last worried glance to Astra, then squared her shoulders and nodded. "Alright. Try and get some rest. I'm sure we'll get this figured out...somehow."

With that, Tallaman showed them out rather gruffly, leaving Astra alone with Keeshiff and Louko.

"Well, I suppose it's good to know we're not the only ones with communication problems in the family," Keeshiff broke the silence with a nervous laugh.

Astra closed her eyes and leaned her head back against the stone wall. Why did things only ever get more complicated?

CHAPTER III

Louko:

An Elf's lifespan was twice that of a Human, meaning after reaching maturity they often remained looking in their twenties and thirties for a good half a century. This was a fact Louko had known, and yet somehow, he still hadn't been prepared for how young Ent and Astra's parents looked. Maybe it was more the shock that, somehow, they now looked almost younger than Ent and more youthful than Astra. It really exposed just how much The War had aged the siblings. Well...The War, and in particular, Tyron.

But even beyond that, Louko had forgotten how uncomfortable family could be. What he wasn't used to was the tension in Astra's, and after having stumbled into the room with Entrais getting...probably reamed out...it was odd sitting there and having to pretend it hadn't all happened. Louko wasn't so used to that anymore.

"So, have we had any updates on The Game since I last...saw you all?" Keeshiff asked, turning the conversation away from the strained family encounter and instead to that stupid board game they were all stuck with. To think Louko used to *like* it....

"Yes," Astra replied, still very quiet. She was rubbing her wrist. "Mariah brought a note when she came."

Louko stiffened at the reminder of his sister. Perhaps he still had some interesting family ties, after all. Funny how easily he forgot about the woman who had done this all to Astra.

41

Sensing Keeshiff's eyes staring into the side of Louko's head, the younger prince sighed and turned to meet his brother's gaze. "Yeah, the note she brought was just another chess log. It makes it even harder to tell if she sincerely had a change of heart, or if she's still helping Tyron in his sick game. Who knows." Louko didn't care anymore.

"The note she brought, at least, is helpful. It said the black queen moves forward by two, and the second white bishop moves diagonally by two." Astra stood up, crossing to the boards. "We know the bishop is Soletuph, but what about the black queen?" She plucked the piece from the top tier. "Could it be Tirzah?"

Louko had caught Astra up on Mitheau's discovery of who Lady Therune really was, but somehow, he couldn't see this new Drogan being the spearhead. "What was the queen's first move, again?"

Astra glanced down at her notes, though Louko knew she had long since memorized them. "This. Well, maybe. We know there are moves that he doesn't tell us about. But this is the first one for the black queen that he's told us of."

"You mean the black queen only *just* moved for the first time?" Keeshiff interrupted. "How much longer is this Game going to go?"

Louko threw up his hands in frustration. "The only person who knows that is Tyron, apparently. I'm not even sure if there *is* an ending, much less any way to win it. For all we know, this is just his means for controlling us."

Astra's sigh mirrored his discouragement. She held up the black, marble piece again. "Is there any chance that she's being controlled? Tirzah, I mean."

"Mitheau said she was one of Ovok's daughters and very dangerous. That she was left behind to take care of things when Ovok disappeared. The only one that would be controlling her would be Tyron and, well, how would he be controlling her?" Louko asked, trying to put the pieces together. There were just…so many that it was enough to make even his brain hurt.

"I wonder if we could find a way to speak with her." Astra placed the black queen back on the board.

"I don't think that's…a very good idea," Louko said, scowling at The Game and trying to analyze the queen even as he spoke. "She seems to already enjoy the way you're at her mercy. Going and talking to her is only going to swell that ego more." He could picture her stupid smile, now. That woman was vicious.

"What did Mariah say?" Keeshiff's question was an unpleasant reminder of their sister. And yet…he had a point: Mariah might know. Louko had been avoiding her for too long.

"I haven't…talked to her since she arrived," Louko admitted with a wince. "I suppose she would be easier to ask than Tirzah."

He saw the way Astra studied him then turned her focus to Keeshiff.

"I think it would be best to start there. She has no sway over anyone, anymore." The reluctance was clear in the way Keeshiff slowly said each word.

Yeah, no sway. Louko wasn't afraid of what she could do…he was afraid of what *he* would do if he was forced to put up with her face-to-face.

But it was time to get over himself. They needed as much help as they could get.

"Are you alright for now, Astra?" He turned to meet the eyes of his friend, closed his book, and brushed off his trousers.

She nodded, sitting down in front of the chess boards. "That is the handy thing about guards," she said dryly. "They may be keeping me in, but they're also good at keeping everyone else out."

All Louko could manage was a weak laugh and, "Yeah. What would you do without them?" as he went over to where his brother was still standing. "Shall we, then?" Half of him wished Keeshiff would change his mind; half of him knew they didn't have such a luxury.

Keeshiff looked as reluctant as Louko felt. "Yeah," He stood up, jamming his hands in his pockets. "Ready. See you in a bit, Pipsqueak."

Astra wrinkled her nose.

Louko blinked. Multiple times. "I'm…sorry?"

Instantly his brother's cheeks turned a bright scarlet. "What? I just thought nicknames were still a thing and I saw it in a book once and thought it sounded like something a big brother would say…."

It took a little while for Louko to register that the reason Astra's shoulders were shaking was because she was trying not to laugh. She had one hand pressed over her mouth as if trying to hide it, but it bubbled up anyway.

"It's still better than your last attempt," she said as if trying to console him.

Now Louko looked at his brother. "Wait. *Last* attempt?" He couldn't help but snort out a laugh of his own. "Pray, tell me what that was."

Keeshiff was red all the way to his ears as he scratched the back of his neck. "Um, you know, I can't recall...."

"It was Shrimp," Astra cut in, laughing openly.

"It-It...what?" Louko barely managed the two words between his own guffaws.

Keeshiff's face was a deep scarlet. "Oh shut up, you two. I thought we were going to go be serious."

With a few coughs to hide the continued laughter, Louko finally got himself under control enough to nod.

But even as they were let out of the cell, they could still hear Astra chuckling behind them.

Louko stood there, wishing for nothing more than to walk away without knocking. The Ethian Guard, Matthes, had already stepped aside so that he could, and yet Louko still wasn't ready to face her. Not even after the days that had passed. No. He could no more stand the thought of looking her in the eye now than he could the day she had proved a traitor. She had been responsible for half of this disaster, and for what? Her petty dislike of him? But he knew he had to get over it. Mariah had been useful so far, and if they wanted to even try and stay in step with Tyron, they needed her. That being said, clearly Tyron had known she would escape; so had she really escaped? Or was she still in league with him?

"So, uh, are we actually going to knock on the door or just sit here philosophizing?" Keeshiff broke through Louko's ever-crowded brain.

"Oh. Yeah. Right." Louko cleared his throat awkwardly, but somehow only went back to staring at the wooden doorway.

Keeshiff knocked.

There was a moment of stillness, then the meek call, "Come in."

You can still walk away, Louko. You don't have to go in. And yet, he did, following Keeshiff as he firmly gripped the latch and entered the room.

Mariah was standing in front of a chair as if she had just gotten up. It was strange how different she looked. Maybe it was just Louko's memory, or maybe it was the lack of cosmetics and fancy dresses. Either way, the Mariah that Louko had known would never have gawked so openly, nor turned her eyes to the floor in shame.

"We're here on business," Louko said, unable to hide the coolness in his tone.

A mute nod. "I...I will help as much as I can."

"How do we know you aren't here to spy again?" Louko thought again of the black queen, and doubt tugged. He felt cornered.

Mariah's hands twitched at her side. "I guess you don't," she said heavily—likely not for the first time. She winced again and her voice dropped. "I know now what I did. And I know that forgiveness doesn't really run in our family." She looked up for the first time. "But I swear: I never would have done any of that if I had known who Kaeden was. If I knew what he was going to do."

Right. All she'd thought would happen was that I would get executed for murder. So much better.

46

Keeshiff sighed. "Let's stop with the self-pitied dramatics and get to where you help make this right."

Louko swallowed but said nothing. Apparently, Keeshiff was a bit more prepared than he was, right now.

"Right, sorry." Her eyes returned to her feet. "What can I do?"

At last, Louko was able to snap himself out of it, knowing Keeshiff was not exactly qualified to answer *this* question. "Lady Tirzah. What do you know of her?"

Mariah's brow furrowed. "Tirzah, Tirzah," he heard her mutter under her breath. "I don't think I've ever heard of her."

"What about Therune?" Louko tried again.

This time, Mariah's expression eased. "Her, I know. She was the daughter of some obscure lord from the northwest of Litash. As far as the rumors go, he began sending her to Court in his stead when he grew too ill to make the trip. He died some while ago and his lands were left to her." Mariah pursed her lips as if thinking. "Some say she was one of the few brave enough to stand up to Euracia. Others think that she came into power because he favored her. Either way, she's considered one of the most powerful figures of the Litashian Court. A bit of a shut-in, though. Very rarely makes any social appearances since The War."

Exasperated, Louko asked, "Were you aware that she's really Tyron's sister-in-law?"

Mariah's lips parted in surprise. She shook her head slowly, looking nearly troubled. "I...when I was going through his desk, I saw a letter. I didn't understand it then, but it was addressed 'Dear Brother'."

Of course. He turned to Keeshiff. "So they *are* in contact." Then, he looked back to Mariah. "And you didn't even think to bring this letter, too? How do we know you aren't still working with him?"

"I-I was scared and hurried and it didn't seem to say anything important," Mariah stammered. "It was talking about Nythrilian tea or something like that."

Louko's entire body went rigid. He didn't need to be a genius to recognize it was code. Code for what Astra's plans had been.

Mariah pressed her hands against her side as she continued. "Even if I wanted to, I wouldn't have any way to contact him. Before, he gave me this pen. He told me that it was part of a set. Anything I wrote, his pen would write out for him. And he wrote back in the same way."

"So he still has those pens, then?" Louko asked. Of course Tyron would have some Gifted relic to communicate discreetly. Idiot!

Mariah nodded rapidly. "Yes, he took it back when I returned."

So then that could be how he was keeping in touch with Tirzah so easily. But why was she helping? Just family ties? "And there is *nothing* else you remember seeing in the letters? Or anything that Tyron said to you?"

Chewing her bottom lip, Mariah did not reply right away. "I don't know," she confessed in a whisper. "He was always so...odd. Distracted. But more than that. You would speak to him, and he wouldn't even notice, or he would reply, and it would have nothing to do with your question. At first, I thought it was the stress of everything. But then I heard that Julyn had been arrested and...." She fell silent, staring at the floor once again.

Louko suddenly turned to his brother, realizing with a pit in his stomach that he had not yet told his brother. But the unsurprised, grim expression on Keeshiff's face proved he had already been told after arriving in Litash. Julyn had been a good man...and a good father to Rufio and Rhumir. Now, he was just another casualty.

"Yes, that fits with Tyron's behavior when..." Louko trailed off a moment, shivering, "When I was there last."

"Great, well it seems we have at least a little information that might be of the slightest use." Keeshiff's tone was harsh as he addressed Louko. Whether because of the reminder of the cost of this mess, or simply because he could no longer stand Mariah's presence; Louko wasn't sure. And honestly, he didn't care; he wanted to be out of here just as much.

"Is that all, then?" Louko forced himself to address Mariah.

She seemed nearly as agitated as them, drumming taut fingers against her sides. Then the incessant rhythm came to a halt. "I don't know if it means anything, but there was this one time I...I had asked him about you again." Her gaze darted up to Keeshiff and back down. "His response was so strange. He nodded and patted me on the shoulder as he said, 'Yes, we do need to go to Nythril, don't we?' and then he walked away." She shrugged stiffly.

A pit formed in Louko's stomach. Was his uncle in danger? Or had that been referring to the former ruler, Dia Tzaro? "Wonderful. If you think of anything further, simply ask your guard to contact us. Understand?"

"Wait!" Mariah looked suddenly desperate. "The nobles...they...they're getting nervous. I think if you were to—" she looked to Keeshiff. "If you were to talk to them, you might be well received. Maybe you could take back the throne yourself."

Keeshiff snorted. "Oh, you want me to walk right into Tyron's hand? How cute. Thank you…but no thank you. I've fallen for enough of your little tricks to do so again."

Mariah shrunk back, not saying another word on the subject. Louko couldn't help but wonder what sort of lunacy had possessed her to suggest such a thing, or did she really think they would go for such a stupid idea?

"Anything *else?*" Keeshiff asked coldly. When no reply came, he spun around, and Louko took that as the cue to leave.

Then, just as they had turned to leave and Keeshiff was already halfway through the door with Louko close behind, Mariah asked, "How is Astra?"

Something snapped a little, and Louko turned to glare at her. "Finally not dying for the first time in two months, but still chained head to foot and possibly getting handed right back to Tyron. So just fantastic, thanks for asking." He should have regretted the words, but he didn't.

Mariah didn't react this time. She just stood there in the same stiff fashion she had before. Like someone bracing for a blow.

Without another word, Louko turned back to his brother and together they left the room.

Again, Louko remember Julyn's death and how he had managed *not* to tell his brother What an idiot he was. "Keeshiff…I'm so sorry there was so much that happened I—"

"It's not your fault," Keeshiff's tone was terse, but he seemed to already know what Louko was referring to. "You didn't kill him. You have your mind on more important things. Besides, Entrais's wife already informed me. I just..." he wandered off a moment. "I don't know how Rufio will react to the news, and I won't be there when he receives it."

Louko understood, putting a hesitant hand on his brother's shoulder. "He'll have the other knights to lean on." Inwardly, Louko wondered how Rhumir would react. He'd always been at odds with his father, but Louko knew that, at the end of the day, Rhumir had loved Julyn. They had all respected him.

Just another casualty in this disastrous bloodbath.

Entrais:

"Ent, just take a breath." Jade's hand was resting gently on his shoulder even as the king struggled to keep himself together.

The crowds, the noise—it blended with the screams and sounds of battle ever roaring in his ears, and it took everything in him to lock onto his wife's voice.

Take a breath. Then another. Breathe. That's all that matters.

Ent gripped the side of the desk as he fought for control. He'd barely made it this far before breaking down in a panic. What a pathetic mess he was.

"They're going to win. This is a trap, Jade," he whispered, getting himself together at last. All he wanted to do was sleep…sleep or scream. Or wipe his desk clean of all the stupid trinkets and letters that littered it.

"Then we'll break her out some other way," Jade said firmly. "We won't let them get her."

"And what if it doesn't work? What will happen to Astra? What will happen to you? To—"

Jade cut him off. "—me and the baby will be just fine, Ent."

But she couldn't promise that. She couldn't promise that failure wouldn't end in death—because it always did. Every battle had casualties, and every loss even more. Ent had a life full of seeing what happened when he couldn't keep those he loved safe. The best-case scenario could still be another nightmare to add to the list.

A sudden knock prompted his hand to instantly go to his sword, and only Jade's hand stopped him from drawing it. The knock was two beats, the first quiet and the second harsher. The code they had for the Ethians.

"Enter," Jade called for him.

In stepped Ascriot, his worried eyes a change from his usual good humor. "Sorry to interrupt. This, um, was just delivered to the guard at the end of the corridor." He held up a sealed piece of parchment. "They said it contains news regarding the stars."

Ent stood up straight, smoothing his jacket and trying to put back some appearance of sanity. "Thank you," he said as he reached for parchment.

King Entrais—

I think it's time we speak face to face regarding the stars.
Join me this evening when it grows dark enough to see them.
No further company will be required.

Yours sincerely,
Lady Therune

Ent crumpled the paper as the fury rose in his throat. He fought the red tinting the edge of his vision, wishing the anger to dissipate. Exhaustion did not help him keep his stupid Elvish Fury at bay.

"What? What did it say?" Jade asked immediately.

"It's Tirzah. She wants to talk about Astra. She knows the code."

"How would she know the code?" Ascriot was the first to ask.

Jade shook her head. "Does it matter? She knows, and now she is using it to try and get your attention without the Court knowing." She looked up at Ent. "What could she want that she's not already getting?"

"I suppose we'll find out," Ent forced the words out.

Ascriot frowned but didn't argue. "How many of us do you want to come with you?"

"None," Ent replied almost too quickly. They were deep enough in the hole already. He couldn't live with himself if any of the Ethians died. They'd lost so many friends—all they had left was each other.

"Fine," Ascriot rolled his eyes. "How many of us who will be there do you actually want to know about?"

Ent glared at him. "None. You need to stay here and make sure no one is going to come snooping around while I'm gone, Ascriot. The last thing I need is for Tirzah to claim I was trying to assassinate her and charge you all with treason."

Ascriot shook his head and walked back out the door, calling, "Got it. I won't tell you any."

"Ascriot!" He hadn't meant to shout, but it was getting so hard to breathe. Everything was spiraling out of control.

"Deep breaths." Jade's voice was steady but so far away. "Ent, deep breaths. Listen, perhaps it's not a bad idea. Just have one of them tag along and stay outside." She had a hand on his arm now. "This way you don't have to worry about losing control."

"Or this is a trap and she knows you all will ignore me and come, and then she'll have reason to kick you all out. Or worse." Ent endeavored to remain calm even as his panic continued to grow. It wasn't working well.

Jade put one hand over his—the one with the still crumpled note. "I doubt she would do that when she's sent us a signed piece of paper with her name on it. And then why would she have tried to keep this so quiet?"

"Perhaps," was all he could manage to say, knowing it was pointless arguing with them. They wouldn't listen to him, anyway. Not that he blamed them; he'd made his share of stupid decisions in his life—gotten enough people killed. He would never get their screams out of his head…especially Astra's. "Do what you want. Just be careful." He turned back to his desk. He pulled a book from the nearby shelf and placed the piece of parchment in between the pages for safekeeping.

"I'm always careful," Jade replied. "Which is why I will be sending Matthes—not Ascriot."

Ent stood outside the door, waiting to be allowed in. Matthes was nowhere to be seen, but the Ethians were all talented shape-shifters, and the unique skill set of being able to shift into seemingly inanimate objects gave them an advantage that any other Bandilarian wouldn't be able to pull off.

But Ent wished Matthes really wasn't here. Worst-case scenarios kept playing over and over in his head; the reminder of every single battle he'd lost and each casualty that had gone with it. He didn't understand why he was even trying anymore.

Because giving up would just mean even more bloodshed.

Right. That.

The door of the manor creaked opening, reminding Ent that he had knocked only seconds before. A scowling face peered out and looked Ent up and down.

"Who are you?" the elderly man demanded.

Ent just sort of stared at him a moment before realizing he was serious. Great. "King Entrais," he said flatly, hating the undeserved title. If he could have found someone more fit for the stupid thing, he would have gladly given it to them. But Jade had needed him to step up while she recovered after The War, and so he'd tried desperately to be enough. Tried...and failed miserably, so far.

"Do you have an appointment?" The man's irritable monotone didn't waver in the slightest.

He had...honestly not quite been expecting this. "I'm not sure it's on the record, so no. I am happy to leave."

The butler peered at him a moment longer, then grunted and let the door swing open. "Fine. This way."

So much for that. Doing his best to remain collected and calm, Ent followed the man, hoping the lack of sleep and general paranoia didn't show too terribly even as he knew he was never strong enough to keep it under control.

They walked through the vestibule, past the parlor, and up a set of stairs. Ent found himself constantly checking the rooms they walked by for any possible traps or exits. It was the only reason he noticed how little decoration there was beyond the first few rooms.

"Lady Therune," the butler shouted, making Ent jump as they stopped by a wooden door. "You have a visitor. Says he's the king."

A muted voice called back, "Bring him in."

Trying to block everything out of his scattered brain, Ent allowed the rather sour-mannered butler to let him into the study. How did entering a simple room feel like setting foot on a battlefield? At least with the latter, Ent had a sword. Here he felt defenseless, unsuited for politics and unable to go verbally toe-to-toe with anyone.

"King Entrais." The greeting was simple and succinct. Rather like Tirzah herself. Gone was the elaborate dress and styled hair. She wore plain, dark clothing, sitting behind a desk with nearly as many papers as

Ent's back in the palace. She held a few of these in one hand. She did not rise to meet him. "Please, have a seat. And ignore my terrible butler."

"I'll stand, thank you," he replied shortly. His height alone made it uncomfortable to sit in most chairs not made for Elves, and he had little desire to bring himself any lower in front of Tirzah.

"Suit yourself." Tirzah shrugged, setting her papers down and shooing away the ill-tempered servant. The door closed with an obnoxiously loud *bang* and Tirzah cleared her throat. "I'll get to the point then: By the end of tomorrow's session, the Court will have what it needs to sentence your sister." She folded her hands and rested them on the desk. "After that, she will be completely under their jurisdiction, with no chance for you to intervene on her behalf. I trust you know everything that this entails, yes?"

Ent remained outwardly unchanged even as panic rose in his throat. "Yes. I am aware. Thank you." They would have her; Tyron would have her.

"Then I presume you also know how slim the odds are should you try any...other methods of freeing her?" Tirzah tilted her head slightly, watching him closely.

His eyes burned as he stared back at her. "I am aware," he repeated. "Is this just to show me again that you intend to hand my sister back to *him?* Because well done on the gloating, you sick animal."

Tirzah raised an eyebrow. "When laying out a deal, I find it best to begin with the terms." Her face returned to its unaffected expression. "The first part is that you wish to save your sister and have no way of doing so. The second part is that you are a miserable king of an ungrateful people. My proposition would solve both." She opened a drawer and pulled out a sheet of parchment, setting it on the desk and sliding it across to Ent. "This is a detailed confession of your illegal actions to break your sister out of prison. In it, you say that you feared for her physical safety and did what you thought best. You told her not to inform you where she was headed so that you could not give the information to anyone else. No one else helped you, you acted alone, and you understand that justice must be served." Tirzah tapped the parchment and looked up. "In short, you will step down from the throne and your sister will go free. Though I recommend she leave Litash in due haste."

Ent felt cold all over. "You expect me to just abandon the people I fought to free? You seem to think very little of them—what do you intend to do?" Was he about to sacrifice his own sister again? His head pounded, and it took every ounce of self-control left in him to keep standing; to keep poised and collected just like everyone always required of him.

Tirzah tilted her head again. "Tell me, King Entrais, what have you actually done for *your* people since you came to the throne? How much do you actually know about the day-to-day running of a country that the Court does now in your stead?"

The truth of his inadequacies were only the same ones that rang in his head day in and day out. "If nothing else, I have kept them from you, Tirzah." He didn't have any strength left in him to play this game of pretend. It didn't matter anymore. He was about to lose either way. "I've seen what your brother-in-law is capable of. Do you really think I'm going to leave the people to this?"

"He has no interest in ruling Litash. Nor does he have any interest in leaving the trail of ash that Euracia did." Tirzah spoke in the same,

58

infuriatingly calm manner as if she wasn't admitting to her false name and to her relation to *Tyron*. "If you have done enough research to know my name, then perhaps you know about my earlier endeavors. Does the village of Routh ring a bell?"

"Are you really claiming their bravery as your own?" Ent's fists clenched at the reminder of the brave souls who had helped provide his group with supplies.

Tirzah's lips pressed together slightly in the manner of a parent dealing with an unruly toddler. "Not at all. Their efforts were commendable and surprisingly well-organized. But one of their members made a deal with the wrong person. A grain supplier, if I recall, who then passed on information to one of Euracia's captains here in Silbyr. Orders were sent out for the village to be ransacked and its inhabitants interrogated one by one." Tirzah folded her hands again, looking Ent directly in the eye. "Those orders never made it to their intended recipient. I have no interest in bloodshed; I want to make it through this with as few lives lost as possible. I believe this is the best way to do that."

Everything seemed to slowly be losing color as the situation pressed in on Ent. "And yet letting Astra go would do nothing but let her possibly walk right into your trap to bring her back to Tyron. Why are you bothering with this at all if you're about to get what you want?" But even now doubts whispered in Ent's ears. Did he really have a choice? Did any of them?

"I don't know what his plans are," Tirzah replied bluntly. "He doesn't tell me that much. But if he did want her back, I doubt I would be able to give you this offer. He would likely have just waited for her sentencing." She gestured again to the parchment on the desk between them. "If you think her odds are better in a prison cell, then by all means, turn me down."

Ent stared at the parchment with his apparent confession. She was right, they were doomed either way. As much as everyone had said they'd come up with some way out of it—no one had been able to get a plan together. Nothing that wouldn't end in death. Astra was about to be turned over either way, and even if he didn't sign this now…would he be forced to sign it when questions of his competency were raised after Astra's sentencing? His shoulders felt heavy as he realized he'd lost. He'd let everyone down and now this really was the best option. No last-minute escapes; no plans getting pulled from the woodwork. Only this deal. But how would the people take it? Was this really about to go into all-out war again? Images of battle and death pressed in as he saw yet another cycle of bloodshed beginning to unfold. No rest. No end to the battles. It had been a daydream to think otherwise.

"Fine. Congratulations. You win." His voice was hoarse and almost a whisper as he spoke at last.

Tirzah gave no reaction. She didn't even speak. She simply dipped a quill into its inkwell and held it out to him.

Ent nearly crumpled the pen in his grip as he signed away his worst failure yet. Every curve in his signature was like a noose tightening around his neck, and he wondered how he'd ever look Astra in the eyes again. How he'd ever look anyone in the eye. Maybe Jade would have been better off without him, after all.

"There." He stopped resisting the urge to keep himself under control and allowed the pen to crumble to dust in his hands, only partially using his Gifting to accomplish it. "But I want to see her before she escapes." The last bit of hope he'd been tricking himself into believing was now gone.

Tirzah pulled the parchment back across the desk, dusting the fresh signature with pounce and then taking melted wax from its holder. She poured a small amount beneath his name and slid the parchment out again. "Consider it done."

"How kind," Ent growled as he pressed his signet ring into the wax, sealing both the parchment and his fate. "Now is there anything else or am I allowed to go? Or is this the part where you tell me this was a trap?"

Reopening the drawer, Tirzah placed the parchment safely within and slid it shut. "That was all. After tomorrow's session, the Court will announce that it is taking three days to deliberate on your sister's sentence. The day after, the evening guards will be picked accordingly and will allow you to pass. That is your window." She folded her hands, once more the perfect picture of composure. "It is up to you whether you want to stay for your own sentencing. The confession will only be brought out once the investigation has begun, so you have time either way. Should you stay, I believe the Court will settle for a simple deposition."

"Thank you for your hospitality," Ent replied tactlessly.

"And thank you for your cooperation," Tirzah returned in the same tone. But as Ent stalked back towards the door, he heard her add, "May you fare better in Cithan than you did here."

He froze, hand clutching the latch on the door so hard it groaned. "You are either as deplorable as your brother, or you have very thick scales over your eyes. If it's the latter, I hope they fall before you become just as much a monster as he is."

Tirzah had already picked up whatever documents she had been busy with when Ent had first come in. But he saw the way that her eyes remain fixed in one place as if not seeing anything at all. "There are two sides to every person," she murmured. "Even monsters."

"Oh, I've seen both sides. Up close."

And with that, he left, closing the door hard behind him as he struggled to breathe. What had he done?

CHAPTER IV

<u>Astra:</u>

Astra, Louko, and Keeshiff all sat in their usual positions. Keeshiff was by the door on the wooden stool, as if guarding from the inside. Louko was on the stone bench, book in hand and pretending to read. Astra was at the chess boards, still pondering the black queen. However, after what Louko had relayed from Mariah, Astra had to agree that Tirzah didn't fit the role.

Sighing, Astra picked up one of the black bishops and went to sit next to Louko. "What do you think of this one? Could this be Tirzah?"

"I mean, it's possible. She seems to act as a spy behind enemy lines, of sorts so…it theoretically would make sense," Louko replied, brow furrowed in deep concentration as he looked up to see what piece she was holding.

Theoretically. There was no way of knowing unless a memory confirmed it or they received another note. Astra couldn't bring herself to wish for either. Still rolling the marble figurine around in her hand, she looked between the princes. Both brothers had been very quiet since visiting their sister.

Perhaps it was time to ask. Astra leaned back against the wall as she cautiously turned the subject. "Do you think she has two pieces like Mariah?"

Louko raised an eyebrow, giving Astra a curious look. "I would imagine so. Every person seems to have two sides on the board."

63

She pressed on. "Which do you think Mariah favors?"

"You are…not very subtle, Spitfire," Keeshiff said, chuckling weakly.

"And you're still bad at nicknames," Astra's comeback was equally lackluster. "I just…you both still seemed upset over her. I did not know how to bring it up."

With a shrug, Louko said, "Well, I suppose this worked well enough." Then, after a pause and a sigh, he continued, "I mean, it's Mariah. I don't really know what else about it is really worth noting. She's seemed to see what she's done, at least."

What she's done. The memory of that night on the mountain when Mariah betrayed them came back in such detail that Astra could nearly hear the rumblings of the avalanche. "I suppose that's a start." She glanced at Keeshiff, noting his sudden preoccupation with the piece of straw he was fiddling with.

Then Astra heard a quiet voice from the other side of the cell door, and the guard opened the door to reveal that…Jade had come to visit.

She walked quietly inside, hands folded in front of her as she gave a gentle smile. "Hello, Astra."

Astra stood up quickly, once again embarrassed by the screeching her chains made on stone. "Jade? It's…" She fumbled for words. "…It's been a while."

The smile turned sad. "Yes, I'm sorry. Ent is still not allowed to see you, but I was able to…be convincing. And he was just called away on business so I thought it was the perfect opportunity. How are you?"

"Doing much better, all things considered," Astra replied. "How have you been?" Jade at least looked much better than Astra last remembered her. At her and Ent's coronation, they had been worried about her being able to walk the length of the throne room.

"I'm doing alright. Things are tense." Jade's gaze wandered briefly to Keeshiff and Louko. "We're trying to figure this out. It's getting more complicated by the moment."

Astra nodded and tried to swallow the twinge of guilt. Perhaps it wasn't her fault, but she still wished she wasn't the source of so much of this mess. "How is Ent doing?" she dared to ask.

There was a long pause, and then Jade looked again to Louko and Keeshiff. "Do you think we could have a moment alone?"

Astra glanced back at Louko. For a brief flash, she wanted to ask him to stay anyway. But Jade had requested it, and Jade was trustworthy; Astra kept quiet.

Louko met Astra's eyes and didn't get up until she nodded in agreement. Soon, it was just Astra and Jade, alone in the cell.

"Astra, Ent is…not well." Jade spoke quietly, wincing at the words as she took up Keeshiff's empty stool. "I don't know that he's slept in a week. It's difficult to get him to eat…. After The War ended, he didn't get enough time to recover from anything, and then when the politics started, it was clear the battle wasn't even over, and…he's a mess, and he's not thinking straight, and I haven't told a soul."

Having her fears all confirmed left Astra feeling sick to her stomach. She sat down heavily. "Will no one do anything? My parents? Tallaman?" Her worried mind began to spin. "What of the other Ethians?"

"Even Soletuph doesn't get it. No one cared during The War when he wouldn't take care of himself—not as long as he got the job done. Nothing has changed. Tallaman—I trust him about as far as I could throw him." Jade's fists clenched, and Astra saw the way her jaw worked back and forth in frustration. "But Ent didn't mean to make you think you were abandoned. I was the one that suggested we not tell your parents about your exile until after you were gone. Things were so divisive as they were that the idea of the Elves marching on Silbyr to intervene was all too possible."

Astra listened silently. If Ent was so unwell with no one to help him, and if Jade was the only one who understood but had no means to intervene, then what could they do? This wasn't so easy as Astra getting herself out of the picture anymore. "Will that be an issue again?" Astra asked, thinking of her inevitable sentencing. If the Elves hadn't liked her exile, then….

"I…don't know. We've been unable to come up with anything, but we have to get you out." Jade ran her hand over her face, a deep sigh echoing around the cell. "Tirzah summoned Ent. That's where he is. Whatever it is, I doubt it is good news."

Astra went stock still. "*What?* And he *went?* Please tell me he wasn't alone." If Tirzah was working for Tyron, this could be worse than a trap.

"No, I would never let him do that. Matthes went with him." Jade reassured quickly. "I doubt Tirzah dares lay a finger on him with everything going on. Not directly."

Somehow, this did little to quell Astra's anxiety. Her grip tightened around the chess piece she'd forgotten she'd been holding. She looked down at it, suddenly wondering how all of this fit into Tyron's Game. Had he been going after Ent, too? Or was it a whole other game? Either way, she didn't understand how targeting Ent helped Tyron get off-world.

Jade slowly walked over and sat down next to Astra, hands now folded in her lap. She seemed to be trying so hard to remain composed. "I'm sorry, Astra."

Astra shook her head. "None of this is your fault." She ran her thumb over the chess piece, turning it over in her hands. "I...I wish I had done more. Before I left, I barely saw him. And then I made so many things worse with my exile and...." She cut herself off, shaking her head again. "Why do people treat me like I'm made of glass while expecting him to hold up the weight of the world? He's been through the same things—no, he's been through more. This isn't right. This—" She sighed and forced herself to look up. "—This isn't helping. Sorry."

"No, Astra, please don't apologize. This is just...this is all a mess. I just wanted to warn you because I don't..." She trailed off, biting her lip. "I don't know what he's going to do. I don't know what we're going to do. I keep telling him we'll come up with a plan, but I really have no idea how, and if we don't, I'm not sure what's going to happen. He's hanging by a thread between the nightmares and the stupid politics and the Elvish Fury keeps coming out—you saw what happened in the courtroom."

"I did," Astra admitted softly. She never understood how Ent could hold back instincts that powerful, but she was thankful that she lacked that one Elvish trait. Who knew how much damage she could do if she gave into it?

Astra took a deep breath and let it out slowly. Then she looked at Jade, taking in the sleepless circles and pale skin. "Thank you," Astra said in full earnestness. "For being there for him. Even when there was no one else."

It was rare for Astra to see Jade so emotional. Even as she spoke in even tones, pain was evident in her sister-in-law's eyes. "We promised each other. We knew we didn't have any other choice so we promised if nothing else we'd have each other."

"What do you mean, you had no choice?" Astra asked, now turning to face Jade better.

"We…" Jade sighed. "We knew I'd have to take the role of queen when the dust settled from The War. I was my father's eldest, making me the rightful heir. If anyone else stepped forward, it was too likely that the Court would use my lineage as grounds to reject them." Her eyes dropped to her lap. "But I was so sick after being…imprisoned by Euracia, on top of my family's history of bad health…." She trailed off for a moment. "We knew I wouldn't be able to keep the country together by myself. Then someone made a comment to Ent that at least we were getting married because otherwise the aftermath of taking down Tyron and Euracia was going to be chaos." Jade's hands squeezed together, closing her eyes together for a moment. Then came the sad laugh. "You know, he apologized to me when he proposed. It wasn't really a proposal as much as an agreement. He knew he was already a mess from what…what Tyron did to him and you, and everything before. He somehow thought I was getting the short end of the stick. The last thing he wanted to do was run a country, but I was still getting my head on straight and I wasn't in a place where I could really help until recently. And by then we were backed into such a corner that it didn't matter. Now the Court won't even acknowledge me as a ruler because they continue to hold up that I am sick even when I am finally recovered."

Astra could barely process all of this. She…she had always thought that Ent's marriage had been a happy ending—one good thing that had survived The War. And all this time, it had been another sacrifice. How many had he made? How much had he lost? Why, when he had given everything, must everything still be taken from him?

"I'm so sorry," she whispered.

"Astra, you are the last person in the world that should apologize. Please don't. I'm just telling you because…well, because you're probably the only person I trust to care. To not judge him or…me for this. I haven't told a soul. No one would understand. They just call him weak and me stupid. I'm done trusting people—not even Tyron turned out to be who I thought he was. You and Ent are the only ones that have ever been what you claim to be, and now even Ent is fall—" she choked up for a moment— "falling apart."

Without thinking, Astra gently placed one hand over Jade's wringing ones. She wished she had more to offer—some kind of plan or solution. But she had none. "It's not just us. There are others," Astra started quietly. "I thought the same thing when I was exiled. And then I met Louko. He has done so much and faced so much for me when it would have been so much easier to walk away. And it's not just him: Keeshiff, Ven, Asher, Mitheau—we've met so many." Astra's voice rose to match her fervor. "And that's how it was in The War. There were so many who were willing to do the right thing. And there still are." She hesitated. "There has to be something we can do to rally them. Litash followed Ent before. Will they not do so again?"

"That is what I am banking on. I just…I don't know what we'll do if we have another war, Astra. I might lose him forever. I'm sure you have the nightmares, too. Every wrong decision playing over and over in your head? He's started sleeping in his study because of how he wakes up. And I know he's not really sleeping there. He's just thinking and brooding and losing himself in it. If he has to face those again—if they have to become reality and not just a nightmare…oh dear, I'm turning into him." She ran her hands over her face.

Astra winced. "It's alright. I-I think it helps to say it aloud, somehow. It feels a little less overwhelming when there's someone else listening with you."

Jade laughed. "Yeah, I suppose so. I'm still sorry to put this all on you. It's not like you can do anything about it—you can't even see him." She slammed her fist down on her lap, irritation briefly pricking her tone before settling down again. "I guess it's just been so heavy to carry alone."

"I understand," Astra said, hoping that the admission was comforting and not grating.

"Thank you," Jade breathed. There was a long silence, and then a quiet, "Do you want to know one more secret? This one's happier."

Astra would be grateful for anything optimistic. "What is it?"

"You can't tell a soul. Only Ent knows. Well, Ent and Tallaman. That's the only reason I put up with that stupid Elf…" A small, whimsical smile crept upon Jade's face, breaking the tension. "I'm pregnant."

Astra's eyes went wide. "You are? Really? Oh, Jade, I am so happy for you."

The smile grew. "It's nice to tell someone who isn't Tallaman," she laughed. "I'm not very far along, but so far, it's been going smoothly. Ent was worried over everything, so he begged me to let Tallaman monitor me. I'm honestly excited. I could use a little life among all the gloom and despair."

"You will be a wonderful mother," Astra smiled, too. "And Ent will make a wonderful father." She determined then and there that, no matter what happened with the Court or Tyron or Litash or any of this mess, she would do anything to make sure her brother made it out with his family all still together.

If anyone deserved that happy ending, it was him.

Was it just her, or was there even more of a crowd than usual today? And for all that, they seemed quieter than usual. Perhaps it was from the tension as Lady Tirzah presented her final statements to the Court.

To be honest, Astra was barely listening. She had spent the night in restless tossing and turning. Those few moments of sleep she did get were filled by nightmares of Ent in that dark room, trapped in the depths of some dark prison, suffering at Tyron's hand. And when she had woken, she had lain there running over the whole, hopeless situation in her mind and wishing she could just see her brother again. But for all those long hours of worry, when Astra had stepped into the grand hall of the Court of Litash, her fears had dissipated. They had left something else in their wake, something Astra had nearly forgotten the taste of.

Anger.

She could barely bring herself to look at the rows of hypocrites that sat in a half circle around her. They loomed over her on their raised seats, nodding gravely in unison to Lady Tirzah's long-winded points, whispering among themselves while glancing not-so-subtly in Astra's direction. But worse, worse were the sideways looks they cast towards Ent. *Entrais.* The one who had fought for so many miserably long years—many of them alone. The one who had endured hunger, freezing nights, torture, betrayal, the loss of all he held dear. The one who had fought so many battles, never even expecting to emerge. The one who had held on when everyone else had given up.

And for what? So that when all of it was over, he had to take up the burden of a throne he never wanted? And then only to find that his fighting had not ended at all! Ent, of course, had taken it all quietly. He had done all he could, taking everything on himself and only thinking himself a failure when he could not carry the whole world. And what did this Court do? Mock him as they added to the burden.

"Princess, have you anything you wish to say before the Court adjourns for the last time?"

The direct address brought Astra back to the present and the courtier who stood before her. Judging by the affectedly polite tone Lady Tirzah used, it would seem she had finally gotten to the end of her final statement. And further judging by her condescending smile, the lady did not expect much of a reply. Indeed, Jade had told Astra that there was no reason to say anything. At the time, Astra had agreed. But now she found that holding her tongue had lost its appeal.

So she cleared her throat and answered, "Yes, actually, I do."

Lady Tirzah arched a blond brow in a sort of amusement, then stepped aside and motioned for her to proceed.

"Ladies and Lords of the Court of Litash, you have accused me of many things," Astra kept her voice clear and calm even while loud enough for all to hear. "The first of which is that I was driven insane by the Great War and am, therefore, unable to cope with peace. You tell me that the fight is over and that all the warnings I have given you are the ramblings of a paranoid delusional."

Some of the nobles smiled to each other in the manner of adults laughing over the antics of a child.

Astra paid them no attention. "But tell me: What do you know of the horrors of war?" There was a shift amid the courtiers, but Astra pressed on. "How many of you could tell me what blood tastes like? How many of you can describe how a blade burns as it slices through your skin? How many of you have held someone's hand as you watched the life leave their eyes? Or heard the screams of hundreds lying wounded across the fields?" Now one hand gestured openly to the crowd behind her. "These people—the ones you claim to rule—all know exactly what I speak of. Because they lived through those horrors, too. They did so willingly, following King Entrais into it all in order to reclaim their homes from Euracia."

There was a growing stir among those raised court seats and Lady Tirzah's gaze flicked from the crowd and back to Astra.

"Just look at all of you!" Astra cried, raising a manacled hand to point at her double-tongued accusers. "Is there any amongst you who did not 'serve' under Euracia? Is there any who can claim to have helped my brother to overthrow that false king? No! You are all far more guilty than I! Would you have the audacity to tell me that all I fought against is gone when all of you still sit in the same seats you held in The War?" The growing hostility in their expressions only made her bolder. "When Euracia fell, you were glad—not because Litash was free, but because it left all of his power open for you to seize. By the time my brother had come to the throne, you had already robbed him of everything but an empty title," Astra spat. "And thus you secured your own places. But you realized a threat still remained: me. And that's why you have set up this mockery of a trial."

Lady Tirzah was talking in undertones with Astra's guard, but she didn't bother to listen in. "Perhaps that's why you try to say that Tyron is dead. It's far more neat and easy for him to be dead than for you to deal with the threat he causes. It's either that, or you are simply working with him."

The accusation caused a ripple effect and one of the courtiers actually got to his feet to shout, "Enough of this! Someone restrain her!"

"Your foolish attempt to ignore him will not work," Astra called out with a fierceness. "Nor will your attempt to silence me. These chains," She raised her wrists and let them rattle in emphasis. "Bind me only because I allow them to. Because I had hoped that there might be someone who would see the truth. But I was wrong."

The protesting grew to a tumult as if to drown Astra out.

"*Silence!*" Ent's command was so sudden and so loud that any other noise was impossible. Stunned, the courtiers looked to their king and slowly resumed their seats. Only then did Ent nod for her to resume.

Astra now surveyed the Court with a withering glare. "You imprison me under the pretense of safety, but I ask you this: Will you be safer with me as a loyal vassal of the king, or as a declared enemy of the crown?" She turned around, facing the teeming crowd that filled the back of the hall. At the top of her lungs, she declared, "May Litash bear witness of my words and take action. May they bring down the Court to its proper place."

Astra turned back to her brother, meeting his gaze before bowing deeply. "And may the king's reign never end."

For a moment, it seemed as if time itself had come to a stop. The entirety of the grand hall stood in utter silence. Even the walls seemed to hold their breath.

And then the moment was shattered. Sound crashed like a wave over the room and chaos with it. Commoners, nobles, courtiers, all of them yelling and shouting over one another—or at one another. Not even Ent could quell the storm. Within seconds, it began to escalate: Fist fights broke out in the lower levels, someone was throwing something up in the nobles' balcony, several courtiers were trying to shout orders to the guards while others were hurrying down their steps.

"Princess, please, we need to get you out of here." One of Astra's guards knelt to unlock the shackles around her ankles.

As soon as the man had finished, he helped her down from the stand and took her by the arm to guide her. The rest of the men fell in around her in a tight formation. Even as they hurried her towards the side exit, she caught glimpses of people trying to climb over the railing that separated the audience from the proceedings. The tumult grew louder and louder until it rivaled even the field of battle. Only when the uproar was muffled by closed doors could Astra think clearly enough to worry for Ent.

Entrais:

Astra's words had been echoing in Ent's ears along with the near riot they had incited. But it didn't matter—their fate was sealed now. He would give up the throne and Astra, at least, would be free. Free being a relative term, anyway. Free to return to whatever sick game Tyron was playing. Free from the physical chains but still very much bound to the invisible ones.

"All set, Your Majesty," the guard announced, opening the door for him.

Taking a deep breath in, Ent crossed over into the cell, memories of all his stays in one as clear as the dampness that hit him. As promised, Tirzah was allowing him to see Astra before her "escape."

"Ent?" The figure in the corner shifted and the rattling of heavy chains made Ent suddenly claustrophobic. "Is it really you? How did you get permission?"

He found it hard to form words, unable to do much other than stare at her and the metal that seemed to bind her head to foot. Somehow, he got past himself and answered, "I, uh, I made a deal. They're going to set you free." He winced. Might as well skip the pleasantries and get right to it.

If their roles had been reversed, Astra would have found a way. She probably wouldn't have even gotten in this mess to begin with…it had all started with *him* getting caught by Tyron. With her being with him. If he'd just—

"A deal? What do you mean?" Now Astra was on her feet, walking towards him.

The scraping of chain against the stone floor made Ent jump, too tired to keep himself together any longer. "I'm abdicating the throne. Tirzah is going to allow you to escape and I'll confess to it. I'll head to Cithan," he replied listlessly, eyes now searching for anywhere else to look besides Astra.

But she stood right in front of him. Her eyes were wide, lips parted in shock, her shoulders slack as she visibly tried to process this.

"I'm sorry," he rasped.

Before the apology was half way out of his mouth, she'd wrapped her arms around him. "Oh, Ent." The sad words were muffled against his coat.

He stiffened, a million alarm bells going off as he fought instinct. "Astra, I don't think you understand," he whispered desperately, arms trapped at his side as she squeezed him. "I lost. I've let you down. I wasn't…I couldn't…."

Astra leaned back to look up at him, but she didn't let go. "Lost what? The crown was never the goal. Nobody can carry what you have been trying to carry—not alone." She shook her head and added fiercely, "And don't you dare say that you've let me down. Not when you've made yet another sacrifice to keep me safe."

Ent just laughed in disbelief. "Everything we fought for is crumbling, Astra, and you're still just...taking it in stride as you always do." He allowed himself to relax enough to hug her back.

"Well, seeing how long your stride is, I had to learn to keep up." Astra pressed her head against him. "We fought to be free of Euracia: We still are. We fought to keep our family safe: They still are. We fought so that lives would be saved: They were. So don't try to tell me that you lost. We will figure this out just like we have everything else."

At a loss for words, Ent found the only thing he could do was return his sister's embrace, unprepared for her collected and kind response and yet somehow not surprised. She was always so good.

Astra didn't say anything for a while, just hugged him tightly. Not until Ent could take deep breaths again did she let go. "So, what is the plan?"

"You leave tonight. Tirzah is arranging it so the guards will be occupied, and then you, Louko, and Keeshiff are going to escape. I'll have your horses waiting outside the city, and then your best bet is to make for Nythril, I think. You could come to Cithan with me but...then the Elves might really try and go to war," Ent explained as calmly as he could manage.

Something troubled flitted across Astra's expression, but she simply said, "It's alright. I'll be of more use in Nythril anyway." She hesitated before asking, "What of Mitheau? And, what about Mariah?"

Right. Mariah. Ent only knew that she was the traitor that had turned Astra over to Tyron. "I imagine Mitheau would want to go with you.

Keeshiff said Ven has since disbanded the Drogan hunters and she will be safe. As for Mariah...I'll do with her whatever you decide."

Astra rubbed one wrist in apparent indecision. Then she sighed. "Send her with me."

"What?" Ent took a step back, already shaking his head. "I am not sending you away with a potential spy, Astra."

"She can't stay here—if Tirzah found her, it could lead to more problems. And I don't see her making it long in Cithan," Astra explained. "Nythril is secure enough. Besides, she may yet have information I need."

Ent wanted to argue but knew it was pointless. Even besides the fact that Astra had made up her mind and was usually impossible to dissuade, she was right. Mariah would probably not make it long in the Elvish city. True, they had come leaps and bounds from even just a few years ago, but they still hated most Humans, and a Human that had betrayed their beloved Astra wouldn't stand a chance.

"Please don't do anything stupid?" Ent could find no other point of argument.

"So long as you promise the same," Astra returned.

Ent couldn't resist ruffling her hair. "Whatever you say, Slip."

Astra pretended to swat away his hand. "If that's the case, then I have plenty more to say."

A smile touched his lips as he tried to look annoyed. "Oh, you and your long-winded speeches."

"On the contrary," Astra nudged him with an elbow. "If I proved nothing else today, it's that I'd make a terrible politician."

Without thinking Ent pulled Astra into another hug, more loath than ever to send her away. They'd always had each other's back during The War, and he'd not comprehended just how much he missed her until now.

CHAPTER V

Louko:

As soon as he stepped in the door, he knew he had knocked too soon. "Oh...were you two hugging...that's why it got quiet—not that I was listening...I just heard, you know, words. Um. Not what the words meant...just...are you both alright?" What a genius. Truly.

Louko, you were supposed to just walk in and pretend you had just arrived, you idiot.

Oh well. The cat was out of the bag, now. Whatever...that...implied.

Astra seemed to find his rambling more amusing the longer he went. Ent, on the other hand, looked somewhere between disconcerted and uncomfortable.

"You know," Louko pointed to the door. "Actually, I think I'm good to go scream at a wall for a couple more minutes…. Carry on."

"No, no, you're alright." Astra moved as if to stop him. Not that she could go more than five feet when chained to the wall. "What is it?"

What *was* he there for? Right. The end of the world—how'd he forgotten? Oh, right. Hugs.

"Well, why is...Ent here, anyway? Is this a good sign? Did your speech actually wake people up?" Louko was more confused than hopeful, and the looks on the siblings' faces didn't exactly offer much reassurance.

"Not quite." Astra glanced up at her brother. "Tirzah offered Ent a deal: He steps down in return for my escape."

Eyes widening, he looked from Astra to Ent. "Wait—you can't be seriously considering it?"

The way Ent shifted in his stance was somehow more ominous than if he'd spoken.

"We leave tonight," Astra said softly.

"W-wait you mean we're taking it?!" Louko tried to process this. Ent was stepping down? What in Eatris?

"Taken. I already signed the document," Ent's reply was barely audible.

Astra put a hand on her brother's arm, the subtle gesture accompanied by her manacles. "We have a lot of planning to do," she said, turning back to Louko. She looked suddenly very tired—the opposite of the person who had been yelling at the Court hours earlier.

It was enough to quell Louko's reaction to the news. Astra didn't need anyone losing their cool or going off and doing something stupid.

He sighed. "So then, planning: What do we have so far?"

Astra looked more hesitant than ever before. "I...I think we should bring Mariah."

Louko stood there, waiting by the horses and wishing he could forget Mariah was standing just a little ways away. He knew it made sense. He knew it was the most logical decision. And yet he honestly wanted nothing more than to never see his sister's face again in his life; the face that was responsible for so many nightmares.

"How much longer?" Keeshiff murmured from next to him. Louko hadn't missed the way Keeshiff kept watching their sister from the corner of his eye, staying between her and Louko.

At least the feeling was mutual.

"I don't know, but it has to be soon," Louko replied, rubbing his hands together even though they weren't cold.

"They're coming. I hear them. Not long, now," Astra's mother, Ameri, whispered. Louko had almost forgotten about the presence of Astra's parents, they'd been so quiet.

"Wait, I don't hear—" Keeshiff cut off mid-sentence when Louko tapped his own ear in emphasis as he mouthed, "Elves."

Keeshiff's mouth formed in an "O."

Mitheau's soft chuckle came from somewhere in the back.

As Ameri predicted, a pair of footsteps soon sounded from around the corner. Then two silhouettes appeared on the secluded garden pathway: one as short as the other was tall.

"You took your time," Destrin said with a nervous sort of chuckle as he walked forward to greet the two.

Louko felt out of place, keeping next to his brother and the horses, and trying to avoid accidental eye contact with his sister.

"Sorry," he barely heard Ent murmur.

"Is this everyone?" Astra asked.

Ameri was the one who replied, "Yes. We've gotten everyone and all the supplies required."

"We'll have to get a move on, though, if we want to get far enough to avoid anyone who's sent after us. I don't care what the woman says, I don't trust her to hold up her end of the bargain." It was Destrin speaking now.

Right. He'd only just informed Louko a few minutes ago that he was accompanying them.

And no one had told Astra.

Her reaction was about what Louko expected. "Wait, Father, I thought you were going to Cithan with Ent."

A quick look passed between Ameri and Destrin before the latter replied, "We decided it was best to divide and conquer. You need as much help as you can get."

Astra stammered a moment, looking from her brother to Louko.

Unsure what to do or which was a worse idea—Destrin coming or staying—Louko gave an apologetic shrug. He had only met Destrin a few times—some during The War and vague memories of when he'd visited Merimeethia. He'd always been kind, but the tension between the family had been unexpected the last few days. Which was worse for Astra? And how much did they really have a choice right now? Allies were allies, and they had to get out of the city fast.

"I'll be alright, just go, Slip," he heard Ent coax. "Be careful. Please?"

Astra nodded, then wrapped her arms around him. "As long as you do the same."

The way Ent hugged her back was so clearly desperate that even Louko was worried. Perhaps because it reminded him so much of the last embrace he'd had with Tyron all those years ago before he'd left.

Before he'd turned into a monster.

The moment ended, but the memory stayed, and Louko didn't say a word as he stepped forward at last to show Astra to Dannsair.

"Astra, I…." It was her mother, now.

Louko tried not to show his impatience. They really did have to go….

"Just, take this." Ameri pushed a wrapped bundle into Astra's arms, then placed a tentative hand on her shoulder. "And stay safe."

Astra froze, then nodded. "I will. I love you, too, Mother."

"I…I love you," Ameri stuttered, seemingly taken aback. "So very much."

Louko, along with everybody else, pretended not to have overheard the exchange, instead finishing up their quiet goodbyes and mounting up.

Back to Nythril it was, then.

The first leg of the journey was tense and quiet. Keeshiff had made a point of staying on the opposite side of the group to where Mariah was; Astra was constantly trying not to seem so uncomfortable around Destrin; and Louko was trying to forget Mariah was even there. Poor Mitheau didn't seem to know who to avoid.

Louko focused on riding beside Astra, gauging her every move and knowing the tumult of thoughts that had to be coursing through her. He could see the warring forces in her strained face, taut arms, and gripping hands wrapped with Dannsair's reins.

And then, after hours of silence, Keeshiff suddenly broke the calm with, "So, when exactly were you intending to tell me you already had a nickname?"

The question was so unexpected that Louko almost choked on laughter.

Astra blinked at him in visible confusion. "You didn't already know that?"

"No, how in Eatris would I know?" Keeshiff waved an arm in emphasis, the exasperation clearly fake. Wait, was he…trying to cheer Astra up? This was strange. Louko had apparently missed quite a bit when he'd been with his uncle.

"I mean, I don't know, I guess you would have heard it back during The War." The attempt seemed to be working; amusement now edged Astra's voice. "Louko knew it." She looked at him. "…right?"

Louko gave a shrug. "I don't know, I was busy trying to survive The War, I wasn't really cataloging you and Ent's terms of endearment."

"And what kind of nickname even is that? Don't go calling my attempts pathetic when 'Slip' doesn't even make sense," Keeshiff grumbled.

Astra opened her mouth then closed it. "I, uh, actually don't know where it's from."

"I do." Destrin chuckled from behind them. "It was from the time you stowed away in your brother's packs when he was headed for Silbyr. He went half a day before noticing." Louko looked back to see Destrin shaking his head. "You were three years old. You gave us the slip, and it stuck."

Keeshiff laughed. "Oh, so she hasn't changed much, then?"

Destrin's smile was faraway and small as he replied, "No, not really."

"And here I thought that Ent was just bad at nicknames," Astra grumbled. "I mean, he…."

Louko glanced at his friend, confused why she'd stopped talking. Her brow was furrowed, lips parted, reins slack in her hands. She looked to Louko with eyes widened in alarm and her mouth moving as if trying to speak, but nothing came out. She slumped forward onto Dannsair's neck.

"Stop!" Louko called out frantically to everyone as he swiftly pulled his own horse to a halt and practically leapt over to Dannsair, keeping Astra from falling off her horse. "Astra, come on, wake up." One look at her eyes told him what had happened—but...but it wasn't supposed to happen when she was awake. Panic welled.

"What happened?" Destrin was the first one to reach him. Then he saw that her eyes were green instead of the usual bright, otherworldly blue. "Oh," he breathed. His voice was calm and collected when he said, "Hold her steady. I'll go on the other side and have Dannsair lay down."

If Louko wasn't so distracted by the fact that Destrin was *not* alarmed, he might have stopped and said something about it. But he *was* distracted, helping ease Astra carefully down onto the ground as the rest stopped.

"What's wrong, is she—is she alright?" Mariah's mousy question came from closer than Louko expected.

"Step back, Mariah. She doesn't need an audience." It was Keeshiff, and Louko was glad for it, unable to form a single word as he took hold of his unconscious friend.

"I didn't realize this still happened," Destrin said, looking at his daughter. He kept a slight distance back. "How long is she usually out?"

Still happened? "I-I don't know. It's only ever happened when she's asleep." Louko again gently shook her. "I don't know how to wake her up...it-it started after the castle...after...."

Destrin's brow furrowed and he looked up. "Are you saying she only sees Tyron's memories?"

"I think so?" How did he know she was seeing memories?

Frowning in thought, Destrin looked back down. "She used to get this when she was a child, but it was always a lot of random memories. Never any one person."

When she was little? Louko looked confused, but didn't have time to say anything more, for Astra began to stir.

And then she bolted upright with a gasp.

"Shh, you're alright, Astra. It's alright." Louko realized he and Destrin were speaking at the same time and saying very similar things. The other man quietly withdrew his hand from his daughter's arm and scooted ever so slightly back.

"Are you alright?" Destrin asked her.

Shoulders still heaving as she tried to breathe, Astra looked around wildly. Her hand went to her mouth and she closed her eyes, which were once more that vibrant blue. When she opened them again, she glanced at her father and then to Louko. "What happened?" He could feel her shaking.

"You...you blacked out." Louko steadied his voice as he followed her gaze to Destrin.

Astra started to move as if getting up and Destrin held out a hand to stop her.

"Easy, now." He still sounded so calm. "If you want to get up, let us help you."

Astra hesitated then nodded.

Slowly, Destrin on one side and Louko taking up the other, they helped Astra up. Louko tried not to show his concern, but she was so unsteady...so pale...and it was hard not to go back to memory of what had made her look like that last time "You alright?" he whispered, asking again.

Her nod might have been more convincing if she wasn't still shivering. "I'm fine. We need to keep moving," she said, visibly gathering her voice. "We can't be staying still any more than necessary."

Louko's grip on her tightened. "You need to catch your breath," he replied firmly. "Please." He tried to ignore the fact that the whole group was staring at them, and he knew Astra was, too.

Though her lips formed a taut line, she did not argue. She waited a minute or so before pulling her hand away. "See? Steady," Astra said, hands raised to show she could stand unsupported.

Louko nodded, fighting the urge to argue further.

"Are you alright, Astra?" Keeshiff was the one that spoke now, "What happened?"

"I'm fine," was all she said, swinging one leg over Dannsair and grabbing a handful of mane as the mare stood up. "Let's just get going."

Even though he knew he himself was little better, Louko wished she would stop saying that. By the looks on everyone else's face, they agreed, but no one said a word as they mounted back up and kept going like nothing had happened. Louko tried not to keep looking over to her, knowing she would only take it as seeing her as weak, but he was so worried.

"Why don't we just keep it at a walk for a bit?" Keeshiff suggested. "The horses all need a breather."

Everyone agreed.

"So, this started again after the castle?" Destrin surprised Louko by coming up on the other side of Astra and addressing her.

Astra also seemed taken aback. She swallowed and regathered her reins before nodding.

"And you only get it with Tyron's memories?" Destrin asked further, somehow remaining gentle.

Looking nearly sick, Astra nodded again.

"Hm." Destrin's expression seemed perplexed. "Perhaps it is because he has also survived the Miadoris. Whatever happened, it must have created a connection between you."

"He...what?" Louko was apparently the only one that was confused in this. Every time he thought he had a story straight....

"When it killed his wife, he came into contact with it," Destrin explained quietly. "Not in as direct a way as Astra, but from when he tried to carry Rhioa to safety."

Louko looked to Astra to find her just as baffled.

"Father, how do you know all of this?" she asked.

Destrin let out a long breath. He looked sad when he began to speak. "We—your mother, Ent, and I—have known Tyron for a long time." He shifted in his saddle, seeming almost lost in the reminder of what had once been. "He was just a boy when we met him. Your mother had been called to consult on a matter at the palace. One afternoon, this boy showed up at our door with an armful of books and asking for help with translating them." He shook his head with a faint smile. "He had to be thirteen, maybe fourteen. But he became a regular visitor at our home. He usually visited monthly, staying for two or three days before returning to the palace."

Louko winced, the thought of what Tyron had once been a painful one. It was far easier to believe Tyron had simply been playing him all along. It was not easy to swallow the thought that Tyron had turned from it. He looked to Astra, trying to gauge how she had taken the information. He already knew she had seen much—and talked of it not enough.

But seeing as she'd only just been forced back into Tyron's head after weeks of blissful silence, Louko decided it was best not to ask what had happened. He would save that question for a better time.

It was quiet the rest of the day, Louko thinking over all that had been said. He worried for Astra, though tried not to seem obsessive in constantly looking over to where she was. What if her eyes changed again? What if one time she didn't come back? He tried so hard not to dwell on those fears, but by the look on both Keeshiff and Destrin's faces, Louko wasn't the only one.

And then there was Tyron. It seemed almost everyone in Eatris had known him at some point, and every story only made Louko more confused. How could he rectify the man he'd known growing up—the boy that Destrin had apparently known—with the monster that had done so much to Astra? Had the sincerity and kindness always been a guise? Would it even matter if it wasn't?

But no matter how much Louko pounded his head with questions, no answers provided themselves. Now they sat around a hesitant fire, warming themselves as they all waited around in silence. It was a dismal evening, though by Merimeethia's standards, it would have been considered beautiful.

After supper had been eaten in the same wordless manner, Astra got to her feet and left the little circle. Louko watched her go back to Dannsair and rummage around in her things. Then she returned to the fireside carrying the gift from her mother, still wrapped in cloth for protection. She sat there with the parcel on her lap as if reluctant to open it.

"You alright?" he asked quietly.

At first, Astra gave no reaction. Her gaze remained on the thing in her lap. Then she gave a slight nod and began to carefully peel back the fabric. Only when the bow was completely unwrapped did she touch it, and then only to run a hand over the wood. It looked almost exactly the same as it always had. Almost. Louko could see the blackened lines that now ran over it like jagged lace.

He was just about to resort to asking his question again when Astra stood up. Deftly, with the speed of long practice, she looped the bowstring around one end. Then she dropped the bow to the ground and bent it around her leg till the string reached the other end. She stepped out, raised the bow, and drew it back as if to shoot an imaginary arrow.

Nothing.

But then, groaning like a tree in the wind, the wood stiffened and flexed and finally settled as it shaped itself to Astra's hand. Astra relaxed the string and sat back down with a glimmer of satisfaction on her face.

"It has its scars," she shrugged halfheartedly. "But that is something we share; it still knows me."

Louko gave a soft smile. "Good. You belong together." It was good to see *any* sort of emotion in Astra other than fear and anxiety.

Even better, Astra nearly smiled in return.

"Your mother said that it was only possible to piece it back together because of how well it remembered you," Destrin spoke up from across the fire.

"...wait." Keeshiff, off to the side, sat up from his bedroll. "Your bow is alive?"

Louko would have answered if he had been certain, but the way Destrin had phrased it left him just as confused.

"Not alive, no." Destrin shook his head. "But it has been crafted with Gifting. That Gifting is what makes it responsive to the wishes of its owner by adapting its shape. It is that bit of Gifting which connects the item and owner and, when used well and long enough, strengthens that connection." He paused as if realizing how little sense his explanation made to someone unfamiliar with how Gifting worked. "Think of it as being intuitive rather than living. It can only respond, not think."

"Huh," Keeshiff mused, staring at the weapon. "That's...interesting."

Louko couldn't help but let a little amusement slip by as he said, "'What? Afraid it's watching you?"

Keeshiff scoffed. "I'm much more worried about her horse than her bow."

Somewhere in the background, Dannsair snorted in an uncanny response.

Louko was sidetracked when he realized how quiet Astra had become. She was looking down at her bow again, still holding it in her lap.

Abruptly, she looked up and called, "Mariah."

The camp went still.

Astra seemed not to notice. "Were you the one who found my bow?"

Mariah. If not for the suspicion that she could still be a double-edged dagger waiting to stab you in the back, Louko might almost have forgotten his sister was among them. She hadn't spoken so much as a word, going where directed and sitting in the shadows. With a pang Louko recalled such an experience all too well. But he had seen what Astra had suffered at Mariah's hand; she was capable of more harm than people gave her credit for, and it made Louko hesitant.

"Yes," Mariah at last answered Astra's question, body stiff and eerily still.

Astra's hands tightened on her bow. "Thank you." Her voice held full sincerity.

Mariah didn't say a word, only pressing her lips together and looking away.

Louko didn't know what to think, himself, and as much as Mariah appeared to sincerely have had a change of heart, Louko couldn't get past the memories of betrayal at the pass and the reality of it at Melye. The weeks in the dungeon knowing who had put them there….

How could Astra?

From his spot to the side, Keeshiff laid back down and rolled over—away from Mariah. The bit of motion dispelled the moment and others got up to do likewise. Mitheau left the fireside for her cot.

Astra said, "You go. I'll take first watch."

Destrin, who had not moved from his spot, raised an eyebrow. "Unlike you, I have not been sleeping in a dungeon and chains for the past few weeks, so I think I can all survive losing an hour or two of rest."

Astra's hands twisted around her bow and Louko could see the tension in her shoulders. But she gave a quiet "Alright."

"Thank you," her father replied quietly. "Try and get some rest, Astra."

Louko reached over and gently grabbed her hand, "Rest would be good." Would it, though? Or would it only bring more memories from Tyron? Would it only make the conflict within Astra rage wilder—just like Louko's own inner war?

He felt rather than heard her sigh. After a pause, she released his hand and dusted herself off. "I need to groom Dannsair first."

Louko didn't say a word, only watched her as she walked off and wished above anything else that he could help carry her burden.

Then Destrin caught him by surprise. "I never did get a chance to say this," his voice was low. "But thank you for taking care of her."

Hands folding awkwardly in his lap, Louko whispered back, "I don't seem to be doing a very good job."

Destrin regarded him with a sad sort of sympathy. "You have done better than her own family," was his soft reply. "Astra's life has never been easy, but I am quite certain that it would be much harder without you."

The young prince was unsure what to say. His eyes returned to Astra, who was keen on getting the white in Dannsair's coat as spotless as possible. An impossible task to keep her from rest. But now he was torn between Destrin and Astra. Louko had known the man during The War—after he had escaped from Tyron's dungeons. But he had also known him from before, and long ago had feared Destrin would have betrayed Louko's affiliation with Tyron to Entrais. He never had, and until now, Louko had never had a chance to ask why. He had always assumed it because Destrin did not remember Louko, but somehow, he couldn't see that being the reason.

"Is that why you never said anything about me and Tyron? Did you know even then?" he asked.

"I knew how much you had been hurt," Destrin said. "I couldn't blame you for your distrust or the way you acted on it." His expression deepened. "Tyron used to speak of you almost nonstop—you kept him going. Before I ever even met you, it seemed like I knew you. Besides, all of us had trusted Tyron: You having done the same would hardly have counted against you." His eyes wandered towards his daughter, now combing Dannsair's mane. "Astra was the only one who never knew him."

"Yeah," Louko murmured, adding after a moment, "What happened? I don't...understand why he's so different." The question was vague and abrupt, and yet it was an overflow from the earlier conversation. Louko wasn't even sure what he was asking—and was afraid to clarify.

Destrin took a deep breath, glancing back towards Astra. He lowered his voice and began, "After Rhioa's death, there…there were many things that happened. His oldest brother, Judican, framed him and exiled both him and Euracia." He tipped his head towards Louko. "That's when he went to Merimeethia. I think he might very well have stayed there permanently if it wasn't for Euracia finding him." Destrin's expression darkened. "He had the Screechers with him. According to Tyron, Euracia used them to intimidate King Omath into cooperation by having them take him over for a few minutes. But he also had them use their control on his own son—Tyron's nephew, Peregrin."

Louko had only been vaguely familiar with Peregrin, remembering how he, like Jade, had been one of several controlled by the horrible Screechers—creatures able to turn someone into a living puppet with a single touch.

"Euracia threatened Tyron, saying that if he did not do as he said, he would torture both his nephew," Destrin's voice dropped further. "And you. So Tyron went with him."

Louko listened to this all without any outer reaction, but inside he digested what they said. Tyron had been forced to leave? Euracia had made him?

Destrin went on. "When Euracia tried to kidnap Astra for her powers, Ameri and I managed to get her out of Litash. So, Euracia sent Tyron, some Screechers, and nearly twenty Bandilarian soldiers to capture us all. Tyron managed to make everyone think he'd killed me, then turned around and introduced me as the new guide. Unfortunately, the Screechers found Ameri before he did and he could not do the same for her. However, he still led everyone on a wild goose chase rather than track Astra down."

"That's how Tyron managed things for years: carrying out Euracia's orders on the surface while undermining him the whole time," Destrin explained, shifting to better warm his hands over the fire. "When Euracia decided to conquer Alarune, Tyron allowed their king to escape and start a rebellion. When the Ethian Massacre happened," here, Destrin paused and had to regather himself. "Tyron smuggled all of his nieces and nephews out to countries beyond Euracia's reach. And so it went for a long time." There was another deep breath. "Too long, I think. I knew the stress of it all was getting to him—I had to remind him to sleep and take his meals. He began taking more and more drastic measures to try and counter his brother. But I think the real blow came when he returned to Merimeethia." Destrin was very somber. "He brought me with him so I could visit Ameri. He went with the intent of getting rid of the men Euracia had left to watch Omath and you, Louko. But when he saw how Omath was treating you…." Destrin shook his head. "I thought he was going to kill him then and there. He had been so sure that your father would take care of you. And to return and see that he had been wrong…." His sigh was heavy, but not as heavy as the sinking in the pit of Louko's soul. "Tyron went into a spiral. He was so erratic: One day, he'd be sitting there chatting away to Rhioa as if she was right next to him, the next, he'd be lining up executions. You could never tell what version of him you would be talking to even from one minute to the next. Him throwing me in the dungeon and forgetting about me probably saved my life."

"He just…snapped?" Louko croaked at last, thinking of the person he had seen in Melye, and how erratic he had been. Then when they had been imprisoned….

"That would be my best guess," came the almost distraught reply.

"How has he managed to remain disguised as Kaeden, then?" Astra asked, startling Louko. He hadn't realized that she had gotten so close to the fire. "If he is truly so far gone, how has he maintained such an act?"

"I don't know," Destrin admitted as Astra sat down across from him. "But he has always seemed to be able to contain the less lucid moments for when he has no audience. Even while he would fall to pieces around me, his men always viewed him as reserved—perhaps temperamental, at the very worst."

Louko remembered such times even as Kaeden. Reserved and occasionally temperamental—that sounded exactly like the "steward." Had Tyron truly lost it? Somehow that only made it all worse. To know that he'd broken and that no one had been there to help him.

"I'm…I'm really sorry, Astra. Your mother and I truly thought he'd died. If we'd known…." Destrin trailed off.

Louko saw the way Astra's gaze was fixed on the fire. "You needn't apologize. You didn't know. With the way I was then, I can't even blame the Court for calling me insane."

The man winced. "We should have been there for you. For both of you."

Louko realized now that he was referencing not only Astra, but her brother as well. As he watched Destrin, he saw the weathered signs of regret and exhaustion playing out on his face.

"You're here now," Astra said softly.

Destrin didn't say a word, only nodded in a way that made Louko think the man wasn't very convinced.

Astra looked like she wanted to say more. She sat there, shoulders tense, one hand wrapped around her wrist as she seemed to roll the words around in her mouth. But all she said was, "Perhaps sleep is not such a bad idea," and got to her feet.

Lips pressing tightly together, Destrin looked from Astra to Louko. He seemed like he too wanted to say something, and yet all too well Louko recognized the fear in his eyes. The uncertainty. The guilt. Instead, the man settled with. "Yeah. You both should get some rest."

Louko didn't argue, wishing he was somehow better able to help the seeming lack of communication.

"Well, goodnight, then," Louko said weakly as he rolled out his cot. Hopefully, time would help the two heal.

CHAPTER VI

<u>**Astra:**</u>

"So that's your plan? Threaten me with them and so press me into your service?"

Out of the corner of my eye, I see Omath flinch as Euracia laughs.

"Do you really think so little of my intelligence? Of course I'm not threatening you—that hasn't worked since we were children." Euracia chuckles as if over some fond memory. "No, I'm threatening him." He jerks his thumb sideways towards where his bleach-haired soldiers stand.

One of the Screechers finally tears its gaze from me. It looks to Euracia, who nods, before it steps aside.

The breath is sucked from my lungs as I recognize the figure there. He is thin, dirty, eyes glassy and unfocused, standing as unnaturally still as the white-haired men, but it is undeniably my nephew, Peregrin.

Every muscle in my body goes taut with the effort it takes to keep from charging forward. "What have you done to him?" I growl, one hand already at my sword.

Euracia raises his hands in innocence, yet that smile still twists his lips. "Oh, nothing. This is their handiwork." He tips his head towards the man closest to him. "It's a neat little trick, really. They can control whomever they want with a single touch. Watch—" He addresses the white-haired man. "Make him raise his arms."

The man doesn't move a muscle. But little Peregrin, in the horrifying fashion of a puppet on strings, raises both hands above his head. His expression remains blank.

"Now make him turn around." Euracia twirls a finger as if demonstrating and Peregrin begins to step.

"Stop!" I can't keep myself from crying out. "Enough of your games—how do I know this isn't a ruse?"

Euracia sighs as if in disappointment, but all I care about is that Peregrin stands still once more. "That's how it is, eh? Fine." He motions again. "Release him."

For a second, nothing happens. It's as if none of the soldiers even hear the order. Then so abruptly that it makes me jump, Peregrin collapses. The weak gasps that echo in the hall are quickly followed by the frantic motions of the boy trying to skitter away from his captors. In two strides, Euracia closes the distance between them and hauls his son to his feet by the collar of his coat.

"Is this proof enough?" Euracia asks.

Peregrin, too weak to even stand, hangs in his father's grasp. Gone are the empty, glassy eyes. Now his face is wild with fear and tears run tracks across his mud-spattered cheeks. "I-I'm so s-sorry, Uncle," he croaks. "I, I d-didn't mean to…."

I don't have time to try and comfort the frightened child before Euracia pushes him towards one of the soldiers. "Shut him up, would you?"

The same man from before steps back so that Peregrin misses him and falls to the floor instead. Before the boy can get up, the bleach-haired man leans over and touches the back of his hand. Immediately,

Peregrin's rigid frame goes slack. In calm, exact, puppet-like movements, he pushes himself upright and stands up beside his father. Those terrible, unseeing eyes stare forward into nothing.

"If you think about it," Euracia draws the words out as if bored. "He's lucky to be alive. The stupid boy followed me and my men through the Forest. If he wasn't so terrible at maneuvering, some monster might have found him before we did. I lost half my men as it was."

I feel violently ill.

"But now, for the first time, he actually has some use," Euracia goes on, paying more attention to adjusting his travel-worn coat than to his desperate son. "See, without him, I was just counting on threatening whatever friends you were bound to make before I found you. Now I have double assurance: If you try to get your new friends to safety, I can still hurt Peregrin."

"Astra?"

Louko's voice interrupted the memory that had been playing on repeat in Astra's head since yesterday. "Hm?" She shifted in her saddle, trying not to shudder as she refocused.

"You alright?" The worry in her friend's eyes made it clear that she had let herself drift too far off.

"Um, yes, sorry, I was just…" Just living memories that weren't hers… "Thinking."

"Alright." As simple as Louko's replies tended to be, they were somehow far from dismissive. It always made Astra feel bad for not telling him everything. But then she'd found that, if she did tell him, she then felt bad for putting all of it on him. It seemed the only solution was to deal with the issue before it occurred, and there wasn't much she could do to prevent passing out and getting stuck with another one of Tyron's memories.

And yet Louko's glances always informed her she couldn't keep things from him. Even when he didn't say a word, it was clear that, tell him or not, he knew.

"So, how many weeks will this trip take us?" he asked instead.

Which made her feel worse. "That depends on what the southern range is like. I've never crossed the mountains there."

She heard Mitheau sigh from behind her. "Flying is so much easier."

"Let's just hope Louko's uncle hasn't done away with all my men before we get there," Keeshiff joked up ahead.

Louko gave a snort of laughter as he replied, "Knowing Rufio's loose tongue, you will probably find one or two amiss."

"I'm more worried about that rascally brother of his," Keeshiff said with a snort. "Rhumir always finds something to get into."

Despite the attempted humor, there was something hollow in his tone. Astra wondered if he was thinking of the news of Julyn and how Rufio and his brother would be taking it. The reminder of the knights turned Astra's thoughts to their newest friends.

Twisting around to look at Mitheau, Astra called back, "Perhaps Grenedil is already back and waiting in Nythril."

"I...I doubt it," Mitheau shrugged, silver hair bobbing. "The original plan before we found you was to get me to safety and then he was going to try and find you and the Guardian, Cyl, and see if he could get to Baeno. That would take him weeks." She bit her lip in worry.

"Well," Astra was surprised to hear Keeshiff was the one who interjected. "If it works, maybe he'll be able to get us some help."

She tried to take this as encouragement, but any optimism eluded her. How long had this Guard been gone again? It would have been before Rhioa's death. If this Cyl hadn't found his way by now, Astra wasn't sure that she dared hope he would.

"He did mention...something about going to a portal site or something?" Keeshiff continued.

"Portal site?" It was Louko.

This time, Mitheau replied, "Grenedil must be talking about the one where Ovok led everyone through. That would be the easiest to reopen."

There was the sound of someone clearing their throat, and only when they spoke at last did Astra realize it was Mariah. "Um. W-what do you mean, portal site?" Her voice was thin and small.

"Why? Are you taking notes?" Keeshiff snapped.

"I just..." It was odd how Mariah somehow managed to sound frustrated and ashamed at the same time. "Tyron just kept saying we had to go to Nythril and maybe that's why. I'm trying to *help*."

"Wait, when did he say this?" Astra cut in. Memories of Nythril rose in a jumble she tried to sort: Anything with the feverish hue was her own, as was anything with Keeshiff and Louko together. But the rest? It was hard to tell.

"I, uh. He just—it was several times. He'd just...mention it. The last time was only a few days before I left," she squeaked.

Astra looked to Louko. Was that where Tyron was headed? Then why wait? Why not just go straight there and get this portal open?

"Mitheau, can anyone open the portal then?" Louko asked, seeming to have caught onto Astra's train of thought.

Mitheau shook her head. "Grenedil has an article of Gifting that allows him to enter through pre-existing cracks. After Ovok let so many people through and under such violent circumstances, he was betting there was a crack there. So, unless Tyron has some special means, the site is useless."

Special means. That meant her.

"So are such articles rare, then?" Louko asked.

"Seeing as it took Grenedil almost a decade to find one, very rare."

Astra met Louko's eyes.

The sigh he let out showed he was thinking the same thing even before he replied, "So then seeing as Tyron wanted Astra for this power she has, and she can theoretically learn to open the gateway or whatever it was…then maybe Tyron is after Astra to open this portal in Nythril?"

The only sound was the plodding of horses' hooves.

"Where is he trying to go?" Her father's question held clear confusion.

Astra adjusted her reins, trying to keep her tension from her hands. "We do not know. And until we find out, he remains hard to predict."

The days wore on with an eerie calmness that Astra was unused to. Though she still tired easily and was sore at the end of every day, she felt stronger than she had in a long time. She could even contribute in the evenings when they made camp. Tonight was their first night inside the Forest of Riddles, meaning their fire would have to burn the whole night through. While her father got the fire going, Astra, Louko, and Keeshiff set to gathering fuel. Mitheau was left with the task of pulling out rations and keeping an eye on Mariah.

"Did you hear that?" Mariah's entire body went rigid. So did the entire camp.

Astra froze, listening carefully. It was just a soft rustling, emanating from across the camp as something pushed through the undergrowth. Then she heard the faint chirp. Before Astra could announce what it was, the thing rolled right out into their clearing.

Mariah squeaked louder than the little grey fuzzball. Its large, owl-like eyes blinked as it waddled on duck feet, squeaking again as if to mimic Mariah. Its beak wasn't visible from beneath the overabundance of grey fur.

"It's just a rubii." Destrin chuckled. "Shameless little beggars, and likely the most harmless thing in the Forest of Riddles."

The little thing tucked its legs and rolled in a circle before bouncing up and chirping again.

"Not unless you kill one," Astra commented, bending to pick up another fallen branch.

The whole camp went dead silent, staring at her.

"What?" Astra straightened. "It wasn't *me*. Soletuph apparently hit one by accident. Ent said an entire swarm came out of nowhere and attacked him. Soletuph had to shift just to get away."

There was a stifled gasp and Astra turned to find Louko staring at her wide-eyed.

"Well, now I'll add that to the list of things I hate about Litash," Keeshiff said as he deposited his load of firewood near Destrin.

"Yeah, still doesn't top the giant Dragon eater that almost swallowed us," Louko mumbled, eyeing the little fuzzball as Mariah threw it a little bit of her rations.

Astra paused. "Dragon eater?" she echoed in confusion.

"Yes, it was huge!" Mitheau chimed in, waving her arms for emphasis. "It almost ate us, too. We had to trick it into tying itself into a knot among the trees. But uh, don't tell Grenedil or he'll rub it in my face. He always did warn me about the dangers of crossing the forest in my Dragon form."

Astra looked between Mitheau and Louko for any traces of a joke. Were they trying to trick her? "I don't remember this…" she said slowly, returning to the fire to contribute her bit of fuel.

Louko rolled his eyes. "Well, that was probably because you were busy hallucinating and, you know, dying."

The rubii was rolling in circles again, trying each person for spare scraps of food. It bumped into Astra's leg and she shooed it away. "I'm not sure which one of us was hallucinating," was her dry reply.

Keeshiff chuckled, only causing Mitheau and Louko to look despondent.

"Great, now no one is going to believe us. You're always the 'sensible' one," Louko replied using air quotes around the word 'sensible.'

"Speaking of sensible," Destrin cut in. "Stop feeding that thing or it will follow us all the way to Nythril."

Halfway through tearing off a piece of bread for the rubii, Mitheau popped the food in her mouth instead. The puffball gave sad chirps and plopped on the ground in response.

"How does it not get eaten by all the other...things in this forest?" Mariah asked quietly. "I could hardly sleep when I went through alone."

Astra hadn't thought of Mariah making the trip alone. How frightened must she have been? To hear of Julyn's execution, to steal papers from Tyron's very desk, then to flee through the Forest of Riddles and across the plains of Litash completely by herself. It would have been easier for her to head to the coast, sail away to Cadbir, and never be heard from again. The question was, was she doing it on Tyron's behalf or theirs?

"Rubiis don't have much meat beneath all that fur." Destrin sat back, the fire now crackling away. "Besides, they're surprisingly agile little things." He paused to accept his rations from Mitheau. "Things are also calmer in the Forest than they used to be. They say the Forest mirrors the state of Litash—I'm not sure if it's true, but this place was definitely worse under Euracia."

"I suppose I should have been more careful when crossing the Forest for that stupid ball last year, then," Louko said with a nervous chuckle. "I didn't really think much of it at the time. And then it was fine when Astra and I went back to Merimeethia."

Astra hadn't thought of that. She settled down at the base of a tree and decided not to think of what could have happened to her friend.

"At least there's the path that the messengers use between Litash and Merimeethia," Keeshiff pointed out. "Makes it easier to keep from getting lost."

Destrin nodded. "It's also one of the narrowest sections of the Forest, and since you learned from Ent how to manage in these woods," He nodded to Louko. "You were probably quite safe. Not to mention that it is always easier with Astra."

At the risk of being told she was hallucinating again, Astra interrupted: "What do you mean?"

"Oh," Her father looked up at her with surprise. "Every time we've ever crossed the Forest with you, we've almost never had any run-ins with animals. Your mother theorizes that it has to do with your connection to the Miadoris. Since the Forest's roots are in Gifting, perhaps it senses yours."

"Well, that certainly didn't help with the dragon eater," Louko mumbled.

Destrin inclined his head to acknowledge the point. "Possibly on account of her, by your words, dying. But who knows; all we really have is theories."

Astra didn't say anything this time. Theories. That's all they'd ever had about her power. No way to control it, no way to learn to use it, just theories. On the bright side, perhaps it could do something besides blowing up buildings, getting her exiled, and having a madman try to capture her for it. On the downside, keeping away monsters seemed a rather paltry trade-off.

Entrais:

"So you do not even attempt to deny it?" the man was indignant as he shouted to be heard above the tumultuous crowd. It was even worse than Astra's hearings. Between news of her escape and Ent's "confession," the whole capital was in an uproar.

"You have the signed confession. What more do you want, a detailed account of my life?" Ent forced the growl even though the fight had long since gone from him. This whole thing was a sham; a simple technicality.

"He's right—why are we wasting our time with this?" An older courtier in the front tier gave an irritated flick of her hand. "He has admitted to the premeditated, illegal release of a highly dangerous criminal. He has betrayed both his country and his status, using his power in favor of his own family instead of his citizens. Let's strip him of his title and be done with it."

From somewhere in the crowd, Ent heard someone yell, "Hypocrites!" followed by the pelting of rotten fruit. The Court had taken the precaution of a few Gifted individuals this time; the fruit splattered on some invisible barrier and dripped to the floor. All the while, Ent felt a strange detachment from it, the knowledge that this was now inevitable drowning out any other emotion. But no emotion was better than the alternative. At this point, Ent was worried he would be unable to hold back the Fury otherwise.

"I think all of us would do well to remember King Entrais's years of service in freeing us from Euracia. Whatever shortcomings have surfaced now, we still owe him the decency of respect." The voice was irritatingly familiar: Tirzah. She stood from among the rows of courtiers and continued, "I believe King Entrais's plight is much like his sister's—The War was too much for any to bear. After all of that, how could anyone bear the weight of a crown?"

At last he felt something: contempt. The ease with which Tirzah spun her lie and played the Court was nauseating.

A lord from the other side of the hall stood. "I believe Lady Therune has a point. One act done for the sake of family does not negate such years of service. Even if the act was unacceptable, is it not understandable? Who wouldn't do anything for their little sister?"

Ent's prosecutor now cut in. "But if he is willing to bend the law to play favorites, how can we trust such a king? He cannot be allowed to keep his position."

"Then give him the chance to step down," Tirzah now argued. "We should give him the chance to retain some dignity. If he will go quietly, then there is no need to drag him out here."

He couldn't help but let out a quiet, hollow laugh. Yes, how gracious of her. The spineless liar.

Stay calm. Stay calm. He repeated the words to himself as he fought to keep the red from his vision. "Seeing as you wanted nothing more than to have me off this throne in the first place, I don't see why you bother letting me have my dignity at all. But fine, you've won. Congratulations."

Whatever Ent's prosecutor said was drowned out by the crowd's turbulent response. However, he did notice the way Tirzah rubbed one temple. Whether it was out of stress or irritation, Ent couldn't help the little bit of satisfaction. *How does it feel? Maybe being in charge isn't as fun as you thought.*

When it became clear that the crowd wasn't going to settle down, the herald gave the signal that the Court had adjourned. The hall doors were opened and the palace guards began to try and move people towards the exit. But people weren't having it. He saw several begin to push back against the guards, shouting and spitting as they did so.

Panic overcame his Fury and reason took hold. People were going to get hurt. Taking a deep breath, he pushed all of his Gifting into projecting his voice above the noise, shouting, "QUIET, PLEASE!"

It worked like magic, and a nearly unnatural stillness settled on the courtroom.

"None of this is helping! You think I want more bloodshed and death?! The last thing I want is another massacre in this city! This is difficult for everyone but thoughtless riots are not the answer. Please, go home. This is my last request as king: Go home and live."

He saw the hesitation, the unsure glances that passed between the crowd, the angry glares that went up to the Court. But when movement stirred, it was a quiet shuffle towards the doors.

Then came the call: "Long live King Entrais!"

Another took it up almost immediately. "Long live King Entrais!"

Soon, it rang through the entire hall at a nearly deafening volume.

Part of Ent was deeply touched, but the rest of him was panicking. How long would they listen and stay home? What if they went to war just as Jade predicted? He felt his hands tremble, and quietly folded them behind his back, attempting to remain collected for the sake of the people even as his worst nightmare was coming to pass. He stared up at Tirzah, locking eyes and willing her to see what he saw; the pain she was causing. The chaos. All for what?

Tirzah did not look angry or worried like he expected, or even irritated like before. Her expression was fully serious as she returned his gaze. Then she shook her head, breaking away to say something to the courtier next to her.

The hall slowly emptied, the chant fading with it. It was only when Ent could hear himself think again that Soletuph approached the stand, stating coldly, "Please allow me to escort you back to your wing of the palace, Your Majesty."

"I will say it again: This is a stupid idea, Ent," Ascriot grumbled as they all stood in Ent and Jade's room, which held plenty of space for all fourteen of the Ethians.

All fourteen of the very, very agitated Ethians, that was.

"We don't have a choice." Ent's own reply felt feeble in his mouth. He knew he looked weak in front of them, and more and more he wondered if maybe he was. Maybe he just wasn't enough…never enough to save those that needed him most.

Matthes threw up both his hands. "Why can't Jade just assume the throne?" The buzz of energy his question brought with it rippled through the room and all the faces; the faces full of disappointment and even outright anger.

They hadn't had any time to discuss this before the trial, and so now, it somehow meant they were deciding to ask all the questions right before Ent was supposed to leave.

"After all, you're the only one getting exiled, aren't you?" Soletuph was leaning against the wall, arms crossed over his chest as he glowered. "Why won't you let her do something instead of just sit there and watch you mess it up?"

"Soletuph! Really?" Jade stepped forward, turning to look each and every Ethian in the eyes. "Ent and I have formulated a plan. I am not renouncing the title my father left for me; I will eventually make a claim, but I am no fool—I am not about to throw myself to the wolves. Let them show the people just how corrupt they are in their leadership. I am not going to jeopardize my unborn child by staying behind and letting the wolves get me. Would you really be fine with me leaving your nephew or niece to be possibly killed by the Court?" Jade looked Soletuph up and down coldly. "Because after Ent leaves, that's exactly what they would try and do. Get me out of the way. They didn't dare do it with Ent here, but if he leaves and I stay, then the Elves go with him. I will have no Tallaman to help me. I will have no one but you behind my back, and let's face it— none of you have any sway over the Court now. You're all next. They want complete control. When was the last time any of you served as lawmakers? Anything other than bodyguards?"

Now she was the one throwing up her hands, face flushed in a way Ent hadn't seen it in a while. And, while it was good to see the color in her cheeks again, it worried him all the same. "We can't fix this from the inside anymore. Ent and I have been trying since The War ended—no. The best play is to do this peacefully and let the people come and ask us. You saw how much they raged during the trial. When the unrest grows, I can step up. But we need the people to unite first."

Ent swallowed hard. No, he didn't want that. He didn't want any more bloodshed. He hoped and prayed that it wouldn't come to that, unsure he could carry the weight of being responsible for the start of a war. He'd tried so hard to stop the last one. But he trusted Jade…she was perhaps one of the only people he could right now.

"Look, we understand you aren't giving up." Ascriot stepped in between Jade and Soletuph, casting a look at each of them. "I think what Soletuph was *trying* to say is that it's hard to watch this and not feel like everything we went through is going to waste." His shoulders drooped. "We all knew that things couldn't last—not with the Court so overpowered compared to the Council. But I think we all sort of expected to make this decision together. And we certainly didn't expect to split up again."

"I know," Jade's voice softened. "But we aren't giving up—right, Ent?" She turned and looked him straight in the eyes, such a mixture of emotions held in that one stare. Fear was shared between them both.

"Certainly not. But I think we can agree I wasn't helping," Ent tried to keep his tone from sounding as listless as it was trying to be.

Some of the Ethians looked saddened. Others looked away.

Matthes sighed. "That's not what we meant, Entrais."

Ent knew that was a lie. There was a reason some of them had looked away. "It doesn't matter right now. What matters is we need you to stay here—to get things ready so that when Jade does make the claim for the throne, we have some footing."

If Jade tried now—after the stunt they'd pulled on both Astra and Ent—all the Court would have to do was claim she wasn't physically fit. If she renounced her title to allow Soletuph to claim it, the Court would simply say he had no right as the second-born. True or not, they would strip the Ethian Council of its last shred of credibility. It disgusted Ent…but unfortunately being disgusted wouldn't change the facts.

"W-w-we will…be r-ready for you to…to come h-home." Peregrin's words, though labored, sounded more certain than Ent had heard since they were all kids.

"Thank you," he whispered. "And truly…I am so sorry."

"Don't be sorry." Ascriot shook his head. "Just don't give up on us."

Right. Keep it together. Just keep going. But Ent just felt as if he'd been dropped in quicksand; the more he struggled to go forward, the deeper he sank.

"Alright. Now it's best if we get down to the courtyard…otherwise they'll send someone up to grab Ent without much decorum." Ascriot's attempt at a joke fell flat in the room, but nonetheless everyone agreed.

Soon, Ent found himself mounting up on his horse in the courtyard of the palace, about to leave much the same as he had once entered; an exile who didn't belong. Most of their things had been sent ahead to Cithan already, meaning all that was really left to do was leave, to run away and admit defeat.

"If you forget anything, just let us know." Ascriot tried to smile as he added, "Then we can all fight over who gets to bring it to you."

"Be c-c-c-careful," Peregrin added quietly, his difficulty speaking just another scar left from The War.

"We will be," Jade again replied after a bit of silence. She seemed to be speaking more to her brother than anyone else. Soletuph stood wordlessly by her horse, refusing to look at anyone.

Ent could say nothing, mind numb as every worst-case scenario of what could happen now ran over and over in his mind. He kept returning to how things had gotten here, going over everything he might have done differently to avoid it. There had been so many things—so many ways he could have fixed this. Always, he was too late to see them.

"And keep in touch. We'll be sure to do the same." Matthes spoke lightly, but Ent caught the meaning. They'd been too closely watched these last few days to establish how to best pass on information. One of them would likely visit soon with a more detailed plan.

How was he supposed to do this? He'd already said goodbye to Astra. Now he had to figure out how to say it to thirteen of the most loyal friends he'd ever had. The friends he was abandoning to clean up his mess. They'd survived The Massacre and The War only to be split up by his bad decisions.

Somewhere behind him, his mother cleared her throat. "We'd best be off."

He managed a nod and spurred on his horse, leading the others to the fate he'd forced them into. But he was unprepared for the sight that met them at the other side of the palace gate.

The streets were quiet—cleared with not a single wagon or carriage. Instead people lined the side of the cobblestone roadway, somber and silent as they watched Ent and his small group ride out the palace exit. A few held flowers that they tossed out into the roadway as the slow procession went through.

"Your sister was right," he heard Jade murmur from next to him. "People still remember—they still support you."

And it was going to get them all killed. Ent wished he could calm the tightness he felt in his chest, but no matter how hard he tried he couldn't shake the reality that something very bad was going to happen.

He should never have signed that confession. He should never have let Astra go to Merimeethia. He should have made sure Tyron was dead, himself.

The funeral-like procession lasted their entire journey through the city, and by the time they reached the city gates, Ent wanted to scream. He didn't deserve this—he'd failed them all and now their stupid loyalty could get them all killed. But all he could do was hold his head up and graciously accept the tribute, knowing to do otherwise would be unfair to those who were sacrificing so much for him.

Only once they had passed through the wide gates and left the crowds behind did Ent feel like he could almost breathe again. Almost.

"Well, that was awkward," Tallaman said as they at last faced an empty road ahead of them. "Humans and their strange sense of loyalty."

At least Humans have loyalty. A suppressed bitterness briefly surfaced as he barely bit back the thought.

"Elves and their strange sense of pride that keeps them from ever admitting they have emotions," Jade grumbled.

"Maybe we should save the arguments for later," Ent whispered. "We need to get going. Cithan is almost two weeks away." He fought to keep himself simply focused on the next task. It was all that was keeping him sane, at this point: Think one step ahead and then there was a reason to stay together.

The traveling was surprisingly uneventful—or maybe that was just because after years of looking over your shoulder with every step, Ent was still unused to the fact that Euracia was no longer here to hunt him. But Tyron was still alive; and he had his eyes set on Astra. That alone was enough to scare Ent.

Regardless, the journey northeast across the plains was safer than had been in the past, with the newly constructed roadway allowing for routes that avoided the wolf-cats and pythanid breeding grounds.

"Ent. You are not going to stay up again," Jade whispered as they made camp once more for the night. It had been four days.

Clenching his jaw, Ent managed to murmur an, "I'm fine," as his throat already threatened to close on him.

"Actually, you're probably on the verge of hallucinations," Tallaman commented dryly from where he had just sat down.

"Thank you for that." Ent forgot how hard it was to have a private conversation with other Elves around. Maybe it was because in the past, none of the Elves had cared to be around him unless necessity forced it. "Nice to see you pretending to care." Had he…really just said that out loud?

Tallaman actually paused a moment, sucking in his cheeks as if mildly uncomfortable. He looked back down at whatever item he'd been rewrapping as he grunted, "Nice to see it makes no difference."

Instead of answering, Ent simply began unrolling his cot and unpacking the rations for the night. He was done talking. Elves had only seen Humans as leeches—able to take on the abilities of the race they married. That had been what led to Tallaman almost killing Destrin when he'd first been at Cithan. It was also what led Elves to despise half-breeds.

The memory of Ent showing up to Cithan alone and lost after The Massacre, only to be turned away, was one he would never forget. No. The Elves hadn't bothered to help until Ent had come to rescue them after Euracia had pillaged Cithan and killed Ent's cousin. They cared for nothing but their own well-being and pride.

"For once, he has a point." His mother's voice brought him back to the present. "Animals aren't much of a worry around here. There's no need to keep watch—get some rest."

Ent didn't realize how much his body ached until every muscle in it tensed from the remark. But instead of replying he handed out the rations, even just the thought of sleep beginning to make it hard to breathe. There was too much—it was bad enough he could see them while awake. He didn't want to be imprisoned and unable to escape in his sleep.

When he handed Jade her supper, she took his hands instead of her food. "Please?"

He let the desperation show as he murmured, "I could get someone hurt."

"We will all stay out of the way," Jade replied. "But you can't go on like this. The longer you wait, the worse it's going to be."

"I—" he stopped suddenly, remembering again that he was in the presence of Elvish ears. "Fine." He shuddered as he said the word, unable to escape the dread.

But Jade only looked relieved. "Thank you." She released his hands and took her rations.

In all honesty, Ent had half-planned to try and simply lay down without falling asleep. He could face the shadows lurking around him even when awake, and knew they'd win over the moment he closed his eyes. And yet as the fire died down and everyone else took to their cots, he found his eyes were much heavier than he expected, and against his will they drooped and gave way to a fitful and frightening sleep.

If only his dreams were just that: dreams. But no, instead they were distorted memories of The Massacre—of Euracia murdering everyone Ent had held dear and scattering the rest to the wind. They were memories of every time he'd failed—every death that failure had brought with it. Of dark cells and interrogations and of him and Astra fighting for their lives as Tyron tried to get information.

Ent jolted awake with a scream half stuck in his throat, hand going to the knife in his coat and holding it out as he heard voices in the darkness. Where was he? Was he still caught? Where was Astra?

"Ent? Ent? Can you hear me? It's Jade." The voice sounded several yards to his left.

"What are you—" he cut off his own question as the darkness slowly faded to something more akin to early morning. He wasn't in a cell. He was outside. Right.

Slowly, he lowered the knife, though still unable to return it to its sheath. "I'm fine. Sorry. Did I wake you?" He noted now that everyone else was awake, Tallaman standing up and Ameri crouching on her cot as if she'd been ready to run to him.

"No, we were all about to get up and get some breakfast," Jade said firmly. He didn't miss her irritated glance towards the others. "Would you like to have some with us?"

"I'm fine," he whispered, swallowing hard and sitting up straighter as he tried to reorient himself away from the nightmares.

Ameri frowned. "You really should—"

Jade cut her off. "Alright. I'll save yours for you. There's a little spare water if you need to freshen up and clear your head."

Taking in a deep breath, Ent nodded, mouthing an apology even as he somehow managed to unglue his hand from the hilt of his knife. He got up, accepting the canteen from Jade and splashing some water on his face. He wiped it off with a sleeve and went to roll up his cot.

"If you had told me that things were this bad, I could have given you something for him," he heard his uncle grumble to Jade.

"I'm very aware what you think of me already and was trying to at least keep some shred of dignity," Ent grumbled before he could catch himself. Well then, he was still apparently exhausted. But he didn't like the accusation in Tallaman's tone when this was in no shape or form Jade's fault. "So leave her alone and keep your acrid tongue to yourself, please."

123

Tallaman's expression was the closest thing to hurt that Ent had ever seen. "I wasn't accusing her of anything," he said stiffly. "I was trying to tell her that I have things that could help."

"Oh, right, because you've always wanted to help me," Ent snapped without thinking. Then he winced. "Sorry. I'm just. Didn't mean that, Uncle. I'm just tired." He turned away. "We should get going."

He could practically hear all of them holding their tongues.

"You're right. *Uncle*, why don't you go get the horses?" Jade suggested tersely.

For once, Tallaman didn't say anything. Ent heard him get up and walk away.

CHAPTER VII

Louko:

"I am the nephew of the Ezai Ru! Louko? Does that not ring a bell?" Louko berated the host of Nythrilian guards that had seized them. This was…new. Why in Eatris was his uncle fortifying the border?

The captain and his lieutenant glanced at each other. Six more soldiers shuffled in uncomfortable silence behind them.

"Do you have any proof to back your claim, sir?" the captain asked.

"I…I don't exactly…know what you would need for proof. My brother, Keeshiff—he literally *just* left only a few weeks ago; don't tell me you don't remember him?" Louko waved his arms frantically in the direction of Keeshiff. "So help me if you put us in prison again I will…do something."

He felt Astra's hand on his arm, though he wasn't sure if it was to comfort him or to calm him.

The captain looked to Keeshiff with mild skepticism. "I'm afraid I haven't been as far north as the capital in a few years, so I have no way to verify your brother's identity either." He glanced at his lieutenant.

"Is there any way you could send word there, then?" Astra now asked. "They would be able to verify us for you."

The captain rubbed his chin. "I suppose we could escort you to Mil-Seo and leave you with the guard there. They could spare a man to play courier."

They didn't really have time to be waiting around, and yet clearly this was the only way they were going to get anywhere except thrown in

125

prison. Again. He sighed. "Fine. Uncle is not going to be pleased when he hears about this."

"Is Dia Jahng any closer than the capital?" Keeshiff surprised Louko by speaking up. "She would be more than willing to verify our identities as well."

Louko blinked. Would she though?

"*Commander* Dia Jahng?" The captain now looked thoroughly surprised. "I presume she is with the Ezai Ru or at the northern border, given everything that's going on."

Here the lieutenant cut in, addressing his superior. "I know one of the men that used to ride in her hunting party. He's the one they have doing the rounds to check the security at border towns."

The captain frowned in thought. "Well, if he hasn't gone through Mil-Seo yet, he'd probably arrive sooner than any reply from the capital."

"The sooner the better, seeing we are currently unwelcomed in Litash *and* Merimeethia. It would be a shame if my uncle found out you all got us caught after all he did to make sure that wouldn't happen," Louko forced his tone to remain calm even as worry pricked. What was going on? What did the captain mean "given everything that's going on"?

"If you don't mind the question, what's caused such a raise in security?" It was Destrin who voiced Louko's thoughts.

The captain seemed to take a moment to realize no one was joking. "Have you not heard? Merimeethia has declared war on Nythril. They stated Nythril had spies in their capital and Steward Kaeden has an army marching for the Merym Pass as we speak."

"Everyone is waiting to hear if Litash will side with its new ally against us," the lieutenant added. "That's why the entire border is being closed."

"*What?!*" Louko couldn't help but gape. War? Mariah's words rang in his head: *Tyron just kept saying we had to go to Nythril.*

He locked eyes with Astra even as he replied, "Then you had better get our identities verified soon because we need to speak with the Ezai Ru as soon as possible."

"Very well." The captain turned to his men and waved a hand. "Two of you with me, the rest to the back. We're headed for Mil-Seo."

Louko was getting tired of all the traveling, and he was really getting tired of being detained. Even if it was in a nice inn with plenty of warm beds. Now he knew Tyron was out for Nythril and the portal site and they had to warn Ven.

A knock from the door made Louko's hopes jump as quickly as he did, but Keeshiff beat him to the door and opened it immediately.

"Breakfast, if anyone wants it," the voice from the hall announced.

Louko felt his disappointment ring around the whole room.

"Oh, uh, thanks," Keeshiff mumbled and reached for a tray.

Mitheau stepped up to help with the other one. "At least they're a little more hospitable this time," she said as she brought her tray over to one of the tables that sat against one of the walls, wedged between two beds.

The room was probably the largest in the inn, likely for wealthier patrons, but was still a little cramped. It had obviously been rearranged to accommodate all six of them at once.

Louko just sat back on one of the beds, frustrated and unable to stop his stupid brain from running through all the possible scenarios with how this newest war could play out. "I suppose that is something."

"How about some food, Astra?" Destrin called.

Astra was on one of the corner beds, though Louko guessed she used it more for TetraChess than for sleeping. "I'm alright for now. Maybe in a bit," was her absent reply.

Raising one skeptical eyebrow, Louko couldn't help but give a "Mmhm. Sure."

Astra's gaze broke away from the boards only for a second. She gave no reply.

"Here they go again," Mitheau sighed, sitting down on her bed with a plate of fish and fruit slices.

"Okay, you two old ladies can get off your rears and come have dinner with us mere mortals, please," Keeshiff said, hands placed on his hips like he was scolding a pair of children.

It was difficult for Louko to keep a straight face as he replied, "Well, maybe we are afraid you *mere mortals* won't be able to stand our presence. It's for your own safety."

"Which one of us is actually expected to live for the next thousand years?" Mitheau shot back, clearly trying to bite back a smile.

"That…is a valid statement. Guess we will have to acquiesce our immortal status to the scaly being and eat our dinner like good little children." Louko sagged his shoulders in mock defeat as he slid off his bed and slowly came over to where the trays were set.

Keeshiff cleared his throat. "He meant you, too, Astra."

"Hm?" Astra picked up her head as if completely oblivious.

Louko just rolled his eyes. "Food. Most people need it."

He saw her press her lips together, looking from the chess boards to the trays of food. Then around the room of people looking at her. She slid off the low bed and picked up one of the wooden plates the inn had provided. After loading it with a bit of fruit and cooked grains, she returned to the bed.

Unsurprised and yet still determined to keep her from isolating herself, Louko brought his own plate of food back over and stood at the end of the bed, eyeing The Game. "Are you alright? Was it another memory?" he dared ask.

He saw the way Astra's eyes flicked up towards him. "At least it was while I was asleep this time," she murmured.

"What did you see?" Would talking about it help or make it worse? Louko really wasn't sure.

"Nothing that gets us any closer to figuring out why he started a war," she said with evident frustration. "And nothing that tells us how to stop it."

"Mariah—" Louko winced even as he said his sister's name, but turned to look at her nonetheless— "Did Tyron say nothing else about how he planned to go to Nythril? If the war is for the portal, wouldn't it have been easier to sneak by rather than start something like this?"

"Um," Mariah froze, spoon suspended in midair. She had placed herself in the opposite corner of the room from Astra. "I-I don't really know." She flinched and set her spoon down. "It was always kind of hard to tell what he was talking about. He never really mentioned a portal." She swallowed. "I tried to talk to one of the soldiers once to see if anyone else knew anything. I guess they were all sort of confused by him, too."

"So do you think he was showing signs of insanity?" Louko asked, having to know. As painful as it was…knowing if Tyron had snapped would maybe bring some closure. Help him mourn the man that had been lost. Know that he had at least once cared.

Mariah bit her lip, visibly uncomfortable with everyone looking at her. "Maybe. Sometimes, anyway. And sometimes he seemed so normal. I-I don't know."

"Wait, insane? You think Tyron has gone insane?" Mitheau was the one who blurted out the question. "Like, acting like two different people?"

"Actually, yes, exactly like that," Destrin entered into the conversation for the first time, turning away from the window he'd been looking out of and leaning against the frame. "Everything went south for him after…after his wife died. He was put in a lot of difficult positions and I guess it was too much for him."

"Do any of you remember how long they were married?" Mitheau asked in the same urgent manner.

"He…not long," Destrin replied, sorrow filling up his expression. "They married in secret shortly after returning to Litash. They'd only just started settling down when Judican discovered his brother had returned to the country. Rhioa died not long after."

Mitheau sat back, slightly deflated. "I guess it still doesn't matter if he couldn't shift anyway."

"As in, into his dragon form? He could," Destrin looked confused even as he corrected Mitheau.

"Wait—but he was Human?" Louko was just generally lost.

"Human?" Astra spoke for the first time since the conversation had begun. "But he's of the royal family—isn't he a Bandilarian? How has he been masquerading as Kaeden?"

Destrin held his hands up as if calling the room to order. "Tyron is Human. His parents were both healers who died in service to the king of the Bandilarians, so he was brought into the palace and given a title as homage to them. Many of the people of Litash only knew him as the adopted son of Jade's grandfather the king, and thus assumed he was a shape-shifter." He turned his explanation to Astra. "He always had some ability at Gifting, however, and managed the guise of Kaeden through illusions and some clever practical effects. His illusion work wasn't very reliable when he first started, which is why he could never manage to keep his eyes a different color."

Louko frowned, trying to wrap his head around it all as he listened.

"As for his ability to shift like a Myrandi, Humans adapt," Destrin addressed the whole room again. "We're a little more flexible than most and tend to take on the traits of those we marry. For example, I'm proficient at certain elements of Gifting. It's not as impressive or practiced as what Ameri can do, but like many Humans—" He nodded to Louko— "I had no Gifting at all before we were married." He looked back at Mitheau with a slight shrug. "Tyron and Rhioa may not have been married long, but they were very close. I have seen him shift into Dragon form many times in the years since her death."

"Then he probably just gave into the Dragon," Mitheau spoke with a grave expression.

"Wait—" Louko's mind was suddenly going faster than a pythanid as he recalled the old and distorted stories of Drogans. "Are you implying Drogan Madness? Is that actually a thing that happens?" He'd sort of thought it was simply exaggeration and legends.

Mitheau appeared nearly surprised. "You know of it? Yes, it happens. We are all trained from a young age to maintain balance. For someone to fall out of that is…" She shuddered. "It has not happened in decades."

"So then, that could be what's happened to Tyron?" Louko couldn't mask his desperation. "He's been through so much and with no one there—do you think the Dragon's taken over? Is there any way to fix it?"

"Hold on, do you mean, like, that he can't control what he's been doing?" Keeshiff sounded nearly incredulous. "What does this 'Drogan Madness' even mean?"

"Everyone thinks of us Drogans as shifters, merely changing our skins like Bandilarians. But we're not. We are both Human and Dragon to the full." Mitheau looked to Keeshiff, hands now held up in demonstration. "It is a balance each of us walks. Tip too far to one side," one hand went down as the other went up. "And that nature will take over. It has happened to many Drogans that they will become so much a part of the world of men that they lose the Dragon part of them. They don't even notice until they can't shift anymore." Her hands returned to her lap. "But worse is when the Dragon takes over. The taste for blood, the cunning, the obsession—it takes over until the person is more animal than man. It has only happened a few times in our history. Usually the signs are seen and stopped by other Drogans. But if all that happened to Tyron, and he had no one to help him rein it in…" The pause was heavy. "He may not have even known the dangers."

"Does it mean there is a way to get him back?" The question was barely existent, let alone audible as Louko breathed it. What if the Tyron he knew was still in there—just as much a victim. Unable to control himself and forced to watch all the horrors unfold. Just like Louko had to when Astra had been caught.

Mitheau looked hesitant. "I…I'm not sure. Like I said, the madness itself is so rare that there aren't many cases to go off of." She bit her lip as if remembering something else.

"What is it?" Louko asked, unable to stop himself.

"I've only ever heard one story in full detail," Mitheau spoke slowly, now tugging at a strand of silver hair. "It was over a thousand years ago. They said that he was well liked, too. But," Her reluctance turned her face into a near grimace. "In the end, he was put down for the safety of others."

Put down. Like an animal.

"I do not think *killing* something is quite getting him back," Louko felt too tense to even breathe.

Tentatively, Astra laid her hand over his.

He looked to his friend, wondering how she was taking this newest piece of information. How would she feel about the possibility of Tyron being captive in his own mind? It was hard to tell anything beyond her troubled expression and pensive silence.

"Grenedil may know something more," Mitheau offered weakly. "He has far more knowledge on such things. He also knows Cyl, and Cyl is thousands of years old and has seen many events in our history: If anyone knows a way, Cyl would."

"Cyl. That's the guardian?" The one that might not even be alive?

Mitheau nodded.

"Well…" Louko murmured. "Let's hope Grenedil hurries up."

A knock on the door interrupted the thoughtful silence that followed.

"Enter," Destrin was the one who replied, and Louko was thankful for it, taking a moment to recover from both the onslaught of information as well as the sudden noise.

The door opened, and none other than Zhahn, Jahng's second-in-command, stepped into the room. His face lit up as his eyes went first at Louko and then Astra.

"Princess Astra! I am so glad to see you've recovered!"

Astra:

Astra…had no idea who this was. Her head was still spinning with Tyron's memories, with thoughts of The Game and now the possibility of madness. She couldn't even start to remember how she was supposed to know this man. Bewildered, she looked to Louko.

"Zhahn, *finally*," Louko stepped forward. "We need to see Uncle Ven as soon as possible and what is all this about a war?"

The name Zhahn rang a faint bell, but Astra still couldn't latch on to any specific memory.

"Merimeethia declared war a little under a week ago." Zhahn's smile had vanished. "Which is why I'm out here. But I'm sending two of my best to take you all straight to Kythdexlentu-Orsha. I've already got men saddling your horses."

Astra watched as her friend deflated, shoulders sagging as he ran his hand through his hair. "Thank you, Zhahn. We appreciate it."

"So are we able to leave today, then?" Astra's father asked.

Zhahn nodded then paused. "So long as the princess is well enough to travel." He looked to her.

Uh. "Yes, quite well, thank you." Astra realized that, however, he apparently knew her, it must have been when she was busy, er, dying.

The Nythrilian soldier looked a little uncertain, but did not argue, only turned to leave. "I'll have your horses and your little pet ready to go by noon. Is there anything else you need?"

"Little pet?" Keeshiff voiced everyone's question.

Turning around, the soldier wore a slightly perplexed expression. "The little rubii? It was in one of the saddlebags and everyone said that it was your little travel companion."

Astra heard her father sigh deeply. "Alright. Who was feeding the rubii?"

No one admitted to feeding the little thing, but everyone voted that Keeshiff would be charged with taking care of it. As much as he'd grumbled and complained at first, it was very clear that the older prince was becoming at least a little fond of the little ball of fur. At least, so Astra guessed by the amount of rations he was willing to share with it.

Their journey to the capital was quick and unhindered, thanks to the escort Zhahn had sent with them. Astra had a feeling it might have been nearly impossible otherwise. Everywhere they went, there were soldiers. Groups of tens, twenties, up to entire companies were marching on every road or camping at every clearing. Astra couldn't help but think of the final days of The War when so many countries had come to their aid. The march had looked something like this. And Astra remembered how many of those people had never marched home.

It only made her more glad when they finally reached the capital. Perhaps they could actually do something here. Perhaps they could find out what was really going on.

The capital was even more crowded with soldiers, and the eyes of every civilian held a wariness. The palace guards were no different, watching them with suspicion until they caught sight of Louko and their escort.

At last, they were ushered into the palace and to the doors of the throne room, a herald having just disappeared to announce their request to see the Ezai Ru.

"Well. This is a bit different than the last time," Louko mumbled.

Astra looked around the gilded halls with their red paneling and stone floors. She remembered the first time they'd been here, when Dia Tzaro had sent them after Mitheau. The memory of their return was more foggy, but Astra could still recall the moment they'd dragged Louko away. "A bit," she murmured in reply.

The herald returned through the side passage, bowing and addressing Louko. "The great Ezai Ru is happy to hear you have returned and will see you now, Prince Lu Quo."

Astra caught the way Louko shifted uncomfortably before replying, "Thank you," and allowing the herald to show them in.

The room was much the same as Astra very vaguely remembered it—with bright colors and elegant pillars, golden chimes strewn between them. The biggest difference was how much busier it was. Everywhere were tables and maps with people bustling around them. Low conversations filled the air and mingled with the deep tones of the chimes above.

For all of the noise and clutter, Astra's eye immediately caught on the occupant of the elaborate throne at the end of the hall. Clothed in brilliant blue and jade, Louko's uncle sat on the throne as if it had been made for him, the air of command tangible even at this distance. It was a stark contrast to the old and senile man that had once sat in the place of power.

"Louko!" An unusually broad smile spread across Aelor Ven's face as he stood up and swiftly made his way down to greet them, of course stopping in front of Louko first. "You look wonderful!" He exclaimed as he put a firm hand on the younger prince's shoulder. "It's good to see you."

"It's good to see you, too, Uncle," Louko replied as he abandoned decorum and embraced his uncle.

Astra was almost surprised with the way Ven didn't seem to mind.

The two separated and Ven stepped back to survey the rest of the group, eyes riveted on Astra. "Oh good, you look marvelously improved. I would have marched into Silbyr myself if you hadn't made it." The smile he'd been wearing settled into the man's usual sardonic expression, and he lifted an eyebrow like some disapproving mother.

Astra was really beginning to wonder how much she'd forgotten from when she was sick. "Then I'm glad to spare you the trip," she replied.

Ven turned and settled his gaze on Mariah and Astra's father. "Who are these?"

Astra had almost forgotten that, without the cosmetics Mariah had once so heavily applied, she now looked completely like her mother—a Nythrilian.

"Uncle, this is Destrin, Astra's father," Louko replied. Astra caught Ven's odd expression, but he did not interrupt as Louko went on. "He's come along to offer support. Litash has…deposed Astra's brother so, unfortunately, there isn't much more support Litash will be offering." Louko then turned to Mariah, but after opening his mouth he clamped it shut and turned to Astra in uncertainty.

There would be no use in hiding it. She squared her shoulders, looked Ven in the eye, and replied, "This is your niece, Mariah."

Ven stood still as a statue. "I'm sorry…what?" The words were as ice.

Astra was beginning to wonder if they should have sent a letter ahead of them. "It is a long story. Perhaps one that would be told better in private quarters."

Ven's attention was now fully on Mariah, a very clear hatred now emanating from him. "Everybody out *now!*" Ven's order reverberated about the hall.

The courtiers that had been in the hall made a hasty retreat until the throne room was completely empty besides Astra's group and the Ezai Ru.

"Explain. *Now.*" Astra was unsure what was sharper; Ven's tone, or the glare he was throwing Mariah's way.

"Uncle," Louko stepped forward, putting a hand forward as if calming some beast. "Please."

This worked only minimally to make the Nythrilian ruler relax, but it was enough that he broke eye contact with Mariah.

"Why is she here?" Something broke in Ven's tone. "I know what she did. She belongs in a dungeon. Why. Isn't. She. In. One?"

Astra kept quiet, knowing Louko could handle his uncle better than she could

"She realized who Kaeden is, Uncle," Louko said, keeping his hand up even as he spoke. "She left and brought us information. We decided it was better to keep her close where we can keep an eye on her rather than leave her back in a crumbling Litash where she could roam free. We do not intend to let her wander, let alone trust her, I can assure you."

"She belongs in a dungeon," Ven hissed, repeating his sentiment once more.

"I know," Louko nodded. "But she might be useful to us, yet. No one is trusting her—she has no power any longer. If you would like to have her under arrest in a room while we are here, that is fine. I request no dungeon; I've spent enough time in one that I wouldn't be able to sleep at night if I agreed to put someone else in one."

That last sentence seemed to finally get through to Ven, making his shoulders sag. "Fine. But I want to know exactly what information she's given that deserves such leniency. And she is to have four armed guards while she is here, and not leave the room I give her unless summoned by one of us. Is that understood?" He turned not to Louko or Astra, but instead to Mariah, who had been intently inspecting the floor during this entire conversation.

Which meant she didn't immediately realize he had been now addressing her.

"I *said*, is that understood?" Ven's tone cut through the air like a knife.

Mariah's head whipped up and her eyes widened with realization. "I-uh—" Dipping her head, she whispered, "Yes, Great Ezai Ru."

"Thank you, Uncle," Louko finally put his hand down as he spoke.

Astra bowed her head, silently echoing his gratitude.

The snort he gave was the least dignified Astra had ever heard him. "Don't speak of it. Ever."

With a wave from Ven, several guards stepped forward. Mariah flinched and began to move back, but then she seemed to remember the agreement that had just taken place, and she went still, taking a deep breath and folding her hands in front of her. Astra tried to give a reassuring nod. Mariah just turned her eyes to the floor and followed her new guards out of the throne room.

"Lhara! Call the courtiers to return. I will be in my study." Ven once more launched his voice across the vast space of the room. Then he turned to Astra and Louko. "Now that the vermin is gone, follow me." With that, the ruler whirled around and led them to the back of the large

140

courtroom and behind his throne where a small, almost imperceptible door led into a smaller back study.

The large study felt small compared to the expanse of the throne room, even with the three full-length windows at the far end and their view of the city. Bookshelves stood floor-to-ceiling along the other walls, and a large table with a map spread out on it was set in the center of the room.

"Anyone who wishes to have a seat is welcome," Ven declared, motioning to the chairs placed around the table. "Though I personally am tired of sitting on that thing outside. Some standing will do me good."

Mitheau also remained standing, her posture having been tense ever since entering the capital and only doubling with the argument over Mariah. Astra couldn't blame her with the way she and her people had been treated by Nythrilians. That being said, Astra and the others took the offered chairs, the long ride more than enough motivation to sit down.

Ven turned away to a long, narrow box that sat on one of the room's many shelves. Astra saw him move a dial and heard a faint whir and click before the lid popped open. Then Ven removed a folded piece of parchment and Astra's heart sunk.

"This arrived ten days ago with a formal declaration of war." Ven turned back to the table. "I have several translators working on a copy, but they say they don't have enough context to fill in for the languages they can't recognize." His dark eyes met Astra's. "I presume it's for you."

Ent being deposed, everyone fleeing back to Nythril.... They'd all known it was Tyron's doing, but to see it happen right on schedule made Astra queasy. She stood and took the note.

Princess Astra discovered in Silbyr, detained—Black Queen forward two

Entrais trades his crown for Astra's safety, leaves for Cithan—White Bishop No. 2 forward/left two, Black Pawn No. 5 forward one, Black Bishop No. 1 forward/left four.

Astra, Louko, Keeshiff, and Mariah leave for Nythril—White Pawn No. 8 forward one, White Knight No. 2 right three, forward two

Merimeethia declares war on Nythril—Black Castle No. 3 forward four

White Knight No. 2 forward three, right two

White Pawn No. 1 reaches the end of the middle board, rises to the top board

Black Queen left two

Folding the note shut once more, Astra tried to keep her voice even as she said, "He knew. All of it."

"Of course he did," Louko said in exasperation, throwing up his hands in the defeat Astra felt.

"What does it say?" Ven asked.

Astra made herself look up. "It says everything that happened within the last few weeks. But if it came ten days ago and all the way from Merimeethia, then it was written before any of it had happened." Her stomach twisted. "We're right on Tyron's timeline." Tirzah may have planned Ent's deposition, but Tyron had known exactly where they would all go from there. She looked to her father, wondering if they were thinking the same thing: How was Ent taking all this? How would he handle the news of yet another war? This must have been why Tyron wanted him off the throne—to keep Litash from coming to Ven's aid.

Her father's hands were folded atop the table and his posture as neutral as usual, and yet his brow showed the stress they were all feeling. Astra could tell he was thinking the same thing she was. "So then we are still playing right into his hands," he more announced rather than asked, briefly meeting Astra's gaze.

"Uncle, what about the portal site? Do you know where that is?" Louko's question broke through the despair.

Ven looked shocked. "Wait, how do you know about a portal site? That's highly sensitive information."

"Because it's where you all drove the Myrandi to." Mitheau's comment was dry.

There was a moment of awkwardness that Ven seemed to refuse to let shake him even as he regarded the young Drogan with a curious expression.

"And because of information Mariah gave us," Louko added.

Ven's expression hardened and he replied, "Well, Tzaro was rather paranoid and had it heavily guarded and watched after the...incident with the Drogans. The portal remained open for a few days before closing. But after more than a decade of it remaining so, it seemed to have been a one-time anomaly and I needed the soldiers for the front. I won't be able to hold off Merimeethia otherwise."

Was that really the cause of this whole war? A *diversion?* Astra was stunned at the very thought. How many people would die simply to give Tyron the access he needed to this portal site?

"That's exactly what he wants," she broke in. "If there is a barracks at the site, then this attack on the front is just a way to empty it." She looked back down at the note in her hands, trying to decipher what these latest predictions meant. They were getting near the end of The Game, weren't they? "What if we made a deal? If all he wants is the site, what if we just gave him access?"

"You'd really give someone out of control with Drogan Madness access to what they want?" Mitheau sounded aghast and a little frightened. "When we don't know *why* he wants it?"

"We know he wants through it," Astra countered. "Which he can't do without one of the Guards. Is war really a better option?" Now she looked to Ven. "If we knew where he was going to be, do you have the means to contain him?"

"I'm sorry but I was still under the impression that Tyron was Human?" Ven raised an eyebrow. "So if I am hazarding the guess that he is apparently Drogan, yes, I still have the means to contain him." There was a look of distaste.

"Human, with Drogan abilities. It's…complicated." Destrin waved one hand.

Astra addressed Ven directly. "What matters is that he can shift, but he's also Gifted. It would take a lot of red-bronze."

Ven seemed to understand that things were too convoluted to explain in detail at this point, but his frown showed his displeasure.

"And he's not in his right mind; we are thinking he has Drogan Madness and that's what is driving his actions. Which makes sense why everything is being done in such…drastic measures. Uncle, can you show us exactly where the site is?" Louko asked, leaning forward to look at the maps on the table before them.

Ven stepped forward, plucking a small, wooden marker from a tray and setting it on the map. It was a ways south of the capital, right in the heart of Nythril. And yet, Astra noticed that there were almost no nearby towns or villages.

"You all can't be serious?" Mitheau stood up from her chair, gripping the end of the table. "Do you have any idea the damage this could do? What if he manages to go through to Baeno and join Ovok? Drogan Madness doesn't just turn off when you get what you want—it's not like a toddler's temper tantrum. It's obsession to the point of madness. Eventually he's not going to care why he's hurting people; he's just going to do it. It's like a rabid dog but with the intelligence and brutality of both Human and beast."

"And what do you suggest we do?" Louko snapped with surprising passion. "Kill him for actions he can't even control? Treat him like the Nythrilians treated you? Like an *animal?* If he's out of balance with the Dragon and Human parts of him like you claim then why can't one find a way to bring back balance? Why do you just throw up your hands and give up?"

The entire table went still.

"After *everything* he's done you *still* want to save him?" Keeshiff asked, voice strained. It was hard for Astra to tell how much of Keeshiff's shock was from Louko's statement and how much of it was from the realization he'd spoken out loud.

This whole conversation had slid terribly sideways. Astra took in the uneasy expressions, the tense glances, and nervous tappings.

"Let's remember that we all have the same goal," Astra said quietly. "And that is to preserve as many lives as possible. If this war continues, the loss will be in the thousands. If there is any way to prevent that, it has to be worth a try." She looked to Mitheau, whose knuckles were still white around the edge of the table. "What would be the safest way to approach Tyron? We can't give him what he wants, but we can't have him walking around freely."

"The Dragon is erratic. Honestly, he must be pretty recently into the Madness because from the tales I'd heard of the Drogan, Bastien, it would be a bloodbath. There's a lot of planning even amid the…violence, right now." Mitheau replied, sighing and slumping down into her seat with seeming defeat.

"Well, I mean, it's been probably ten years…" Destrin offered hesitantly.

Mitheau just threw up her hands. "Look, I don't know. I'm only sixty-three and I've just been trying to survive the Drogan hunters and my whole people disappearing into thin air. I wasn't exactly sitting around being a scholar. If you wanted more information then you should have asked Grenedil but he's gone, too, so I don't know what to tell you."

Astra felt a sudden wave of guilt. Mitheau was on her own with near strangers in a hostile country, simply hoping that her one friend made it through this alive. Astra knew what that was like. "If we were able to contain him, then," she offered slowly. "We could hold him until Grenedil comes back—or maybe even finds Cyl. Perhaps they would have a way to restore him to his right mind. And then any threat he poses would be nullified."

"I would say we could consult the Drogan Hunters…" Ven paused and took a moment to show his disdain. "But I have used the excuse of war to convert them into soldiers at the front until I can formally have this country rid of the disgusting sport," Ven's nose wrinkled and he seemed to be addressing Mitheau at this. "So, we will not easily have access to the weaponry or knowledge unless I were to pull Jahng from the front to lend her former…expertise. Which I do not feel is wise."

"If we can't be sure that we can contain him, then luring him out will only put everyone in harm's way—and make him angry." Astra knew his anger well enough to know better than to tempt it. "We would have to be absolutely certain that we can hold him."

"Then I shall write to Jahng and see what she might be able to offer us in regards to information. Though I am unsure as to how much it will be of use without her presence. And that we cannot afford," Ven announced.

"Then we need a different angle. What about Merimeethia? Wouldn't it be wise to have Keeshiff stake his claim on the throne?" Louko spoke up, his suggestion taking Astra by surprise. He had never mentioned this before. And why was Keeshiff frowned in seeming displeasure?

"Is that likely?" Ven asked, brow furrowed as he looked to Keeshiff. "Merimeethia isn't exactly known for its…loyalty to the royal lines."

Louko's cheeks flushed, clearly unsure how to proceed and apparently not confident in the idea, himself. "It might be worth a shot. Keeshiff always seemed fairly popular among the people."

Astra's attention went to Keeshiff. The older prince looked uncertain, staring at his brother. "Sneaking me back into Merimeethia seems…unwise seeing the last time we were there. Certainly if I really held so much sway, Killyan and his men would have let us alone when chasing us halfway across the country? But perhaps I could go to the border…see for myself the situation?" He added hesitantly.

"I, for one, have no wish to rest the fate of my country on the possible loyalty of a few Merimeethians." Ven cleared his throat. "But another body at the front wouldn't hurt. Jahng can use all the help she can get. Jhang could use a fresh set of eyes apart from Itso, and you would have a better idea as to the Merimeethians' tactics." He looked around the room as if scanning for any disagreement.

If there was any, they—like Astra—held their tongue.

CHAPTER VIII

Keeshiff:

At last, they'd been dismissed to settle in, but Keeshiff had one more thing to do. It had been a difficult decision to keep the knights here at the capital—but with some still recovering from the minor injuries of the tower siege, it had been a foolish notion to even think of bringing them to Litash. Aelor Ven had proven himself trustworthy; it had been the logical choice to leave them with him.

Still, Keeshiff had been loath to part with them, and there was that constant nagging in the back of his head that something might happen to them while he was gone. It wasn't anything he'd brought up to Astra or Louko, as they had enough on their plates, but he was relieved to be back at last.

"They are in the courtyard sparring grounds," the servant explained as he led Keeshiff through the halls. They must be bored if they were out there this close to sunset. Or perhaps they just didn't want to be in here where they could get in the Nythrilians' way. The Nythrilians had been tolerant and some—at least those with Jahng—even fairly cordial since Aelor Ven's take over, but there remained an element of tension and Keeshiff wouldn't blame his men for avoiding the glares of the soldiers that had been their enemies not so long ago.

When they at last arrived at the courtyard entrance, the servant announced, "I will remain here by the door, should you need me. They're just down the main path and to the left."

With a nod, Keeshiff walked down the paved walkway and followed the sound of sparring wafting through the elegant azxi trees until, at last, he rounded the corner and found his men, all spread out on the sparring grounds. Gavin was using a target to practice his marksmanship, Coryn and Lucian were sparring, and the rest were talking or giving input into the match.

"Oh good, you didn't get yourselves killed while I was gone," Keeshiff said loudly, not bothering to hide the enormous grin glued to his face.

"Keeshiff!" Farian called out as all the knights spun to face the prince.

"You idiot, what took you so long?" Rufio was the first to reach him, throwing one arm over his shoulder before prodding him in the ribs. The others were close behind him, and soon Keeshiff was well surrounded by his friends.

Asher broke the mood and asked hesitantly, "Is Astra…?"

"Much better. And here—you'll see her and Louko when we leave," Keeshiff replied, shoving Rufio back and allowing the mood to lighten as relief rippled through the knights' faces.

Asher seemed especially relieved, relaxing his shoulders as he processed the information.

Gavin was the next to ask a question. "But what about you—and what do you mean when we leave? Where are we going?"

"To the front—we have to try and help Dia Jahng settle this whole war problem." Keeshiff again thought of Mariah and her suggestion…and the fact that they'd decided she would be going with them.

"We aren't…going to fight, are we?" Ivinon spoke up, a shadow crossing over the joy that had been there only moments before.

A heaviness settled deep inside Keeshiff. He knew exactly what was now going through their heads. He didn't want to deal with the possibility any more than they did, and yet Keeshiff felt as if there was no good way out of the problem ahead. He had to hope that he was enough to get the whole Merimeethian army to change their mind...somehow. "Hopefully not," he spoke at last. "I'm going to discuss with Dia Jahng once we reach the front and see what can be done."

He again bit back the suggestion from Mariah. The nobles wouldn't care, would they?

"As long as there's a plan," Bandon said firmly. "I do not want to spill any of my countrymen's blood."

With a nod, Keeshiff replied, "I understand. I will do my very best."

Putting an arm over Keeshiff's shoulder, Gavin said, "Oh, loosen up, we know you will. We can worry about it on the journey. You look exhausted and I imagine the last thing you want to do is talk about this." He steered Keeshiff to a nearby bench and sat him down. "Catch us up on your adventures in Litash—how did you stand the company of that ill-mannered shape-shifter all the way back to Litash?" he asked as everyone took various comfortable positions, some leaning against trees, others sitting on the ground or the other bench nearby.

Keeshiff rolled his eyes, remembering how barely a word had passed between him and Soletuph the whole time. Soon he found himself recounting not just the journey, but the trial and everything in between, stumbling only when he came to the bit about Mariah having shown up and come with them. It was amazing how her very name could transform everyone's mood for the worse. First, Aelor Ven, now Keeshiff's men. Not that he blamed them.

"And then I heard…." Keeshiff choked a bit when he came to the news of Julyn. He turned to Rufio.

"I know," Rufio replied, voice taut. "We got word shortly after you left. There was nothing that could be done." The knight looked away, taking a deep breath and adding, "Though it has hit Rhumir hard. He's hardly left his room. I would like to bring him with us…if that is alright with you. He needs something else to focus on."

"Of course," Keeshiff whispered, wishing he could do more than offer an empty condolence. When his father had died, there had been a measure of twisted relief. But Rufio and Rhumir—even if at odds with each other at times—had always loved and respected their father.

Clearing his throat, Rufio made a motion with his hand. "Please, continue on," he requested, clearly wishing not to dwell on the pain.

Wishing he had the understanding and comfort to give his friend, Keeshiff decided it was best to at least respect this one request and resumed the story.

When at last Keeshiff got to the end of the tale, with them all arriving back at Nythril and getting here, he realized he had to break the news to them…. "So, yes, after the meeting, the Ezai Ru has agreed that we should bring Mariah to the front with us."

A collective grumble rippled through the group. Farian put a hand over his eyes. "You can't be serious. Keeshiff, she was a *spy*."

"She's heavily guarded and will remain that way. But I would much rather have her with me and far away from Louko and Astra, especially since Louko refuses to put her in the Ezai Ru's dungeons."

Asher rubbed his temple, murmuring, "Of course he would."

"How do you know she wasn't the one to give up my father?" Rufio's tone was bitter.

With a wince, Keeshiff replied, "Because that's what shocked her into reality. And I am not saying to trust her—I am not asking you to treat her as anything other than a prisoner and possible source of information on Tyron. That is how I am treating her and I don't plan on doing anything else; she is a traitor and deserves whatever she gets. It is Louko alone that stays my hand."

"Fine. I can't wait to explain this to Rhumir," Rufio's reply was hard. "But if she makes one wrong move...."

Keeshiff nodded. "I understand. She will be carefully watched."

There was a long silence, everyone trying to digest the situation in their own way.

"You must be exhausted, Keeshiff. I think it's about time you go and get some rest—we'll have the whole journey to the front to talk and catch up." Asher was the first to speak up.

"Except that traitor will be there the whole journey, too," Rufio growled under his breath, receiving a stern, yet somehow sympathetic, glare from Asher.

No one else spoke, and so Keeshiff nodded and hoisted himself up from his seat. "It...it is so good to see you all...and to see you all safe.

Please know that." The words were difficult to say through the growing lump in his throat.

"Oh please, you're the one we need to worry about," Ivinon said with a laugh. "You can't get rid of us that easily. But Asher is right; get some rest. We can talk more later, you oaf."

But as Keeshiff bid them goodnight and walked back to the courtyard entrance, he couldn't help but think of Rufio and Rhumir and wonder if it really had been a good idea to bring Mariah. Hopefully he wouldn't live to regret this.

Entrais:

"Of *course*, I played right into their hand!" Ent slammed his fist against the wall as he took in this newest information. War between Merimeethia and Nythril, and now he was powerless to help. The population of Cithan was far too small to risk extinction in a war, and while Elves were a force to be reckoned with, the scarcity of them bearing children left any sort of conflict a dangerous gamble. They had already come close enough when Old Cithan was destroyed during The War.

Ent had lost his only cousin to that. The only Elf that had actually supported him when he'd tried to ask the Elves for aid originally. Now, she was just another casualty.

Jade, still holding the letter that Ascriot had brought, looked up. "At least it seems that Litash is divided about offering Merimeethia aid," she said. "Some of the Court is citing the new treaty we have with

Merimeethia. Others are citing recent instability as an excuse to stay neutral." Ascriot's letter had included the murmurs of dissent among the citizens of Litash. Ent hoped it stayed at that.

"I should never have left." Ent ran his hands over his face and took a deep breath, turning around to face the window. They had arrived at Cithan only a day ago, and since then, things had only spiraled. At least there weren't spies here like the ones crawling all over Silbyr. But the Elves were asking after Astra and now with war between Nythril and Merimeethia being declared, she was once more the one in danger. Once more facing the war while Ent just sat comfortably in an estate others had *apparently* built for him.

"Given the position they had put you in," His mother's voice came from the chair where she sat, index finger tapping on the armrest. "I'm not sure that staying would have been any better. They would have forced you to carry out this war instead."

"We don't know that," Ent replied as he looked out to the spacious city streets. It was new, like Silbyr, and yet with their Gifting and knowledge the Elves had still managed to create something as beautiful as Old Cithan. The bright marble and glass buildings glittered in the sun, only brought out more by the clean-cut cobblestone that made up the streets. "We'll need to send word to Astra and see what her next move is." And besides, Astra would want to know that everyone was alright.

For now. Who knew how long that would last.

Jade set the letter down and joined him at the window. "Matthes was already working on getting some of the fastest shifters set up for a relay to Nythril. They should be ready within a few days."

"Good, thank you." Ent hated the inaction. It left so much time to think…to realize how tired he was…how useless he was. He needed to do something, and yet as usual he was too far away to do much else than worry. Why was Tyron doing this? What was the point?

"For now, is there anything we should send back to the Ethians with Ascriot?" Jade asked.

"Just to keep an eye out on how the Court proceeds." Ent wished there was more they could do.

He heard his mother get up from her chair. "Well, since you have done what you can for now concerning Litash, come be part of your other people. A Litashian king is expected to stay on his throne, but an Elvish one is meant to be seen in his streets."

"Ah, yes." Ent was too tired to bother hiding his displeasure. He'd stayed away from Cithan for more than one reason. The blatant hypocrisy was hard for him to take. For years, when Ent was on the run and his parents imprisoned, they'd refused to let him in—Tallaman had been too bothered to see his own nephew, ashamed of a half-breed. But then Astra had come and charmed them all and now they all fawned over her like some goddess. Then once he'd saved them after the burning of Old Cithan, Ent was suddenly wanted and a hero. He'd seen the way they'd ignored the blood and death around them during Euracia's reign, and he'd experienced first-hand how little they really cared about him. He was tired of pretending.

Ameri sighed. "I know the Elves are too proud to apologize out loud, but one day you will have to forgive them anyway."

"Yes, I know. I'll get over it," Ent replied quietly, straightening and folding his hands behind his back. Just suck it up and get over it. If only he was better at doing such a thing.

He turned to see that his mother still looked...was it worried? Or displeased? Ent didn't want to ask. It was a cruel trick of fate that had Ent become the ruler of the Elves instead of his mother, who was far more suited to the task. If not for the fact that she had renounced her title and fled with Destrin all those years ago, then this all would be different. Instead, it was Ent who was left trying to pretend he could stand the sight of the ones that had repeatedly turned a blind eye to him and others in need.

"Maybe your mother is on to something," Jade broke the silence. "It's a good day for a walk."

Ent tried to turn his grimace to a smile, but gave up quickly and instead said, "Yes. Some fresh air would be good." He walked over and offered his arm to Jade. "Would you like to come?"

Jade gave a little smile as she accepted his arm. "I think I would."

He brought his other hand to where hers rested and squeezed it gently, looking to his mother. "Well, I suppose it's settled. Lead the way."

They made their way downstairs and to the ground floor where Tallaman was currently sitting down, absorbed in a book.

Upon seeing them, however, he quickly got up and asked, "What is it, now?" in the usual show of irritation.

But something in his lingering gaze seemed just the slightest bit lonely.

"Mother is bringing us out for a walk," Ent explained. "You're welcome to join us, Uncle." He could already feel the way Jade's grip on his arm tightened ever so slightly, but Ent didn't take back the offer.

Besides, Tallaman was clearly out of sorts if he didn't glare at Ent for using the term 'uncle.' Ent saw him glance towards the doors of the hall and then briefly towards Jade. He didn't make it as far as Ameri.

"I'm afraid that I have much more important things to do than go for a stroll." Tallaman cleared his throat and sat back down. "But by all means, enjoy your little social trivialities."

Ent couldn't help but show a little confusion as he replied, "If you're sure," before allowing his mother to show them out.

It was so bright outside. Ent had thought it bad enough in the estate with all the windows, and yet outside was definitely even worse.

"Why don't we start with the old sector?" Ameri suggested, tone as brisk as her long-legged stride. "That was the only section that was stable enough to repair, so it's the most finished sector of the citadel."

He allowed his mother to lead them wherever she wished, seeing the way her eyes lit up at being home. Ent only wished people would stop staring or smiling or stopping them to give their respects. As suffocating as it was, he did nothing but return the smiles and wish them well.

It was strange how much the city already looked like it had before The War. Perhaps the stone buildings were cleaner and newer, the metal archways less tarnished, the wide gardens younger and thinner. But this only made the city seem brighter than he remembered. Certainly much more so than the day he'd watched it reduced to a pile of ash.

As they walked down the street, Ent took in the bustling shops that lined each side. Food, textiles, gleaming white Elvish pottery, crafters of jewelry and fine clothing, and then—of course—the weapon masters.

"They've certainly recovered quickly from The War," Ent commented to his mother, trying to make some form of conversation.

"To some degree, at least," Ameri replied. "It will be a while until the entire city is restored."

It would be a long time before anything anywhere recovered fully from the destruction. If ever. Ent pressed his lips tightly together and tried to keep the train of thought from getting out of hand, but already the reminder of what was going on between Merimeethia and Nythril was hard to ignore.

They stopped at a food booth, a chatty Elvish cook eager to show off his culinary abilities to Cithan's king. In all honesty, Ent had little appetite, but Jade's pointed steering in this direction was enough hinting.

But even as the baker was grabbing some of the braided sweet bread from one of the racks, Ent was suddenly distracted by a pair of gossips chatting away while they waited in line.

"What do you think he'll do about the riots?" one man asked.

"Well, seeing as he's here and not in Silbyr, he probably gave up on the Humans and all their infighting."

"But if this doesn't clear up soon, Merimeethia and Nythril might not be the only ones at war...."

Riots? Ent froze, barely registering the bread that was put in his hand by Jade as he tried to figure out what in Eatris the strangers behind them were talking about. What riots? Ascriot's letter had only said whispers. Had he played it down? Had this only just happened?

"So what? If we learned nothing else from Euracia, it's to stick to the citadel. Let the Humans and Bandilarians drive themselves extinct if they want to."

Before Ent could listen for more, however, Ameri led them away, using her bread to point out a newly constructed bridge over the canal. Ent handed his bread off to a young Elvish child and their mother, ignoring Jade's displeased glares.

"Mother, what riots?" He had no idea if his mother had been paying attention to the gossips, but he was too confused to bother giving context.

The way she sighed told him that she'd overheard. "I'm not sure. But I know who would."

Ent looked to his wife, seeing the same concern he was feeling. "I suppose we should try and find out what they're talking about, then. If you don't mind, Mother?" Everything felt suddenly close and suffocating, the whispers of riots seeming to be on everyone's lips now.

"This way." Her little tour cut short, Ameri now doubled back and led them through unfamiliar streets.

The polished, finished buildings they'd passed earlier now tapered off into those still under construction. Half-formed walls and empty water channels now bordered the unpaved road, and in some places, workers were still hauling off charred stone and warped metal.

As they caught sight of the citadel walls, solid homes and streets resumed. Ameri charged on until they reached the front gate itself. She rapped twice on the gatehouse's wooden door.

"King Entrais and Governor Ameri, here to speak with Passyl." She announced.

Ent winced at his title, but knew one day he'd have to get used to it.

The door opened quickly and a woman dressed in the Elvish soldier's uniform stepped out hurriedly, bowing deeply to Ent and then giving a respectful nod to his mother. "How can I be of service?"

"You have a sharp ear and a taste for news—did anyone come in today speaking of riots in Litash?" Ameri asked.

Passyl looked from Ent to his mother, then replied uneasily, "It's all just talk, really. One of the Elvish traders just returned from his route and said the people are rebelling against the Court in Silbyr after..." She looked back to Ent and bowed in apology, "After your most unjust deposition, My King."

Ent paled. "Rebelling?"

"Yes. The Court wants to get involved in The War with Merimeethia but the people refuse to go to arms. The local militias of the surrounding towns are gathering and there's even talk of them sending a courier here. My humblest apologies, I was sure someone would have told you, My King. But then the trader only returned today and they are still just possibly rumors."

Ent could do nothing but stand there, processing the newest nightmare that was rising up as a result of his poor decisions. He'd been a fool for hoping that abdicating the throne of Litash would be the end of it—for thinking giving up and running away would have been any better than facing this all head on. For thinking the end of The War would be the end of the death and bloodshed.

But no. It was only the beginning, and the knowledge of that was too much for Ent to bear. The roar of battle seemed to already be ringing in his ears as the reminder of the horrors of war played over and over in his mind. He couldn't do this again. He couldn't watch everyone around him die. Not for him.

"Ent?" he barely heard Jade's whisper. "Ent?" She turned to Ameri and said, "Perhaps we should get back to the manor."

"That is probably best. We need to plan," Ent managed to reply, cutting through the echoes of shouts and cries. Were they real? Or just in his head. "Thank you for the information." He barely registered that he addressed Passyl.

He didn't wait for his mother to lead the way this time, nor did he wait for Passyl's reply. He needed to get out of the open.

The noise of the city around him was enough to make him dizzy, and he couldn't breathe as the very buildings lining the street seemed to close in, threatening to burn like so many had during The War. Barely, he made it back to their estate, rushing into the house, past a confused Tallaman, and into his study where he shut the door behind him. But the screams were still echoing, the clamor of battle still present.

Desperate for peace, Ent put both hands over his ears, shouting, "Get out of my head!"

The sound of a door behind him made him jump and instinct had him draw his dagger.

"Ent, it's me, it's Jade." The figure had both palms raised. Jade. And behind her was Ameri.

Get yourself together! Ent dropped the knife and took a few steps back, struggling to breathe. "Sorry, I didn't realize I...left you. I'm...I'm fine I just need...a minute. We need to figure out what to do before...before people get hurt. Before people die. I can't let that happen—not again."

"We'll figure it out," Ameri assured, staying a step behind Jade. "This could even work out for good. If the people want you back, then—"

"Work out for *good?!*" Ent's panic rose with the anger. "Since when did people killing each other get labeled as working out for good? Do you know what this means? It means we never won The War—nothing changed, nothing is *ever* going to change. I'm stuck in a cycle of killing and death and I can't stop it! I can't even pull myself together and walk down the street like a normal person and all these people decided it was a good idea to *die* on my behalf! This isn't working out to any advantage. Just more chaos and bloodshed. If they wanted change, they shouldn't have followed me because the only thing I seem to do is leave a trail of destruction behind me."

"The only destruction that you leave behind is that which your enemies wrought before you stopped them." It took Ent several seconds to realize that his uncle had come in behind Ameri. "If you didn't do anything, the destruction would be ten times worse. So stop trying to take responsibility for the wrongs of others—it's making you sound like your sister." Tallaman stopped beside Jade, glancing at her and clearing his throat as if in discomfort. "Besides, if you can convince someone like me to change, you can probably change anything in Eatris."

Ent stared at his uncle, the shock of the uncharacteristic response enough to drag him out of the nightmares.

Tallaman only looked more uncomfortable, shifting slightly and tugging at a shirt sleeve. "I have said what I wanted to. I meant it, and I will not be repeating it. But for goodness sake, stop acting like you've caused all of these problems when you're the only one trying to stop them."

"For once…I agree with him," Jade said quietly, taking a step forward.

"I…I can't keep doing this. I'm not strong; I'm sorry. I can't keep watching people die," Ent whispered, the shock mixing in with the fear of what was going to happen next.

Jade reached out a hand, cautiously laying it on his arm. "You have always been strong. But you've carried too much for too long. We'll find another way."

Ent gave in, finding himself again in her embrace as he whispered, "I'm sorry."

What other ways were there?

CHAPTER IX

<u>Louko:</u>

"You know, being all sad like that isn't going to make this any easier," Keeshiff said nervously as they stood together in the garden of the palace.

Louko rolled his eyes and tried to manage a smile, but it fell short. "Come on, you can't blame me—after all, you would manage to stab yourself with a spoon if you were left alone too long." More than anything, Louko wanted to accompany his brother to the battlefront. But Astra needed him here, and Keeshiff was capable enough on his own. At least, that's what he kept telling himself.

"Seeing as I survived just fine on my own before, I think you're the one I should be worried about when handling a spoon." Keeshiff chuckled and nudged Louko with a shoulder. "Just. Don't come up with any stupid ideas?"

His brother went stiff as he said the last bit, making Louko realize just what Keeshiff was talking about.

Tyron.

He couldn't get Mitheau's words out of his head. If she was right about the Drogan Madness, then Tyron was a victim, too. Perhaps he wasn't completely to blame for what he had done. Had this been why it was so difficult to rectify the sadistic maniac he'd seen in Melye with the kind, open man he'd known as a child? And then there was Mitheau's statement that the only way to stop it was to…to put them down. Surely there was another way.

He had to believe it.

"I don't know how you could even contemplate anything but judgement," Keeshiff murmured.

Louko went stiff. "Well, if it's not really him, then maybe options are worth exploring."

Now, Keeshiff locked eyes with him. "You don't want to cure him just to stop him, do you?" His voice was low. "You actually want him back. After everything he's done, you want him back."

Louko's lips pressed together and he couldn't help but look away. He didn't want to reply; to acknowledge how much he wanted Tyron back.

"You really can forgive anyone, can't you? Me, Tyron…." Keeshiff sighed. It was as if he wanted to argue, but couldn't find a way to do so.

"You?" Louko raised an eyebrow. He had never thought himself one to forgive easily, and the thought of Mariah only pricked at him.

"…you're joking, right?" Keeshiff looked at him dubiously only to shake his head in disbelief. "I sat on the sidelines for *years* while Omath did, well, everything to you. I even dragged you back to him after The War in Litash ended. And then you made that promise and I—" he cut himself off, looking flustered. "Oh, never mind. I'm not the point. The point is that you would take anyone back—no matter what they've done to you. Just, be careful not to let someone in who's only going to do the same thing all over again."

His brother seemed to forget the pressure Omath had put on not *just* Louko. The need for perfection, the walking on glass. Louko had always seen it in Keeshiff's demeanor. And then his last comment…. Perhaps he was right, perhaps Louko was too much a mat to be walked over. Yet the prince could not let Tyron go. No matter how he had tried, he could not reconcile the man that had tortured Astra with the man he had grown up knowing—and now he knew why. Tyron was just as much a victim; just as much in need of help…and no one had been there for him.

But after everything that had happened to Astra, who did Louko even think he was? How could he say or think such things after what Tyron had done to her?

Keeshiff said nothing more, but he didn't have to; questions were written all over his expression.

"What is it?" Louko pressed, the uncertainty in the silence unbearable.

Keeshiff looked uncomfortable. "Just, I mean…say he does come back. Then what?"

Louko's shrug was limp. "I don't know."

"Sorry." Keeshiff rubbed the back of his neck. "I know that that's not helpful. I just," He gave a hollow chuckle. "Well, I guess I don't know."

Louko knew it didn't make sense. What in Eatris was he even thinking? "There's nothing to be sorry for. I mean, I'm the one not thinking logically."

"No, you're just taking the higher road as always." Keeshiff's expression was rueful.

Louko gave a wince, accompanied by, "I think this is quite a selfish thing, this time, Keeshiff." Again he thought of Mitheau's words, and the realization of the Drogan Madness. How had he not considered? Well, yes, of course he hadn't known Rhioa was Drogan—but still! And now, too late, they knew. Now, when they needed to *stop* him, Louko faltered, for the thought of what *stopping* meant was almost too overwhelming to process.

"Selfish?" Keeshiff folded his arms in front of him. "Try me."

The dare was surprising enough to coax an arched eyebrow from Louko's dim countenance, "I'm...sorry?"

"I fail to see how sparing the life of a literal madman is selfish," Keeshiff said. "And I wanted to see how you could possibly rationalize it as such."

"I can't lose him, Keeshiff," Louko's voice cracked. "I can't. After everything, I still can't let him go—even after all of the horrible, *horrible* things he did to...." His gaze trailed to where his words had run away. "He's all I had for so long, and I just.... If it's not him doing this, then he needs help, too, right? If the Dragon or whatever took him...then...then...." He didn't keep going; this was enough.

Keeshiff's shoulders drooped and he leaned back again. "Still don't see how that counts as selfish," he mumbled. He took another deep breath, still looking troubled. "If that's how you feel about it all, I guess I have no right to feel otherwise. And I'm sure Astra wouldn't go against you."

He didn't say the last part, yet Louko heard it all the same: *She won't go against you...but will she go with you?* And did she deserve to be dragged along? *No.* That was the problem. It had always been the problem—even during The War, when he'd been fighting Tyron and knowing he wouldn't be able to kill him if he'd had to. But if it came down to Astra or Tyron, he knew the choice. Even if he knew the choice would kill him.

"What's gotten into you?" Louko suddenly asked his brother. He did not recall his brother being so...well. This.

"What do you mean?" Confusion made Keeshiff tilt his head.

Louko made a wild gesture that motioned to his brother. "I don't know...*this*. You are not usually....this...." The gestures continued. Louko was an idiot.

"Er, nice?" Keeshiff suggested when Louko couldn't find the word.

Frowning, Louko said, "Perhaps 'pushy' is the right word? Or wise...or mildly annoying." The last bit was said with a hesitant grin.

It earned him a mock glare. The look quickly softened to something more sheepish. "Blame your," Keeshiff caught himself. "Um, friend. I was stuck with her for a week when we were separated in Nythril."

Louko narrowed his eyes in suspicion at the cut off comment, but replied, "That suddenly does make a lot more sense."

"She is certainly something," Keeshiff grumbled. "I mean, she was the one dying, and somehow she made me talk about *myself*."

"Yeah, welcome to Astra," Louko chuckled. "She has...issues."

Keeshiff laughed quietly. "That's one way of putting it. Issues." He laughed again. "And somehow, she still makes us all look bad by comparison. Still, she couldn't have chosen a better..." This time, he cut himself off with a smirk. "...friend."

"I'm sorry, am I missing something?" Louko feigned brittleness. In all honesty, it was a strange thing sitting here, joking with Keeshiff. And yet...not in a bad way. The warmth it brought was both unfamiliar and pleasant.

Keeshiff's smug expression remained. "I guess that depends: Have you, you know, talked to her yet?"

"About...Tyron?" Louko asked hesitantly. She'd seemed in agreement when they'd gone over their plans, at least.

"No, no, I mean," Keeshiff looked nearly embarrassed as he cleared his throat. "I mean have you *talked* to her?"

"I'm sorry but no amount of you saying the same vague sentence is going to change my confusion, Keeshiff." Louko threw his hands up in frustration.

Keeshiff sighed with equal exasperation. "Fine. Have you or have you not expressed how you feel about her and asked her if she feels the same?"

Louko actually laughed. "What in Eatris, Keeshiff, we're just friends. I can't tell if you're joking or you actually think that, but I think you were in the Tower a little too long...."

"Oh, come on, *everybody* knows," Keeshiff replied, then adding under his breath, "Except maybe you two." He shook his head. "Why do you think everyone always looks at you two funny? Your uncle, Asher, the knights, Astra's family—seriously, everyone knows. It's hard to miss when you both can't go a minute without either talking about each other or holding hands. You're inseparable and the very thought of being apart from her clearly upsets you."

Oh no.

Louko's eyes widened as the nagging thought he had unconsciously been stuffing down at last came into full realization, too quick and too overwhelming for him to pretend to ignore. And Keeshiff said *everyone* knew? "This is bad," he whispered. He'd never expected to get this far in life, but now, of *course*, he'd been an idiot and fallen for Astra. How in Eatris had he let this happen?

Keeshiff blinked at him. "Wow, you really didn't know," he muttered. Then he regathered himself. "What do you mean, bad?"

Louko ran both hands through his hair as he almost shouted before remembering that there was the slight possibility his voice could carry from the garden—and he did *not* want Astra to somehow hear this. "I like her and we're supposed to just be friends! How did this happen? Why did you have to tell me?!" Louko had apparently gotten so good at repression that he'd done a fabulous job at staying ignorant about this, and yet now he couldn't *unsee* it. Oh boy. Yeah, he really did like her, didn't he?

Now Keeshiff was the one that looked confused. "Why do you have to just be friends?"

"Because she thinks that's what we are!" Louko whispered harshly, running his hand through his hair. This was a mess.

"How do you know if you haven't talked to her?" Keeshiff tipped his head, brow scrunched up.

Louko couldn't manage to say anything at first, only letting his mouth fall open as he tried to formulate a coherent thought. "I...I...because if I don't know, then there's no way she caught on."

"Well, if she does feel the same way and just hasn't realized it yet, then don't you think someone should tell her?" Keeshiff's lips pressed together as if he was trying not to smile.

"But…what if she doesn't? This will ruin *everything*. Maybe we just don't tell her…I'm sure it'll be fine." Louko somehow found himself pacing back and forth, running his hand through his hair more obsessively.

"So, on the off chance that she doesn't feel the same way, you'd rather never tell her and go through life wondering?" Keeshiff asked, mystified. "What if she *does* know and has had the same worry? Besides, Astra's a good enough person that she wouldn't let a single question ruin your whole friendship."

"Easy for you to say," Louko grumbled, forcing himself to stop pacing and take a deep breath. How was he letting something so stupid get him all riled up when there were far more important things to worry about?

Keeshiff raised both hands. "Look, do you really think I would have even said anything if I didn't think she felt this way, too?"

"I…" Louko made a face. "Do you really think so?" Somehow, the possibility was still just as frightening.

Looking absolutely certain, Keeshiff nodded. "The only time I ever see her smile is when you're around. You should see the way she looks at you."

Feeling suddenly strange, Louko's anxiety deflated, leaving him exhausted and…he didn't know. Something else. "Really?"

"Really. The moment you walk in, she brightens." Keeshiff grinned. "She'd be as lost without you as you'd be without her."

"Well then…if that's the case. If she really does like me…then how am I supposed to ask?" Louko replied, strangely stuck on Astra's smile.

"Oh, um, well," Keeshiff was back to rubbing his neck. "I mean, maybe you could try bringing up future plans. If she starts thinking about how she doesn't want to be separated from you after this is all over, maybe she'll start to realize it, too."

Making a face, Louko replied, "That sounds…like a really depressing way to approach it.

With a roll of his eyes, Keeshiff said, "Well then, do it your way. You know her better than I do anyhow."

"I'll think about it," Louko grumbled, looking up at the sky and trying not to scream at it. It seemed silly to be talking about this when so much hung in the balance. So many lives. His brother. Ent. Tyron. Astra. Would things ever stop being this complicated?

"I suppose we should get going to meet the others. The knights should be waiting now," Keeshiff broke into Louko's melodramatic thoughts.

"Yes…I suppose you're right." But Louko couldn't shake the two problems now before him; one with Astra, now wrestling with if and when to tell her how he felt, and then with Tyron. How could he even think of getting him back—and think of it in the same breath as Astra. Would Astra hate him for it?

Now standing by the palace gate, Louko was still unsure how to say goodbye, and even as he found himself once more wrapped in his brother's fierce embrace, he wanted nothing more than to force him to stay. To stay where it would be safe. To stay with him.

"Come back soon," he managed to whisper before they separated. "And watch your back." The last bit was aimed at Mariah, who was already atop a horse with four Nythrilian guards still surrounding her as well as the whole group of knights—who had been very pleased to see Louko and Astra again.

"Stay out of trouble." Keeshiff said back, giving Louko a playful punch on the shoulder and turning to Astra, who was also in the courtyard to see them off. Extending his arms, Keeshiff walked forward and gave Astra a hug as well, albeit a much shorter and gentler one than he had given Louko, and then said, "Keep him in line for me?"

"Only if you promise to stay in line, yourself," Astra said, returning the hug before stepping back. The worry that showed in her fidgeting hands added to Louko's uneasiness.

Giving a nod, Keeshiff replied, "I'll do my best. But I'm sure Asher will take good care of me." He looked back to the older man who arched one eyebrow in amusement.

Another shot of anxiety sprang through Louko as he watched his brother mount up, remembering the last time they had been forced to part ways. Why were people always leaving?

It was mere minutes before the troupe was gone, but Louko remained in the courtyard, staring out to the gate that had closed behind Keeshiff and his knights.

He felt Astra step up beside him. "Are you alright?" Her question was soft.

Clearing his throat to try and rid it of the tears stuck in it, Louko gave a raspy, "Yes. Just worried."

"If I am Tyron's target, then perhaps being further away from me will keep him safer." Astra scuffed the paving stones with one shoe.

"Don't think that way," Louko whispered, grabbing Astra's hand without thinking. And then…then he began thinking. Did Astra see it as a romantic gesture? Was this a bad time to ask? What was he supposed to do now?!

To make it worse, Astra's only reply was a quiet sigh as she squeezed his hand back.

Louko wanted to scream. Especially at Keeshiff…who had been nice enough to point this all out to Louko so that he could now spend every moment with Astra in pure agony.

Marvelous.

Astra:

"You both have been staring at this game for over an hour and have come to no conclusion other than everything is the same as it was an hour ago." Destrin broke the tension hanging in the air.

Ven, who was currently sitting behind his desk, added, "Even I have given up looking over it. And that is saying something."

Did Ven even know how The Game worked? Was that another thing she'd missed while sick? Astra decided the question wasn't worth asking.

With a quiet sigh, she looked up at Louko who sat on the other side of the boards. "Any better ideas?" she asked.

Frowning deeply, Louko didn't look up as he suggested, "Maybe fresh air…."

"I think that would be a great idea, actually," Destrin interjected, now. "What if we went somewhere you could practice some Gifting, Astra?"

She froze, bewildered. It took her several seconds of staring at her father before she realized he was serious. "I can't—no, no, that's not a good idea." He, of all people, should know what could happen. He'd been there when her power had first risen, then when her uncle had failed to train or contain her, and surely he'd heard of what she'd done to get herself exiled.

"Clearly trying to suppress it hasn't worked, and from the stories I keep catching from Louko…you have been trying to use it anyway when in danger." Destrin gave a look that seemed very unimpressed. "There has to be somewhere with a wide space that we could practice, surely?" He turned to Ven with the question.

"How wide are we discussing, exactly?" the Ezai Ru asked as he sat forward in his seat, leaning his chin against his folded hands.

Astra couldn't believe they were actually considering this. She glanced towards Louko, certain he'd be on her side.

"I, uh, I think it would have to have no people by or even near it?" Louko said timidly. "I mean, she was able to heal me and remain in control. I'm sure she—" He abruptly changed to address Astra directly. "I'm sure you could get the hang of the other parts of it?"

Healed him? Astra had a vague recollection of healing, but was unsure if it was her own memory or Tyron's. "That must have just been luck. I've lost control so many times—it wouldn't be safe." Her hand twisted around her bare wrist and she wondered if she should be wearing red-bronze.

"Wait, you healed someone?" Destrin's eyes bulged. "Yeah...I think it would definitely be good to get you some guidelines. Is there anywhere outdoors and away from populated areas, Ven? Somewhere we could get to within a day or so but far enough away from the border to be beyond any possibility of Merimeethian intervention?"

Why was it bad to heal someone? Had she messed something up?

"The Wildlands to the west are uninhabitable," Ven mused. "And far enough from the front. It's a few days, but I could send some soldiers to accompany you."

"And Mitheau could come as well?" Louko suggested. "For both extra protection and the ability to stretch her wings. She's seemed to be uncomfortable doing that here, but she said the other day she really needs to be in her Dragon form more."

"Then it's settled. We could leave first thing tomorrow?" Destrin swiveled around and tilted his head as if waiting for Astra's final agreement; as if she hadn't been against the idea from the start.

"But what happens if things go wrong? I-I've leveled entire sections of forest. I took out half a building." She looked to Ven for support. "Even when I was sick, I kept nearly setting your entire manor ablaze, didn't I?"

"I, uh…" Ven did seem to flash a bit of uncertainty at this. "The Wildlands are uninhabitable. There is not much you could do to them…. But, Destrin? What of other people…is this a good idea?"

Astra's father did not waver as he folded both hands in front of his chest and answered, "If Astra can learn to harness her ability, then I think Tyron might lose his power as a threat. Tallaman had his…ahem…attempt at teaching her, but I think it's my turn—and there's no Elf to step in the way and scream about it."

Every argument that Astra had suddenly evaporated, leaving her grasping at a mist of unintelligible words. Did her father really believe that she could have the power to stop Tyron? Did he truly think she had the strength to control it? She couldn't understand how he would have such faith in her after so many disasters of her own making.

"Are you sure?" Ven asked. "Astra?"

Astra blinked at him. "I, um…." *Tyron might lose his power as a threat.* She swallowed and nodded.

"I shall make the arrangements, then," Ven said with a nod, giving one last look to Destrin.

Before the day was out, everything was packed and every last detail settled. Astra's secret hope that Mitheau wouldn't want to go, and thus give her some excuse to stay, was just as quickly dashed. If anything, the young Myrandi seemed more eager than any of them. Or so Astra gathered by her perpetually asking how much longer until they reached the plains.

On the third day of riding, the soldiers Ven had sent as their escort announced that they should be far enough from civilization to make camp. Mitheau had taken off flying the moment the tents were up. Louko, on the other hand, seemed reluctant to take more than a few steps from his tent. He'd been unusually quiet for the entire journey. Astra understood. She kept wondering when the next note would arrive—*how* it would arrive—and whether it would bear news of Keeshiff.

"I'm sure he's alright," Astra said in what she hoped was a comforting tone.

"Huh? Who?" Louko jerked his head to face her in confusion, only to quickly add, "Oh, right, Keeshiff. Yeah...he's fine."

Astra wasn't sure if Louko was so worried that he was trying to cover it up, or if he was worried about something else. "Are you alright?"

Stiffening, her friend blushed and looked down. "I, uh. Yeah. Just was...thinking...."

The way he trailed off doubled her concern. "Thinking?" she prompted.

"Of, you know." He shrugged, frowning and blushing more than ever. "About what happens after this is over."

Astra's brow furrowed. Was he worried about how long they were going to stay out here? "I'm sure we can head back after a few days. I don't think it would be wise to stay for too long."

"No, no, I mean..." He sighed in seeming exasperation. "Like. *After*, after. When we have some time to breathe...relax. Not be...you know, dying?"

"I...I don't understand," Astra admitted.

"I was just...you know, thinking that—that maybe—uh—after when we aren't so busy fighting or running for our lives or dying that—that we could do something?" He gave the weirdest, most embarrassed looking smile she'd ever seen.

Astra wasn't sure if she was supposed to smile back. "...something?"

"I, uh—you know—uh, like..." His unfinished thoughts sputtered to a halt, and all in a moment, he seemed to deflate. "We, uh. Could go out...go out and get a pet? Like maybe a cat?" Another one of those weird grins.

Now Astra was truly concerned. "Are you sure you're alright?" she asked, looking him over. "Don't you dislike animals?"

Louko coughed—or rather choked—saying something indiscernible in between it all.

Suddenly, Destrin came up, starting to speak until he seemed to notice Louko's sudden coughing fit.

"Are you alright?"

Waving a hand away, Louko nodded and almost instantly regained composure, though his face was still scarlet as he said, "Never better— what is it? You need something?" The last bit was said almost too eagerly, as if he wanted nothing more than for Destrin to need something...Astra wondered what she had done that Louko wanted so badly to change the subject.

"We still have a few hours of daylight, Astra." Her father took another moment before redirecting his attention towards her. "Why don't we try something small?"

Anxiety filled her mind with all sorts of excuses to delay. "Alright," she managed to say instead.

"Louko, since you seem to remember more of Astra using her Gifting than she does, would you like to accompany us?" Destrin turned back to her friend.

With one more awkward cough Louko replied, "Yes, of course. Whatever she—er—you both need." He again muttered something about stupidity and cats under his breath.

Destrin glanced at Astra out of the corner of his eye.

Astra shrugged.

"Just to make sure everyone is comfortable," Destrin's gaze now turned up towards where Mitheau's white wings could faintly be spotted darting through clouds. "Why don't we hike out a short ways?"

Astra was quick to agree.

The three walked out until the tents were small white flecks in the distance.

"The soldiers just said we'll have to keep an eye out." Her father scanned the horizon. "Apparently storms move in pretty fast and hard around here."

Astra was mostly worried about storms that she might cause. "You brought the red-bronze in case, right?"

Destrin's shoulders sank almost imperceptibly. "I have things under control, Astra. Focus on the task at hand and trust me?" Somehow words that would have sounded like an order coming from anybody else sounded instead like a gentle request when coming from her father.

Astra wished it was an order. She was better at defying those. "Alright," she murmured, only because she knew he could transport himself and Louko away if things went wrong.

"Thank you." Her father gave a nod with the word, then beckoned her to come closer to him. "You stay over there, Louko. Maybe take a seat; this will be a little while."

Watching her friend sit cross-legged in the grass, Astra stepped forward to await instructions.

"Alright. Let's start with transportation, perhaps?" Destrin asked.

Astra remembered the times her brother had used Gifting to whisk them away from trouble. If nothing else, mastering it would allow her to get away if she became too volatile. She took a deep breath and nodded.

"The first thing you need is a clear picture of where you want to go in your head. As Tallaman…explained once to you, you can never—nor should you ever—try and go somewhere beyond your normal physical limits. If it's not somewhere you could run continuously to without water, sleep, or food, then don't try to go there. To put it dangerously simply, Gifting merely speeds up processes that would otherwise take much longer, but uses all the energy you would normally give for that process in a matter of seconds. Hence why the act of healing someone is often much more painful to the patient than if they were to heal on their own—"

"Wait…I, uh. I never felt anything when Astra fixed my jaw," Louko piped up ever so helpfully from the background, causing Astra to wince.

Destrin just sort of stared from her friend to her, blinked, and closed his eyes as if summoning a great amount of patience. "We can discuss

182

the nuance of healing at a different time, but it is best you know never...*ever* do that again, Astra. It is incredibly dangerous to heal someone without proper anatomic understanding—and on top of that, taking on the pain for your patient could result in you losing focus and doing something like rupturing a major artery."

Astra could practically hear Louko's quiet dismay in the background. She was no better. She could have *killed* him....

Destrin seemed to catch onto the panic and quickly added, "But you're a very quick learner and it's clear you have watched your uncle very carefully. Just...wait, next time." He offered a small smile.

He did not have to tell her twice. "I will."

"Good. Now let's get started. Transporting?" He waited for her to give a nod of affirmation before continuing on. "So as I was saying, never go further than you would be able to physically run. In the same vein, you will never want to transport more people at a time than you would be able to carry in one trip."

More people than she could carry? Astra was beginning to realize why Ent had always been so sick and tired all of the time during The War.

"So why don't we just start with trying to transport a few feet. I know you've likely gone further before in your own...experiments...but we are under no doubt of your ability. We are learning control. Our goal is to be deliberate and feel as if the move is planned. Understood?" Destrin raised an eyebrow at the last bit.

Astra nodded yet again. She thought of those few lessons with Tallaman and the exercise he'd given her of trying to light a candle. She'd nearly burned his entire house down. What was the transporting equivalent of that? Would she move them all miles from camp and not know how to get them back?

Destrin leaned over and plucked a small stone from the ground. Then he crossed to Astra and set it in front of her. "Study this spot. How it looks, how it feels—where it is in relation to everything else around you."

Eyes glued to the rock, Astra tried to obey.

A minute or two ticked by in silence. "Good," Destrin finally said. "Now walk over here."

He walked a few yards away and Astra joined him.

"Visualize what you just saw and move yourself back there with Gifting."

Astra summoned up the image of the small, blue-grey stone. Nervously, she reached for a little of the power that hummed constantly in the back of her mind. But as soon as she did so, the hum turned to roar and nearly threw her backwards. She gasped and immediately released what little power she'd drawn out. "I don't think this is a good—"

"I think you are more afraid of it than you need to be. If you get on a horse and show fear, that horse will respond accordingly. Gifting is very much its own force of nature. You can't hold onto the ground and it at the same time, much like you cannot ride a horse without leaving the ground." Destrin explained, ever patiently. "It's time to get on the horse, Astra. You can't hurt anyone out here, and there is no Tallaman to get in your face, however well intentioned."

Astra couldn't help but think of how a horse was much less likely to wipe out her father and friend in one blow. Nevertheless, she did her best to steady her breathing. She allowed herself one last glance towards

Louko, who gave a small smile as if to encourage her, before closing her eyes.

First, she thought of the stone a few feet away. Her father's words echoed in her mind: *How it looks, how it feels—where it is in relation to everything else around you.* Then she reached for her Gift. This time, she was ready for the roar. And when it charged, just like with a horse, she did not turn and flee. Instead, she stood ready, challenging it—daring it—to run her over. It never did. There was a split second of strange, familiar sensation as the ground beneath her feet changed.

Then a distant voice called, "Very good!"

Astra opened her eyes to see her father waving his arms in the distance.

It worked! Astra's elation was only somewhat marred by having gone a hundred times this distance she was meant to. She hadn't brought either of them with her, or moved miles away, or any of her other fears. Grinning, she raised her arms to return the wave. "Should I come back?"

"Yes, but don't rush it—keep working towards that focus," Destrin called back.

Astra closed her eyes again and pictured the stone. Her Gifting roared and swept through and carried her back, but instead of steady ground beneath her feet, she landed on something soft and uneven that tipped her over before she could catch herself. It wasn't until he yelped that Astra realized she'd landed directly on Louko.

"I, uh. Hi there...am I...distracting you?" he asked as he awkwardly tried to disentangle himself from her, looking very flustered.

Astra felt her face go hot. "Sorry." She managed to get back on her feet and offered a hand to help him do the same. "I didn't mean to...." Astra slowly realized that Louko had been sitting and withdrew her hand. "...sorry."

"Remember, Astra...focus. On the terrain you want to go to...not your—friend." Destrin coughed inconspicuously. Astra seemed to have missed the joke. "Let's try again."

Face still flushed, Astra crossed back to her father to repeat the exercise.

After an hour, only two successful attempts to land directly in front of the stone, and five more unsuccessful landings on Louko, they all agreed that there had been enough practice for one evening.

"Perhaps," Destrin cleared his throat as they walked back towards the camp together. "It would be best for Louko to remain by the tents for tomorrow's practice."

"Oh, uh. Sorry. I didn't mean to make it difficult," Louko mumbled.

"It wasn't your fault." Astra started to nudge him with her elbow before remembering he was probably pretty bruised from her falling on him.

Again, Louko blushed. What was with that lately? Was he feeling alright?

Her father cut in. "It's not anyone's fault. Today went quite well—you never once lost control."

That was only true if they left out the instances of Astra not controlling how far she transported. But, in the larger sense, he was right. No one had gotten hurt. She didn't even feel shaky like she always had when using her Gift in the past. Perhaps…perhaps her father's faith in her wasn't entirely misplaced.

"Thank you for the help," she said quietly. "And for trusting me."

Her father gave her a soft smile, making her feel a warmth and love she had forgotten she craved. "Thank you for listening."

As they re-entered camp, Astra finally let herself believe that maybe…just maybe, this wasn't going to be another catastrophe.

CHAPTER X

Keeshiff:

The journey had been more difficult than expected. Rhumir had done nothing but glare at Mariah and mutter murderous threats, and Rufio had been fraying at the ends just trying to keep his brother in line. Even when talking with the other knights, there was this cloud of apprehension that hung over each word. Maybe bringing Mariah hadn't been such a great idea, after all.

Somehow, things had gotten even more stressful when they'd discovered the rubii had apparently stowed away in Keeshiff's food pack. It hadn't been found until a day and a half down the road, and so it was just another problem for Keeshiff to deal with, and didn't help that the squirming thing was more difficult to work with than Mariah.

In truth, Mariah hadn't spoken a single word, and yet somehow that was worse. It was like waiting for the other shoe to drop—for her ulterior motive to become known, because there always was one with her. It left him thinking about her one suggestion about him reclaiming the throne of Merimeethia. Was he just playing into her plan? Did she even have a plan to play into?

"Prince Keeshiff, good to see you again." Jahng's greeting came in Merimeethian as they entered the Nythrilian camp—which was a lot larger than Keeshiff had been expecting, in all honesty. Even Jahng had changed, no longer wearing the armor of a Drogan hunter and instead the leather and metal mixture of a Nythrilian commander.

Dismounting quickly, Keeshiff found himself handing his horse off to an attending soldier. He then walked up and extended his hand to Jahng, who clasped his arm with a firm grip and a small smile.

"Glad you would have me," he replied.

Jahng dipped her head and released his arm. Then her attention turned towards Mariah, confusion marking her brow. "Who is this?"

As usual, Mariah came back into the conversation like a bad headache. "My…sister, unfortunately. She is to be carefully guarded at all times—here, Astra wrote a letter explaining it. As did the Ezai Ru." Keeshiff handed the woman two sealed letters.

Accepting both, Jahng asked, "In that case, do you wish to leave her under our guard or under the guard of your men?"

"Under your guard. I think mine might be less patient with her," Keeshiff replied with a wince, looking back to his men and especially Rhumir.

"Understood." Jahng waved up two soldiers. "Take her to the central ring and give her a tent. I want one man at the entrance at all times."

Both men bowed, stepping up alongside Mariah. Keeshiff caught the way his sister flinched, but chose to ignore it, instead looking back to Jahng. He was done with Mariah taking up space in his mind.

"So. How can I be of assistance? As I'm sure the letters will explain, we do have a few ideas of how to proceed…but it's all very uncertain as of yet," Keeshiff asked. He didn't like saying anything so out in the open—not even in Merimeethian. Tyron's spies could be anywhere, after all.

Jahng turned, motioning for him to follow. "Leave your men with mine to get settled in camp and follow me," she said.

With a quick nod to Asher to make sure his knights would cooperate, Keeshiff turned and followed Jahng.

"So far, there have been no direct attacks," she explained as they walked. "But we have tracked several of their scouting parties trying to get around the flank. We thought you might have the best idea of where they were headed."

Keeshiff remembered the discussion with Aelor Ven and the possibility of Tyron searching for some old portal site. "I might, yes." He remained vague, however, until they had arrived at last at the command tent. Jahng ushered him inside to find a table strewn with maps and surrounded by what Keeshiff could assume were generals—based on the insignias on their Nythrilian uniforms, that was.

"Prince Keeshiff, this is General Tahrin, the head of our defense tactics." Jahng nodded towards the oldest of the three. Keeshiff tried to copy her gesture as she went on. "General Laosim, who runs our intelligence and counter tactics, and General Itso, who has oversight of our scouts and the southern flank. General Xianti, the head over the combined cavalry, is currently occupied."

Keeshiff felt almost unsure what to do. Usually this sort of environment was something he was very comfortable with, but not like this. Not with the generals of a country his people had long deemed enemies. What did they even think of him? Clearly, General Itso had his opinions, based on the glare he was shooting Keeshiff's way.

"It is an honor, thank you, Commander Jahng," Keeshiff replied at last, keeping his shoulders straight and hoping not to betray too much of his uncertainty.

"We are glad your journey was swift and safe." General Tahrin was the first to speak. His Merimeethian was heavily accented, taking Keeshiff a moment to decipher. "Do you come with any news from the Ezai Ru?"

"Yes," Keeshiff answered, clearing his throat as discreetly as possible. Knowing that they were all speaking Merimeethian on his behalf somehow made him feel more conspicuous. "I have given the correspondence already to Commander Jahng, but we believe that Steward Kaeden is after something behind your border." It still disgusted Keeshiff the way they could not talk openly of Tyron's identity since half of Nythril would still likely think them crazy. Most everyone Astra had ever tried to tell thought so.

Laosim, the general Jahng had pinpointed as overseeing intelligence, was quick to interject. "Do we know exactly what? Or where?"

Keeshiff looked to Jahng, battling his instinct to stay quiet among strangers. These were her generals, after all—if they couldn't be trusted, they'd already lost. Right?

Jahng met his gaze and nodded slightly.

"It is the site where the Drogans disappeared—the Thikao Ruins. He believes in the ancient stories of it being some portal and wishes to utilize it," Keeshiff said with a deep breath.

Frowning, Laosim immediately began sorting through a pile of papers.

"Commander, shouldn't we start with the direct correspondence from the Ezai Ru himself?" General Itso was still looking right at Keeshiff.

As offended as Keeshiff would have liked to be, he knew that was by far the worst possible move he could do right now. Oh, he despised politics. "Yes, please, Commander, the letters will phrase it much more clearly than I will." He tried his best to sound genuine, but felt like the words came off exactly the opposite of how he had intended.

The rest of the meeting comprised of Itso's glares, Laosim's doubts, and Jahng's attempts at being impartial. Itso had especially disliked the idea of Keeshiff trying to regain the Merimeethians' loyalty. Keeshiff, in the meantime, did his best to keep his opinions to a minimum and make a decent first impression. If he was going to get the Merimeethians to eventually cooperate then he really needed to have equal footing with both the Nythrilians and his own people, and it seemed like that might be fairly difficult. Would he really be able to cross a barrier that had been there for generations? A barrier that not even the marriage of his father and Louko's mother had broken?

Well, perhaps that was more because of what his father had done afterwards that had been the problem.

All that being said, Keeshiff was very relieved when at last Jahng called the meeting to an end and dismissed the other generals. "I'm sure you would now like to return to your men and perhaps get settled?" Jahng asked once they were alone.

"If it is not too much trouble, that does sound like a lovely next step, thank you, Commander." He dipped his head.

The corner of Jahng's mouth tipped up in a slight smile and she said, "You may call me Jahng when not in a formal meeting, if you wish."

Why did Keeshiff's cheeks feel suddenly warm? "Then I am bound to return the favor, Jahng. Besides, I'm really not a prince of anything, at the moment."

"Hopefully that will change, Keeshiff," She replied with a raised eyebrow. "Now, to your men and accommodations? A tent should be set aside for you by now."

Keeshiff nodded and together they left the tent.

Clearing his throat awkwardly, Keeshiff asked, "So…how have you been, Jahng?"

Jahng looked at him out of the corner of her eye just long enough for him to nearly take the question back. "Busy," she replied succinctly. "I presume you have been about the same."

"Yes.…" Keeshiff struggled to find something *else* to talk about, and yet he was about as good at making casual conversation as that rubii was at staying where it was told to. "Though it seems you have been doing well, keeping things organized here."

"As much as I can." Jahng glanced down a row of tents before straightening her shoulders. "Our army functions differently from yours. Each general is leading troops from their regional state, meaning there are some differing ways of functioning among both leaders and men. I am set as the Ezai Ru's chosen commander, meaning I am technically their head, but not everyone is thrilled about answering to a former Hunter."

"I'm sure they will see your true qualities soon. You seem a capable leader," Keeshiff replied. Astra was always better at this sort of thing…what would Astra say?

"Hopefully, this will all be over before we have to find out," Jahng said grimly.

"Hopefully." *Come on, Keeshiff think of something more helpful to say!* Keeshiff came to the acknowledgement that he was very bad at talking, and that shutting up was for now a much better option than making a fool out of himself in front of the commander. He'd need to get better at that if he was going to try and stop this war....

Louko:

Louko sat there dejectedly, watching Mitheau as she swooped and climbed through the air above him. Destrin had proclaimed Louko was too distracting to sit in on their lessons, and thus, today he was stuck with Mitheau. She'd offered to let him fly on her back but after everything that happened the last time he really, really didn't like the idea. Still, anything was better than sitting in a tent or awkwardly waiting with his uncle's soldiers. The distance allowed him some privacy for his thoughts.

But he just...he couldn't stop thinking about it—about Astra, and about what Keeshiff had said. About how Louko had gotten so close to asking her only to bow out at the last minute.

"Did you want to get a cat...what were you thinking, idiot?" He grumbled to himself, rubbing his forehead and imagining Keeshiff's reaction if he'd been there for the embarrassing moment.

And then there were Destrin's comments. What sort of distraction was Louko? A good kind, as in she wanted him around? Or an uncomfortable, bad sort of distraction?

"Oh, would you just quit it? You sound pathetic." Louko threw up his hands in the air as he berated himself a little too loudly.

"Am I interrupting something?" The calm voice came from behind him.

Louko recognized the voice even though his logic told himself it was impossible, and jumping up he whirled around to come face-to-face with none other than Tyron.

"W-What are you—how—" Louko's eyes were wide as he stumbled through the words, panic fighting every movement as he now struggled to reach the sword at his side.

Tyron looked up, seemingly more preoccupied with Mitheau overhead than with Louko. He stood with hands folded neatly behind his back as if unbothered by the weapon Louko was now pointing at him. "Let's skip the pleasantries, shall we?" His green eyes turned down to Louko, inspecting him in a glance. "How long has Astra been practicing?"

Louko's eyes only grew wider, faced once more with the nightmare and the desperation to bring the Tyron he knew back. "No!" It was the only word Louko could form as he tried to move—tried to use his blade. But was it Tyron's Gifting or was it Louko's own weakness that kept him rooted in place?

Tyron's sigh held both disappointment and thinning patience. "A few days, perhaps?" He studied Louko intently. "Yes, a few days. Has she lost control at any point?"

"Stop!" Louko still could manage no more than one-word cries, but was now desperate for someone to realize—someone to see. It was as if he was drowning a mere inch from the shoreline, everyone's head turned away. How was Tyron *here?!*

"No? Good. Very good." Tyron nodded to himself. Then his attention turned back up to the sky. "Call for your friend."

Somehow now seeing Tyron *wanted* him to call for help made Louko go silent. What was happening—what was happening!? Panic swelled until Louko felt as if his vision would fail, and all he could do was whisper. "Stop. Tyron, please. *Please.*"

Tyron showed no reaction to his plea. "Ah, perfect, she's already seen us."

Something inside Louko broke. "Please."

There was a gust of wind as Mitheau landed nearby, teeth bared and neck arched. Her tail whipped back and forth as if she was ready to pounce. "Who are—" Her draconic voice cut off suddenly and her whole posture relaxed until she began to sway.

"Run, Mitheau!" Louko managed to croak the words.

"Don't fight it, young one." Tyron spoke quietly, tone somewhere between soothing and taunting. "It will only make it harder when you wake up."

All Louko could do was watch in horror as Mitheau collapsed, breathing hard. Her eyes flickered, then closed, and she slowly shifted back to the form of a young girl. Tyron crossed to her and knelt, feeling her wrist a moment.

"Leave her alone!" Still Louko could not move—but not for lack of trying. This was a nightmare, such a nightmare.

Tyron pulled out a piece of folded parchment and placed it in her motionless hand. When he stood, a chilling smile crossed his lips. "I'm not here for her."

Louko couldn't even fight back as Tyron pulled the sword from his numb hands and stabbed it point-down into the ground.

"You'd best hold still."

Without any other warning, their green surroundings melted into black and the whole world vanished.

Astra:

"I'm pretty sure I'm getting worse at this—not better," Astra grumbled as her father stomped out the small fire she'd started. She couldn't seem to focus on anything today.

"No, definitely better. Nothing has exploded in a while," Destrin replied with a bit of a smile.

Astra was about to say something dry in reply when her ears picked up the sound of frantic footsteps coming their way.

Both her and Destrin turned to find several of the soldiers running towards them, shouting something.

Then one sentence broke through the muddled noise: "The prince is gone!"

The words made no sense to her. Astra looked up at her father, trying to see if he knew what was going on.

"What?!" Destrin's voice rang as the soldiers at last caught up to Astra and her father.

"The lady Drogan wished to practice further off—the prince asked for space—we were still in sight and checked in every half hour in person. But then we saw the Drogan land and not stir for a while and when we went up to check on them the prince was gone and she was unconscious…she still has not woken."

Shock made her limbs feel paralyzed even while her mind lurched into action. Was it Tyron? How could he have gotten this far? Where could they have even gone? Surely no one could have taken Louko far in such a small span of time.

"Where is she?" her father demanded.

"We brought her back to camp," the soldier replied between gulps of air.

That feeling of the ground melting away beneath her feet came on quickly, but Astra hadn't reached for her Gifting. Not until they all appeared in the circle of tents did she realize her father had moved them.

There Mitheau was—laying on the ground in her Human form and groaning with one of the soldiers leaning over her. Everyone else seemed to keep their distance, eyeing the Myrandi with a mixture of suspicion and uneasiness.

"What if she did something to him?" Astra heard one of the men mutter.

Astra pushed through them and kneeled down by Mitheau. "Mitheau, can you hear me?"

"I…I'm…sorry…" Mitheau murmured. "I…couldn't stop him…." Her whole body shook as she tried to get up, eyes fluttering open as she grimaced.

"Don't try to get up, Mitheau." Destrin was right next to Astra. "Wait until you're steady."

"Him? Who is 'him'?" Astra asked urgently.

"I-I-It was…Ty—" She looked around at the soldiers that surrounded them, eyes wide. "It was *him*, Astra. He used Gifting…he's…gone with Louko…."

"Where? Which way?" It took every ounce of Astra's will to not shake Mitheau by the shoulders.

"Gifting. They Gifted away," Mitheau gasped, putting a hand to her head. "I'm so sorry." The words were barely understandable through the choked sob. A tear ran down Mitheau's cheek. "I'm sorry." She held out one hand and Astra's breath caught at the sight of crumpled parchment beneath her fingers.

As if in a trance, she reached for the note and opened it.

Dear Astra,

I see you've been practicing. To ensure that you don't get distracted or attempt to cut our Game short, I've decided that some extra motivation is in order. Hopefully a raise in the stakes will motivate you to keep up your studies.

—T

Prince Keeshiff goes to the Nythrilian front—White Knight No. 2 forward three, right two
Prince Louko captured—White Pawn No. 1 reaches the end of the middle board, rises to the top board

White Castle No. 3 takes Black Bishop No. 1
Black Castle No. 4 back three, White Pawn No. 4 reaches the end of the bottom board, rises to the middle board
White Pawn No. 1 remains in his place

Astra pulled back, already looking towards the low hills around them. *No. No, no, no.*

"Astra," Destrin whispered in her ear and put a hand on her shoulder. Mitheau was now openly sobbing.

"He'd head for the border," Astra heard herself say. "He couldn't go farther than he could carry Louko, right?"

"We don't know how long it's been...and if he changed to a Dragon he could be leagues away by now, Astra. We need to stop and think—we need a plan." Destrin's grip tightened on Astra. "Astra...."

"If he gets away, we'll never get Louko back." Astra was already reaching for her Gifting.

"Wait—"

Her father's cry was cut off by the roar of her power as Astra wrenched away, willing herself far from the camp.

Her feet hit the ground with enough force to make her stumble forward. The motion scattered small stones down the steep hillside. She spun around, eyes catching on the distant cluster of white spots—the camp. She craned her head back to search the sky in every direction, scanning for any possible sign of Tyron or Louko. Nothing.

So Astra turned herself northeast and fixed her attention on the furthest hill she could make out. Another wave of Gifting carried her there. Again, she combed the skies, came up empty, and moved herself further northeast. Then again. And again.

No! She nearly screamed at the barren sky above her. This couldn't happen! Louko couldn't go back there—back to *him!* They had to be somewhere—how far could Tyron have possibly gotten? Astra's heart was pounding so loudly that she could barely hear her own thoughts. What if he wasn't heading for Melye? Or what if he wasn't taking a direct route? *What if Louko was already dead?*

The thought nearly spurred her to transport herself all the way to Melye. It was Tyron's note that stopped her. If he was taking Louko as leverage, then he couldn't risk harming him, right? If Astra did catch up to them, would it prompt him to hurt Louko just to stop her?

But what would happen when Tyron found out she couldn't open the portal? Her stomach twisted. *He would kill him.* He would kill him and take someone else, and then someone else…over and over again until Astra had no one left for him to use against her.

Panic made her thoughts spin too fast for her to keep up with. There had to be something—some way to get Louko back. But if she couldn't give Tyron what he wanted, she needed another way to get whatever he was after. How could she manage that when no one knew what his goal truly was?

…*that's not true.* The realization brought the very world to a stop: Tirzah. If anyone in the world of Eatris knew what Tyron was chasing, or what he planned to do with Louko, it would be Tirzah. And Astra knew exactly where she was.

Astra looked southwest towards the camp, despite being too far to see it anymore. The setting sun had turned the green hills a dusky red. Did she dare? She remembered her father's warning to never go further than she could walk. What happened if she tried? Would she appear somewhere halfway? Would it just kill her and leave her where she was?

Part of her wondered if they would ever find her body. The other part of her didn't care. If there was any chance that this could help save Louko, she had to try. Astra closed her eyes, tuned out the whistling of the breeze around her, and summoned up an image of the streets of Silbyr. Her breath was no longer shaky as she inhaled slowly. Without another thought, she reached for her Gifting and flung herself into the image.

She didn't land on the cobblestone. For a moment, she was suspended, entirely weightless in a sea of black. The city she had pictured so clearly mere seconds before now faded until she couldn't even remember what a street looked like. Fear rose, an instinct that clamored for her to fight back against the dark that had swallowed her whole. But that clamor, too, faded to black. Silence such as Astra had never heard reigned absolute.

It was then that she saw the stars. They were dim at first, coming into focus one at a time. But then they were everywhere, cold and brilliant, in colorful swathes above her head and beneath her feet. The sheer wonder of it all made it hard to remember why she was ever frightened to begin with.

Just as the stars had seemed to reach their full strength, they shifted. The weightlessness started to lift as if she was falling in slow motion. She tried to reach up towards the stars, but her hands swung in empty air above her head. Then her feet hit solid ground and the darkness evaporated like fog to reveal an empty alleyway. Sound hit her with deafening force, making her clap her hands over her ears. She must have stood there for minutes until her senses readjusted enough for her to discern the distinct timbres of voices, animals, and carts rattling over cobblestone.

She'd made it to Silbyr.

Astra had no time to wonder about where she'd gone in between. She quickly pulled up her hood, ducking to the side of the alley. A rodent, the sole witness of her arrival, scurried off around the corner. Now what? She needed to find Tirzah—fast. Who would know where "Lady Therune" lived?

Astra had an idea.

Three hours later, thanks to the gossip of the laundresses in the courtier's city quarter, Astra sat on the floor of Tirzah's small study. The contents of the nearby desk half-surrounded her, with everything she'd already sifted through strewn to her right. Agricultural logs, tax reports, details of a territorial dispute—nothing that gave Astra any information. The only thing of use had been the riot reports. Astra had found eight of them so far, all from different settlements, and all apparently over her brother's removal.

Nothing from Tyron. Nothing about Louko. Astra wanted to scream, to throw all the papers in the hearth and Gift herself back to the front to see if she could find Tyron herself. *Louko. He had Louko.* Louko had spoken of trying to cure Tyron and now Tyron had taken him. To where? To what? Astra tried to tell herself that Tyron wouldn't harm him if he was using him as a hostage. But if Tyron truly was insane, then there was no telling what he would do.

The sound of creaking wood drew Astra's attention upwards. Someone was walking up the stairs. Not the butler—Astra had avoided him earlier, waiting until he'd left for the night to search the house. This person was steadier, lighter, and heading right for the study door. There was a pause as they reached it. Then the handle turned.

"Astra Verzaer, to what do I owe the pleasure of you ransacking my house?"

Tirzah's appearance was jarring, triggering memories of far-off times and places that Astra had never seen. All of it was overlaid by the days that she had spent before the Court in chains.

"Where is he?" Astra growled.

Tirzah surveyed her study, now littered with Astra's search, and raised an eyebrow. "Right to the point, I see. Just like your brother." She stepped in but left the door open. "If you are speaking of Kaeden, he is still in Merimeethia—presumably in the castle of Melye. Considering the public nature of that information, I'm not sure why that has merited—"

Astra lunged towards her, dagger drawn, stopping short only because of the desk between them. It was just enough of a delay for the logical part of her brain to remember that she stood little chance of overpowering the Drogan. Not without Gifting. Did she dare use that when she was already seeing red?

"You have thirty seconds to tell me where Louko is," Astra hissed, gripping the desk with her free hand.

Tirzah had sunk into an angled stance with one hand on whatever weapon was tucked inside her coat. "Louko? The Merimeethian prince?" Her voice had lost any pretense of casualness. "The last I knew of him, he left with you for Nythril."

Astra was already questioning her resolve to not use Gifting. "Where your brother-in-law promptly abducted him. Where did he take him?"

Something like surprise flitted across Tirzah's expression. "When was this?"

"This afternoon." Astra forced herself to let go of the desk.

Tirzah seemed to process this slowly, straightening as she did so. Her right hand stayed by her weapon. "I'm afraid I know nothing of this. But if this is as you say, Louko is safer where he is than he would be if you tried to rescue him."

"Safe? *Safe?*" Somehow, Astra was laughing, a horrible, joyless sound that bubbled out without her permission. "You really have no idea what he did to us, do you?" With one hand, Astra drove her dagger into the wooden desk. With the other, she yanked at her sleeve until the scars it hid were on full display. The ragged, ugly shapes nearly covered her entire arm, glowing red in the light of the fireplace.

"I was fourteen the first time Tyron nearly tortured me to death," Astra spat. "I was a *child*. And he did it all in front of my brother to get him to talk. The second time, I was sixteen. I didn't see sunlight for a month. And Louko was trapped down there for every second of it." She pulled her dagger free of the desk. "You think he won't hurt Louko? Think again."

Astra saw the way Tirzah's gaze was glued to her scars. When the woman looked away, the motion seemed to take effort. "In all of that, he never directly laid a hand on Louko, did he?" she murmured.

Through grit teeth, Astra admitted, "Not directly."

Tirzah closed her eyes for a brief moment. When she opened them again, she met Astra's gaze without flinching. "Then he is safe for now. If Tyron has taken him, I presume it is either as collateral against you or to, in his mind, ensure his safety. His well-being will not be jeopardized so long as Tyron continues to feel in control of the situation." She took a deep breath, crossing to the chair that sat across from the desk and taking her seat. "You must understand, this is all because of—"

"The madness, I know," Astra cut her off. She did not sit down. "And I know he wants me to open some portal. But I have no way to do so and no one to show me how. When I fail, then what happens?"

Tirzah's jaw went taut.

This upset her. *Good.* Even if Tyron was the only person Tirzah was concerned for, concern gave Astra a better angle. "This madness—if it's true and he is still in there, what do you think it will do to him when he wakes up to find that he has hurt or killed Louko?" She finally sheathed her dagger.

She caught the way Tirzah swallowed. "I'm afraid that, even if I wanted to help you, I have nothing to offer. Besides, he probably has as many people watching me as he has watching you." The Myrandi's voice was low. "I don't know where he is keeping your friend. I don't even know what his full plan is. All I know is the orders that he sends me."

"Then what is his goal?" Astra pressed, frustration rising. Tirzah had to know something. "If I know that, I could try and find some other way to give him what he wants. Or at least to convince him that I cannot give it to him."

Tirzah shook her head slowly. "I don't think either is possible. He's trying to find my sister."

Astra's anger was suspended by a moment of pure confusion. "Rhioa?"

Brow furrowed, Tirzah nodded. "You know of her?"

"In a way." Astra had no intention of explaining her shared memories. "But he was there when she died. Surely, even his state, he knows she is gone."

Again, Tirzah shook her head. "She's not dead. Myrandi have two forms and both must be killed in order for them to die. Rhioa had both when she was struck by the Miadoris."

Unable to even muster a reply, Astra felt herself sit down.

"Tyron thought, initially, that she had died because her first form never faded. The Miadoris does not interact well with Myrandi, so our best guess was that it was responsible for the death of both forms," Tirzah explained. "But when I took up my role as Lady Therune, I learned that that was not the case. Her body had vanished the day before her burial. Thinking Tyron would go mad with grief, his brothers did not tell him."

Astra tried to process this. She could remember the day of the funeral—a rainy day on the plains outside Silbyr's walls. She could remember the stone being set over the casket. *He didn't know...he didn't know the casket was empty.*

Tirzah was looking down at her own hands as she continued. "After we found this out, we realized that Rhioa must have reappeared with my father. Slain Myrandi reappear to the ones they are closest to—we had presumed that would be Tyron or myself. But my father had left for Baeno before anyone could inform him of what happened. We believe she is there with him."

Rhioa was alive. Astra could hardly believe it. "That's why he wants the portal," she whispered. "He's trying to get to her."

Tirzah nodded. "By the time we had pieced this all together, Tyron was already too far gone. Instead of pulling him back to his senses, the idea of getting her back became his obsession. The Dragon will stop at nothing until it is fulfilled."

Sitting back in her seat, Astra tried to think through all of the ramifications. All her fears were being confirmed: She could not give Tyron what he wanted, and there was no way to stop him. She could only think of one other option.

209

"Is there any way to convince him that I can't do what he wants?" she asked, more desperate than before. "I would gladly help try and reunite him with your sister, but this Door—I can't open it. I don't know how and I'm not even certain that I would be able to even if someone did show me."

The pained look on Tirzah's face said what she did not. It was a long moment until she said, "I'm sorry. If I knew how to stop him—to cure him—I would do it in an instant. I've gone along with all of it because I hoped that somehow reuniting them would restore him. I didn't realize that..." She let out a shaky breath. "...that this was his plan. And that you were unable to open it."

Astra wanted so badly to hold on to her rage—to be so angry that she didn't have to feel the way fear made her hands tremble. But it was too late. She was already consumed by the thought of what was going to happen to her friend and how little she could do about it.

"He was the kindest person I'd ever met." Tirzah spoke softly, eyes fixed on the desk and yet not seeming to see it. "And the most persistent. All he ever wanted to do was help others." She looked up at Astra. "I don't know if that person is still in there, but please; if there is any way to save your family and still spare his life, I beg of you to do so."

Mere weeks ago, Astra had stood in the Court while her brother begged for her to be spared. Now the same woman who had sought her demise was begging before her. Astra wished that she had the strength for revenge. But here they both were, tired, afraid, and unable to help the ones they loved.

"I do not know if there is a way to save any of them," Astra said, suddenly exhausted. "Not when this 'Dragon' controls The Game."

Something appeared to give Tirzah pause. "Game?"

"TetraChess," Astra explained wearily. "He sends notes. They compare people to particular pieces, detailing things that have happened and predicting what will happen next. I suppose it's his way of gloating."

Tirzah's brow furrowed. "These predictions…do they always come to pass?"

Astra nodded, feeling sick. Even Louko's kidnapping had been predicted. And she had missed it.

"Perhaps," Tirzah's shoulders straightened as if brightening at the thought. "Perhaps that's more than just gloating—perhaps that's his way of trying to feed you information."

Narrowing her eyes, Astra didn't get a chance to speak before Tirzah plowed on.

"He did that during The War, if you recall. One of the spies in your brother's camp—she was a double that worked for Tyron. He always provided her with whatever information he could get on Euracia's movements." Tirzah spoke quickly, the closest thing to excitement that Astra had ever seen from her. "If the real Tyron is still in there, then there is a chance that this is his way of doing that now."

Astra's gaze remained narrow. "I know about the spy. She was revealed when she tried to kill me. If he is trying to give me information, what's to keep it from doing the same?"

Tirzah winced. "I suppose there is a certain risk involved." She sighed quietly. "Either way, the best advice I can give you is to play along—at least outwardly—as well as you can. If the Dragon does not feel threatened, it is unlikely to hurt your friend. Whatever plans you make, keep them as quiet as possible. He has many spies."

Play along. Play The Game. What happened when they reached its end? "You're telling me to just leave him there?" Astra felt her ire stir.

"Even if you found him, how do you plan to keep him safe?" Tirzah's question was like a slap to the face. "And even if Tyron didn't come for him, you have too many others you love. He would just take someone else."

Astra's thoughts raced to Ent, Keeshiff, her parents, Ven…. "Is that why he sent you after my brother? Just to threaten me?"

Somehow, Tirzah's pursed lips made her look troubled. "I presumed it was to keep Litash and your brother from coming to your aid. You are an easier target when isolated. But your guess is as good as mine," she finally admitted. "He does not explain his orders; he simply expects me to follow them."

Astra couldn't help but stare. "That's it? An entire country thrown into uproar and you went along because of following *orders?* Do you know what my brother sacrificed—what every person in this country sacrificed—to bring peace?" Astra got to her feet, unable to hide her disgust. "And you threw it all to the wind on the whim of a madman."

At least Tirzah had the decency to look ashamed. "Like I said, the Dragon will stop at nothing."

Astra did not look away. "But what will you stop at?"

Tirzah opened her mouth as if to speak then closed it.

"I hope you figure out the answer before it's too late." Astra did not wait for a reply. She had gotten all that she would be able to get from Tirzah. With the thought of her father and the camp she'd left behind, she pulled at the world around her and whisked herself away.

CHAPTER XI

<u>Entrais:</u>

"This is the eighth town that's sworn allegiance to us and denounced the Court," Jade said, still poring over the open letter in her hand.

Ent couldn't muster anything to say in response, instead continuing to look over the map in his own hands as he scanned all the documented towns and villages. Litash only had three large cities: Silbyr, Cerdris, and Takarast. But most of Litash's military came from the towns and villages scattered throughout the country, and when the Court had tried to call them to arms against Nythril…well, it seemed they were slowly answering to Ent instead.

War was coming whether he wanted it or not. It was all he could do to keep himself together.

"Ent?" His mother's voice was muffled through the door, a brief warning before the handle turned and Ameri walked in.

Taking in a shuddering breath, Ent straightened and took in the confusion in his mother's expression. "What's the matter?" Did he really want to know?

"The gatehouse just sent word. They say a representative from Silbyr is at the gate and asking for you." Ameri frowned. "No entourage, and refused to give her name. The guards have not yet let her in."

Her. Why did he immediately go to Tirzah? Was she coming with yet another ultimatum? He worried what the Court would do in retaliation against the blatant insubordination. But then again, without the people of

Litash, did they even have an army to do so? Or maybe Tirzah would come and say that the Court would actually accept Jade as the head monarch and then this could all end.

He saw his mother glance towards Jade and back to him. "What do you want to do?"

"Let her in," Ent replied, folding up the map in his hands and placing it in the drawer of his desk.

Ameri nodded and stepped back out of the room.

"Do you think it's Tirzah again?" Jade asked the second the door had closed.

"I don't know," he whispered. He walked over to join his wife where she stood, forcing himself to quietly reach out and take her hand even as he fought the instinct that told him to keep away for fear of hurting her somehow. But the comfort that came with the warm touch was undeniable.

For nearly twenty minutes, they waited, and by the time the knock came on the door, they had sifted through three more letters.

Ent steeled himself. "Enter."

With one guard in front and another behind, Tirzah walked through the door.

"Lady Therune of the Court of Litash," the first guard announced, eyeing his charge with thinly veiled disdain.

Something broke in Ent as his fears once more proved true. "Oh great, to what do we owe the honor of such a visit? Am I to give myself up for execution? Who do you want me to turn over to the mercy of Tyron? Any more lives you would like to upend? Or is an entire country thrown to chaos not enough?"

Tirzah appeared entirely unaffected. His mother, on the other hand, looked suddenly ready to kill someone. The two guards glanced at each other uneasily.

"Your sister paid me a visit last week," Tirzah said in monotone. "I thought it might be wise to catch you up on some of the situation."

"Wait, what?" Ent narrowed his eyes. "That's impossible, she's in Nythril." He let go of Jade's hand, reaching for the hilt of his sword even as he took a step towards Tirzah. "If you harm a single hair on her head—"

"—She's already gone," Tirzah interrupted. "Back to Nythril, I presume." Her expression verged on annoyance. "She must have transported herself if she got in and out so quickly."

There had only ever been a few times where Ent had picked someone up by the collar of their shirt, but them rolling their eyes in response was a new reaction. It didn't stop him from plastering Tirzah against the nearest wall. "Choose your next words carefully: I don't have much left to lose." Panic swelled as he wondered if Astra had actually been dumb enough to transport across an entire country. "Why are you here?"

"Guards," Jade's voice came from behind him. "Please take up post at the door. No one in or out until we say so." There were footsteps and the sound of a closing door. Then Ent felt a hand on his shoulder. "Ent, why don't you let her go so that we can get some real answers?"

"Fine," The vehemence was directed not at Jade, but at Tirzah as he glared at her. Slowly, he put her down. "Now what have you done to Astra?"

Tirzah took a moment to adjust her collar and take several deep breaths. "Nothing," she finally said. "I came home one evening to find she'd broken into my study. She asked me for a variety of information and then left. That was it."

Astra was in Nythril...there wasn't time for her to have gone all the way back to Litash unless she really had used Gifting....

"What information did she ask for?" It was Jade, sticking to task as usual.

"She wanted to know what Tyron was after and where he might be keeping Louko," Tirzah replied.

"*What?!*" It took all of Ent's self-control not to shove her back up against the wall. "What have you done to *Louko?*"

Tirzah looked past him to Jade. "You hadn't heard yet? I'd presumed they would have sent word. Apparently, Tyron is holding Louko hostage until Astra gives him what he wants."

"Ent, snap out of it!" The shout was accompanied by the sting of cold water as someone dumped a pitcher of it over Ent's head.

Gasping, his vision cleared from the red that had overtaken it and he found himself being restrained by Tallaman and Jade, at the other end of the room, where he'd sworn he had been only moments before.

"He just *had* to inherit your tendency for the Fury," Tallaman spat.

"At least he didn't inherit any of *your* tendencies," Ameri shot right back, setting down her now empty pitcher.

Ent realized suddenly that he was struggling against them and, taking a few deep breaths, surrendered. Stupid Elvish Fury. Stupid Elvish blood.

"Is it bad?" Jade asked.

Ent looked at her in confusion, only to realize she wasn't asking him.

"It's not deep," Tirzah grumbled. "I'll get it stitched up in Silbyr."

"It-it's not deep?" Ent stuttered, looking around until he set eyes on where Tirzah was on the opposite side of the room.

That's when Ent realized he was holding a knife. And it had blood on it. He let go of it quickly and the sound of it clattering to the floor only caused him to jump.

"Relax, she'll be fine...unfortunately." Tallaman's reassurance was rather lacking.

Part of Ent wanted to apologize, but the rest of him still had that unnatural anger pumping through his veins. "Did I hurt anyone else?" Ent turned his attention to his wife and the others who had been restraining him. He'd fought so hard to keep this stupid thing under control and yet still it got the better of him. Elvish Fury. The thing that made Elves so deadly in a battle. The reason Ent had been such a formidable figure during The War. The thing Astra had been lucky enough not to inherit.

"No, no, we're all fine." Jade still had a hand on his arm.

"Sorry," He murmured hoarsely to his wife, looking her up and down once more to make sure she was telling the truth. The Fury did not always tell friend from foe.

"As I was trying to tell you," Tirzah's explanation was interrupted by the sound of ripping fabric. Ent watched her begin to bind up her arm with what used to be the hem of her tunic. "Tyron told me nothing of this plan. I didn't know what had even happened until your sister told me." She used her teeth and free hand to knot the loose ends of the fabric.

"And then why are you here again?" Ent growled, clenching and unclenching his fists in an attempt to allow the anger to flow out of him somehow. He needed to relax. He needed to not think of the fact that Louko was apparently in Tyron's hands. He needed to not recall all too vividly his own time in Tyron's dungeons.

Tirzah wiped blood on her breeches. "Because Tyron has abandoned his interest in Litash." She pulled a parchment with a black seal from her pocket and held it up. "He is no longer sending orders; he is no longer monitoring me."

Ent's laugh was cold. "Wait—so now that he is no longer helping you, you've just decided why not come and have a little fun on the other side of things? I'm sorry, is this some sort of sick game to you? Seeing the way you've thrown all of Litash into a frenzy gives me the feeling I know the answer."

Tirzah simply waited for him to finish ranting. "I told you before: I have no interest in bloodshed. I am doing whatever I think will spare the most people."

"Prevent *bloodshed?*" Ent shouted, everything again tinted with red. "Do you have *any* idea what you have put my sister through? I've *seen* her scars—I saw them put there! So let's cut to the chase and tell me why you're really here and why you decided out of the *goodness* of your twisted heart to come and lend us a hand after you've done nothing but *cause* bloodshed and death." Memories and images bubbled to the surface of his mind and overshadowed Ent's vision.

He felt Jade tugging on his arm as if trying to bring him back to the present.

"If I went against Tyron, there would have been no telling what he would have done." Tirzah's reply was low and terse, the first sign of emotion she had displayed so far. "I had no backup. I did what I could. I hoped that, somehow, if he got what he wanted then his insanity could be cured."

Ent ground his teeth together, forcing himself to remain at least a little in control of his temper before replying, "I'm sorry, insanity?"

"You—" Tirzah suddenly addressed Ameri. "You knew my sister, did you not? Did you know what she was?"

"Yes, she was Myrandi. Tyron told us when he returned to Litash with her." Ameri's voice was taut.

Taking in another deep breath, Entrais found his hand clasped in his wife's.

"And I take it you are also familiar with the way Humans adapt to their spouses," Tirzah continued.

"Yes," his mother again replied.

What was Tirzah getting at?

"Myrandi have a weakness that disposes us to madness. If we do not keep it in check, it takes over." Tirzah locked eyes with Ent. "Think of it as our Elvish Fury. Except Tyron did not know how to balance it. After he thought Rhioa died, he succumbed and it drove him to all of the actions that you know him for."

"Wait," Ameri sounded completely taken off guard. "What do you mean, *thought* she died?"

Tirzah let out a deep breath. "Perhaps you should all take a seat."

No one sat down, but nonetheless Tirzah quickly explained Rhioa and how she was potentially alive and on this other world, Baeno.

"So Tyron wants Astra to open the door, but she can't," Ent summarized as Tirzah finished. He barely held in a groan. "And so now you want to help because you want Astra to learn to open the door?" He asked, not bothering to hide the hostility in his tone. "Because being on our side seems the perfect opportunity to cultivate that. And you still want your sister, I assume." That was the angle, wasn't it? Ent knew there'd been one somewhere.

Tirzah pressed her lips together. "Did you ever know Tyron? I mean really *know* him—before all of this mess."

"I'm not asking about him. I'm asking about you," Ent countered.

"If you did not know him, then you have no way to understand me." Tirzah's reply was terse.

Ent let go of his wife's hand, taking another step closer to Tirzah as every inch of him burned. "Yes, I knew him. I knew him when he was nothing but curious and full of kindness. I watched how he cared for those he loved and bore those he didn't. I knew him when he helped my parents and risked his life to heal and help others. I knew him as the devastated widower who was wrongfully accused all just to cover up someone else's mistakes." Ent suddenly brought his hand up to his collar—the collar he always made sure was fully buttoned and hidden behind the even taller collar of his coat. In one motion, he practically ripped it open, revealing the horrible scar that snaked around his neck and down to his collarbone. "And all too well, I remember the wicked grin as he made this. So, yes, *Tirzah*. I know him. I know him like I know every scar on my sister's body."

Now Tirzah clenched her jaw, looking away. There was a long pause before she seemed to recover her voice. "He was the best person I had ever known. He…he rescued my sister—he was the only person I would have ever trusted with her." Tirzah swallowed and looked back to Ent. "If she were to see what has happened to him, she would be devastated. If he could understand, he would be, too." Her shoulders were slumped. "I want to spare them both any more horror. If I can keep Tyron from doing anything worse, or if I can find some way to return him to what he was, I will do whatever it takes." She looked down. "And if that means I do not see my sister again, so be it."

Ent wanted nothing more than to just give into the Elvish Fury and be rid of Tirzah. He felt cornered—like this was just another trick, another play of words and deceit. "So what exactly are you suggesting?" he hissed.

"I'm suggesting that we cooperate with one another so far as it will minimize damage," Tirzah answered dully. "For starters, that would mean getting the Miadoris out of reach from that bickering Court before they blow something up with it."

"I see. So you realized you have no idea how to get into the vault, didn't you?" A brittle smile somehow cracked Ent's dry lips.

"I know quite well how. But since I do not possess any kind of Gifting, that knowledge does me little good." Tirzah's expression had returned to its usual deadpan.

"Then why do you think I would ever hand such a thing over to you?" Ent's mind was already racing, realizing how stupid he'd been for not already trying to get the Miadoris out of the Court's grasp.

"Why would I want it?" Tirzah scoffed. "Or Tyron?—if that's what you still suspect. Euracia used it to harm my sister. I'd like to keep the Court from repeating the affair. But keeping them at bay is growing more and more difficult with the growing riots. While some may yet be talked into following you," She gave a pointed look at Jade. "Others might yet be stupid enough to try and use the Miadoris to enforce peace. There is already talk about using it to 'suppress' rioters."

At the mention of the riots and the thought of the Miadoris being used against them, Ent's blood ran cold. He turned to Jade, trying desperately to remain expressionless. "What do you think?"

Jade pursed her lips, surveying Tirzah before meeting Ent's gaze. "Perhaps we should get in touch with your sister first. See what she has to say about making friends."

"Alright. I will do that, then," Ent replied, stone-faced as he addressed Tirzah. "We'll let you know what we decide."

Tirzah's eyes darted from Ent to Jade. "Understood." She got to her feet, keeping her injured arm close.

The guards were called to escort Tirzah out.

Ent turned to his mother as soon as Tirzah was gone. "We need to send word to Astra as soon as possible," he said, rubbing his temple as a headache slowly began to sink in.

"If it's possible." Ameri's remark sounded troubled. "If Astra was back in Silbyr so soon after leaving, I can only think of two explanations: Either she never made it to Nythril, or Tirzah spoke the truth and she Gifted herself all the way back."

Ent paled at the prospect of either. "Uncle? Would it even be possible for Astra to get all the way to Silbyr from Nythril?"

A glance passed from Tallaman to Ameri. It was the first time Ent had seen anything besides hostility go between the two siblings.

"I'm not sure," Tallaman admitted gruffly. "No one has ever been stupid enough to try it, but your sister...." He shook his head. "We've spent too much time trying to contain her power to ever see how deep it went."

Straightening his shoulders, Ent noticed for the first time the stain of blood on his right sleeve, left behind from when he'd attacked Tirzah.

Hopefully that would be the last of the blood spilled. Somehow, he felt it was only the beginning.

Louko:

Louko was once more acutely aware of how much he hated flying. If he'd been bolder, he would have tried to fight the draconic figure of Tyron as he'd carried him across the country in the shadow of night, but the fear of falling had been too great.

Now, Louko was in some sort of structure—a prison room perhaps?—with no windows or a door. Or light. He must have blacked out during the flight as he didn't recall being put *in* here.

Here. Captured by Tyron. Taken away like some helpless child. He could still remember Mitheau's limp form as Tyron had Gifted them both away.

Terror set in. Terror and anger. Of all the *stupid* things to happen! He thought about how panicked Astra had to be and wondered who would even be able to tell Keeshiff.

Louko suddenly felt like he couldn't breathe, the walls closing around him as he saw just how horrible this situation was. He was going to die, wasn't he? Stupid, useless prince!

"Would you like some supper?"

Louko could feel all the life drain out of his body as the voice echoed about the space: Tyron.

"Who's asking?" Louko spat, trying to will the anger to outweigh the fear. "You or the Dragon?"

"Neither would gain from poisoning your dinner." Light flared, momentarily blinding Louko. His eyes adjusted in time to see Tyron hanging a lantern from its holder on the wall.

Breathe. Keep your head. Don't panic. Louko was definitely panicking. "What do you want, then?" he asked, forcing himself to meet the gaze of his captor as he desperately tried to find anything but madness in his eyes.

It was hard when Tyron just stood there studying him, and it was even harder when Louko couldn't tell what he was thinking. One moment, he seemed utterly tense as if poised to strike. The next moment he was frozen in place, almost terrified himself. Then he looked tired, worn to the very bone.

Tyron leaned down and set the plate on the floor, sliding it across the stone to Louko. "Usually food is to keep one from starving," came the late reply.

"Usually, but I would also like to think not kidnapping someone keeps them even safer and well-fed," Louko replied even as he struggled to keep steady. Over and over he reminded himself that it was not Tyron doing this but the Dragon. Over and over he searched for signs that the Tyron he'd known once was still in there, fighting. Somewhere. Anywhere.

Tyron gave no reaction. He might as well have been a statue. Then Louko blinked and the man had vanished.

"Could you…not?" Louko forced himself to keep talking, hoping maybe if he pretended to not be falling apart at the seams, he could trick himself into believing it, and thus forget how this wasn't his worst nightmare.

Idiot, you'd wanted this, in a way. You wanted to be able to bring him back. Yeah, but not like this. Not this way.

Louko nearly jumped right out of his skin as Tyron reappeared. He was holding out a…blanket?

"What are you going to do?" Louko took a step back only to find his back met a wall.

Tyron looked at the blanket then up at Louko. He appeared tired again when his brow furrowed. "I'm sorry?"

"I said, what are you going to do?" he asked again, forcing the words out in a mangled mess.

In a matter of seconds, Tyron's expression went from weary, to cold, to livid, and settled back on weary. He slowly folded the blanket and tossed it next to Louko's untouched plate. "Nothing for now."

Louko did not budge. "Well then take the blanket back until you figure out what it is you are going to do."

Tyron tilted his head, making a shudder run down Louko's spine. "You will be safe until Astra is ready." Each word was clear, precise.

"Got it. So I'm just useful to you again. You're going to keep me alive to kill me later. Wonderful." Louko fought the despair, instead trying to find something—*anything*—that would snap Tyron out of this insanity. Yet even a month of begging had done nothing when they were imprisoned before. What could he do now? Just wait and watch, like he was always forced to do.

There was another shift in Tyron's posture as he tensed, fists clenched, then turned away. "Not killed, not yet," he hissed in an undertone. His hands went to his head and his voice trembled when he whispered, "Stop, stop, stop."

Something cold ran up Louko's spine. Great. Tyron was talking to himself. This was...this was a nightmare.

Tyron turned back, only to stop abruptly. His eyes went wide with horror. "Are...are you real?"

Louko blinked. "Um...I am...less sure by the moment." Tyron hadn't been *this* off the walls last time.

"Oh no, oh no no no." Tyron's hands were visibly shaking as he put them back to his head. "Are you hurt? Did I hurt you?"

"I am...not sure...." Louko laughed nervously as he plastered himself even further against the wall. "I am pretty certain you were threatening to kill me a minute ago, though...."

Now Tyron was the one stepping back as if afraid. He had taken to running his hands through his hair. "We need to get you out of here. We need to get you back."

"Well...yes, that would be nice." What was going on? Was...was this...the *real* Tyron? Was this another ploy just to play with him? The panic looked so sincere, as if Tyron had just woken up and was seeing everything for the first time.

"Wait, is she..." Tyron shuddered. "Is she alright?"

Was he talking about Mitheau? "I have no idea!" Louko waved his arms in the air. "I was a *little* busy being kidnapped by my worst nightmare, so not sure what else to tell you."

Tyron winced, face twisted up as if in pain. "I'm so sorry, I'm so sorry, I couldn't stop it." He shuddered again.

Louko had no idea what to do other than breathlessly ask, "And what couldn't you stop? Tyron, *what* is going on?" He needed to know. He needed to know for sure—to know this wasn't a trick or his own mind willing things to seem the way they were. He needed to know Tyron was still in there—the kind, selfless man he'd once known. But one question begged to be answered; Would it matter? Would he even be able to stop the *other* side of Tyron from killing not only him but all of his friends? From killing Astra?

"It, me, I...." Tyron froze. "I need to get out of here. It's not safe—I'm not safe."

"It's...is it the Dragon?" Louko could hardly make the words come out between the rapid beating of his heart and the roaring in his ears.

For a brief second, Tyron's green eyes locked on to Louko's. He opened his mouth as if to reply, but no sound accompanied the motion. There was a faint puff of blue as Tyron disappeared.

Louko almost screamed. Alone in a cell with no door, trapped by the man he had wanted to grow up and be like, and knowing the man was now as equally trapped as Louko. This was his worst nightmare.

CHAPTER XII

<u>Louko:</u>

This had gotten old very quickly. The only way Louko could tell time had passed was with the meals, and even then, Tyron seemed prone to forgetting. Or at least so Louko's stomach informed him.

Louko had spent way too much time thinking, trapped alone and knowing that it was quite likely that he was, at some point, going to die. So to try and avoid *that* reality, he'd been instead trying to find out how to get the Tyron he'd known to come out and to keep from angering the Dragon. He'd slowly become aware of the two different personalities, and yet the triggers for each were…a little less clear. If there even *was* any clear trigger to them. Louko was beginning to worry there wasn't. He was beginning to worry it would only be a matter of time, now.

"Breakfast?"

As usual, Louko received no warning as Tyron materialized out of thin air.

The one and only thing that Louko *had* learned, at least, was that casualness was key.

So without so much as a reply, Louko loaded his spoon full of some of his leftover porridge from last night—or at least probably last night—and flicked the contents towards Tyron with expert aim.

Tyron watched the cold glob splatter a few inches from his boots. "If this is how you plan on protesting my cooking," he began dryly. "Then this is probably a good time to inform you that Graece made it—not me."

Louko's heart choked at the mention of Graece, but he kept any reaction hidden. Hopefully, she wouldn't end up like Julyn…. The last thing he needed was the Dragon utilizing a weakness. "Well I'm bored and I had nothing to do so I figured I'd use what I had at hand for some entertainment."

Setting down the fresh plate—carefully beyond the porridge, of course—Tyron pushed it across towards Louko. This is how he always did it, never getting close. "Perhaps I could bring you a book or something of the like."

"Some history books would not go amiss," Louko replied, guardedly taking the food and poking at it. He would have liked to be of some use and maybe look into the portals, though even if he found anything he wouldn't be able to get the information to Astra. Defeat again weighing heavily, Louko pushed the mostly empty bowl from last night back towards Tyron.

Tyron bent to pick it up but he didn't simply Gift away, pausing instead. "If you say anything, there is the chance she will see."

"Well, isn't that comforting…." So she might see his screams if anything happened. Great. Wonderful. "Well at least, for now, I'm fine. And bored. Very bored. And I still want to get a cat." Louko had no idea what possessed him to blurt out the last bit, but for some reason her dying and not knowing how he felt about her was…shaping up to be the worst regret of his life thus far. And that was saying a lot.

Tyron blinked. "A…cat? I thought you disliked animals."

"I *do*. I just…I was trying to.…" Louko sputtered to a stop, realizing there was no explaining this, and that he really shouldn't be explaining it to his kidnapper. Even if it was the currently *sane* side of him.

But Tyron was still staring at him.

"Look, it was an accident, alright? Stop looking at me like that."

"You…accidentally…wanted a cat?"

Louko threw up his hands in exasperation. "No, I was trying to ask something else and then for some reason I decided asking for a pet was a safer option."

Tyron's eyes went wide and Louko braced for another shift back to the Dragon. "Oh, no.… You were trying to ask her, weren't you?"

"What? I…wait, no, stop it." Louko had a mixture of confusion and panic as he realized he'd let that slip. Would the Dragon use it?

Well, genius, seeing as the Dragon already kidnapped you to threaten Astra…I think it's pretty safe to say it knows you're close. So.

"And I interrupted before you got the chance to try again, didn't I?" Tyron looked nearly as aghast as he had the last three times he'd remembered he kidnapped Louko.

"Well, you didn't interrupt me, I was sulking…but you could have been decent and well, not come at all, ever," Louko said with a scowl.

"Sulking?" Tyron's brow furrowed. "When was this?"

"I have no clue!" Again he waved his arms frantically around the room. "No windows or doors in here, if you haven't noticed. I mean there's not even a mirror—what if it's been like three years and I look completely different?"

Tyron looked nearly as panicked as Louko felt. Not that it helped when Tyron vanished into thin air. Before Louko had even made it through a full sentence of complaint, Tyron reappeared.

"It's only been three days," he said, looking relieved.

Louko looked unimpressed as he replied in monotone, "Well, time is simply flying."

Now Tyron ran a hand through his hair, looking around the small space. "Perhaps I could find you a book or something of the like."

This was…not a good sign, seeing as he'd suggested that only a few minutes ago. The Dragon was coming back. Louko was learning the signs. "Yes…that would be…lovely. I'd love one of the volumes on Nythrilian history." His shoulders sagged.

Seeming to latch on to this plan, Tyron began to nod. "Yes, alright, I'll go fetch that." He Gifted away once more.

He didn't come back.

Once more alone in his dimly lit cell, Louko sat against the wall and tried not to think of Astra. Of what this was probably doing to her and to Uncle Ven and to Keeshiff. Of what his death would cause.

Astra:

It was well into the night by the time Astra stepped out of the strange, starry pathway and into the grassy Wildlands. At first, she couldn't see anything but the light of the moons. Had they left without her? Oh no…what if Tyron had come back?! Just as adrenaline began to seep through her fatigue, she spotted the warm glow of a fire in the distance and her pulse slowed to its normal pace. She had just landed a bit further than she'd intended.

Defeated, she trudged back towards the camp. *Tyron had Louko.* She had been too late. She'd been right there—just right on the other side of the hill!—and she hadn't even known.

"Who goes there?" The half-familiar voice of a Nythrilian soldier broke through the night.

"Astra Verzaer," she called back. "I've returned."

"ASTRA!" The voice shattered the air as Destrin suddenly appeared next to her, grabbing her by both her shoulders. "What in EATRIS!? I thought you were *dead!*"

Instinct made her pull away, raising her hands to shield herself. "No, no, I'm alright."

Astra didn't have time to process as her father...scooped her off her feet and carried her quickly inside one of the nearby tents, leaving her frozen in a confused sort of panic. The light of lanterns greeted her as Destrin deposited her on a chair that was inside.

"Are you dizzy? What happened—where did you go?" Destrin asked quickly as he began fussing over her—checking everything from her eye tracking to her pulse.

As the shock finally wore off enough to let her, Astra pulled her hand from his. "I searched a few areas northeast of here, hoping I would spot them. I didn't find anything at all. Not a single trace of either of them." She shuddered. "So I went to Tirzah. I thought that, if anyone knew what he wanted, or what he was going to do with him, it would be her. But she didn't even know that Tyron was going to take him. She told me that all I could do is play along with whatever Tyron wanted."

"Wait—you went to *Silbyr?!*" Destrin's eyes were wider than Astra had ever seen them. "I—wh—how are you alive, Astra?!"

Astra wasn't really sure how she was supposed to answer him. She looked down at her hands, then back up, before saying, "I really am alright. I'm a little tired, but that's it."

"You don't get it, Astra," Destrin knelt before her. "This isn't possible— I don't care how powerful you are, this would shatter all of the rules of Gifting. You should be *dead.*"

But…but she wasn't. How wasn't she? "I…." Realization dawned slowly. "It was different this time. It didn't feel like when we were practicing. That was always instant: I would be one place, then another. It wasn't like that this time. I…I was somewhere else, and then I stepped out where I wanted to go."

Destrin's panic subsided only a little before it was replaced with a deep look of confusion. "Somewhere else?"

"It was, I don't know, um…." Astra rubbed her face and was distracted when her hand came away wet. Why was she crying? "There were stars everywhere—not just overhead, but underfoot, too."

"Okay…okay…." She felt him suddenly take her again in his arms, but this time for an embrace. "I'm sorry…it's alright. We'll figure this out and we'll get him back."

Astra hugged him back, but she no longer knew if he was right. All she knew is that Louko was gone, and he was completely at Tyron's mercy.

Ven was unmoving, drained of all color and seeming ten years aged as they stood before his throne.

"But you are alright, at least?" The question was near a whisper.

Astra nodded mutely, throat feeling thick. She should have seen this coming. It was even in Tyron's previous note—*white pawn no. 1 moves to the top tier.* How could she have been so *stupid?!* "I'm sorry," she scraped out. "Tyron did this because of me. If I hadn't—"

"No." The word carried through the hall even as softly as it was spoken. Slowly, Ven rose, coming down from the dais so he stood in front of Astra. "You have done nothing but be there for my nephew. You—" His breath caught. "You are not allowed to blame yourself."

Somehow, this made Astra's eyes well with tears. She wanted to explain the note, what it had meant, how she had missed it, but she knew arguing wouldn't help Ven. So instead she replied, "I will do everything in my power to bring him home."

"Thank you," Ven choked, wincing a moment before regaining his composure.

"We may have a lead on that," Destrin spoke from behind her. "We know what Tyron is after. And there is the possibility that Astra may be able to barter with him. But first," his voice dropped. "Someone had to have passed on information. Information that led to the kidnapping."

Ven's hands clenched into a fist, and it took a moment before he replied, "How is that possible? I am para—" he stopped short a moment— "prepared on all fronts for spies—gah!" He threw a hand up in the air at last. "But clearly not enough. I will have a thorough search done.... We will find whoever leaked this information."

The horrible thought sank in slowly: She saw Tyron's memories. Logically, then, he saw hers in return. Had he seen their location through her? "I...I have no way to be certain, but...but it could have been me."

Everyone froze. "What?" Ven's question echoed the confusion in the room. "Astra, it couldn't possibly have been you." The tone was gentler now.

She swallowed, glancing at her father. "I, um, I see his memories," she sputtered. "Tyron's. It happens at random—I can't control it. I...I don't know if he can see mine, too. But if he can, it might have been me."

Ven's eyes widened. "And you can't control it?" There was almost panic in his expression now. "Then why have you been included in our meetings? We should have been taking more careful precautions—what if—"

"Woah, let's all take a deep breath." Destrin stepped forward so that he was nearly between them. "Tyron has been sending us our every move on a piece of paper before we've even made it. What he may—or may not—see from Astra would not be enough for that. Clearly, he has enough of a network that nothing is secret to him. Besides," he addressed Astra now. "You said you didn't see any memories while locked up, correct? That the red-bronze stopped them?"

Astra took a shaky breath as she nodded.

"But isn't that unhealthy for her—and I don't see you wearing it now?" Ven was leaning forward in his throne, a war of emotions rippling through every inch of his body.

Astra's hand went to her bare wrist.

Her father sighed. "Yes, it is unhealthy. That's *why* she is not wearing it now." He turned to face the dais. "My point is that not all of this could be Astra—even if Tyron is seeing some things through her. There *has* to be others."

Ven stood up quickly, his anguish seeming to rise with the movement. "I think then it might be best if we discuss things…but Astra should not be present if Tyron might see through her eyes." There was regret tracing every word.

This really was her fault, wasn't it? Not just for her role in The Game, but now for giving Tyron information simply because she was too weak to control her own power. And now Louko was paying the price. "Just give me the red-bronze."

"Astra—I—" The pain dripped from Destrin's voice. "It'll hurt you," he whispered.

"And it will keep everyone else safe," she countered. *Safe from her as well as Tyron.*

Slowly, Destrin reached into his pocket and took out the small cuff of red-bronze, reaching it out to her as if he was fighting every muscle in his body to do so. Astra couldn't look him in the eye as she took it.

She was accustomed to the sudden exhaustion that washed over her, accompanied by that slight dizziness and moment of nausea. She felt her father's hand steadying her, and within a few seconds, she was stable enough to let go.

"Are you alright?" Ven asked, brow furrowed in what looked to be deep concern.

She nodded. "I'm fine. It will buy us some privacy."

"Alright." The Ezai Ru's reply was hoarse. Nonetheless, he continued on almost flawlessly, stating, "So then what of the Drogan Hunters? Jahng had sent a letter that some of her hunting weaponry might be at her estate and not yet disposed of, but that Tyron's use of Gifting would likely render it all useless when compared to most other Drogans."

"It's too dangerous to think of trapping him anymore." Astra shuddered at the thought of what could go wrong. "Even if there was a way to suppress his Gifting effectively, it would be too risky with Louko as a hostage. He took him so easily; if we try anything and fail, he will kill Louko and take someone else."

Ven took a deep breath and nodded, "Alright. We won't do that, then."

"As Tirzah said, our best bet is to play along—at least outwardly," Astra said. "We have to find a way of settling things between Nythril and Merimeethia, while keeping Litash out of it."

Still looking pained, Ven said, "Then it is time for me to catch you up, for I'm afraid I have some…news on Litash. I remain unsure what kind of news it is, however." His brow furrowed with the last bit. "Apparently, the common people of Litash have not taken your brother stepping down well, and I have been receiving report after report of riots. Litash is a mess, to put it simply."

Astra's heart sank as she thought of her brother. "I don't think it was ever quite cleaned up after what Euracia did. It was simply quieted for the past two years," she murmured. "At least this means Litash cannot send aid to Merimeethia."

"Yes, that is a start. But I am very aware of what the Litashians hide in their vault. It may be wise to warn your brother of such as well." Ven looked again from Astra to Destrin. "From what you've told me of your visit with that courtier, the vault is not in good hands."

He meant the Miadoris. Astra knew Ent would not forget such a thing. Whether or not he had the means to do anything about it was another matter.

"Astra," Destrin whispered. "Please. Stay. Here."

"I'm not going to try it," Astra mumbled.

Astra realized Ven was staring at them, one eyebrow raised in a way that reminded her all too painfully of Louko. "It is rude to whisper in another's presence on any occasion, but in my own throne room a mere three feet away from me, I find it especially annoying." There was a weak twitch at the corner of the Ezai Ru's lips, however, that gave away the attempt of humor.

"It's nothing," Astra shook her head.

The conversation turned back to the task at hand. They discussed the portal site, Litash, and the next step, all the while, both Ven and Destrin appearing uneasy. Astra didn't miss the glances to her wrist. What a fool she was for thinking she would be safe from Tyron's eyes.

At last the meeting came to an end, and Ven, appearing to have aged years since the news of his nephew's kidnapping, announced, "I think it is time you both get some rest. You came right here upon your return...you must be exhausted." Ven snapped his fingers—looking apologetic when Astra winced at the abrupt sound—and a servant came quickly to his side. "Please escort these two to their rooms."

The servant bowed towards Astra and Destrin before motioning for them to follow.

But before Astra did so, she brought up one last subject. "We have to send word to Keeshiff. He needs to know." Already, her heart sank to think of what such news would do to him. *Keep him in line for me*, he'd said. Instead, Astra had let him be taken by Tyron. She wished she could break the news to Keeshiff herself…and to apologize in person.

"Right. I will see to it," Ven's reply was thin. Thin and weary.

With quiet thanks, Astra turned and followed her father and the servant from the throne room.

No one said a word as they walked through the grand halls. Whether from the looming war or the kidnapping of their prince, it felt as though the entire palace was holding its breath. The tension made even their footsteps feel loud.

Upon reaching their rooms and now left alone by the servant, an uneasy silence clung to the air like some unspoken cry.

And then the cry spoke, in the form of her father whispering, "You can take it off now, Astra."

Astra's hand froze on the door handle to her room. "I can't. Not now that I know Ven's plan."

"Astra, I don't think keeping it on is a good idea…." He dug both his hands in his pockets, worry permeating every inch of his features. "It isn't good for you…it's not just some accessory. No one should have let you wear red-bronze for as long as you had."

"But they did and there's nothing anyone can do about that now." Astra released the door handle, turning back to her father and trying to swallow her rising frustration. "And seeing as I cannot control it, and Tyron can apparently control me through it, it's the best defense I have."

The hall ached with the tension between them, and yet Astra held firm.

"Astra—" Destrin cut himself off, shutting his mouth quickly and looking away to the left for a moment. "I still do not think it is wise. As your father—for what it's worth—it's hard to watch you do this to yourself."

"Then don't watch." The words left her mouth without her bidding. "If this is what it takes to bring Louko home and to keep from losing anyone else, then so be it."

There was no reply, and no visible expression when he turned his head back to face her. For a moment, he looked blank—devoid of anything living except his eyes, which stared unwaveringly at her. "I'm sorry, Astra."

Astra had been ready for an argument—not an apology. Was this about him feeling guilty for other things? The thought cooled some of Astra's ire. "You have always done what you could. This isn't about any failure on your part."

"This is about it, Astra. This is about my daughter asking me to give her a bracelet that will make her sick because that's all I've ever done for her—give her a temporary fix and ship her off to be torn apart again. I'm not doing it; I'm done. I know I wasn't there when Tyron took over—I know I wasn't strong enough to protect you or Ent, but I'm done pretending like that means I have to give up trying." Destrin spoke with an uneasy calmness, but Astra still caught the way his hands dug deeper in his pockets and how his otherwise steady tone occasionally shook.

She looked away, unable to swallow the lump in her throat. It was hard to process her father's words—much more so her own tangled feelings. "None of that was ever your doing," she finally murmured. "It was always the result of circumstances beyond anyone's control. It was not your fault then and it isn't your fault now." She steeled herself before meeting her father's gaze. "Yes, red-bronze might make me sick, but it will be a thousand times better than being made a tool by which I lose another loved one. I," She swallowed. "I can't lose anyone else."

Her father remained silent and motionless, his gaze never leaving hers as he silently begged.

But Astra could not afford to give in. "I can't take it off."

Destrin closed his eyes and looked away. "I understand."

Why did him giving in make her feel worse? "Thank you," she said quietly, ignoring her own tugging conscience. After a pause, she added, "For all of it."

Destrin's only reply was a taut nod and, "You should get some rest."

Somehow, sleep no longer sounded appealing. "I'm just going to check on Mitheau first," she replied. Mitheau had been ill for nearly two days after Louko had been taken, though she seemed to have been feeling better as they reached the palace.

His shoulders sank just barely. "Alright." He looked as if he wanted to say something else, but whatever it had been, it was never said. They parted ways once more: him to his room, and Astra a few doors down to where the servant had said Mitheau was.

She knocked softly on the door. "Mitheau? It's me—Astra."

"Astra? Is everything alright?" The reply came softly from the other side of the door.

Astra wished her presence wasn't so associated with things going wrong. "Yes, I just wanted to see how you were doing."

A moment passed before the sound of Mitheau fumbling at the latch filtered through the quiet. Then Mitheau's head appeared from the opened door. She looked exhausted, with dark circles and tousled hair. Worse was the weariness in every line of her features: the tight lips, the drawn brow, the tired eyes. "I'm doing better, thank you," she mumbled as she looked Astra up and down. "Had the Ezai Ru heard anything?"

Throat feeling suddenly tight, Astra shook her head. "No. He didn't know until our letter arrived ahead of us. There have been no sightings of either of them."

"I see…." Mitheau's already knotted brow furrowed further. Then her eyes traveled down to Astra's wrist. "Why are you wearing that again? Is it because you transported so far?"

Astra had forgotten how self-conscious the red-bronze made her feel. "No, it's to try and stop the memories. The transport never bothered me."

"Didn't you…didn't you go all the way to Silbyr?" Mitheau opened the door a bit wider and was now in full view of Astra, looking a bit more with it than before.

"Um," Astra glanced down the corridor towards her father's room. "Yes. But I really am alright."

"Yes but…" Mitheau wrung her hands in front of her, looking down at them as if confused by her own action. "I've been thinking. Astra, do you remember how Grenedil told you of Cyl? The Guardian of the Doorway?"

Astra was not sure how these two topics were related, but she tried to follow along with a nod. "Why?"

"Well, um, he could transport across long distances—distances that seemed impossible even to the strongest user of Gifting. I just…I can't stop thinking about the similarities and the fact that Grenedil had even said you were going to be a new Guard. Grenedil said you would be able to use it, too, right? Before he left?"

Was she…was she implying that Astra had used the Door and not Gifting? "Yes, but he said Cyl would have to teach me. And it didn't work before when I was…" Astra fumbled for a softer term. "…trapped." The possibility of being able to give Tyron what he was after—of having something to barter to get Louko back—was dizzying. "Is there any way to test it?"

"I mean, I have no idea. I have no expertise in Gifting and even less expertise in understanding the Doorway. Did it feel any different?" Mitheau looked somewhere between intrigued and concerned.

"I…yes, actually." Astra's stumbling words came in a rush now. "Yes, it was as if I was somewhere else before I arrived in Silbyr—like I was somewhere in between. I remember that it was dark, but there were lights, like stars, all around me. It only lasted for a flash before everything appeared."

Mitheau's eyes widened. "Yeah…that *has* to be it. I knew it! I wonder if we could get you to do it again…maybe you don't need Cyl in order to learn it." If possible, her eyes widened even more. "Or maybe Grenedil found Cyl! Maybe he's the one who made it so you could do this. We *have* to try and replicate this."

Astra's hand went to the red-bronze at her wrist. "Theoretically, if I could still transport while wearing red-bronze, it would have to be the Doorway, right? That could prove it?"

"Oh, yeah, that would work. But haven't you used Gifting with red-bronze before?" Mitheau asked, curiosity clearly winning out.

"It always shatters the red-bronze," Astra explained. "So, I guess, the measure could be whether or not the cuff remains intact."

"This is true...and...well, I guess I'll feel it if you use Gifting, but I won't feel it if you use the Door—wait." Mitheau's thought process seemed to come to a full stop as her expression changed from excited to perplexed and frustrated. "You aren't...considering trying to give Tyron what he wants, are you?"

Astra bit her lip. "I don't know. All I know is that he has Louko, and he always seems to know what we're doing. Even if we're searching for an alternative, I need to look like I'm playing along."

Mitheau did not look very reassured.

"I have not forgotten about what you said about his obsession," Astra continued. "And how it cannot be cured by giving into it. But if he is seeking a person, is there any chance that person could help us?"

"That person is *dead*, Astra. That person is probably Rhioa—because she's the reason Ovok went off the wall, too, from what I've heard." Mitheau waved a hand in exasperation.

Astra took a deep breath. "What if I told you that Rhioa is with her father on Baeno?"

Mitheau just stared at her, seeming to realize Astra was dead serious. "I, uh...um. Well then, I think...that would change a lot of things."

CHAPTER XIII

<u>Keeshiff:</u>

Louko was gone. It was that simple. Keeshiff couldn't believe it. Not even as he stared down at the letter, writing it all out so plainly, could he believe his younger brother was gone. Too late. Keeshiff was always too late.

And then there was Astra—what if she got herself killed trying to save Louko?

No! Don't think that way.

"So then what is our next move, Commander?" General Tahrin asked, hand to his chin as he looked grimly at the map on the large table. Little red and blue markers littered the large parchment, representing the Merimeethian and Nythrilian troops. The letter had arrived in the middle of a war meeting, and Keeshiff—the fool he was—had hoped it had contained some form of information that would be useful to them. Not this.

Jahng looked at Keeshiff as she replied, "I was hoping the Prince of Merimeethia might shed some light on how we might best move against his country. We must tread carefully."

Keeshiff couldn't find the words to reply. How would he tell everyone here? All he could do was stare at the words, so eloquently written on the page. Louko was gone.

"Prince Keeshiff?" Keeshiff wasn't even sure who called his name.

"He's...he's gone," at last, he got the words out, vague as they ended up being.

The tent went still.

"What do you mean, *he's* gone?" Itso spat, leaning forward as if he might somehow catch a glimpse of the letter even from across the table.

"Louko. Somehow T—Kaeden got through to kidnap Louko." The words felt so foreign in his own mouth. They didn't sound real.

"*Prince* Lu Quo?" General Laosim sounded aghast.

There was a series of murmurs as Jahng reached for the letter.

"Has the Ezai Ru given any instructions?" General Tahrin asked urgently.

Giving the letter a quick read, Jahng replied, "He says to hold our position and to make sure we have no information leaks...."

Did this mean Tyron could show up and take Astra next? What was the point? And how did they know Louko was...was even still...alive? Keeshiff felt like he might vomit.

"He wants us to wait until they've used the prince against us?" General Itso grumbled. "Or worse, publicly executed him to demoralize our troops? We either have to show that we're doing something to get him back, or we need to find a way to wrap this war up quickly."

"Any wrong move could spell death for him—the Ezai Ru must have information we don't," Keeshiff cut in suddenly. Astra had to be talking with Ven, clearly. They had a plan...right? Maybe just one they couldn't share through a paper trail?

"Is that your excuse to continue withholding information about Merimeethian tactics?" Itso's narrowed glare fastened on Keeshiff. "Because I don't feel comfortable fighting with someone who might help my opponent instead of me."

"Enough." Jahng's gaze hardened as much as her tone. "We are not here to point fingers, General Itso. The prince has shown himself nothing but honorable." Then she turned to Keeshiff. "But blood will be shed either way. We need to be as swift as possible to avoid a bath of it. If you have any ideas that could shorten this war, we need them."

Cold all over, Keeshiff turned his attention instead to the map, remembering Mariah's suggestion—that he take back the throne. She claimed the nobles would be sympathetic, and yet she herself had done nothing but deceive. It seemed more likely she had been trying to lure him into a trap.

But maybe he didn't need the nobles. All he needed to stop this fight was to get the army on his side. He could deal with the rest of this mess from there.

"If you really want to end this, then I need to take my country back. I know most of those generals who are camped across the line from us. If we can convince them that I'm at least a better option than Kaeden, they will lay down their arms." He eyed General Itso. "And we won't convince them if I'm out there fighting against their men."

The haughty general did not back down, returning the gaze full force as he came back with, "Why should we fight to give you back your country? Merimeethians have only ever stabbed us in the back."

Keeshiff's grip folded around the table, splinters digging into his fingertips. "Because, like it or not, I know my country's forces. I know they are more than yours—I've seen both sides, remember? They're more used to inclement weather, food shortages, and fighting for what they have, and if you intend to fight them all the way to the capital to get Louko back, then you will find yourself drowning in a swamp. Our terrain is dangerous and often unpredictable. But if I get my country back, then not only will Louko willingly be returned, but you will have more of your soldiers to greet him upon his reunion."

A begrudging glance was thrown back and forth among the generals. Even Jahng seemed unsure. But she was the first to break the silence, asking, "How do you suggest we go about this?"

"If I can get in contact with Killyan—arrange a meeting, perhaps. That could be the first step. I know these people and they know me. They know I would never deceive anyone. If I can talk to them, then I can tell them what is truly going on." Keeshiff hoped he sounded a lot more certain than he was. Rhumir had claimed Killyan had aided in letting Astra and Louko get away, and yet the man had shown no reservations when chasing them across the country. Had seeing what Tyron did to Astra opened his eyes? Or would he pass Keeshiff off as a power-hungry, exiled prince? There was only one way to find out.

General Laosim now rustled a few parchments before pulling one out. "Killyan, as in the captain? He is not very high ranking. Will he have the sway that you need?"

"He is immensely popular among the soldiers. He was the first one sent after me when I fled, and he has connections that lead up to the highest-ranking officers. He is a captain because he preferred the active role, not because he was unworthy of a higher rank." Keeshiff was able to speak with confidence here, even if the reminder of all the soldiers on the other side of the border left another knot in his stomach.

"So you think that he would be able to get you a private meeting with his commanding officers? One that Kaeden wouldn't be informed of?" Jahng looked up from the maps.

Keeshiff nodded. "Yes. If anyone can, he will be able to." This had to work.

With a thoughtful frown, Jahng turned to General Laosim. "Would you be able to arrange a private message to this captain?"

"Of course, Commander." He bowed his head.

"Then see to it." Jahng dismissed him with a brief gesture. "General Tahrin, in the meantime, I want the trenches deepened on the riverbanks and northern flank. We play the defensive until we see how this captain pans out."

General Tahrin bowed, following Laosim out of the tent.

"Likewise, General Itso, hold all scouting parties on our side of the river, but keep your archers at the front of the line. We should appear peaceful while remaining prepared if they decide to take offense at our letter."

With a last glare towards Keeshiff, the general bowed his head. "As you say, Commander." He marched from the tent without another word.

Frustration and despair boiled inside of Keeshiff, and he kicked at the ground, his foot hitting something solid under the table. A little squeak followed and Keeshiff bent down, pulling up the table cloth enough to find none other than the little troublesome rubii blinking back at him.

"Oh you stupid little thing, come here." He went to grab it, but the rubii tucked its little legs into its fluffy body and rolled away with a squeak, only to be apprehended by the stone-faced Jahng who had quietly moved to intercept it.

Squirming and giving out relentless high-pitched—albeit rather adorable—squeaks, it looked quite odd in the arms of a figure so formidable as the Nythrilian Commander.

Keeshiff huffed. "Sorry. Someone in our group fed the stupid thing and then we thought we left it with Mitheau, but it apparently stowed away in my food pack…" It felt ridiculous to have to keep an eye on this little pathetic creature while also worrying about Tyron murdering his brother.

"I…see," Jahng arched an eyebrow as she offered the thing back to Keeshiff.

Hesitantly, he took the little thing, glad that it had at least stopped squirming.

"Are you…" Jahng cleared her throat. "Are you alright?"

No. No, he wasn't. He wanted to scream—to tear up the letter and force it to take the words back. "Yes. We should speak with Mariah," he replied, listless. "She might know something." What if Mariah had leaked information to Tyron somehow? Logic dictated she was nowhere near Louko and Astra and thus it would have been impractical for her to have helped…but Keeshiff just wanted someone he could catch—someone he could blame. Someone who could bring him back his brother.

Jahng seemed to be thinking through the same trail of logic, but she did not argue. "We have a detainment section near the center of the camp." Jahng hesitated, looking towards those that were busy poring over troop placements in the back of the command tent before asking, "Do you want backup?"

Any other time Keeshiff would have been thrilled to actually get some time with the commander, but now all thoughts were wrenched away other than one, shattering truth: Louko was gone. Still, he could use the company, and so replied, "Backup would be appreciated. If it's not too much trouble."

Jahng simply nodded and motioned to Keeshiff to follow as she ducked out of the tent.

Swallowing and trying to keep himself composed, Keeshiff followed Jahng outside, probably looking as awkward as he felt as he held the little white fluffball in his hands.

They walked in silence for the first minute or two, only interrupted by the occasional guard snapping to attention. Jahng released each with a nod of acknowledgement. They were almost in sight of the camp center when she asked, "Are you sure you are well enough for this?"

Keeshiff took another deep breath. "I am not. But I can't afford to be anything but fine. We don't have time for that."

Jahng took this in quietly. "I understand."

Keeshiff was desperately trying to find something more to say, and yet he was just struck by the fact that someone else understood, for once. He could see the responsibility and weight in Jahng's shoulders. The worry she had for those under her command. But did she know the pain of having one of the last people you cared about ripped from you? Keeshiff so desperately wanted to not feel alone, and yet the only thing that could fix it would be Louko's safe return.

"The last time we all planned a rescue, I'll admit, I thought it wasn't going to work," Jahng said, sounding nearly uncertain of herself. "I'm still not sure how it did, but everyone made it out." She stopped before a row of tents. "If all of you can make it through a plan involving a coup, a siege, and freeing a Drogan to fly to Litash, I have no doubt that you'll find a way to get your brother back safely."

"Yeah. Thank you," Keeshiff replied. "And for all you've, er, done."

Jahng seemed suddenly occupied with adjusting the sword at her hip. "You have Ven to thank, not me." She cleared her throat. "Unless you ever really need to be thrown in prison again. I suppose I could help with that."

Keeshiff couldn't help but let out a snort. "I mean you did also help us survive. So I feel like you made up for it."

"I'm not quite sure that's how it works, but I'll keep that in mind," was her dry response. Then her humor—if one could call it that—faded. "This is it."

A picketed fence formed a ring around a circle of tents, the only opening guarded by two soldiers in full armor. They parted as Jahng stepped forward.

If it was up to him, Keeshiff would gladly live his life without ever seeing his sister again. And yet here he was once more, hoping she'd have information and not more lies to lead them astray.

"Would you prefer I stay outside?" Jahng asked, stopping in front of one of the tents.

Keeshiff sighed. "I suppose that is probably best." He wanted nothing more than to have her come in, but his sister wasn't her problem. She was his.

With one more deep breath, he walked inside the tent, somehow managing to hold the stupid rubii with one hand and open the tent flap with the other.

"Keeshiff?" Mariah practically squeaked his name. She sat in the back of the space, looking startled. "What's going on?"

Keeshiff couldn't help but wonder if maybe Astra's propensity for giving people a second chance had gone a little too far this time. "Here, I brought you a stupid toy to play with," Keeshiff said curtly, ignoring the question and instead placing the rubii down on the ground to run free. It quickly rolled over and jumped on the cot in the corner, burrowing under the blankets.

Mariah's expression only turned more puzzled. "I don't…understand. What's happened?"

"Oh. You don't know? Or are you just pretending, as usual? Louko's gone. Tyron took him." Keeshiff didn't bother mincing words. He didn't care about breaking it to her gently—and he still didn't know if she was somehow working for Tyron. Honestly even if she wasn't, it wouldn't change his response.

Mariah gasped, jaw hanging open. "*What?* No, no, no, we have to get him back. He can't go back there. We can't—"

"*We?* Please stop, you're making me nauseous. Now, is there anything you can give to help us or are you just going to play the drama up like you always do?" Keeshiff didn't regret the words. The words that had been in his mind for years. The words he'd always wanted to let out "Because I want a good reason to believe you're not the mole feeding Tyron information."

Her lips quavered. For a moment, she was frozen, silent. Then she began to stammer. "I didn't give him anything. How would I have even gotten anything to him? I've been watched the whole time—with you and—"

"—That hasn't stopped you before." Keeshiff folded his arms. "And Tyron clearly has someone feeding him information." Mariah was, after all, the one that had consistently and deliberately tried to put Louko in harm's way.

"Then there has to be someone else," she said, nearly desperately.

"Oh? Oh, yeah? Who, Mariah? Who? Who else has been with us enough to hear our plans and is anything but undyingly loyal to Astra and Louko? Who else wanted to ruin Louko's life?" Keeshiff didn't bother hiding the emotion in his voice.

Mariah's expression crumpled. "I, I didn't want to—" She cut herself off, swallowing. "Alright. At first, I did," she whispered. "I blamed him. I blamed him for Mother's death, for the way Father acted—for everything. It was easier that way." She looked down at her hands. "But I promise on my life that I didn't know what Tyron was going to do. And after I found out, I...." She looked back up. "I understood. And I understand why you hate me. But I *swear*, I did not do this."

"I wish I could believe you," he managed to get the words out. But he wouldn't believe her, not completely. Never again. She seemed sincere...but she had in the past, too. For now, he only had enough evidence to doubt it was her. But if they couldn't find an actual culprit.... "Then do you have *any* idea who it could be?" The question was double-edged. He wanted to see if she would find someone to try and spread doubt, or if maybe she would give genuine help. Either way would further give proof to her innocence or treachery.

Mariah bit her lip, looking half-panicked as she seemed to scour that empty brain. "There was Dia Tzaro's advisor, Dahg?"

"Aelor Ven already dealt with him," Keeshiff replied, not bothering to hide the irritation.

Throwing up her hands, Mariah replied, "Well then I don't know! Kae— Tyron never talked about his informants. I only knew Dahg because there were letters to him sometimes. I didn't even think they were anything suspicious so it was a guess. It wasn't like Tyron trusted me any more than you all did. I just wanted you *home*."

Keeshiff scoffed. "Home? When was Melye ever a home for any of us? If Tyron hadn't killed our father, it was only a matter of time before I deposed him myself." He cut himself off and forced himself back to the subject at hand. "If you don't know about any of his informants, do you at least have any guesses where he would have taken Louko?"

"Back to Melye is all I can think of," Mariah said sharply. "I don't know why he'd bring him anywhere else. Wherever he kept—" she broke off a moment— "kept them the first time." The last bit was accompanied with a hard swallow.

The thought of Louko repeating that nightmare made Keeshiff sick. "Then if you are of no further use, I see no reason to keep you here. I will make the recommendation for you to be sent back to Aelor Ven for him to do as he sees fit."

"I've already told you—you need to talk to the nobles!" Mariah said in exasperation. "If you meet with them, privately, I *know* they'll side with you. Take me with you and I could even help—I could be useful."

Keeshiff felt his face twist up in disgust. "You have more audacity than even I realized. Do you *really* think I would bring you anywhere near Melye?"

"I—" Mariah looked desperate, rasping out, "I only want to help—to try and make things right. I don't want you *or* Louko hurt and you are definitely going to get hurt if you don't listen."

"I've listened to you before. Do you remember where it got me? Do you remember what happened to Louko and Astra?" Keeshiff jabbed a finger towards her. "How do I know that this isn't just another one of your traps? For all I know, any one of those nobles could double-cross me and hand me over to Tyron. They didn't like Father; why would they care about me?"

"Because you aren't *like* him, Keeshiff! They hated him and you are everything he wasn't." Mariah's pitch was fevered.

The statement was probably the only thing that could have caught Keeshiff off guard. He shook his head as he recovered his wits. "Then it's pretty ironic, isn't it? That I ended up being everything he wasn't, but you turned out to be everything he was."

She looked stricken, standing there with her eyes wide and mouth half open.

There might have been a time when her pain moved him. But not anymore. "Goodbye, Mariah." He turned back to the tent entrance.

"Keeshiff, please," Mariah whispered.

Keeshiff did not look back. He stepped out to find Jahng still waiting in the deepening evening. Wordless, they walked side by side and out of the guarded circle of tents.

Not until they had cleared the fence did Jahng comment, "I think she's telling the truth."

Keeshiff swallowed if only to prevent from growling in return. "She is a good liar. I wouldn't put anything past her. Until we find a spy, we need to assume she is it."

"Then I think we need to arrange a test." Jahng sounded much calmer than he felt. "The Ezai Ru's letter mentioned spies, which tells me that he suspects there is a leak somewhere. If she is a spy, you can carry out your threat to send her back to Ven. If she isn't, we can still use her to rout out the real traitor."

"Fine," Keeshiff forced his shoulders to relax. "What sort of test are you suggesting?"

Jahng waited until they passed by a group of drilling soldiers. "Information. We act like we trust her, feed her some false information, and see if that information ends up in enemy hands."

That was…a good plan, actually. Keeshiff sighed. "Good point. Sorry."

Jahng looked at him oddly. "What are you apologizing for?"

"I am not thinking clearly," he replied, shaking his head as if that might help.

"With a situation such as yours, I can't blame you." Jahng's tone was dry when she added, "I don't think I've ever been so glad to be an only child."

He let out a humorless chuckle. "Louko was never a problem."

CHAPTER XIV

Entrais:

Ent hated waiting almost as much as he hated sleeping, not that it seemed to stop either of those things from happening all too frequently. He had sent word to Astra days ago, and while it made sense not to have yet heard back, every day brought with it new possibilities of how things could have gone wrong. What if their relay was intercepted? What if Tirzah was, indeed, lying? How much of this all was a trap?

"So, if we go through with this and you do get the Miadoris, what are we going to do with it?" Jade was sitting at Ent's desk, watching him pace. "Tirzah will almost undoubtedly betray us as soon as we have it out of the vault. We'll need a plan for that, too."

His fists clenched as he remembered how much pain the power source had caused. "I wouldn't mind destroying it, if that was an option." Even though he knew the suggestion was a bad one, he couldn't help but let the words slip off his tongue.

Jade's quiet sigh was understanding. "It's not. Even if that were possible, and even ignoring the risk of it simply killing anyone within a hundred miles, it would cause more problems than it would solve. No one really knows if it is the source of life or if all life is connected to it, but either way, destroying it would end in catastrophe."

"I know," Ent replied, rubbing his forehead. "But it would be nice to have it gone." That being said, this was no time to be indulging in such a stupid fantasy. "Our options right now, then, would be to hide it, bring it to Cithan, or give it to Astra, am I correct?"

Jade nodded. "Seeing how hiding it went for my father, I think we can rule out the first option."

"Yes, no hiding it. And seeing how it interacts with Astra…" Ent trailed off a moment, remembering how close it had gotten to killing her during The War. "Perhaps that is unwise as well." He couldn't do that to her again. Not after everything else.

"Then Cithan it is." Jade leaned forward, resting her arms on the desk. "We can speak with your mother and uncle about what it would take to build a secure vault for it."

Ent wasn't sure whether the ringing in his ears was from stress or exhaustion, but the thought of bringing the Miadoris here was certainly as present in his mind as the sound. "What if the Elves decide to use it for…their own gains?"

Jade appeared nearly amused. "You do recall that you are their king, don't you? And despite the variety of their flaws, they do seem to share a strict sense for following the rules." Her demeanor softened. "They have received you well and followed your every word. I don't think that will change when you hold the Miadoris. Careful not to fall for the same trap they did; do not be as biased towards them as they once were to you. I think they are learning from their mistakes."

With a wince, Ent surrendered to the point. He knew she was right, but it didn't make it easier to swallow. Right now, the Elves were the only people that hadn't turned on them—and that was quite ironic considering they had once been the first to abandon him. "You're right. I know you are. Cithan it is, then."

As if on cue, there was a knock at the study door.

"Enter," Jade called while Ent composed himself. Why did everyone always knock so loudly? And why did he always have to calm himself down after it? Pathetic.

"Sorry to interrupt, your majesty, but there is a commotion downstairs." The attendant stepped into the room, bowing his head. "The Governor Ameri asked me to inform you that your sister is here."

Ent just stared at the Elf for a very, very long time. "I-I'm sorry? She's...here?" A million theories flew through Ent's muddled mind, including that he had completely misheard the attendant.

The attendant nodded. "She came up to the front entrance and, um, knocked. She asked if you were here."

"Tell Ameri we will be right down," Jade was the one who replied, putting a hand on Ent's shoulder. "Thank you."

The door shut and Ent turned, wide eyed, to his wife. "How in Eatris?" He breathed the words in a panic. She was going to get herself killed—or had something happened? Was she here because something had gone wrong with Nythril? How did he even know she hadn't traveled on foot? Maybe she hadn't Gifted herself away at all, but instead she was running here because Nythril had also abandoned her. Or worse.

"He didn't seem rushed, so I'm sure she's alright," Jade spoke calmly and quickly. "Before we jump to conclusions, let's go see what she has to say."

"Right," Ent struggled to get even that word out, forcing himself not to launch through the door but instead take measured steps to leave the study and go downstairs, Jade close behind him.

"Maybe she never even left Litash after speaking with Tirzah," Jade suggested hopefully.

Ent might have been more encouraged by the thought if it weren't for the raised voices he could already hear coming from the front vestibule.

"What were you thinking? There's so many people trying to kill you and now you're trying to do it for them?!"

"Mother, please, yelling is only going to give everyone a headache," Ent butted into the argument as he pulled himself together, entering the room and locking eyes with Astra in a desperate, '*Please, tell me you aren't dead*' stare.

"Well, I hope Astra *does* have a headache after transporting across a country and a half," Tallaman mumbled. He was glaring relentlessly at his niece, as if the gaze itself could make her shrivel up and repent.

Ent tried to ignore the fact that apparently Astra *had* used Gifting to cross the country again.

"Could you all calm down for a *single* second?" Astra's tone matched their mother's. "I am trying to tell you that I didn't use Gifting." She wrenched her hand from Ameri's grasp and pulled down a sleeve, revealing a red-bronze cuff.

Why did Ent always see a shackle before he registered it was a cuff? Every time. And every time it reminded him of her in chains, always because of him.

But that did not matter at the moment, what mattered was…. "Wait, what exactly do you mean?" Ent broke in, hoping this would stop his mother from any further berating for now, at least.

He caught the brief flash of gratitude on Astra's face before her exasperation returned. "You remember what we told you of Grenedil? All the things about Guards and some Door?"

Brow furrowed, Ent slowly shook his head. "I…" Wait. Door. "The supposed door to other worlds?" That, at least, he remembered.

"Yes, that." Astra nodded rapidly. "It's what Tyron is looking for. And he took…" She glanced at their mother, down to the floor, and then back to him. "He took Louko to make sure that I would learn how to open it, and then let him through."

"We heard…" Ent trailed off, knowing an apology would do very little. He could only hope the look of understanding that passed between them was enough. "So…then you used this door somehow?"

Astra's irritation had dimmed now. She looked smaller when her hand went to her wrist. "Yes." She sighed. "Sort of. Our best guess is that Grenedil has finally reached the Guard, Cyl, who has done something to open the Door for me. We've been running tests—under Father's supervision." The line seemed to be directed towards both Ameri and Tallaman. "Mitheau, being Myrandi, can sense Gifting. We started with small distances and worked up to this. But I can't seem to do anything more than move myself from one place to another. I don't know how I'm supposed to get to this 'Maze' or some other planet."

"So, you aren't using Gifting, then?" Tallaman mused aloud. "I suppose that makes sense why you always broke the rules of Gifting…I knew I wasn't crazy."

"But then, wait, Astra. What are you learning this *for?* Do you think you can find Louko?" Ent asked, worried about the other possibility…that she was going to give Tyron what he wanted.

Astra's hesitation reinforced his misgivings. "I don't know yet. Even if I did find Louko, I have no way to keep him safe—or anyone else, for that matter. To bring him home, Tyron must be dealt with. Until I know how to do that, I have no choice but to play along with his Game."

"Well, we might have other factors at play from this side." Ent turned to the issue of the Miadoris. Maybe *somehow* that could help combat Tyron. The very thought made Ent uneasy, however.

Astra's brow furrowed. "What do you mean?" Then she held up a hand. "Wait, give me one moment."

She vanished into thin air without warning. But before anyone could even react, she reappeared with another figure beside her.

"Des!" Ent's mother exclaimed as she realized before even Ent who was standing before them.

Destrin blinked, a slightly dazed smile appearing as he saw Ent and his wife. "Well, this is a nice surprise."

"Nice for some," Tallaman grumbled.

"It's alright, Tallaman, I missed you, too," Destrin replied without skipping a beat. He stepped forward to embrace Ameri, then turned back to look at Astra. "What did I miss?"

"Nothing yet," Astra said. "Ent was about to fill me in."

"Tirzah came for a…visit," Ent said bluntly, overwhelmed by the sheer amount of absurdity that was now taking place.

"She came with an offer," Jade chimed in from next to him. "She apparently wants to help steal the Miadoris."

Ent winced as he realized he probably should have given more information. "Right. That."

Astra's eyes went narrow. "To what purpose? That doesn't make sense—Tyron hates it more than anyone after it killed his wife."

Ent suddenly realized he couldn't really remember half the conversation with Tirzah…everything was rather hazy.

Fortunately, Jade was the one who answered, "She claims that Tyron has cut ties with her. She says she is no longer being monitored and that she came of her own volition. According to her, the Court is feeling the pressure of the spreading riots and is looking to the Miadoris as a possible…solution."

Ent could see Astra thinking this over. "The black bishop," she murmured. "The black bishop gets taken by the white castle." She glanced towards Ent then back to Jade. "Did she say anything else?"

"She…she was the one that told us of Louko being kidnapped. And about Rhioa." Ent spoke slowly, brow furrowed, as the memory of the conversation slowly came back. Why was his brain so slow? And why were there so many people?

Astra's shoulders drooped. "Then I think she is telling the truth. I don't know if she is to be trusted, but she is probably right about the Miadoris."

"But then what do we do with it?" Jade asked. Ent could feel her glance sideways at him.

"Just don't let it anywhere near Astra." It was Tallaman, gruff and to the point as ever.

Destrin looked like he had been ready to cut Tallaman off, but then he paused. "Well, would you look at that? We actually agree on something."

His uncle arched an eyebrow, looking down at Destrin and giving a non-committal noise.

"See?" Destrin grinned. "We're on the same side."

"Absolutely not." And yet…the reply was said with the slightest of smirks. It seemed Ent wasn't the only one taken aback by the interaction, and the room was silent for longer than it should have been, given the dire situation.

Right. The situation. "I'll retrieve it," Ent spoke up. He had to be useful for *something*. All he'd done so far was fail at just…being. Being a brother, being a son, being a husband, and definitely being a king. He wasn't even much use ruling Cithan thus far—his mother and father seemed to have been doing a good enough job as his proctors before he'd shown up. Oh, right—shown up *banished*.

"Is that a good idea?" Astra's eyes had widened ever so slightly. "It would be risky—you're needed here. Why not the Ethians? They're already in Silbyr and they are all very capable."

"They are risking themselves politically enough as it is. The last thing we need is to give the Court an excuse to banish them as well—especially with them working to help establish Jade in good report among the nobles. Besides, only the king had access to the vault and so I'm the only one that knows the ins and outs of how it functions. I'm also supposed to be half-decent at Gifting, which I think would be a little more useful than just shape-shifting." Ent ignored the pounding in his chest as he listed every quality he had to pretend to have confidence in. In reality, he was just willing to bet his life more than anyone else's, at this point. He'd only seemed to keep sending people to their deaths.

Whatever argument had been forming in Astra's half-open mouth was cut off by Destrin. "Who would be your backup?" his father asked, calm as ever.

"There are plenty of options," Ent replied as vaguely as possible.

"And here I thought that I sent you with the rash child," he heard Ameri grumble.

"Entrais kept a rebellion alive for nearly a decade without us." Destrin laid a hand on her arm. "I trust him to know what he's doing with this one. I think our efforts are better spent on figuring out how to keep the Miadoris safe once he has it. Astra," he turned his head. "Why don't you go inform Ven that all is well and we will be here a few hours more."

Lips pursed, Astra nodded once and disappeared without further warning.

This all felt unreal—Astra traveling across a country…his father being suddenly right here. The fact that Ent was about to steal from the country he'd tried to save. What was next?

"So is she actually doing alright or is she just as good at hiding things as her brother?" Tallaman asked with very little tact.

Destrin sighed, rubbing the side of his head. "She is…focused. For now, that is holding her together. But I fear it is leaving her blind to other things."

"You're taking care of her, right?" Ent wished he hadn't said the words. It was his father—*Astra's* father. Of course he was taking care of her. And yet too many reminders of Astra *not* being taken care of rattled around in Ent's mind.

His father's dark eyes held his for a long time. "As best as I know how," Destrin finally replied. Then he glanced towards Tallaman. "I take it that my charming brother-in-law has done the same for everyone here?"

"Of course—wait. No. Yes." Tallaman was uncharacteristically confused. "Stop doing that," he growled at Destrin.

"Are you…alright, Uncle?" Ent couldn't help but ask.

"No—yes!" Tallaman waved one hand. "But if I have to agree with one more Human, I might not be. Can we get back to whatever terrible plan it is that we're supposed to be making?"

Ent swallowed. "Yes. I suppose we should, shouldn't we."

Louko:

Louko was beginning to wonder if boredom was actually an underused method of torture. He'd been trying to keep track of the days, but with no windows…or doors…or regular meals…he'd given up keeping a tally. Tyron had seemed to be very erratic with his visits, and that included rations. It also included which version of Tyron that Louko got. Sometimes he was draconic: hostile, threatening, always rubbing in Louko's helplessness. Other times he seemed lost, confused to the point where he wouldn't recognize Louko at all. He always mentioned Rhioa in those moments. The rest of the time he seemed to vacillate between panic and despair, saying little besides quiet apologies.

"Breakfast."

As usual, the sudden announcement and Tyron's simultaneous appearance startled Louko.

And I..." Tyron was looking down at the hand not holding the food tray. "I don't know why I'm holding this." He looked up, brow furrowed. "Was this for something in particular?"

Louko sat up straighter, hope igniting that perhaps boredom was at an end. "Oh! You promised you'd get me a book." Actually Tyron had left...at least four times in the last few—visits? Could they be called days?—with the promise of returning with a book to pass the time. But then either he would never come back, or he would return with something totally unrelated. That was, if the more lucid, calm Tyron came back at all.

Tyron looked nearly relieved. "Oh, really? Then here you are." As usual, he set the tray of food on the floor—along with the book—and backed up to the opposite wall.

Louko launched himself forward, ignoring the food and instead grabbing the book, afraid it might evaporate at any moment. Only...no sooner had he opened the precious volume than he realized the horrible truth; it was in Pershizarian. Tyron had grabbed a volume on Pershizarian history.

Louko did not know Pershizarian.

Disappointment was an understatement as Louko now turned to his food, wishing he could somehow get a volume on Nythril or *anything* that might pass the time. Yes, but also perhaps help him understand Drogan Madness or the portal issue or anything that could actually be of use.

Anything to get him to stop coming up with the thousands of different ways he could end up dying, and the hundreds of different ways Astra might react to it.

Tyron ran a hand through his hair. "You can't read Pershizarian, can you?"

It was hard to watch Tyron in this state—as the man he had actually looked up to—and know that in a few minutes the regret and worry and nervousness would be replaced by the ruthless and sadistic Dragon. It hurt almost more to know the kind man was still in there somewhere, frayed at the edges and fighting a battle he couldn't win.

Except that Louko was desperately trying to find out how to make it so Tyron *could* win. The *real* Tyron, that was. If he could save Tyron, maybe everything would be alright. Maybe…maybe Astra would be safe. Louko didn't want to think of what would happen if the Dragon won, because he knew where that would leave him.

And Astra had dealt with enough loss already.

"My apologies. I thought…." Tyron trailed off, a frequent habit, as if he knew he didn't have time to waste on unnecessary words. He scoffed to himself before shaking his head. "Here, tear out one of those pages and I'll write it down. Maybe that will work."

"Do you have something on you to write?" Louko asked, knowing full well if Tyron left this room he would not remember.

Tyron felt his pockets before shaking his head. "But Gifting will do."

Hesitantly, Louko tore off one of the index pages in the volume and held it out for Tyron. "I want...uh...just something in Litashian or Nythrilian. History was always my favorite subject, so maybe something in that area?" He tried to be vague enough in order to keep the Dragon off the scent of what he wanted it for.

Tyron reached for the page, paused, then took it very quickly. A haze of blue engulfed the parchment as the ink rearranged itself. "Alright. I will try."

"Thank you," Louko said very, very slowly and very, very hesitantly. His eyes wandered back and forth from Tyron to the book in Pershizarian, wondering which one was safer to consult with at the moment. Both seemed equally as fruitless...Louko had still failed to figure out what would trigger Tyron in and out of lucid moments like this, and it seemed like anytime Louko tried to make conversation with Tyron, it only landed them both in trouble.

"Don't thank me. Don't ever thank me." Tyron's green eyes were fixed on the page as he folded it with shaking hands.

"Right. Okay. S—" Wait, no, an apology would probably be equally as bad. Louko's head jumped through each response he could give and how it might trigger the Dragon to return, but at the same time, he knew he had to say *something* so that the stumble in his words wouldn't be latched onto. Gah! "So then do you know Pershizarian?"

Tyron looked up, visibly lost. Then he looked down at the book and his brow furrowed. "I studied it once. I've only been to Pershizar a handful of times, so my speaking is poor." He tucked his note into his overcoat and shrugged lightly. "Rhioa is fluent, though. That's where I met her."

Oh no, not Rhioa again. But also wait—they met in Pershizar? "Do you think you could teach me? It seems to work off a different alphabet system and I am no good at deciphering those." Louko's strategy when in regards to Rhioa was to ignore and pretend he had not heard her brought up in conversation—no matter how confused or intrigued he became.

"You…you want me to teach you?" The baffled question came slowly.

Something inside Louko screamed. He didn't know what he wanted—he just knew he wanted to not talk about the dead wife or the fact that they were sitting in a dungeon or the fact that both of them were probably going to die by the end of this all. "Yes," he replied with a shrug. "Seems like some experience is better than none, after all."

He couldn't tell if Tyron was still confused or if he was going through the same thought process that Louko was. Either way, looking very unsure of himself, Tyron sat cross legged on the cold, stone floor. "Push it over here."

It felt as if a knife had been shoved right into his chest, it was so hard to breathe. For a moment, just a moment, it was like old times—and it hurt. Just Tyron and Louko, sitting alone with no one else, trying to act as if everything was alright. Louko didn't want to believe that Tyron was fraying at the ends. He didn't want to believe the Dragon had them both captive. He just wanted to get lost in a book with Tyron, with the closest thing to a real father he'd ever had.

And instead, he was constantly wondering when the man might kill him, and how much it would tear Tyron up inside when that happened.

In halting measures, Tyron began to point out each letter and explain their sound. He took another page from the index and used Gifting to make a chart with rough explanations. "Grammar is the most difficult part, I'm afraid. Pershizarians came across the Ocean of Xzarial from the south west—a very different background than either Nythrilians or Merimeethians—so their language has a very different structure. But...."

The way his voice faded made Louko brace for the sudden switch back to the Dragon. Yet when Tyron looked up, he only looked pained.

"Are you sure you want this? Even if the circumstances weren't...." Tyron shook his head. "This does not seem like it would bring up good memories."

Louko froze. His next words could mean the difference between keeping his old mentor and receiving the madman instead. "I, uh. Just don't know what else there is to do." *Idiot!*

Laying the book back on the floor and pushing it towards Louko, Tyron replied, "Perhaps it would be better to see if the note works and I could bring you something of interest."

Yeah...that had never been a good idea. "Or alternatively we could play word games?"

Tyron barely reacted. "If keeping me here is your attempt at preventing me from going off and doing more damage, I can at least assure you it makes no difference. He will return when he wants either way." His gaze dropped to the book. "If anything, I think he sends me here on purpose to keep me too busy to undo his work. I...am not good at leaving when I should."

"It just seems like...the longer you are able to stay yourself, the stronger you get," Louko couldn't hide the hopelessness from his voice any longer. "I was just trying to help." Trying to do the impossible and avoid the inevitable.

"Help...." For a moment, Tyron's expression twisted into something like agony. He seemed to swallow hard in an attempt to contain it. "You have always deserved better. I am sorry that you ever met me. And I am sorry that it came to this."

Louko looked right in the eyes of the man he both admired most and most feared. "Well, I am not sorry. For all that...you became...you made me what I am—and I would rather be that than my father."

Tyron's laugh was soft and bitter. "You don't remember, do you? Your father hated you because of *me*." He jabbed one shaking finger at himself. "The abuse, the isolation, that wretched deal he forced you to make—that was all because of me."

"Yes. How dare you try and make things better. I remember being forgotten and uncared for. I remember it being better when you were there...and I know now that it was not worse because you left. It was worse because your brother came. Because Euracia forced you to leave." He forced himself to remain calm and keep eye contact. This probably was not going to help...but something deep inside him needed to say this all—needed Tyron to hear it.

"...who told you that? Wait—Destrin. You've spoken with Destrin Verzaer, haven't you?" Tyron raked a hand through his hair. "It doesn't matter. I left, I returned, and then I sat and watched while your father tried to break you. I—" he sucked in a ragged breath. "It doesn't matter."

"You're right," Louko clenched both fists as he spoke, allowing his tone to harden just a little bit. "It doesn't matter. Because I *am* going to save you, and we *are* going to get out of this, because I'm done giving up. Not when you didn't give up on me."

Tyron recoiled. "No," he said vehemently. "Don't try to save me. There's not enough left. After all I've done, to you, to her, to…" He was tugging at his hair now. "No, if you find a way, kill me. That is the only hope for any of us."

He wanted to argue, and yet if ever there was a way to trigger the Dragon…that would be it. All Louko could do was stare at Tyron, unable to speak and unwilling to give in and agree. Maybe he was right; maybe it was easiest to just kill him in the end. But Louko couldn't forget the way Mitheau had talked of it…*put down.* As if Tyron had been a dog or a rabid animal. Even deeper than that, in the end—even after everything that had happened—Louko didn't think he could do it. He didn't think he would ever be able to end Tyron. After being told he was the reason for his mother's death so long ago, could he really carry the weight of *actually* being the death of his oldest friend?

Suddenly, Tyron's shoulders relaxed and his hand returned to his lap. "You needn't look so concerned. It wouldn't work even if you tried." He tilted his head. "Not even he's managed to succeed there." He stood up, straightening his overcoat.

Louko took a deep breath, hiding the grief and panic as he realized he'd again lost his friend and instead coaxed out the nightmare. "I see," he said simply, knowing the worst thing to do was dare the Dragon. It only loved the challenge.

Tyron narrowed his eyes and leaned forward, nearly looming over Louko as if he was going to take a step towards him. Then he looked down at the still-open book and gave a chilling smile. "Enjoy the book." With a wisp of blue, he was gone.

No, the boredom wasn't the worst part of this, after all. It was watching his friend fall apart over and over every day and being able to do nothing about it.

CHAPTER XV

<u>**Astra:**</u>

Astra sat on the floor of her borrowed room, the three-tiered chess board in front of her and Tyron's notes laid out chronologically beside her. Not that she really needed them; she'd long since memorized them. All of them besides the newest one, anyway. That one had been waiting for them this evening when she and her father had returned from Cithan. Ven had been incensed that no one, neither guard nor servant, had any knowledge of where the note had come from. It had simply been waiting in Astra's quarters.

Yet Astra could not bring herself to be upset. Not when the note had information on Louko:

White Castle No. 3 takes Black Bishop No. 1—Lady Tirzah aids King Entrais

Black Castle No. 4 back three, White Pawn No. 4 reaches the end of the bottom board, rises to the middle board—Litash riots, Court continues to lose control

White Pawn No. 1 remains in his place

Black Bishop No. 3 forward/left four

White Knight No. 2 forward two, left three

White Castle No. 3 right three

Black Queen forward one

The white pawn was still alive. Still trapped behind the black queen, but alive. However, there were no predictions regarding it, so how long would Louko remain safe? The key to finding out was discovering the identity of the black queen. The piece had been mentioned before in the note Mariah had brought after fleeing Merimeethia, but in the next note, there had been no explanation of the previous prediction. Why would Tyron give away the identities of other pieces and not this one? Now the piece was predicted to move again—still keeping in between the white pawn and the white king.

And there was another piece she didn't know—the white king. It hadn't been mentioned in any of the notes. Louko had been the one to guess at its movements, using the positions of figures on the other boards to extrapolate the information, but not even he could guess who the person behind it was. And if Louko, with all his learning and strategy and skill could not figure it out, what hope did Astra have at doing so?

Helplessness and exhaustion settled over her like a heavy blanket, nearly suffocating. What would happen if she failed? What would Tyron do to her friend? What would he do to Ent and Keeshiff and Ven and…. Astra wouldn't let it happen—she couldn't. No matter the cost, she would play The Game and she would win. Even if she couldn't decipher the other pieces, even if the white queen was lost, Astra knew it didn't matter: To win a Game of TetraChess, all you needed was to take the king.

Resolved, she began. The first rounds were muscle memory by now, their explanations echoing in her mind with the same eerie, calm tones that Tyron had spoken in during her capture.

Princess Astra rides to Merimeethia; White Queen moves forward three.

Kaeden kills King Omath; Black King forward one.

Then came moves that had not been dictated by the notes. These brought back Louko's voice as he had thought aloud: *Well, we know this pawn is Mitheau, right? Since this black pawn moves here, and we know she escaped the capital around this time, it only makes sense that she moves over here…right?*

On the cycle went, Tyron's voice narrating the notes, Louko's relaying his thoughts, and Astra reliving everything that had transpired since she'd left for Merimeethia. How long ago had that been? Eight months, maybe? She couldn't recall. It felt like a lifetime.

Only once Astra reached the last note did her pace slow. Yes, she now understood the predictions of the white pawn and the black castle, but what did these new ones mean? Astra plucked Tirzah's black bishop from the board as she moved Ent's white castle to take its place. She rolled the dark, stone figurine in between her fingers as she thought.

Was it possible that Tirzah was right? Was Tyron using The Game to feed them information? If he was battling another half of himself the way Mitheau described, could it be his way of trying to work around the draconic side? But how could Astra know which side of him sent the note—what if the Dragon sent her false information?

She picked up the latest note and studied its three predictions. The first one focused on the third black bishop and its movement towards the second white knight. She knew the white piece was Keeshiff, but who was the black? She frowned at the boards. The black bishop had, by

283

Louko's estimation, moved in the last round. The round where he had been kidnapped.

But wait…. Out of the four black bishops, they knew two of them had been spies. What if this was another? If so, what were they going to do to Keeshiff?

A knock startled Astra into the present.

"Just decided to check and see if you were alive," Ven's concern made its way through the door.

"And bring you breakfast," her father added.

"And that."

Astra was confused. What time was it? Ven had given them rooms in the very heart of the palace for security reasons, meaning she had no windows by which to tell the hour. But she'd thought it was still sometime during the night. She regathered herself. "I need to go to the front. I think the spy is there. Whatever they're going to do next, it involves Keeshiff."

The door opened and in came Destrin with a tray of food, followed by the king of Nythril.

Her father calmly set the food down by the chess board. "Is that really a wise move, Astra?"

"Someone has to warn him," she replied adamantly. She placed the bishop she'd been holding down with the other taken black pieces.

"I agree. But considering how you seem to be Tyron's biggest target, I don't think that 'someone' should be you. If he thinks that you will be there regularly, it could lead to greater harm." Ven's brow furrowed, and for a moment it allowed Astra to see just how tired Louko's uncle seemed—tired, and strained like the rest of them.

"Astra...you haven't been to the front, have you?" Destrin asked hesitantly. "As helpful as it would be, I don't know that it would work. We've already practiced enough to know you can't transport precisely if you don't know where you're going—and the front is too volatile a place to not be precise."

Astra gestured to the boards. "But this is too important to delay. If I don't go, and something happens to him, it will be far worse than me appearing somewhere I didn't intend."

"But if that somewhere is in the middle of the Merimeethian camp...then you would be putting those in Litash at stake. We don't need to give that idiotic Court any more reason to think about getting involved," Ven added.

The point was valid enough to make Astra hesitate. "But what else can we do? He *has* to be warned."

"I will send word immediately to Jahng—and I will send the courier of my old estate rather than anyone here. He is well trusted," Ven replied, sounding so sure of himself. It was somewhat of a feat considering how paranoid he usually sounded whenever trying to trust another person.

Astra bit her lip, looking back down at Tyron's most recent note. A hundred scenarios ran through her head, each worse than the last. What would she tell Louko if something happened to his brother and she did nothing to stop it? But Ven and her father were right: She might cause more damage than she would spare. She would have to trust Ven's courier to arrive in time.

"Alright," she gave in with a whisper. "Send word."

Ven gave a nod and left her room, leaving only her and Destrin.

"What about this Game, Astra—did you find anything else?" Her father asked.

Astra's gaze dropped to the boards and the notes scattered around them. She hoped she was making the right move—for Keeshiff's sake. "I think Tyron has predicted that Ent successfully steals the Miadoris. But I don't know what happens with it afterwards."

"I see. But it is at least with us and not the Court or Tyron?" Destrin's question was more a remark as he turned away from the chessboards.

"For now, yes. That could change with the next turn." Astra felt her stomach twist. She had been the one to tell Ent he could trust Tirzah long enough for the heist. What if this was another trap? What if she lost not only Louko, but Keeshiff and Ent as well? "I need to find a way to get this Door open to this other world. I should go to the portal site."

"Not alone, you aren't."

Astra had been prepared for pushback, but not this kind. She'd expected him to not want her to go at all. "Alright. Not alone, then. But we'll need something from Ven to allow us into the barracks."

Destrin gave a nod. "I will go speak with him as soon as he's done with that letter for Jahng. Where would you like to meet afterwards?"

Thinking for a moment, Astra asked, "What time is it? Do you think Mitheau is up? She may want to come with us."

There was a flicker of sorrow as he replied, "It's midmorning." Then, clearing his throat, he added, "So Mitheau is awake and about. I think she was stretching her wings in the little back courtyard Ven allowed her to use. Should still be there if you wanted to ask her."

"I'll meet you there, then." Still feeling disoriented, Astra started to repack the chess. Should she change before going down? Or maybe find something to drink? In times when everything felt dire and drastic, such little things felt silly to even think about.

"Don't forget your food by the desk. Maybe some water before leaving would be a good idea. I'll have things packed just in case," were Destrin's last words before the door separated them. He didn't stay to supervise her and make sure she ate, just suggested it and left.

Astra felt a swell of gratitude. She knew her parents mourned the lost time with both her and Ent. She also knew that they had done everything they had in order to keep her and Ent safe. And yet, when Astra was with them, she could not help but feel out of place. As though she wasn't supposed to be there. As though the daughter they'd once lost was gone forever and now all they had was her—a small, broken reflection of the child they missed. Astra did not know how to make it up to them.

When the boards, pieces, and all of Tyron's notes were safely stowed away, Astra hid the case behind the wardrobe. She tried to tidy herself up a little bit, then take some breakfast like her father had asked. After that, she strapped on her sword and headed for the back courtyard. She was nearly familiar with these halls now, with their bright mosaics, their wooden framing, and their jade and blue panels. Funny how the same corridors that were so daunting the night of Dia Tzaro's ball had become the closest thing Astra knew to safety.

Just as her father had said, Mitheau was indeed in the little fenced courtyard, her small draconic body weaving in between the tall, thin trees that lined either side of the paved walkway. Leaves drifted to the ground as the young Drogan's tail hit the branches with each sweep, and the whole courtyard seemed alive with movement even though Mitheau was the only living thing to be seen.

Astra decided not to interrupt. Mitheau had few good things to hold onto, and Astra figured her father would probably take a little while to join them anyway. She sat down on the doorstep and waited.

As Mitheau rounded another tree, Astra saw her bright eyes shift to where she was sitting. The Myrandi landed in front of Astra with a flurry of feather-like scales and wind, front legs becoming arms and scales becoming hair as she returned to her Human form. "What is it?" Mitheau asked. "What's going on?"

Astra felt a twinge of guilt that Mitheau would again immediately assume something was wrong in order for Astra to come see her. "I'm headed for the portal site, my father and I. I wasn't sure whether or not you'd like to come."

A strange cloud fell over the girl's face. "The portal site?" Her voice was quiet. "Yes, I'd like to come," she added at last, hands twitching at her side. "Are we using the Door? I'm assuming I'm still not allowed to fly beyond the palace walls?"

"It's still safer for you not to. Since Louko was taken, most of Nythril is on the lookout for Dragons." Not everyone would think twice about the difference in color from Mitheau's silver to Tyron's black. "So yes, we'll take the Door. If I can manage it." Astra was still working on being able to transport to places she hadn't been. They'd had some practice with pointing out places on a map, but she wasn't always accurate. And she still couldn't seem to find a way off-world—not even into the Maze that

Grenedil had talked about. "I'll go myself a few times before bringing you and Destrin."

"Alright. I'm for it. Just…why are we going?" Her arms folded in front of her as she asked.

Astra recalled the way Mitheau had been so against giving Tyron what he wanted, and how fearful she had seemed of the Madness she'd described to them—how scared she had seemed after her own encounter with Tyron. But Astra answered honestly. "To see if there's anything that can help me figure out how to reach one of these other worlds."

The Drogan's entire body stiffened, but she said nothing, only biting her lip as if to physically bite back an argument. At last, she gave in. "Alright, then let's go see what we can find."

<u>Keeshiff:</u>

"She said *what* now?" It was Lucian, looking incredulously at Keeshiff as he finished relaying what Mariah had suggested.

He hadn't been able to get it out of his head. Even as much as his logic screamed that trusting her was a bad idea, something in her words made him wonder. Had he really left such an impact on the nobles? If they could skip the middleman and go right for the heads of the territories, wouldn't that be a safer option? But he had long set the foundations among generals and the Merimeethian soldiers for a coup to overtake his father. Surely, he could persuade them to join him once more?

"She's probably just trying to send you to your death, too," Rhumir growled. "That little witch has done nothing but try and play everyone else with her games. To think *anyone* else could be the spy is foolishness."

And yet Keeshiff wasn't convinced…it seemed such an easy explanation, but he found himself hearing the sincerity in her tone when she had begged. Was he falling for her trap again? Just like always?

Keeshiff turned to see what the other knights would say on the subject and found Gavin frowning in thought, setting down the crossbow he'd been cleaning. "I mean, is it possible, though? I don't know anything about nobles, but it's no secret that no one liked Omath—no offense." He tipped his head towards Keeshiff. "But if Kaeden's gone off a cliff and started wars and random executions, it could be that they're not so fond of him either."

Indeed, Kaeden had executed Julyn—Rufio and Rhumir's father—who had been a very well-liked man, even if he was technically staff. Keeshiff turned to Rufio. "What are your thoughts?"

Rufio rubbed the side of his face, glancing at his still-scowling brother before letting out a deep breath. "I don't know. I don't know if Mariah acted out of malice or just out of sheer stupidity, but neither makes me want to trust her on this account." His shoulders rose and fell in a tired shrug. "Though none of us really know anything about nobles or socialites or politics. Lucian's the only one who ever moved in those circles."

"Don't ask me," Lucian grunted, holding up both hands. "My father disowned me over twenty years ago when I left to become a knight."

Rufio shrugged again. "All I'm saying is that, out of anybody in this camp, you and Mariah are the only ones who would know anything about this. And you would know better than anyone whether you could trust her."

"But you also would be the first person she could fool," Rhumir cut in. "She's playing on your emotions and trying to play into your pride. Who has always shown and told you of their support? Killyan and the soldiers. Who have you never heard from? Any of the pompous aristocrats on their high horses. Those are *her* friends. What if she's trying to take the throne for herself?"

Keeshiff sighed. Rhumir was right. Mariah was playing into his fanciful ego and he knew it. Of course he would like the idea that not being like his father would appeal to the nobles. But they had never seemed to care. His best angle to stop this bloodshed was the army, and his best approach to that was Killyan. He couldn't understand why in Eatris he kept lingering on Mariah's words when every ounce of reason mocked him for doing so, but this was no time to gamble on the word of a liar.

"All she's ever done is use her status to her advantage. She did it before and she'll do it again." Rhumir was on his feet now, anger rising by the word. "You still haven't found the spy—it could still be her! Would you really take advice from someone who might be *actively* betraying you?"

The other knights murmured in agreement, and the last bit of Keeshiff's doubt vanished. He remembered how Mariah had always charmed everyone growing up. Always gotten her way—seemed to convince people of ideas when it should have been impossible to talk them into them. He wouldn't be falling for that again.

Keeshiff was so sick of feeding this rubii. He'd tried three times now to give it to Mariah—hoping to give her something semi-useful and harmless to do—but it was constantly getting away from her, and she claimed all it did was bite at her with its little beak and try to scratch her with its feet.

Seemed there was at least one consensus: Beasts and people alike found Mariah insufferable.

But of course, that wasn't the only thing they'd given Mariah. Upon leaving the tent with the stupid little animal and finally admitting defeat in *that* department, Keeshiff and Jahng had made sure to talk a little louder than usual and drop hints about them setting up a group on the side to possibly flank the Merimeethian army to the south. A completely false plan, but one that would perhaps show if Mariah was indeed sharing information with the enemy once again.

Now, out of earshot and back in Jahng's command tent, Keeshiff's shoulders sagged—at least as much as they could while holding the squirming rubii. "So then the plan remains? Fake camp so that if she's a spy then it will send any soldiers to the opposite end of the front from where Killyan and I are meeting?"

Jahng nodded, giving the animal a dubious side-eye in the process. "Yes. A few of my men will be waiting in the spot you let your sister hear, should anything come of it. But this thing with Killyan could be a trap too."

"I'll be careful. Besides, you'll have backup there as well. And Killyan would never resort to deceit." Keeshiff forced confidence into his reply.

Something in him didn't like this plan, but perhaps it was the possibility that he might have to once more fight his own people up close…and this time there wouldn't be the option for sparing them should Killyan somehow, indeed, be luring him out. Before they'd been fleeing to Nythril and it had only been a patrol. Now it was an army and this was a war.

War held no scruples nor friendships, and it threatened to break anyone who did.

Jahng glanced around the empty tent before replying in a low voice, "If I may, I still think it's unwise that you're going. You are our best shot at getting the Merimeethian army to question its loyalty to Kaeden. Kaeden, Tyron—whoever he is—knows that. He can't afford to let you win, and we can't afford to lose you."

"Killyan has already agreed. And this *is* that shot at getting the Merimeethian side to question who they want to follow. I can't just sit here and let this chance slip by." He had to do anything in his power to avoid spilling more Merimeethian blood. To avoid having to kill the very soldiers he had trained with growing up. "And with the men you're sending, I'll be fine even if this *is* a trap. Killyan is a soldier, not a spy. If he were the latter, he would have known better than to suggest a meeting at all."

Jahng held his gaze for what seemed like an uncomfortably long time. Then she let out a breath and shook her head. "Stubborn Merimeethians," she muttered in Nythrilian. Keeshiff had been desperately trying to pick up Nythrilian during his time here, but the reason he understood this particular phrase was because she had said it at least twenty times in the past week. "We go on as planned, then," she returned to Merimeethian. "When do you leave?"

293

"Tomorrow afternoon. Killyan wants to meet under cover of darkness to keep identities concealed, but we want to be there before nightfall to scout the area." Keeshiff had agreed that was a good plan, worrying what Tyron might do should he find out the captain was no longer loyal to "Kaeden."

Jahng nodded. "I will send orders to supply to make sure you and your men have rations packed for the day, then. Do you all have the equipment you'll need?"

"Yes," Keeshiff replied, already going through a mental list of what they had. "We have our own weapons, and we still have the coats you provided. All we need is the rations."

The night was inexcusably normal for a covert meeting. It wasn't even that windy—which for the edge of Merimeethia was fairly good weather. One of the moons sat just over the top of the distant mountains, casting dim light over the small hollow where Keeshiff stood waiting.

Their Nythrilian backup was over the crest of the nearby hill and Rufio, Ivinon, Gavin, and Coryn waited in the copse of trees not far off. They'd checked the entire hollow for any marksmen that might have been trying to take any of them down. Still, Keeshiff felt uneasy about all this. What if this was the wrong call?

The sound of muted footsteps through the brush set Keeshiff's already taut nerves on edge. He remained in the shadows, trying to identify who or what was the source of the sound. Then came the whistle: a low, whooping tone like a retha warbler.

He dared not allow relief to set in even as he replied to the whistle with one of his own. The sign he had told Killyan to use.

The response was more footsteps and a dark figure appeared, descending into the hollow. "I wasn't sure you were serious about meeting," Killyan's familiar voice low.

"I wasn't sure you would come," Keeshiff said with a very sorry attempt at amusement. He felt like he might puke from the stress of this. But he'd told himself Killyan had never lied to him before—had never done anything but act honorably even when they were on opposite sides. So, surely nothing had changed now?

"If I was smarter, maybe I wouldn't have," Killyan's reply was nearly rueful. Keeshiff saw him glance back over his shoulder, then at their surroundings. "The girl—did she make it?"

"Astra?" It took Keeshiff a moment to understand what he was referring to. It felt so long ago from everything that had happened in Merimeethia. Oh. He was talking about her imprisonment, wasn't he? Swallowing hard, Keeshiff replied, "Yes. She made it. Barely. But she hasn't been the same with Louko being taken."

"Wait, Louko was taken? By whom?" Shock edged Killyan's question so vividly that Keeshiff didn't even need to see his face to know he meant it.

Aha. Again, Killyan was no spy: The shock was genuine. "By Tyron. Well, who you call Kaeden. He's the one who murdered Omath. He's using Merimeethia to get to Nythril and he is using my brother to get to Astra." It was hard to remain calm with the reminder of just how messed up this all was, but Keeshiff forced himself to do just that. It's what Louko would have done.

Now there was nothing but stunned silence. When Killyan did find his tongue again, he murmured, "Kaeden has blamed Omath's death on you and your brother. Few believe it, and those that do don't care. But this…this is a hefty accusation. Do you have proof for any of it?"

"Only witnesses. Lots of witnesses…but none that anyone would trust. And then—wait. Astra has been receiving letters from Tyron. But he never signs them." Frustration grew. Of course, they would want proof.

Killyan's gloved hand tapped the pommel of his sword nervously. "What kind of witnesses?"

"Astra—the Ezai Ru—all of my men?"

Still shifting uneasily, Killyan let out a terse breath. "I…I want to believe you—and I do. I saw what happened to Astra and your brother. But it's going to take a lot more to convince everyone else. No one likes what Kaeden is doing, and no one trusts him, but you'd have to give them a really good reason to trust you." His shrug was stiff. "You know how Merimeethian rulers go. Few Merimeethians are willing to die for someone they think will get overthrown in a year or two."

"Yeah, well, I am done with the way things are," Keeshiff spat. "If we are loyal to nothing then what even is the point? I could tell them exactly how many days it has been since he came and took Louko, but that is only my word. If no one's word holds any power then why bother?"

Killyan's hesitation told Keeshiff that the captain knew he was right. "Perhaps if we could—" he cut himself off sharply, head turning and hand wrapping around his sword. "Did you bring backup?" he hissed.

Keeshiff drew his own blade, whispering, "I had them waiting in the bushes in case…Gavin?"

No response. Then some distant voice called, "Watch out! From the back!"

Keeshiff put his sword to Killyan's throat and snarled, "Really, a trap?" as he put his other hand to the knife at his belt, torn between keeping with Killyan and running to help his men. Where was Jahng's backup?

Instead of pulling his blade, Killyan held up both hands. "It wasn't me—I told no one, I swear!"

The prince didn't have any time to reply, instead tackling the man head on as an arrow headed right for the captain's head.

"Well, I guess I believe you," Keeshiff muttered as he spit out the mouthful of dirt, rolling off Killyan and quickly out of the way as another hail of arrows came down at them.

"Come on! My men are over there—" He tugged Killyan's arm towards the few trees on their left, barely visible in the thick darkness of night. His words were nearly drowned out by a clamor of steel and shouting.

Both the captain and Keeshiff rushed to make for the trees, Keeshiff's head pounding as his worst fear was realized.

"Watch out!" Killyan blocked a blow that had come from some unseen enemy behind him.

Keeshiff turned around to find two shadows of soldiers, one having just tried to take a swing at Keeshiff's back. Another attacker was right behind, this one swinging for his head. Keeshiff deflected the sword with his own and used the momentum to drive his pommel forward. It went over the soldier's grip and connected with his metal helmet, creating a ringing sound as the man staggered back.

Everything was chaos, the sounds of the skirmish only made worse by the terrible visibility of night. No torches—no light—only darkness and the cold, unforgiving edge of steel waiting for you. With no ability to tell numbers, Keeshiff felt swallowed in a sea of endless foes, drowning under the blades of his assailants and having no time to even *think* of how to get them all out of this. He barely heard Killyan shouting useless orders for their attackers to stop. Where was Jahng's men?!

The very real, raw thought that they all might die permeated his mind.

But then, suddenly, it all faded to nothing, replaced by an intense pain that spread through his entire body. The ringing of steel against steel faded into oblivion, and Keeshiff looked down slowly at his middle, mystified as he stared at the edge of a blade protruding from it.

Oh.

He felt his body begin to shake, the panic taking over as his body realized he was slowly dying even though he himself could not register it. All he could do was look at the sword, wondering if whoever had put it there was going to take it out again. How much time had passed?

Then, all of a sudden, the pain cut through the haze, and Keeshiff crumpled to the ground, coughing up blood and nearly choking as whoever had stabbed him in the back withdrew the blade. He desperately tried to use his arms to brace himself against the ground, but nothing was working—everything was weak and impossible to move. Why was he so cold? Desperately he tried to crawl to help, but where help was, he had no idea; and every time he opened his mouth to cry out, he found himself coughing and panting. Shaking, cold, and lost, Keeshiff found himself unable to move any further, wet all over as his own blood poured out and left him alone in the darkness.

That's when the pain faded. At first, the violent change from agony to tranquility was terrifying, but a strange peace fell over Keeshiff as, all in a moment, he found himself face-to-face with people he loved: his mother, his friends, Louko and Astra. His entire life played out before him—the adventures they'd lived through. The warmth of his embrace with Louko. His brother's wistful expression when Keeshiff had finally said how he loved him. The memories washed all over Keeshiff with a warmth, and his last conscious thought was wishing he could give Louko one more embrace and tell him this wasn't his fault.

CHAPTER XVI

Entrais:

Ent had apparently *un*pleasantly surprised Tirzah when he'd announced he would be the one breaking into the palace vault, and she'd been trying to make him change his mind ever since.

Which, of course, only made him more resolved to do it. Now he was just wondering more of what her plan was in double-crossing him rather than *if* she was planning to. He'd even taken the precaution of sending a letter to the Ethians still in Silbyr, informing them of the full plan in case anything should happen. Hopefully that wouldn't be the case.

"And you're sure that thing will keep the Miadoris from blowing us up the moment we take it out?" Tirzah's monotone held a touch more irritation than usual as she followed him through the dim tunnel.

"Yes," Ent replied, ignoring the skepticism and wondering if he should bother telling her this wasn't the first time he'd done this sort of thing. Last time he'd handled the Miadoris, he hadn't even had a contraption from the Elves to help him. "The entrance is up ahead. Just do what I instructed and we'll be fine." Ent had used Gifting to alter her face to Commander Erhail, then once inside, she'd go to the emergency entrance and let him in through the back. The entrance was heavily Gifted and could only be used from the inside, so there was no need to guard it as anyone let in was already carefully checked and on a list of those allowed inside the vault.

"And you're certain that me touching the red-bronze in their security check won't disrupt the illusion?" Tirzah, already wearing the uniform of the palace guard, glanced up and down the tunnel.

"Trust me, I don't want you thrown in prison. How am I supposed to kill you later if that happens?" Ent asked, completely straight-faced.

This seemed to reassure Tirzah more than anything else he'd said. "Fair enough," she muttered.

"Then see you out back. I'll be waiting." They'd come to the end of the tunnel where they would need to temporarily part ways, and the only thing keeping Ent together was the knowledge that Tirzah could not physically get the Miadoris without letting him in the emergency entrance.

Her borrowed face narrowed its eyes, but she nodded and turned without another word.

Now out of sight of each other, Ent didn't have to try hiding his shaking hands anymore. He'd been trying so desperately *not* to think about things going wrong, but with being forced to go with Tirzah, he couldn't help but worry what she'd do if the plan went sour. Ent didn't want anyone to get hurt—the soldiers guarding the vault were technically the loyal ones, after all, trying to stop anyone from getting their hands on the Miadoris again. They didn't know the agenda of the Court, nor understand that Ent only wanted to keep them safe.

He didn't want to kill anyone.

With that thought burned eternally in the back of his mind, Ent tried to focus on the task at hand. The back entrance was small, more like a mine shaft barely big enough to fit a Human, let alone an Elf. It was only meant for extreme emergencies such as cave-ins, and the entrance was technically not visible from the rockface. Ent just happened to know where it was. Being the paranoid person he was, he'd studied all exits and entrances in and around the palace—especially the vault. Seemed being obsessively suspicious had finally come in handy.

But he really, really didn't like waiting. Too many things could be going wrong, especially when he was relying on Tirzah to open the door within the next ten minutes. What if she didn't? What if his illusion slipped and she didn't get through the door? Or what if this really was a trap and she was sending guards to his location at this very moment? Well, whether or not it was a trap, if she didn't show up in the next ten minutes, he would be explaining himself to the next patrol that walked by.

Just as his spiraling thoughts threatened to squeeze the air from his lungs, there was a sound from the other side of the metal door, then the clicking of a latch and the groaning of unused hinges. Ent grabbed the edge of the door as it slowly opened, trying to minimize the sound. On the other side was a disguised, but still visibly disgruntled, Tirzah.

"When you said it was small, I didn't realize it meant I had to crawl just to fit," she grumbled under her breath.

Ent went to lean down into the small space. "You're not almost seven feet tall so you can relax."

Still almost on her hands and knees, Tirzah's only reply was a grunt as she shuffled back up the shaft.

Nothing was as pleasant as trying to crawl through a three-foot-tall hole when you were a seven-foot-tall Elf with serious issues about closed spaces...but if nothing else, Ent had become very disciplined in curbing his panic. Or maybe it was that the years of spending time in various dungeons had forced him to get over the issue with dark, cramped places.

It was longer than Ent would have liked before they had made it through the crawlspace and into the vault. The second tiny door gave an eerie creak as Ent closed it behind them, standing up and brushing himself off as he now stood in a back corridor of the vault—where countless dangerous items were kept from greedy and corrupt hands. At least, supposedly.

He couldn't help but remind himself he had led Tirzah right inside it. Of course, they were here to steal the *most* dangerous of all the things kept here.

"Which way?" Tirzah murmured, glancing up and down the corridor.

Ent tilted his head towards their right, quickly using his Gifting to change into Commander Erhail and switch Tirzah's disguise to that of an attendant, knowing enough about the Bandilarian official to be able to impersonate him if necessary. Not that it would help too much if someone was aware enough of who had been let inside to know Tirzah hadn't come with any companions. But technically Commander Erhail was the only officer allowed inside the vault, so it was the best chance they had if they were sighted.

Down the corridor they went. Each section of the vault was connected to the single, main hallway that led out of the guard room. To get to the chamber that housed the Miadoris, they would have to go into the main hall and past two other chambers. Now they just had to hope everyone stuck to their patrol schedule and nobody would be checking the hallway while they were in it.

Right as they came to the threshold, Tirzah stepped up past him, leaning into the corner to check and clear the hallway.

Ent walked right by her, shoulders squared as he rounded the corner. "If we look like we're sneaking around, when someone *does* see us, no disguise will erase suspicion," he whispered calmly.

"If we're not seen at all, there's nothing to suspect," came Tirzah's thin reply.

He didn't say a word, only continued to lead on as they made their way through the vault, Ent's fingertips tingling as the power of this place seemed to radiate from the very walls.

He hated the vault.

"Footsteps," Tirzah whispered the warning half a second before Ent caught the sound himself.

Of course there would be someone else inside. This was *his* luck, after all.

What he wouldn't do to trade his stupid sight for Astra's ears, right now.

Apparently, it was time to test if he could back up his claim on them being able to brush off someone seeing them.

From up ahead on their left, a guard stepped out of one of the corridors and stopped in surprise. She barely remembered her salute before sputtering, "Commander Erhail?" Ent noted her insignia; she was the minimum rank for vault duty, which was probably why she had been the one sent on the rounds. "My apologies, sir, I wasn't informed that you would be in today. Did you need anything unlocked?"

"Checking on the Vial of Enervation from the vault. But I also wanted to make sure you were on mark with your new duties, and it would seem I am left wondering…" Ent said calmly without missing a beat. The other reason he'd chosen Commander Erhail? His voice was similar enough to Ent's to make it easy to come off sounding like him. "Which chambers have been checked this hour?"

"The Miadoris, the casings, the unidentified relics, and the preservation room," she rattled off the list. She seemed a touch nervous when she added, "I know I am a few minutes behind schedule, sir. I am trying to be extra thorough. I will attend to the rest right after this."

"Good. Sounds like you are a little more prepared than you first appeared. You may continue your rounds," Ent said with a short nod even as he processed the relief of her having already checked the Miadoris. That would give them more time.

"Thank you, sir." With another salute and a quick glance at Tirzah, the guard continued past them and into the next corridor.

Ent didn't dare let loose a comment telling Tirzah he was right, but he did give her a look that said as much.

She ignored him.

They continued down to the end of the hall, glanced back once to make sure that the guard wasn't watching, then took the last corridor on the right. This one led to a massive door Ent had visited only once before. The metal was completely smooth—no handle, no keyhole.

Taking a deep breath as he dropped their disguises, Ent stepped up to the door and placed a hand on it, closing his eyes and feeling the lock that was hidden inside. Slowly, he felt the pins and springs, coaxing them to click into place with the energy pulse from his hand. There was a small groan, and then the door made a hiss, lazily sliding to the side and allowing them into the first room.

The small observation room was unlit, yet the blue light that emanated from the thick windows made it easy to see. Ent checked over his shoulder one last time before waving Tirzah in and letting the door slide shut behind them.

There was a second door in front of them, this one made of red-bronze in order to keep the Miadoris firmly inside its walls. But this door also had a proper lock, and Ent always preferred picking with actual pins rather than Gifting when he could. The former took less energy.

He knelt in front of the door, taking out the two picks he'd stored in his pocket and setting to work on the lock. It took a few moments, but he'd had long years of experience in this, at least. Somehow, he'd thought such skills would be of little use after The War.

Apparently not.

"There," he dared whisper, as the satisfying click finally resonated through the small observation room. Keeping the lock picks in place with one hand, he used his free one to open the door. "Shall we?" he asked as he turned back to Tirzah.

She didn't answer right away. Ent was almost ready to repeat the question when she nodded. "Let's just get this over with."

Ent suddenly noticed she looked...off. "Is something wrong?" Had he missed some sort of gas installation? Something that was triggered by an attempt at picking the lock? That would have had to be installed after he'd been dethroned, and surely there hadn't been enough time to change the defenses of the vault that much?

"No. Let's hurry it up," she snapped. "We only have so much time before that guard makes it back to the guard room and mentions you."

Ent didn't waste words on further questioning, instead slipping into the room and coming face-to-face with the thing that had caused his family so much pain. The thing that had spurred Euracia to the Ethian Massacre; that had almost killed Astra as a child; and that had later made her almost lose her mind during The War.

The Miadoris.

The blue Essence sat on a pedestal in the center of the room, surrounded by narrow, silvery bars that made up a cage that could fit in the palm of your hand. Tendrils of energy swirled and splashed up against the bars, even coiling around them, but never slipping beyond them. It was nearly mesmerizing to watch. At least it would have been if Ent wasn't keenly aware of how fast the Miadoris's mood could change. Strange how something this small could be deadly enough to reduce a country to ash.

Slowly, he took from his pocket the small, cloth-like, folded panels that were to go around the cage. As delicate as they seemed, they were woven with more than cloth and hopefully would be enough to keep the Miadoris quiet.

He placed one around each side of the cage, the cloth sticking to the sides on their own. The buzz in the room lessened slightly as Ent placed the final piece along the side, hating how his hands shook at the process. One wrong move, and he could have brought this place down.

But there was no time for imagining worst-case scenarios. Not right now. Now they had to get out of here...and quickly. Sparing no time for hesitation, Ent grabbed the covered cage containing the Miadoris and left the room, meeting back up with Tirzah who—by some miracle—was still there waiting. He'd have been lying to himself if he hadn't half-expected her to be gone. In fact, he'd gone through several backup plans in case that had happened or if she had alerted guards.

But he was distracted suddenly by how increasingly pale she looked.

Ent gave no verbal communication, merely nodded that he had secured what they'd come for and then led the way back out of the room. Tirzah followed almost clumsily behind.

Not good. She should never have come—what in Eatris was wrong? Ent's ears roared as they carefully retraced their route back to the emergency exit. Anything at this point could go wrong; the Miadoris could be too powerful for the cage to hold it; Tirzah could...just fall down and die with the strange way she was acting; and the guard could have realized something was odd and come back to check on them.

But nothing happened. They found their way back without any mishaps, and yet still Ent refused to believe it as he and Tirzah slipped into the narrow emergency tunnel and back into the main tunnels running under the palace.

"Now to hope no one checks on the Miadoris for another few minutes," Ent murmured as he readjusted his hold on the case.

Tirzah didn't reply.

"Is this the part where you try and take it from me, then?" Ent didn't mince words as he turned to face her, beginning to think she was feigning illness so as to catch him unawares. It would make sense.

To her credit, she gave a very convincing expression of confusion. But she still couldn't seem to think up a reply in time.

Ent took one hand away from the Miadoris and snapped it to one of the knives hidden in his coat. Patrol. He heard them round a distant corner, and Ent flashed an accusatory look at Tirzah as he stayed flat against the wall. Was this the moment then? Was she going to call out when the patrol passed the tunnel they were hiding in? Ent should leave—he was clear of the protected vault, he could transport himself and the Miadoris away...but what if she wasn't faking it? What if exposure to the Miadoris had made her ill and he left her to get caught? What would keep her from telling everyone that he'd stolen the Miadoris and taken it to Cithan?

Before Ent could decide, the footsteps reached the entranceway. Instinct spurred his Gifting to pull the shadows closer around himself. He watched breathlessly as the guards came into sight, glanced casually down the corridor, then kept walking. But Ent didn't have time to let out his breath before he heard a thud from behind him.

He snapped around to find Tirzah had fallen to the floor, unconscious. What in the world? The echo rang along the tunnel, cutting through the ringing ears and the roaring panic, and Ent ran quickly over to Tirzah, gripping the Miadoris hard in case this was a ploy. But he was beginning to think this really wasn't.

"Tirzah! Wake up!" he hissed even as his mind raced through the different scenarios that this might turn into. She might wake up and take the Miadoris, the patrol might have heard her, or she might even take a moment to dispense of Ent first and take the Miadoris.

Tirzah's head lolled to one side, but there was no other response.

"Did you hear that?" a voice questioned from down the hall.

"Yeah, it came from back...."

"You there! Identify yourself!"

There was no time to think. With a mysteriously limp Tirzah next to him, Ent used Gifting to transport them away, envisioning Silbyr's streets and hoping their backup plan wouldn't just make things even worse. But they couldn't go across the plains—the Bandilarians would outrun them easily.

The clamor of people in a city of unrest soon filled Ent's every sense, and he found himself kneeling over Tirzah in an alleyway, the Miadoris still in his free hand. How was he supposed to carry Tirzah *and* the Miadoris? Clearly, this wasn't a ploy—if she had wanted him caught, she would have called out to the patrol when she'd 'fainted.' No. Something was very, actually wrong.

Fortunately, Ent knew the city fairly well, and they were hidden in a side alley where no eyes would have seen the unexpected appearance of their former king with a fainted courtier.

But the alarm was already tolling through the city, and shouts of soldiers were beginning to mingle with it.

"Tirzah, wake up, you idiot!" Ent growled as he shook her, not bothering to be subtle anymore. He couldn't carry her!

At first, nothing. Then her eyes half opened, closed, and opened again. Her gaze roamed listlessly without catching on anything.

Ent didn't know what else to try; he shook her again.

Tirzah snapped to it, breaking his grip and pulling free. "What's wrong with you?! Let go of me!"

"What's wrong with *me?*" Ent's question was cut off by the sound of soldiers getting closer to their general location. "We need to get *out* of here and I can't carry you!" His last strand of sanity felt as if it had finally snapped.

Apparently noticing her surroundings for the first time, Tirzah's eyes widened. She pushed herself upright and then to her feet, teetering dangerously for a moment before steadying herself against the wall. "How far can you transport yourself?"

"Not far enough and I don't dare pull from the Miadoris. How likely are you to pass out again?" Even as Ent replied, he took a knife from the slot inside his coat, familiarizing himself with the weight even as he began to plot out a few exit paths.

Time to find out if he was still together enough to manage it.

"As long as you don't use Gifting again, I'll be fine," Tirzah grumbled. "I underestimated that stupid thing." Her gaze went to the hand still holding the Miadoris.

"We're already in the eastern sector of the city. Can you make it to your house from here?" If they could get to it….

Tirzah seemed to remember their backup plan. "Not without being spotted. We'll need a distraction."

"Great. Distraction…I can lead them off and then transport to your house. Just let me in." How was Ent suddenly putting so much faith in this woman? She was still quite possibly only out to get the Miadoris herself. Sure, now it was pretty clear she wasn't working *for* the Court. But she might still be working for Tyron.

Frowning, Tirzah shook her head. "Neither of us can afford to be identified. You head for the house; I'll shift and lead them off. No one here knows I can shift, so it won't be traced to me."

Right. Astra and Mitheau had both explained the whole Drogan thing…. "You hardly seem in a state to be leading anyone anywhere," Ent commented. But they were running out of time. If she insisted, he knew he'd have to play along or risk them both getting caught anyway.

With a glance up and down the alley, Tirzah stepped back. Her change from Human to Dragon was surprisingly swift—faster than even some Ethians who had spent decades in practice. She shook her silver head as her deepened voice growled, "Just get to the house." With a leap, she clambered up the wall of the nearest house and disappeared over the rooftop.

Get to the house. Ent collected himself, gripped the Miadoris a little harder, and disappeared into thin air, the worry of this all being some elaborate trap still whispering in the back of his head as he left for the house of his enemy.

Louko:

"Wait, I thought it was pronounced *kjarta*?" Louko asked, perplexed as he stared at the Pershizarian tome in front of him and Tyron.

"That's the wrong diacritic." Tyron pointed to the word, tracing the thin line that ran next to the almost-familiar lettering. "If it was a half-length, you would be correct. Because it is a full length, it is a hard sound— *kharta*."

"Oh, I see…" It had been…a while since Louko had been able to sit down and study anything except that stupid chess game. Come to think of it, at least as long ago as it had been since Astra had first come to Merimeethia.

When this had all started.

"I suppose I am a bit rusty at this," he mused as he tried to commit the difference in the two diacritic signs to memory. Though, honestly, he only cared about it in the hopes that, somehow, he'd stumble upon *something* useful in the mound of books he was accruing.

Indeed, it was quite a mound. Apparently having Tyron write himself a reminder was too effective—he'd shown up with a new armful of books every time he'd come to visit. The room was beginning to get a bit crowded.

"If you can conquer Nythrilian lettering, your Pershizarian diacritics will be just fine," Tyron reassured quietly.

Now if only Louko was good for conquering something actually useful. Like Tyron. Or this doorless prison. Or anything more than stupid symbols on a page.

Louko sighed, trying to keep up the facade of normalcy as he replied, "Yes, well, I suppose with you teaching me there is a chance."

Tyron's eyes remained fixed on the page between them. "It has nothing to do with me. You did quite well for yourself in these years without me."

"I mean," Louko looked up from the book and dared look his friend and captor in the eyes. "You were still there, in a way. You just didn't tell me." As Kaeden.

Tyron shook his head vehemently. "No, that wasn't me. Maybe a little bit—maybe at first." His voice was as hollow as his stare as he looked off into nothingness. "I hadn't been there in years."

"What do you mean?"

When the silence began to stretch out, and when Tyron's empty stare didn't even waver, Louko began to think he'd lost him again. Then Tyron drew a shaky breath and raked a hand through his hair.

"The Dragon," he muttered. "I was too weak. I couldn't find a way out or around him. All I could do was watch."

"It was that bad? None of it was you?" None? The killings during The War. Astra and Entrais's capture? Had Tyron not been able to stop it either?

"I..." Tyron's laugh was sudden, bitter. "How can I tell? How do I even know which one *is* me? For all I know, I am both and am simply deceiving myself to play two sides. Black, white—what does it matter if I play both kings?"

"Wait, you're both kings?" The confused question slipped from Louko before he could think twice.

Something dark and dangerous flashed across Tryon's expression. He looked like he was going to get up or reach for Louko. Then that exhaustion returned and he leaned back against the wall. "She doesn't know, does she?"

Louko somehow managed to shake his head even through the sudden panic at Tyron's change. Every time he thought Tyron was getting better, he was reminded at how quickly he could revert to madness and choke Louko out on a whim. Only time would tell whether Tyron could break that or if it would break him.

Tyron's shoulders drooped. "I have to find a way to tell her," he murmured as if to himself. "Yes, it's me. I am both. I was the one who challenged him to the Game. I...I didn't know what else to do...." His words trailed off, lost to despair.

"What do you mean, you're the one that challenged him? You challenged Astra...." Louko's chest grew tight. Had they misunderstood this *entire* time?

"He went too far when he captured you and her. I couldn't stop him, I couldn't...." His hands trembled violently. "Strategy, competition—it appealed to his pride, his desire to dominate. He accepted the challenge. It forces him to play by the rules." For the first time in the entire conversation, Tyron's gaze met his. "Your friend...she is the means of victory or defeat." He leaned forward slightly. "For both sides. Do you understand?"

So Astra had never been in control. None of this—none of the moves, the sacrifices, the mistakes. Tyron was playing against himself and desperately trying not to lose. Yet Louko was not sure he understood the last part. "I…I think so," he replied all the same, walking on eggshells. It was clear Tyron was teetering on the edge right now, and at any moment, the Dragon could return.

"Does she know?" Tyron's question held an urgency. "Does she know she is both sides?"

"Wait, but…you said you were both sides?" Louko was starting to lose his patience and ability to think rationally.

Tyron seemed equally flustered. "Yes, I am both. I am the same for both. Don't you see?"

"I…I'm trying. I'll understand." Alarm bells were ringing as Louko noted the change in Tyron, which only made it harder for him to concentrate and remain calm himself.

"But you don't, do you?" Tyron's tone dropped to something menacing.

A chill ran down Louko's spine. "I never said I did. I said I would." He forced his tone to remain completely even and not betray the growing sense of dread.

It worked up until Tyron smiled, head tilting to one side. "Do either of you have any idea how much you repeat yourselves?" He chuckled. "And he calls *me* obsessive. At least I'm not as dense as his pupil."

Don't insult him, don't insult him. Louko had done *that* before…. Instead, he remained motionless, deciding against speaking to avoid angering the Dragon further.

"What? Are we playing dumb now as well?" Tyron's eyes narrowed.

"Just trying not to say something to wound your fragile ego," Louko bit back.

Tyron's narrowed gaze remained, now lit up by a grin. "Fragile, is it? Isn't that a tad ironic coming from you?" He stood up slowly.

"You're weaker than he is, whether you realize it or not, and I know he'll beat you." Louko forced the confidence to break through the fear, knowing he was being beyond stupid. But Tyron could fight this—he could beat the stupid Dragon. He had to, or else Louko knew he was going to die.

Before the words had even finished echoing in the little room, Louko found himself slammed up against the stone wall with Tyron's hand around his throat. No amount of preparation could help Louko swallow the panic—not that he *could* swallow; he couldn't even breathe. All the while, Tyron looked completely unaffected, regarding him calmly even as Louko gasped for air.

"No," he smiled. "I don't think he is going to beat me. I think he is going to watch you die. Him and that little redhead of yours. Tell me, do you love her?" He leaned in, insane, green eyes boring into Louko's. "Do you think she loves you? Or will she realize it after it's too late?"

Louko was going to pass out. At least, that's what he guessed by the black closing in around his vision.

"No...no, no, no...." With the way Louko's ears were ringing, it was hard to tell if Tyron was speaking or if he was just hearing things. But it kept coming. "No, no, NO!"

Tyron's grip released all at once, causing Louko to collapse on the book-strewn floor.

Coughing and sputtering as he rubbed his throat, Louko somehow eked out, "I think you...dropped...me on a book...and that hurt...."

Tyron was half-hunched against the opposite wall, hands tugging at his hair. He let out an unearthly scream that made Louko jump.

"I'm so sorry—I'm so sorry. Are you alright?" Tyron's jumbled words were as breathless as Louko felt.

Although he had opened his mouth with the intention of reassuring Tyron, he instead found himself letting loose another fit of coughing. How delightful. At last, he was able to clear his battered throat and wheezed out, "Just great." His neck felt numb; the kind of numb that hurt a lot.

"I'll go, I'll get out of here, I...." Tyron sputtered to a stop. "May I check to make sure I..." he winced. "To make sure I didn't cause damage?"

Louko managed a nod, sitting back against the wall and constantly trying to clear his throat, even if it only made it hurt more. That being said, on the bright side.... "Hey. You broke through." The words were barely understandable through the rasps.

Hesitantly, Tyron took a step forward. Then another. Then he knelt next to Louko. "Don't talk," he murmured. "Let me look first."

There was a faint, blue glow and then a nearly scratchy sensation all around Louko's neck.

"This may sting a moment."

Sure enough, the itching was replaced by a mild stinging. Then both faded and Tyron pulled back.

"There may still be some swelling, but no other damage," he whispered.

"See?" Louko wished he sounded more properly optimistic, but the bruised vocal cords rather dampened the effect. That being said, this really was a large step. Tyron had never come *back* once the Dragon took over.

Tyron's head fell into his hands. There was no reply.

Louko had to say something—do something. Tyron had won the fight...but if he collapsed now, then the Dragon could easily take over again. "I wouldn't say no to water, though," he whispered.

With a listless nod, Tyron vanished.

Wait. Why did Louko do that? He hadn't written a note; he wasn't going to remember! Sure enough, minutes slid by without a trace of Tyron. *Idiot. You should have—*

"Here," Tyron rematerialized, setting two cups down between them. One had steam rising from the top. "The tea should help your throat."

"Oh. That was, uh, fast," the prince replied as he gingerly took the hot cup of tea, breathing the sweet scent in with a hunger. He hadn't really had much besides the simplest of food and water for...well, however long he'd been in here. So long, that apparently his mouth had decided to water from the mere smell of the tea.

"Is there anything else that will help?" Tyron asked quietly.

Slowly taking a sip of his tea, Louko thought a moment before shaking his head. No. This was good tea. Louko had forgotten how much he liked tea.

Getting nearly killed had definitely been worth this.

"I will go." Tyron sounded so tired. "I will try to return in an hour to check on you. I..." His voice wavered. "I am so sorry."

Louko set down his tea and leaned forward, feeling the most hope he had in a while. "But Tyron, don't you see? This is a good step. You beat him this time."

Tyron stared at him, visibly horrified. "I...I *hurt* you."

"Yes! Exactly. The key word here is *hurt*. Not killed, hurt. Progress!" Louko gestured wildly with his hands to add emphasis, only for him to ponder his words and add hastily, "Okay that sounded better in my head, I'll admit...but still."

Now Tyron just looked ill. "I'll be back within an hour," he mumbled. He vanished before Louko could say anything more.

"What an idiot you are," Louko chided himself as he rubbed his neck, wincing at the memory more than any residual soreness. "Oh great and now you're taking to talking out loud to yourself...please don't tell me you're also going crazy." A nervous laugh escaped as Louko decided it would be best to keep his thoughts to himself in the future. Inside his head where it made him look less like he had also decided to emulate Tyron's insanity.

But of course, that resolution did not last very long, and in the lonely darkness, Louko began to lose track of what part of his thinking was happening out loud and what was in his head.

"Okay this is good...we learned some things, right?" Louko turned his attention to what had aroused the Dragon's anger. The chess game; Tyron had said *he* was the one playing it, not Astra. "But...what does he mean, she's both sides? I thought he already said he was. He was both kings." Both sides, both sides. What in the world did he mean, both sides? Wait. Both sides. Tyron said he was the king of both sides, but that Astra held the key to victory for either. Maybe he wasn't meaning Astra was the player of both sides, but was trying to remind Louko that she was a piece on both sides? They hadn't figured out her piece yet and—

"Oh. I am…an idiot." Of course. Louko ran his hands through his hair as he tried to will some way in Eatris he could get this information to Astra.

Tyron was the king on both sides…and Astra was the queen.

The *black* queen.

CHAPTER XVII

Astra:

Astra was aware of three things: the hard stone under her knees, the cold breeze tugging at her coat, and Mitheau's impatience emanating from a few feet to her left.

"Anything?"

Astra sighed, opening her eyes. "Nothing."

How was she supposed to 'feel' something when there was nothing here? Nothing but ruins, anyway. The nearly vacant barracks that ringed the hill were somewhat scattered in order to avoid the crumbling structures. But while there was evidence of buildings everywhere, time had erased all traces of the portal that had once stood on the hill, leaving only a wide stone slab. Her best guess was that it had once been the floor to some ancient structure.

Mitheau huffed in exasperation. "I should have made Grenedil tell me how he did it. He had some sort of relic that helped him, but surely there was a sense. I mean, can't it be like flying? You just have to sort of…take the leap and go for it? Gah!" The young Drogan threw up her hands.

"Where would I be leaping?" Astra asked dryly, getting to her feet and brushing herself off. Too many nights sleeping in Dannsair's stable was leaving her sore. It was still better than sitting in her bedroom and getting no sleep at all, she supposed.

"I don't know. That would be your part to figure out." Mitheau's grumbled response was hardly helpful.

Somewhere nearby, Astra heard her father sigh. "I do not think that is particularly useful advice," he chimed in. Astra turned to find him kneeling over the cracked stone floor of the ancient…thing they were standing in.

Astra felt frustration stir and swell. What kind of Guard was she? She couldn't find the stupid Doorway—much less use it. How was she supposed to keep a world safe when she couldn't even stop someone from taking her closest friend? As if responding to her emotions, she felt the red-bronze cuff around her wrist begin to ache.

"It's getting a bit dark…maybe it's best to return? I know this place is no Litash, but I still don't like staying in the middle of nowhere after dark." Destrin eyed their surroundings in the typical fashion of a Litashian—a fashion that Astra understood. Litash had rightfully earned its reputation for strange and dangerous creatures.

Astra let out a deep breath, looking around at the barren valley one last time. The deepening dusk and the accompanying chill told her that her father was right. "Alright," she conceded. "Hold still."

With a thought and a tug at the world around them, they appeared in their usual garden behind the Nythrilian palace.

"Now what?" Mitheau asked as she stretched, looking around the garden.

Destrin began to head for the nearest entrance inside as he said, "Now we get some dinner, I think."

Astra followed, wondering as usual if Louko was given any food.

Into the palace halls, they walked. While there were always people bustling through the corridors since the war had broken out, the place was somehow quieter than Astra recalled it being. As if everyone was holding their breath.

"Princess Astra?"

The voice startled her from her thoughts. Astra stopped in her tracks and turned to see a servant rushing towards them. The man paused, bowing hastily.

"The Ezai Ru has been looking for you," he said, glancing from her to her father to Mitheau. "It is quite urgent."

Urgent? "Where is he?" Astra asked.

"The throne room."

Without pause, Astra pulled again at the space around them, whisking Mitheau and her father with her into the Nythrilian throne room.

"There you are," Ven's voice was dead calm, as dead as his face was pale. "I just received a message from Commander Jahng. It is not regarding Louko, so you needn't worry there." But there was something in his tone, and the way he was looking her in the eyes as if to try and console her made Astra's throat tighten. "Keeshiff has been mortally wounded. The letter is dated two days ago. She said then that the doctors didn't know how much longer he would hold on. She also said one of his men is also wounded and faring poorly."

Astra stood there, numb. She felt strangely detached, as if she had somehow pulled herself away again and yet forgotten to bring her senses with her. *Two days ago.* Was...was Keeshiff...dead?

"I will be back by morning," she heard herself say.

Whatever interjection her father was about to make was cut off as the ornate palace dissipated around her.

Astra's feet hit soft ground as a blast of cold wind hit her face. The setting sun outlined rows upon rows of canvas tents. For a split second, she wasn't sure which side of the front she'd landed on. Then her eyes adjusted enough for her to make out the flags of jade and green that confirmed she was in the right place.

"You—" Astra called to one of the guards, skidding down the short hillside towards the perimeter of the camp. "Commander Jahng. Where is she?"

The soldier looked confused, clearly not having seen Astra appear from nowhere and also not recognizing her. "The same place she's been for the last two days"

"Take me there."

"I can inform her you are looking for her, but I will not be letting anyone into this camp without authorization," the soldier replied, straightening his shoulders even as he looked uncomfortable.

The guard next to him nudged his companion. "Wait, I think this is the Litashian—the one the Commander sent for," he whispered.

"Wait, how is she here already—" The two soldiers exchanged looks before seeming to have something occur to them.

The first replied with, "I will inform the Commander," and quickly disappeared into the sea of tents.

Urgency growing with each delayed second, Astra looked at the remaining guard. "Just tell me where she is. There is no time to waste."

"The command tent. It's in the center of camp. The one with the red trim," the soldier answered, seeming to now understand the situation.

"Thank you." Astra was gone before she'd finished the words.

Astra transported twice before she found herself in the dead center of the camp, facing the red-trimmed tent. The slack-jawed guards didn't even stop her as she strode in.

"Wait, stop—"

"What's going—Astra!" Jahng had turned around from the table she was standing at, eyes wide along with every other officer in the tent.

Astra ignored them. "We received your note. Is Keeshiff still alive?"

A deathly quiet hung over the room, Jahng's already sleepless face looking somehow even more drained.

Oh no. No, no, no—

"Astra…" Her voice was hoarse as she whispered, "He's…he's dead."

Astra heard what Jahng said. Logically, she knew what each word meant. But somehow her mind could not put them together. She stood there, completely numb, unable to register anything besides the ringing in her ears. The strange detachment made it feel like she was watching herself when she finally replied, "I want to see him."

"I—" Jahng choked up, turning to the officers. "Will you give us a moment?"

The men nodded and left without a word. Astra had just enough feeling in her legs to step out of their way.

A single tear welled in Jahng's otherwise fierce eyes. "He looks very different now, Astra. I rather wish I hadn't seen him."

"I need to see him," Astra rasped.

"Alright. Come with me," Jahng's reply was quiet as she slowly moved from her spot to lead the way out of the tent. As they walked through the camp, Astra now noticed the eerie quiet that hung over the entire camp.

327

Everyone watched Jahng and her, stopping what they were doing and just giving knowing glances. No one said a word.

At last, they came to a tent where Gavin and Coryn stood guard, red-rimmed eyes accentuated by the dark circles under them. They were both in much more formal attire than Astra had ever seen them in—attire that she recalled seeing from the royal guards at Melye. Only in the back of her mind did Astra have enough wherewithal to wonder how they'd acquired the uniforms. The rest of her still didn't believe this was actually happening.

"She wants to see him," Jahng's tone held a gentleness Astra had never dreamed of hearing from the commander, and it only made the whole nightmare feel that much more surreal.

Both Gavin and Coryn stared at Astra, the former choking as he said, "I'm sorry…we couldn't keep him safe."

"Neither could I," was all Astra could muster in reply.

Whether in grief or in guilt, both knights bowed their heads as they pulled open the tent flap to allow Astra through. She half registered Jahng murmuring something about staying outside as Astra stepped forward.

The first thing she noticed inside the tent was Asher, sitting on a stool with his shoulders drooped. When he raised his head, his reddened, ringed eyes matched the two knights outside. Unlike them, tears had traced paths down his cheeks. He said nothing, getting to his feet and stepping back as if to give Astra space.

And then she saw him: Keeshiff. Astra had seen death enough times to know what it looked like in the face of a friend. She knew the way it took one's features and set them still, the way it took everything that made the person familiar and left only a shadow. The man before her looked more like some painting or statue—a likeness of Keeshiff instead of Keeshiff himself.

They had laid him on a cot, arms folded over the sheathed sword on his chest. He was dressed head-to-toe in Merimeethian regalia, wearing even a buckled cape around his shoulders and a crown-like band atop his neatly combed hair. His eyes and mouth were closed in an almost peaceful expression.

Her footsteps seemed loud as Astra approached the cot and slowly knelt beside it. Instinctually, she slid off her red-bronze cuff and laid one hand over Keeshiff's. The same steady hands that had once carried her to safety were now stiff and cold. But she pulled at her Gifting anyway, sending it through her palm and willing it to search out any spark that might be there. It felt nothing like that time when she'd healed Louko. Then, she could feel every bit of life and vitality that coursed through his veins. Now, there was nothing. No life rose up to meet hers.

Keeshiff was gone.

Astra pulled her hand away, drawing a ragged breath. The numbness that had overtaken her earlier now evaporated and left her acutely aware of the crushing pressure against her chest. Her eyes welled until tears spilled over and she could barely see.

A gentle hand found itself on Astra's shoulder as Asher came up behind her. "Astra I...I am s-so sorry." Never before had she heard the man so torn up—so lost for words and unable to get through a sentence. "We should never...n-never have encouraged him to go. He-he didn't want to tell you. He knew you might not approve and he thought—" There was a shaky breath. "We thought it was the right move."

The right move. Was this...was this part of that stupid Game? Had Keeshiff died for a *Game?* Astra looked up at Asher, voice thick and gravelly as she demanded, "Who did this to him?"

"It was...an accident," Asher croaked. "Keeshiff was meeting with Killyan at night—to try and see if he could convince the Merimeethian army to switch sides...someone—someone informed the Merimeethians and Keeshiff and Killyan were ambushed. They even had a counter ambush to...the Nythrilian back up. The Merimeethians had only meant to capture Keeshiff, for when he—when he f-fell..." Asher took a moment, trying to keep the tears in check so he could finish the story. "When he was wounded, they all stopped. They actually...helped get him and Rufio back t-to camp. But it was...too late."

If Astra had come when she had found the spy on the chessboards, if she had warned him or somehow intervened, could she have prevented this? Would Keeshiff still be alive? A new, worse thought nearly shattered her all over again: What was this going to do to Louko? They had only just gotten the chance to be actual brothers—to be a family. And now it had been ripped away. Keeshiff wasn't even able to have the peace of knowing whether or not Louko was safe.

"Rufio...R-Rufio still hangs by a thread. I..." Asher's tone trembled. "I can't do anything and I don't know what you've been told. I just know...if anyone could help him, perhaps...."

Astra did not want to leave Keeshiff. Not yet. But she knew he was already gone. She could not save him, but there was a chance she could save one of the people he cared about. Slowly, with one last look at the friend she'd considered as her own brother, Astra pushed herself to her feet and turned away. She wiped her face with one sleeve as she said, "Show me."

It was hard to leave the tent—to leave Keeshiff behind. Astra kept reminding herself he wasn't there to leave, and yet that only made it feel worse.

Jahng was still outside, her expression unreadable.

"Commander. We...we need to show Astra to the other wounded knight, please. She might be able to help." Asher sounded as if he squeezed the words out with great effort.

From behind her, Astra heard Gavin and Coryn stiffen.

Turning to Astra, Jahng gave a curt nod and said, "Alright. Follow me," as she led the way once more.

The medical tent wasn't far, meaning the tent for Keeshiff had likely been pitched soon after his death. Astra didn't want to think about it. Instead, she tried to think ahead. Her father had warned her never to heal again after she'd told him of the time she'd healed Louko. He'd told her that it could cause more damage than help if she lost focus or mended something incorrectly. But even if she couldn't heal Rufio, she could fetch someone from Cithan who could.

The two Nythrilian guards that stood watch at this tent let them in without a word. Astra spotted Rufio almost immediately, lying motionless on a cot with his chest and most of his arm wrapped in bandaging. But there were no physicians around his bed. Astra could already hear why—

the horrible, scraping sound of his breathing that meant he was already dying. Rufio was out of time.

Panic washed over Astra in a wave. Did she have time to go for help? What if her uncle refused to treat a Human he didn't know? Wait…what if he wasn't even there? They'd put forth the idea of him going most of the way to Silbyr with Ent in case the heist went wrong. What day was that planned for? Today? Yesterday? Her uncle could be anywhere from Cithan to Silbyr.

But Rufio was too close to death for her to risk healing him out of ignorance. She remembered her father's warning all too well. "I will return in a few minutes," she told Asher in a rush. "Do not let them move him."

As soon as Asher nodded, Astra summoned up the mental image of Cithan and pulled herself away.

Astra appeared in the streets of the citadel, directly in front of her uncle's house. It was late enough into the evening that both moons were out but no Elves were, but Astra spared no thought for those who might be sleeping when she started pounding on her uncle's door. "Uncle? Are you here? Please—I need your help!"

The door opened much quicker than expected to reveal Tallaman, still clothed and looking with wide-eyed confusion. "*Astra?* What in the blazes—"

"—Please, Uncle, there's no time." Astra cut him off, breathless. "A friend is dying. I don't know what to do."

"Where?" Tallaman breathed.

"Nythril. I can take you."

"Alright," he said as he quickly came into the lamp-lit streets of Cithan, his tall figure casting an even taller shadow over Astra.

Astra needed no other prompting. She whisked them both back to the medical tent in Nythril, startling everyone in it as she did so.

"This is my uncle," she explained as quickly as she could. "He's here to help."

Tallaman pushed by the few in his way and knelt beside Rufio, putting a hand to the knight's chest and closing his eyes in concentration. The rasping coming from Rufio turned to gurgling. The awful sound made Astra feel like she was going to be sick.

Astra could feel the hum of Gifting emanating from her uncle and Rufio's body began to twitch, eyes opening unnaturally as they rolled back. Her uncle muttered something under his breath, bringing his other hand up and shifting his position.

Minutes passed, and Tallaman did nothing except mutter about Humans. After what had to be nearly half an hour, the crowd that had gathered waned a little bit, those besides Asher, Jahng, and one of the physicians, going back to whatever they'd been doing before.

Astra had not witnessed a healing since The War. Even then, she'd been the patient more often than the spectator. She'd forgotten the difficulty involved for both parties. The occasional growls or huffs from her uncle were hardly comforting, and no matter how long this went on, neither were the unnatural sounds from Rufio. Every minute, Astra was sure he would stop breathing altogether. It was as if they were watching two wills at work; nature trying to claim what rightfully should be dead and the Elf trying to stop it.

The gurgling ceased. Not a living soul in the tent moved as the noise that had plagued the place for over an hour suddenly vanished.

Desperate, Astra watched for the rise and fall of Rufio's chest. At first, nothing. Then, almost imperceptibly, it moved, an unsteady, quiet breath escaping Rufio. And then again and again. Not the last breath of death's kiss, but one of life.

Tallaman let out a sigh. "I think the healing has…taken," he said, words coming out in labored breaths. He tried to get up, using Rufio's cot for support, but failed, stumbling and remaining instead on his knees. Astra instinctively moved forward to help.

"Stupid Humans," he mumbled, blinking rapidly. He did not, however, shy away from Astra's aid, allowing her to help him up. "I could not…completely heal him. But he should be in a state that will…recover now. When he…first wakes he will be in a great…deal of pain."

Asher was now at Rufio's bedside, checking the knight over with widened eyes. "Alright, yes, thank you." His voice was thick with sincerity when he looked up at Tallaman. "Thank you," he repeated.

Tallaman said something unintelligible as he waved his hand. The healing process had clearly been quite difficult—Astra had never seen her uncle so drained after using Gifting on someone.

"Are you alright?" She kept her question low. "Do you need to sit down?"

"I need to go home…and sleep this off," he grumbled.

A twinge of guilt rose to the top of Astra's already knotted emotions. "I'll be back to help sort everything out," she told Jahng.

Lips pressed into a thin line, the commander gave a bow of her head.

"Hold on," Astra told her uncle.

After she was certain he was steady, she bent the world around them once more until they were back in the streets of Cithan. Then she helped him up the steps to his door and opened it for him.

"I-I'm sorry it took so much," she found herself murmuring. "I didn't know who else to go to. I…." *Keeshiff was dead.* The reminder took her breath away. Rufio was saved, but Keeshiff could not be.

"Don't mention it. Ever," Tallaman replied as he stumbled through the doorway, using the wall inside to steady himself. "Just don't make me have to do it again."

Astra didn't know if her uncle had meant it that way, but his words struck her square in the chest: *Don't make me.* Was she responsible for all this? Was her role in Tyron's Game what had brought all of this about? And now she was using her own family to try and fix it all. Try as she might, Astra could not stop the tears that streamed down her face as she bit back the threatening sob and managed a nod to acknowledge her uncle.

"Oh, uh, Astra he'll be fine, I…uh…" Tallaman's stuttering now seemed more awkward than exhausted and he put a hand on her shoulder. "You came to me just in…in time."

Astra had to press her hands over her mouth just to keep herself quiet. It took her several seconds to regather herself even enough to shake her head. "I-I didn't. I was too late for Keeshiff." The words were all half-stuck in her throat. "The prince—Louko's brother—he…he's…." The sickening truth nearly left her doubled over.

Tallaman's eyes widened, "Wait. He's…the prince is *dead?*"

The sob that Astra had tried so hard to suppress now broke free. She could barely even cover her face as she wept.

"Oh, Astra—" Suddenly, Astra was pulling into an unexpectedly tight hug, brought close to her uncle in an embrace she never could have expected. She sobbed into his shirt as she leaned into him.

"Sometimes…sometimes we're too late for the ones we need most," he whispered. "I don't know why…no one does." He squeezed harder. "When someone's time has come, there's nothing we can do about it— not even Elves. I'm sorry our blood has made that harder to accept."

Astra could barely speak through the tightness in her throat. "It-it's so wrong," she cried. "It sh-shouldn't have been him. He isn't…he wasn't even Ent's age. He never even g-got to go home."

"He is home now, Astra," his voice was barely audible. "I know it's hard to accept. But he doesn't need you anymore, Astra. He's free now— you have to let him go."

"But I need him." Astra was nearly begging. "Louko needs him. How can I let go?"

"I don't know," The words came out with a shuddering breath. "But every day, learn to need him less. Don't forget him…but you can't live in the world of the dead, Astra."

For what might have been seconds or eternity, Astra poured out her grief. She was helpless against its tide as it swept over her. Only when the first waves had passed and left her empty did she have enough strength to step back.

"Why?" The broken question had echoed in her mind since the first day she had seen war and its toll. "Why does death take those who least deserve it? This was all because of me—it should have been me. Why was it him?"

Tallaman let out a long sigh, putting both hands on her shoulders and looking her right in the eye. "Because the living need you too much. Your brother needs you too much, your parents certainly need you, this Louko needs you…and I need you. I need you to stay here. Please." Never had Astra seen such earnestness in all her uncle's features. It far outweighed the exhaustion—the years of bitterness he'd built up to protect himself.

It took all of Astra's crumbling will to keep from bursting into tears all over again. She forced herself to swallow and scrape out a hoarse, "Thank you, Uncle. For all of it."

Clearing his throat, Tallaman let go of her shoulders and used the wall to support himself. He quickly broke eye contact. "Well, yes, uh, anytime." He coughed.

The ache in her chest and the exhaustion that pressed down on her shoulders returned in full force. "Is there anything you need?" Astra asked now, feeling guilty once more for dragging him out in the middle of the night without warning. "Or any way I can help?"

"Just sleep and…for you to be careful, please. With yourself." He again made eye contact, though the exhaustion had once more taken over his expression.

Astra did not have it in her to make any promises. "I will try."

"Thank you…if you need anything, just please let me know—let Ent know."

Ent…she was going to have to tell Ent…. Astra had just enough presence of mind to decide that it could wait until morning. For now, she needed to return to the front and help figure out what they were going to do now. "I will try," she said again, wiping her face in an attempt to dry it. She stepped out the door only to hesitate. "I hope you know that you can do the same."

He gave a weak smile. "Of course. Now go back to your friends. *They* need you. And…I need sleep."

Astra dipped her head. "Yes, sorry, goodnight, Uncle. I love you."

"I—uh—I love you, too, Astra. Please be careful." Her uncle sputtered out the words like a lost puppy.

With one last nod, Astra steadied herself, took a deep breath, and transported herself back to Nythril.

"Astra!" Asher's voice made Astra jump. The physician was still at Rufio's side, but he looked nearly panicked.

"Asher, wh—"

"Hurry, you're just in time: Rhumir is trying to kill Mariah."

CHAPTER XVIII

Mariah:

Mariah had done everything she could to remain as normal on the outside as possible. She had continued to eat the rations given to her and had kept herself clean and neat so as to not draw attention to herself.

But the truth remained. Keeshiff was dead. Keeshiff was dead, and if Mariah had acted differently…if she had never allowed Kaeden—Tyron—to use her, then maybe he would have listened to her. Maybe he would still be alright.

Mariah almost wished she *was* this spy they were looking for, as she felt just as responsible as if she was.

Don't cry. She chided herself, taking a shuddering breath from where she sat motionless on the stool in her tent of a prison. *Breathe. In and out. You aren't the one who deserves to mourn.* No. Not after what she'd done. Not after what she'd let happen to Astra.

Voices outside the tent drew her attention.

"I think you have the wrong tent." It was one of the Nythrilian guards. "She's already been given her evening rations."

"I'm not here to give her food." This voice was familiar, and had a Merimeethian accent, but Mariah couldn't tell who it was. The flickering torchlight outside her tent reduced the person to a dark silhouette. "She's the sister of the Merimeethian who died. I'm supposed to give her his effects."

Mariah stiffened. She was the last person who should be getting Keeshiff's personal items. What was this?

"With all due respect, sir, I am under strict orders not to allow anyone in who is not Djoa with rations or Commander Jahng herself," the guard replied.

There was a pause and a frustrated huff. "Fine. If I give you his things, can you just give them to her?"

"Yes, of course."

This wasn't right. Mariah clenched her fists against her dress.

She heard a shuffle of footsteps and watched the two silhouettes trade something off. The guard, shape evident by the helmet he wore, turned around and a hand started to pull at the opening of her tent. But then Mariah saw the outline of the stranger raise something over his head. Before she could cry out to warn the guard, the stranger brought it down over the guard's helmet with a loud crack. The guard yelped and fell sideways.

Eyes widening, Mariah quickly stood up and backed away as close as she could to the back of the tent, unsure what was going on and half of her petrified it was the spy from Tyron, come to force her back to Melye. The stranger charged through the opening of the tent.

Suddenly, Mariah found it difficult to breathe. She opened her mouth to call for the guards, and yet nothing came out. In the back of her mind, she knew no one would really care except for the fact that if this was the spy, this was the chance to catch them. But her throat felt thick and closed from the hours of repressed tears.

"*You.*" The growl was almost indiscernible. The lack of light in the tent meant Mariah still couldn't see the man's face. But the torchlight outside was enough to make his dagger glint as he held it up.

"D-don't you come near me!" Mariah finally found her voice, disgusted at how weak it sounded. Stupid and weak.

"Or what?" The man scoffed. "You'll do what you did to Keeshiff? Or to my brother? You don't have anyone to do your dirty work, this time."

Wait. This wasn't a spy. This had to be a knight, come for revenge. "I-I—" Words failed as she could come up with nothing. Nothing to save her sorry hide and nothing to try and convince them there was a different spy in camp. No one believed her, and she didn't blame them.

An unexpected shout came from outside the tent, soon joined by a chorus of voices and footsteps. The man twisted around to look back towards the tent entrance. Then he turned back with a snarl, lunging towards her.

Instinct drove her hands up to protect herself, and a sharp, unfamiliar pain greeted her efforts. Alarm bells went off in her head, and Mariah let out a cry, half of her wondering why she'd done so. The other half registered the blood now dripping from her hand as she tore away from her attacker, feeling suddenly dizzy as she frantically dove to the side.

The shouting all around her grew louder as she tried to drag herself further away. The sound and the dim lighting left her too disoriented to even tell which way her assailant was. Then a pair of boots stepped right in front her. All she could do was wrap her hands over her head.

"Grab him! Hold him down!" A voice boomed from directly above her.

She didn't move, only thinking what a coward she looked huddled on the floor, waiting for the knife to sink its icy teeth in her and end her miserable existence.

Why are you such a drama queen? Get over yourself.

There was scuffling and grunting and, "Let go of me!" from the other end of the tent.

"Get her up and check her over," the deep voice ordered. "But tie up the rascal before he hurts himself."

"I'm fine, I'm f-fine," Mariah dropped her hands to hoist herself from the ground and was rewarded by a splitting pain racing from her right hand up to her arm. She let out another sob, instantly hating herself for it and yet unable to stop from doing it.

A pair of strong hands grabbed her by the arms and practically dragged her to her feet. "She's bleeding, sir. Somewhere from her hand or forearm, I think."

"My…stupid—AH!—hand," Mariah groaned as she struggled to stand. She didn't want to look at it, worried the sight of whatever had happened to her hand would only make her faint and look that much more pathetic. Funny how she'd spent so much time acting the part of fragile princess to slow down Keeshiff all that time ago, that she had never stopped to think maybe she was just that.

"What's going on here?" Mariah recognized the stern voice as Commander Jahng's.

The captain who had been giving orders now held open the tent entrance and waved one hand. "Everyone out of the tent. Line them up for the commander."

Mariah began to walk forward in an attempt to obey, hand going to her pounding head. *Gah! Stop using that hand you imbecile!* She somehow managed to keep the scream inside as she pulled the wet, bleeding hand away from her head.

"Not so fast—you stay with me." Whoever it was that had pulled her up had not let go of her other arm. The soldier leveraged it to half guide, half push her out of the tent and into the torch-lit circle where the prisoners' tents were.

What had happened again? What was going on? Mariah was finding it difficult to remember. Her hand hurt...she was bleeding...but now her head hurt too from the throbbing of adrenaline. Was the wet only from her bloodied hand? Had the assailant actually landed a second blow? Was she...dying?

Would serve you right.

"Let me *go!*" Her attacker was brought out behind her, struggling wildly between the two soldiers who held his bound arms.

"This man knocked over one of the guards stationed here and forced his way into the tent," the captain reported, ignoring the protests of his newest captive. "He attacked the prisoner with a knife, clearly intending to kill her."

Jahng's stony gaze flicked towards the assailant and her eyes narrowed.

Mariah swayed, beginning to wonder how much it would hurt to just...fall on the ground. It couldn't be *that* bad, could it?

Then a smaller figure stepped up alongside the commander. "Jahng, she's bleeding."

Yes, yes, she was. Mariah was beginning to think maybe she'd get to apologize to Keeshiff face-to-face, soon. Not that she'd be going to the same place he would. *Would you quit being dramatic? It's just your hand.* Was it? Right. She was pretty sure…maybe?

Now Jahng was staring right at her. "Take her to the infirmary. Get her patched up and keep her there. I will take her testimony myself when I'm done with this miscreant." Jahng turned back to the attacker. "Fetch me the knight, Lucian—or whoever those Merimeethians have put in charge of themselves."

Several soldiers bowed and scurried off, including the one still gripping Mariah's arm. She stumbled along next to him as she tried not to end up face first on the ground.

"Careful with her." The smaller figure that had addressed Jahng now caught up to them. "She is in shock. We don't need to add a fall to her list of injuries."

Were they talking about her? Mariah couldn't tell. She felt someone else take up her other arm as if trying to steady her.

Down through the rows of torches and tents they went, finally stopping at one of the larger structures. More muffled voices and dizzying lights before someone pushed down on her shoulders and she found herself in a seat with a blanket draped around her shoulders.

Someone washed the side of her face and she barely registered someone going, "She's not hurt here. Just some blood. Must have touched her face."

That apparently had been the easy part, however, and Mariah attempted with little success to keep herself together as someone looked over her hand. If not for the strange, faraway feeling she might have jumped from the seat when he applied some form of salve to it. Then came the stabbing and she squeaked as she registered a needle being used to sew her back together.

She was going to puke.

Yes, you would do that wouldn't you, you little brat? How do you think Keeshiff felt when he was dying, hm? Just breathe, no one is worried, clearly. She tried to keep her breathing regulated, but it was difficult when the constant jab of pain surprised her every other moment. Tears welled in her eyes, but mostly from the thought of how much pain Keeshiff had to have been in if this is what a mere scratch on the hand felt like.

"Could someone get her some water?" The soft, scratchy voice came from beside her. It was quieter when it added, "Don't look, Mariah. Looking makes it worse."

Right, of course. Mariah wanted to do nothing more than squeeze her eyes shut, but instead she forced herself to look straight forward. Her vision was more in focus now, and soon the people around her were more than just shapes. But she'd been able to see her hand so clearly...was she just that bad at noticing the others around her? She turned again to look at the person caring for her hand and jolted away in horror as she realized it was Astra.

Astra jumped back as if startled. "Woah, woah, it's alright—you're almost done." She reached for her hand.

"What are you *doing?*" Mariah asked as she kept her throbbing hand to her chest. What was Astra doing here? Why was she *helping* her? Mariah had seen the scars—she'd figured out how badly Tyron had hurt her. How Mariah had been the only reason it had happened. "I'm fine it's just a sc-scratch." *Oh nice, added that wince in just to show how pathetic you are? Really convincing.*

"You took a slice to the hand." Astra's tone was slower and deeper as if trying to calm Mariah down. "There are a lot of interwoven muscles in there. If the wound is not stitched and treated properly, it could limit how much you will be able to use that hand in future."

Shaking, Mariah slowly returned her hand, wishing she'd had the strength to refuse. To be strong and tell Astra to leave. But instead she allowed Astra to finish, desperately trying to keep from showing how much the stitches hurt, to stop from showing how pathetic she really was.

"There. Done." Astra cut the last bit of thread. She measured out a length of bandaging and began to wrap Mariah's hand with well-practiced motions. "They will likely not have much bandaging to spare. See if they will give you a second piece so that you can alternate between the two and wash whichever is not in use. Try to keep your hand dry and use it as little as possible."

"Alright," Mariah whispered, eyes averted to the ground. She thought of the knight who'd given her the wound—so distraught over the death of Keeshiff.

Footsteps made her flinch and Mariah's first thought was that the knight had escaped and come back for her, but when the tent flap opened, it was Jahng who stepped in. Her steely eyes went from Mariah to Astra.

"How is she?"

"She's alright," Astra replied. "A few stitches in her right hand and still working through the shock, but she got lucky. What of Rhumir?" Mariah noted now the red-rimmed eyes of the half-elf.

Jahng grunted. "That idiot almost got himself killed. Lucian has agreed to leave him in our custody for now. In the meantime, we explained how we've vetted Mariah and that his brother will live. He calmed down after that."

"His brother?" Mariah asked weakly, knowing she shouldn't be talking even though she couldn't help but ask. Had someone survived, at least? She'd worried for what other casualties might have been with Keeshiff, and yet even good news was bittersweet. One had survived, but not Keeshiff.

Astra's shoulders dropped only slightly, but it made her look very tired. "Rufio," she murmured. "He was wounded. But he'll be alright."

Mariah was about to say something undoubtedly stupid when she was suddenly distracted by the bag Jahng was holding. It...it wiggled. Blinking rapidly numerous times, she dared not ask and yet couldn't stop from staring. Was she hallucinating, now?

"What is in the sack?" Astra's furrowed brow nearly made Mariah sigh in relief.

Jahng, if possible, looked even more irritated. "Apparently, Rhumir handed it to the guard and said it was for Mariah as a distraction. It's that stupid rubii that always followed K-Keeshiff around." She scowled at the wriggling bag. "I tried to take it out, but the thing nearly bit me."

Mariah remembered the stupid creature and how it had constantly escaped even from her. "I...I can take care of it...if you need it off your hands."

The bag let out a series of sad chirps.

"By all means, take it." Jahng stepped forward, holding out the bag. "It has no place in a camp."

Mariah reached out with her good hand to take it.

Astra cut her off. "Wait," she interrupted. "Let me see if I can calm it down first."

Recoiling quickly, Mariah caught something strange in Astra's tone.

Judging by the confusion on Jahng's face, Mariah wasn't the only one. The commander hesitated, shrugged, and handed the bag to Astra.

Strangely, Astra took it and retreated several steps. She glanced around the large tent as if eyeing the few occupants at the other end.

"It's probably just scared from being tossed around," Astra said almost too casually. But her gaze kept moving back and forth from Jahng's eyes to the sword buckled at the commander's side.

Why in the world was Astra telling Jahng to be on guard for...a rubii? What was she missing? Mariah's eyes darted from Astra to Jahng and back again, desperately trying to figure out what was going on.

Astra undid the tie around the mouth of the sack and reached in. There was a series of high-pitched trills and nearly frantic squirming before Astra lifted the little furball out and let the bag fall to the ground. "There," she continued in that strange voice. "That's not so bad, is it?"

Jahng still had a hand on the pommel of her sword, but Mariah couldn't figure out the threat.

"Here, hold on." Astra tucked the rubii under one arm and reached down to grab the sack. Just when she was about to pick it up, she suddenly shoved the rubii to the ground and used her free hand to slide her copper bracelet over one of its scrawny legs. Before the shifter had even returned to Human form, Astra had a foot on their chest and a knife at their throat.

"Who are you?" The question was like a snarl.

Eyes wide, Mariah stared in disbelief at the *Human* form in front of them.

The spy.

"I have nothing to say to you, half-breed!" The woman shifter spat.

"Jahng, get me four guards and a pair of red-bronze shackles," Astra said, eyes never leaving the Bandilarian. "Quickly."

The commander had left almost before Astra was finished with her instructions, and it was mere seconds before she'd returned with reinforcements. "The shackles will be here shortly," she announced grimly.

Mariah did not move, watching breathlessly as Astra kept her dagger pressed against the shifter's skin. Not until another soldier jogged in with the shackles and clapped them around the shifter's wrists did Mariah breathe in and Astra warily step back. The guards hauled the woman shape-shifter to her feet.

"You know, watching you all argue like idiots was getting too entertaining for my own good," the shape-shifter said as she spat into the dirt. "I suppose no good thing lasts forever."

Astra acted as if she hadn't even heard the jab, instead looking to Jahng. "Do you have anywhere we can take her for a private conversation?"

"Yes. I think we still have a prisoner's tent that is still unoccupied," Jahng replied, looking dazed by the turn of events.

"Perfect. Then let's go." Astra paused, glancing towards Mariah. "Stay here. If anyone asks, you're still waiting for the commander to take your testimony."

Her what? Mariah blinked, still in disbelief over what had just happened. The spy had been…the rubii? All along?

Without another word, Astra followed the rest out of the tent and left Mariah alone with her questions.

CHAPTER XIX

<u>Entrais:</u>

"I knew you weren't really the king," the butler grumbled under his breath as he poured the tea, spilling half of it in the saucer as he did so.

Ent hated tea. Why did everyone think soaking a dead leaf in water was somehow delicious?

"I am not currently the king, so yes, of course, you are correct," Ent at last replied with forced patience as he resisted the urge to pace in the kitchen. He was just sitting here, idling like some peacock as if he didn't have the Miadoris in his pocket; as if he hadn't just stolen it and split up with his accomplice.

The butler turned and set the kettle on a stand with a loud clunk. "Well, *Your Highness*, I hope you don't expect palace service. Lady Therune works well into the evening most days, so you're in for a long wait."

"Oh, don't worry, I was expecting no such thing. Especially from you, good sir." Ent might have been amused if he hadn't been trying to control the tightness in his chest. His hand went to inside his coat, where the small box that held the Miadoris still resided. He'd never wanted to lay eyes on this accursed thing again, and yet here he was stealing it.

A knock at the door jolted his pulse into double time.

"Two visitors?" The butler was already heading for the door. "Lady Therune is not going to be happy."

Ent immediately stiffened. Would Tirzah have knocked? They hadn't exactly had time to plan *how* they would meet at her house, only that they

351

would. It took Ent mere seconds to decide on three exit plans, two of which he had already half formed the moment the begrudging butler had showed him into the room. The third of which was probably the worst of the three, but there was no harm in being over prepared, right?

As soon as the butler was out of sight, Ent crossed silently to the hallway and listened as the front door creaked open.

"What do you want?" The butler's irritation was somewhat muffled by the distance.

"A day off, but that's not happening." Ent immediately recognized that voice. "I would settle for a visit with Lady Therune, though. Any chance she's home?"

Not bothering to wait, Ent quickly exited the room and made his way to the hall. "Ascriot! Come in!" He called out, if only to make sure the butler couldn't deny the Ethian entrance.

Ascriot appeared within seconds, followed by the butler—who, if it was possible, seemed even more disgruntled than before.

"Is that tea I smell?" The Ethian was as nonchalant as ever.

Ent let out a nervous chuckle. "Yes, please help yourself to the soggy leaves." He motioned for Ascriot to follow him back into the sitting room. "No one has caught Tirzah, have they?" He had assumed Ascriot wouldn't have asked for her had they taken her into custody. "Does anyone suspect her?"

Ascriot picked up the kettle and rummaged through the cabinet for a cup. The butler, mouth half open, stood and watched. Then he turned and walked out, muttering something along the lines of "I'm not paid to put up with this."

Spooning sugar into his tea, Ascriot shrugged. "Does he work here? My bad. With manners like those, I thought he was a burglar." He stirred the tea and turned towards Ent, scanning him quickly. "So far, no one has an inkling Tirzah helped. They all think it's some rogue Bandilarian. I'm not on any of the teams, but I did hear reports of a small, silver dragon.'

Somehow that did little to ease Ent's tension. What if she was caught? Did red-bronze impact Drogans shifting? Most likely not...but what would happen when they couldn't force her out of her dragon form?

"So what happened to the 'leave the city instantly' plan? You did get it, right?" Ascriot sipped at his tea and made a face.

Don't grab it, don't grab it. Ent forced himself not to reach for the box once again, instead giving a sharp nod.

A brief flash of seriousness crossed Ascriot's expression. "You're not wounded, are you?"

"What? No, I'm fine," he replied, shoving his hands in his outer coat pockets if only to avoid the paranoid need to check on the Miadoris every two seconds. Where was Tirzah?

Ascriot's former casual air returned. "Just checking. I presume we're going to the backup plan where you take her carriage to the gate?" He leaned to the side and poured out his tea in the fireplace.

"Yes. Just waiting for Tirzah." Or proof she wasn't coming. Or signs she'd betrayed them...but if she had already come through on her promise of masquerading as a dragon to pull their pursuers off the scent, Ent doubted that betrayal was likely to happen at this point.

Which only puzzled him more. Maybe she was waiting until they were both safe so she could make off with the Miadoris? That had to be it.

"Any idea on the timeline?" Ascriot set the tea kettle back over the fire and started rummaging through the tea cupboard. "I have to make sure the right guards are at the gate when you go through."

"I do not have a window. Tirzah did not deign to provide me with one," Ent said with a sigh. "But she's come through so far."

Ascriot paused, a tea box in hand. "Wait—the Miadoris is with her?"

"No. I'm not an idiot. But if she really is helping us now, then she's got a well of information on Tyron and is worth waiting around for." Ent's fists clenched from their place in his pockets.

"Maybe so, but the Miadoris is worth more than any information." Ascriot began measuring tea into the steaming kettle. "It's just past dark. If she isn't back by an hour before dawn, you should go and leave the cleanup to us."

Ent let out a pent-up breath. "Alright."

"I'm glad at least someone had a plan if I didn't make it back."

Ent did not think, only reacted to the alarm bell that went off at the sound of an unfamiliar voice, instantly taking hold of the small knife in the left pocket and throwing it at the intruder by the doorway—intending to pin them to the wall. But they were fast, sidestepping as the knife buried itself in the carved door frame.

A clucking sound came from behind Ent, followed by Ascriot's remark, "Oh, what a shame. That looks like real dritus wood."

Eyebrow raised, Tirzah replied, "It is."

Ent forced slow, steady breaths, squaring his shoulders and calmly saying, "Good. You made it."

Tirzah paused, then tugged the knife free of the wall and held it out handle first. "Had to wait until dark to get back into the city."

"I see," was all Ent managed as he gave a quick look up and down to make sure she was unharmed before taking the knife. "Well, it seems we won't be needing to wait then, Ascriot."

He turned back to see Ascriot pouring the fresh tea. "Alright. I'll get them set at the next change of guard, meaning you have about two hours."

"Perfect. That will be more than enough time to get clear of here," Ent replied, locking eyes with Tirzah. "If everything runs smoothly from here on out."

Tirzah rolled her eyes but gave no reply.

"I suppose I should get going then." Ascriot downed his cup in one swig. "Enjoy the tea."

Oh, Ascriot. Ent couldn't help but shake his head at the Ethian as he left the house without another word, leaving Ent once more with Tirzah. "So are you going to tell me what happened back there?"

Tirzah crossed to the fireplace, lifting the lid of the kettle and peering dubiously at its contents. "I did not have enough Ithynian Gasper to protect me from the Miadoris, it seems. My kind do not tolerate Gifting well."

Well, that certainly would have been nice to know before they walked into the vault full of dangerous, Gifted relics to steal the source of all Gifting.

"Are you going to tell me what you are going to do with it?" Tirzah selected a cup from the nearby shelves.

It. The Miadoris. Was this where she planned to try and take it? Ent decided to remain standing, still listening for any sign that someone had found out where they were. "We will keep it locked up in Cithan. Somehow, I doubt anyone would want to challenge the city full of Elves for it."

"What's to keep the Elves from using it?" Tirzah's voice remained level as she replaced the lid.

Ent turned his attention to the window—which had its curtains covering them and offering the security of privacy, but gave him little reassurance. "My mother. Me, though perhaps that is little comfort to you. My uncle is also loath to see anyone take it after seeing what it did to Astra. In fact, most of the Elves are. Their pride would keep them from doing anything except proving how much better they are at keeping it safe compared to you lot."

The silence was marked by the crackling of the dying fire and Tirzah pouring herself some tea. "Fair enough." There was the sound of ceramic against wood as she set her cup on the table. "But as long as such power exists, people will seek to possess it."

"This is true of any power. A throne, for instance," Ent couldn't help but give a small, dry smile to emphasize the fact as he locked eyes with her.

Tirzah seemed unbothered as she sat down. "Thrones can't be dropped in the middle of the sea and forgotten about. People would simply rebuild them." She gave a pointed look at his coat pocket. "*That* can't be remade."

"Thrones also don't hold the life source of the entire planet. Thrones can be rebuilt, but life, once lost, is gone forever," Ent shot back without hesitation. Jade would be laughing at him if she could hear him now.

"I think we've all seen what the Miadoris does to life." Tirzah's eyes narrowed slightly.

Ent sighed. He was going to have to tell Jade she was right, of course. But for now, he just had to use her wisdom on Tirzah. "But it lives in everything on Eatris. It's what allows the Gifted to heal others. It's what helped the Wildlands heal from the corruption millennia ago. It is only dangerous in its full concentration, and it is not the Miadoris as much as the people who seek to use it."

Tirzah took this in quietly. She took a sip of her tea and set it back down before asking, "Would your sister agree?"

"Unfortunately, yes," Ent replied with a twinge of hopelessness.

"I'm not sure mine would." Tirzah's gaze dropped to her tea. "Not if she saw what has become of the world."

"I'm not sure I can completely agree with it either. But I know it's right, and I know it would be worse to destroy it or leave it forgotten. Forgotten would only allow it to be found one day by the wrong person," Ent echoed Jade's sentiments.

Tirzah did not reply this time. Ent decided to take this as her knowing he was right—even if she wasn't willing to agree out loud. Several minutes of silence told him that the conversation was finally over.

At least, that was until he heard her take a deep breath. "When…" He saw her swallow. "When did Tyron hold you captive?"

Ent went completely rigid, replying curtly, "During The War."

She gestured loosely with one hand. "Yes, that, but how long ago?"

Paralyzed by the unexpected questions, Ent could only manage to say. "Around two years ago."

Tirzah's taut posture drooped slightly. She was still looking down at the cup in her hands when she asked, "And you said…you said he had both of you? You and your sister?"

"Is there a point to this?" Ent hardly recognized his own voice; it held such an edge to it. "You never believed Astra when she was on the stand testifying, so I can only imagine you are trying to garner a reaction out of me now. Are you happy with what you're getting?"

Tirzah still would not look up. Her hands tightened and relaxed methodically around her cup until Ent half thought she was going to break it. "I did not believe your sister because I did not think it possible for Tyron to do such a thing to a child." Her voice, though it's usual monotone, held an unfamiliar rasp.

"Well, he did. I saw it all," Ent's voice was hollow—as hollow as he felt inside. Hollow…and trapped by the memories.

When Tirzah raised her head, pain had cracked her usual stony expression. "He really made you *watch?*"

Detachment, that is what Ent felt. It was that, or he would be completely overwhelmed with the reminder. "He needed information I had." It was like trying to scream while suffocating—that was the sort of quiet Ent felt. "He…questioned me first. Made sure I knew exactly what he was going to do to her if I didn't give him what he wanted…made sure I knew what she would feel." What was he doing? Part of him wanted to stop, warning him that this was just more information Tirzah could use against him. But she had already used everything she could.

He had never told a soul about what had happened inside that nightmare; he'd never wanted to put that sort of guilt and pain on anyone. Somehow putting it on someone who had caused Astra so much harm seemed like a lesser evil, and Ent found that once he had begun, he couldn't stop—as if he was in some horrible trance. "I had never allowed myself to bring anyone along with me on missions except Soletuph—and even then. I never wanted anyone used against me in an interrogation scenario. I knew the ropes...I'd been there enough." He choked.

"Then Astra came along. She would come whether I let her or not." The smile was without joy. "She became such a spitfire. Challenged the Elves and actually changed their minds. Set Euracia's fortress on fire. It made me think maybe we really could take on the world together. That she was right—we'd keep each other safe." Ent closed his eyes as he allowed the dark memories to consume him, unable to battle them any longer. "And then we were caught. I could have stopped it...I could have stopped it all if I'd just caved. If I'd told Tyron what he wanted to know. But I had a camp full of desperate fugitives and refugees to think of. If I told him what he wanted...then we could lose The War—we could cause the death of hundreds."

His voice grew colder as the feeling of utter self-loathing became more intense. "Who does that? Who can let that happen to their own family and just watch when they have the power to stop it? Forget stupid morality. I knew exactly how much pain she was in—I'd felt it. I would never have asked anyone to be under that. And yet I did. I did and I created the ghost Astra has become because of it. Every single scar and every single nightmare she has…is because of me."

Ent somehow couldn't find the will to open his eyes, sucked into the realness of it all now that he was explaining it. The words poured out without his permission and he didn't even remember he was talking to anyone. "I can't even look at her without seeing the scars I put there. But to show that would only hurt her more. It's not her fault; it's mine. All mine. And then the Court wanted to use her…I found out Tyron was in the Court somewhere and," Ent paused, breath catching suddenly as he struggled to keep his lungs from freezing up completely. "I tried to send her as far away from Tyron as I could. As far away from me so that it couldn't happen again—so she'd be safe. Instead, I gave her right back to Tyron *again* to be picked apart *again*," he growled, fists clenching and eyes finally snapping open as he could no longer bear the shadows dancing behind his closed lids.

"I am haunted by many ghosts, but she's the most real. She was the one good thing I had left in my life for so long…and I killed her. *I* killed her." A single tear traced down Ent's cheek, the last sentence the final nail in the coffin. The unspoken truth he had been too afraid to say out loud. "Even Louko has done better to keep her safe than me. He rescued her from Tyron. He saved her and brought her back to Litash for care. He even rescued both of us the first time during The War. I have only ever given her up for slaughter. And for what? Nothing. We're right back where we started anyway. Just another war and more bloodshed. It was for nothing." At last, he was spent, unable to continue and now fighting the way his whole body trembled. He didn't look at Tirzah, wondering whether she would laugh, feel disgust, or simply do what everyone else had done: Say nothing and pretend it had never happened.

The way the silence stretched out left him resigned to the latter.

"Your sister is many things, but she is no ghost." It took Ent a moment to register the voice as Tirzah's with how different it sounded—it was soft, nearly shaky. "No ghost stands up to an entire court while in chains, nor fights back against a madman who holds her family as leverage. And it was certainly not in vain. You saved those lives, did you not? They made it home." He heard her shudder and exhale. "But I know it doesn't matter. It does not undo the horror that was wrought on you or your sister. I..." Her tone was dull and lifeless. "You did not do this. You did not kill her; you did not bring this war. Do not forget who held the knife...do not forget who made him. Euracia. The Screechers. Me. ...Blame us—not yourself. You have already been through enough. I am sorry for that."

There was some small, strange sense of solace in hearing those words for the first time. But it was mostly drowned out by the screaming in Ent's head. The shouts that never stopped. "Blaming does nothing. I blame the dead, and they aren't here to pay for it. I blame the living, and it doesn't make me feel any better. It doesn't change what happened and it doesn't change the fact that I still put other people's lives over my sister," Ent replied at last, eyes staring almost sightlessly at the wall. "I get to live with my choices, and I gave up on living after that one."

"I'm afraid making the other choice is little better," Tirzah murmured.

"Don't tell me. I don't think I want your tragedy stuck in my head, too, do I?" He gave a sad, strange laugh as he finally pulled his eyes back to face the woman he had, only a little while ago, called an enemy.

She was still looking down at the tea cup in her hands. "No, probably not." She gave a terse shrug. "But you still have your sister. She is still here. Perhaps learning to live comes slowly."

Ent gave another quiet, sad sort of laugh. "Perhaps."

"She seems to have enough determination for both of you." Tirzah finally met his gaze.

"Yeah," His voice cracked with the word. "She does, doesn't she?"

There was a brief flash across Tirzah's face—something like sorrow. It vanished too quickly for Ent to tell. She swiftly looked back down at her tea, picking it up and swirling it once before draining the last bit. She set the empty cup down as she got to her feet. "I should change. We'll have to set out in a few hours. I'll see if I have a cloak long enough for you."

Unable to muster the energy for any more words, Ent nodded, managing to meet her eyes as he did so. He had never expected to speak of any of what had happened to another living soul, let alone someone like Tirzah. And yet it had been easier to tell someone he wasn't afraid to hurt. He was unsure whether actually allowing the worst whispers of his conscience to escape had been a wise idea, but as much despair as it had brought to the surface, it had brought a small amount of relief. It felt not far off from disinfecting a wound. It hurt, but perhaps, it would help even a little bit to stop it from festering.

Only time would tell.

CHAPTER XX

Louko:

Louko was going to go insane. He had all this information…and yet no way to get it to Astra. All he could do was sit here and wait. Wait for one of his oldest friends to accidentally kill him…wait for his best friend to rescue him…wait for his two friends to kill each other. The possibilities were rarely anything but grim. All he could do was desperately cling to the hope that Tyron was getting better. The fact that he'd been able to come back from the Dragon had to mean something—it showed he really wasn't willing to kill Louko. It showed that Tyron was getting stronger, not weaker like he feared.

But how could he be of any help? Everything he did seemed to just be a roll of the dice.

"Oh, my apologies." Tyron appeared without warning. "I did not mean to intrude on your study."

"I, uh," Louko blinked, quickly taking in the clear confusion in Tyron's expression. Aha, he was not quite in the here and now, was he… "Are you alright?" With all the books and things, Louko must look like some scholar holed up in his room. It was sometimes hard to tell he was still in a dungeon, these days.

"Actually, I seem to be quite lost. I'm not even entirely sure how I got in here…." He trailed off, brow furrowing. "I was just walking with my wife a moment ago. Any chance you've seen her? Tall, long blond hair, brown eyes."

Oh. "I, uh. No, I haven't seen anyone…I could come help you search?" Louko offered as casually as possible. It was very difficult, however, to act casual when talking to Tyron about his dead wife and trying to trick him into letting him out.

Tyron's expression eased. "That would be most appreciated. To tell the truth, I can't even remember where I am. I must have…." He turned around as if to gesture to something, then froze. "Why…why are there no doors?" He looked back to Louko with fear in his widened eyes.

"I, uh. Remodeling. I just need a lift from the room and we can go searching. What's your wife's name?" *Idiot! Remodeling? What sort of pathetic excuse was that?* Louko's brain was melting from being in here too long.

Tyron was already backing away from him. "Oh no; no, no, no, Rhy…." He began feverishly raking a hand through his hair. "I lost her, I lost her—she's *gone.*" His voice cracked and he turned away, seemingly having forgotten Louko was even there.

Louko dared not reach out or say anything, knowing this spiral all too well.

"Not gone—missing," he growled. "You'll find her. You *are* finding her. They won't stop you: not Astra, not Entrais, not Ovok." Tyron's sudden, bitter laugh was jarring. "And then what?" The weary tone had returned. "What makes you think she will want to see you after everything you've done? Do you think she'll be *proud* of the blood you've spilled for her sake? I doubt she'll even recognize you."

Wait. Louko hadn't heard this before. What was he talking about? "Wait, is Rhioa…alive?" It seemed that Louko had grown so accustomed to talking aloud to himself in here...that in the moment of confusion, he had quite forgotten to say the thought *in his head. Idiot!*

Tyron spun around, visibly startled. "Louko?" He looked around as if he'd already forgotten his surroundings again. "Where are we?"

"Um. In my cell..." Louko just owned up to it now.

"Cell...." The stages of realization and horror were familiar as they played out on Tyron's face. He sat down heavily, as if too exhausted to stand. "My apologies," he murmured. "What did you ask?"

Louko cleared his throat nervously. "You said something about Rhioa being alive. I was, uh, confused."

Tyron looked up at him, lips parted and yet silent. Then he looked back down. "Do you remember anything I taught you of Drogans? Of the Myrandi?"

Oh he was, he was still acting half sane. "I, uh. Yes."

"How many forms do they have?"

"Th-They have two." Louko decided it was best not to explain that he had also recently learned a lot more about them since meeting Mitheau. He needed Tyron to stay focused. He seemed strangely...with it. Again, beating the Dragon.

Still looking down, Tyron drew a shaky breath. "To kill a Myrandi, you must kill both forms."

"Yes," Louko nodded.

"When...when Rhioa was killed, she did not fade. I thought that because of the properties of the Miadoris, it had killed both forms." He fell silent, as if too tired to continue. "I was wrong. I did not know until nearly ten years later that I had buried an empty casket."

Louko's eyes bugged out. "*What?*" Rhioa was *alive?*

"My so-called brothers concealed it from me." He nearly spat the words. Louko feared the Dragon was returning, but then Tyron's shoulders drooped. "When they lose their first form, Myrandi appear to the one they are closest to. I'd thought that would mean myself or her sister. When months had passed and neither of us had seen her, we drew our conclusions." He rolled the dull, gold wedding ring around his finger. "But she must have appeared to her father. He left Eatris and now no one can reach him."

"Yeah, he left in a frenzy. We met a young Drogan who was left behind. She said Ovok fought the Drogan Cyl?" Louko said slowly, trying to process this. Rhioa being dead had been a cold, hard fact for almost all his life. Rhioa had been killed, and Tyron had always been a widower. But...if she was alive. All this. All Tyron's pain had been for nothing? No wonder he had broken—Louko couldn't imagine finding this out after having grieved for so long. When *had* he found out?

Tyron nodded slowly. "And now Cyl holds the Door shut so that Ovok cannot return."

"So...you are trying to get off-world to get Rhioa?" It all made sense. But why did Rhioa just leave?

"Yes...no, *he* is." Tyron tugged at his hair. "I've been trying to convince him she won't want anything to do with me."

Aha. So the Dragon wanted off-world.

"I...Louko, I..." Tyron seemed more and more agitated—desperate, even. When he looked up, his eyes were rimmed with tears. "I cannot even say how sorry I am. For every last bit of it—for leaving, for those I've killed and betrayed, for the war I waged and let my brother win, for what I did to…to Astra, oh no, Astra…" He was back to tugging at his hair. "I made you watch. What have I done?"

Oh no. He was slipping again. This always happened right before… "Tyron, please, I know…it's alright I know it wasn't you just stay with me, please."

"But it was—I'm still in here!" Tyron pointed to his temple. "I know what he wants to do to you. He's going to…going to…." His expression contorted and he covered his face with his hands.

"Yeah, I think I got the gist of that." Louko forced himself not to show the way the knowledge put him on edge. Funny how he'd been through his share of life and death situations and yet somehow sitting here knowing the possibility of what could happen was still nearly unbearable. "But he's already tried and you didn't let that happen," Louko said the last bit with true conviction. He knew Tyron was stronger.

Tyron's hands dropped, allowing Louko to see him fighting to regather himself. "I have failed for so long. I don't know that I can make any difference now."

"You didn't fail with me, Tyron. I'm still here and I really don't think I would be if not for you. The stupid Dragon can take a good long walk for all I care, but you are not the failure. I mean look at you! All the Drogans I've talked to have said fighting the Drogan Madness is impossible, and yet you defied it." Now granted, all the Drogans Louko had talked to meant the one Drogan he had talked to. The one, very young one. But he felt the statement was still true—based on Mitheau's knowledge of what the madness was and did.

367

"But it's not consistent. I cannot pick when I have that control." Anxiety laced every word. "I may have intervened a few days ago, but I still can't get you out of here. Not without him stopping me."

"Well, there are clearly things that snap you back—and one of them is the thought of harming me, apparently. We need to find those things and use them against the Dragon. We need to get as much of a plan together as we can, and you need to have some faith in yourself because that's the only chance we have and I believe in you. Alright?" Louko's bravado was hopefully convincing, but it wasn't all fake. If anyone could beat this, it would be Tyron.

All of Tyron's nervous movements stilled and he simply sat there, staring at Louko.

Wait, what had he said? Had he triggered something? Had he—

"I do not know that it means anything coming from me, but I hope you know that you have grown up to be a more remarkable man than any I have ever met." Tyron's green eyes dropped. "You are right. We should plan as well as we can."

Louko was not sure whether he could be truly impacted by what Tyron said yet. Only because he was still unsure himself whether he was setting Tyron and Astra up to fail. Was this really a good idea? What if it got them all killed?

Swallowing hard, Louko nodded. "Alright."

Astra:

"All of the damage she caused, and she doesn't have a single thing we don't already know." Jahng said in bitter summary as they exited the tent. "Nothing but a mercenary, working for the highest bidder."

"So it would seem," Astra murmured. Feelings of rage and grief and exhaustion swirled so thickly that she nearly felt dizzy. Keeshiff was dead. Gone. Uncovering the person responsible only to find out the woman knew nothing just made it all worse.

"You need to tell the Ezai Ru about the spy." Jahng's comment broke through the fog of Astra's thoughts. "I assume you are going to return and update him."

Astra nodded, the pit of dread already forming in her stomach at having to relay the news again. Part of her rebelled, wanting to stay behind with Keeshiff as long as possible. But there was no time to waste. "Yes. I can bring any letters or other news you might have." Astra paused and looked out over the rows of tents. Dawn was beginning to turn the horizon pink. "You said you were communicating with the Merimeethian line about Keeshiff's ceremony. Do you know when it will be?"

"This evening. They called a truce after the event and wanted to discuss…a funeral." Jahng's breath caught for a moment before she regained her composure.

It was the closest thing to grief Astra had ever seen Jahng wear. "He…he admired you very deeply, I think," she said quietly. "I believe you gave him hope—hope that people could see right from wrong and make the choice for themselves."

Jahng said nothing, giving a nearly imperceptible nod. But Astra saw the way she swallowed hard.

With no comfort left to give, and none left for herself, Astra took a deep breath. "I will be back by this evening."

Jahng gave a bow of her head in parting, and Astra pulled at the world around her as she envisioned the palace.

She appeared in her borrowed room. After a few misadventures during her first attempts to transport, Ven had asked her to refrain from randomly appearing in public spaces. She had been limited to her room or to the back garden after that. It took a moment for her eyes to adjust to the dark of the unlit space before she could cross to the door and let herself into the hallway.

The palace staff were already bustling through the corridors, nearly soundless as they carried out the many morning chores. Astra tried to stay out of the way as she went down one hall and to the left to reach her father's room. Tentatively, she knocked. Nothing. She opened the door a crack, just enough to stick her head in and scan the room. Empty. She stepped back out and closed the door.

Guessing that perhaps he was in some conference with Ven, Astra trudged towards the throne room. The guards outside the great doors took one look at her and let her in without a word.

Inside was a flurry of courtiers talking between each other, the hurricane of bodies and sound revolving around Ven, who stood over the table full of maps. Next to him stood Destrin, both of them looking distressed and holding conversations between themselves as well as those who constantly interrupted them.

But all of this movement stopped the minute the door closed behind Astra.

"Astra!" Destrin's voice was the first to echo back through the room, its tone almost desperate. He ran over from where he was and grabbed her firmly by the shoulders. "What happened?"

Astra went rigid, instinct making her pull back but not completely away. She tried to speak but nothing came out. *Just spit it out.* "Keeshiff is dead." The words were hoarse. "I was too late. He's dead."

Her father's eyes went wide, grip tightening on her shoulders.

No one spoke for a while.

"Astra…this was *not* your fault," her father whispered at a volume that only an Elf could catch.

If Astra had any tears left to cry, she wouldn't have been able to hold them back.

"Everyone stay here," Ven's voice boomed deep and almost angry. "Astra. Destrin. In the back, now."

Astra's feet felt leaden as she followed her father around Ven's throne and into the private room hidden behind it. At the king's motioning, she slumped into one of the chairs at the long table.

"So…he's dead." Ven didn't ask this as a question, rather instead as a defeated answer.

"How bad is it, Astra?" Destrin came up next to where she was sitting, again putting his hand on her shoulder.

Astra put her head in her hands. "It's bad." As best as she could, Astra recounted everything she'd been told about: the attempt to trap the spy, Keeshiff's meeting and the ambush, followed by the Merimeethians bringing him back. From there, she went into the events of that night: Rufio, Tallaman, Mariah, Rhumir, the spy.

Ven took in a deep breath. "So at least Merimeethia will be in no state to continue its assault on the front."

"What do you mean?" Destrin asked.

"If they've called a truce and they didn't mean for…well, things to go the way they have," Ven only barely faltered in his words before continuing, "Then Keeshiff's sacrifice was not in vain. Knowing Merimeethian politics and the fact that clearly no one on the Merimeethian side actually wanted Keeshiff harmed, there will no doubt be infighting and Merimeethia will implode."

Astra tried to wrap her mind around this newest problem. "So what can we do? How can we stop it?"

Ven regarded Astra with a strange look before slowly replying, "The best thing we can do is nothing. Tyron will no longer be able to get through to the portal site. It's only a matter of time before they retreat and storm Melye, if I were to guess. Tyron—or Kaeden, rather—had kept a lot of sympathy by not touching Keeshiff. He had given no kill order—only live capture. With that undone…as horrible as it is…it is good news for us."

"Good news?" Astra repeated, aghast. "Keeshiff died trying to win his country back from a madman, and instead all of it's going to go up in flames. How can you call that good news?" She glanced towards her father, hoping he was on her side. "I think we've all seen what a civil war does to a nation. What we don't know is what Tyron is going to do in response. He still has Louko, and this turmoil will give us even less chance of rescuing him."

"I think what the Ezai Ru is trying to say, Astra, is that it is good news in the attempt to stop Tyron," Destrin said quietly. "But I don't know that there would be any way we can help the Merimeethians now. Not without getting Louko back first—"

"My nephew will not be dragged into that political mess anymore. We are getting him back *alive* and then he is never to be forced to take one step in Merimeethia again. Is that clear?" Ven was suddenly vehement as he interrupted Destrin.

Astra sat back in her seat. "Then what about your niece?"

Ven's cold stare turned on Astra. "Excuse me?"

"What about Mariah?" Astra did not back down. "She has a rightful claim. If she could gain pledges of loyalty before they retreat, then—"

"—I'm sorry, what?" came the chilling interruption. Somehow it being a whisper was worse than if he'd screamed the words. "Astra. You are not thinking clearly—Mariah is the last person we should trust with anything. We'll figure something out but that wretched soul is not the answer."

Astra swallowed. "I know she is the last person. But we have come down to the last. We don't have time to figure this out; if Merimeethia falls, it will take Louko with it."

"I saw what trap she led you to, Astra." The words were desperate as they left the Ezai Ru's mouth. "How can I even think of allowing her any power?" He turned to Astra's father. "You can't possibly agree."

Destrin ran his hands over his face. "I…I don't know." He pressed his lips together, his sorrow and worry evident as he looked at Astra. "Perhaps it would be wise to get some rest before anyone makes any further decisions."

"There's no time for that," Astra nearly interrupted. "Keeshiff's funeral…." She stumbled over the unfamiliar sound of those two words together. "The ceremony is this evening. Jahng said they expect the Merimeethians to begin withdrawal tomorrow. If Mariah is to win anyone over, it must be done *now*." Her voice cracked as her throat constricted. "I know what she did to me. I don't think I will ever have the luxury of forgetting. But this is not about me, and it's not about her: It's about Louko. I would let her betray me to the same fate all over again if it meant getting him back."

"Don't say that," Ven's voice cracked. "Please don't say that."

Astra looked away, trying to blink back tears. "I…I'm sorry. I shouldn't have said that. I meant," She drew a ragged breath and looked back. "I meant that no matter what she has done, she is still our only means to keep Merimeethia intact. Even if that is only for long enough to find someone else to take her place. We cannot disregard her even with her past."

Astra thought she saw Ven's hand tremble as he brought it up to rub his forehead. He closed his eyes, took a deep breath, and said at last, "Fine. If this is what we have to do to get Louko back…I will speak with her and judge for myself whether we can use her."

Knowing this was the best she would get, and that even this much surely cost Ven dearly, Astra bowed her head in acceptance.

"Then it is decided. I think the next course of action is rest…or at least, we should all pretend we can get some," Ven announced with an emptiness.

"You said the funeral was this evening?" her father asked.

She nodded mutely and got to her feet. "I told Jahng I would return by then."

"I will wake you," Destrin whispered softly. "And Astra…this is not your fault," he said again, gently touching her arm.

Astra fought to keep her expression from crumpling. She wasn't very successful. But she did manage a nod before she turned and pushed open the heavy door. She shut it quietly, leaning back against it and attempting to compose herself before she had to walk past anyone. What did it matter if this was her fault or not? Keeshiff was gone. There was no changing that.

Unable to bring herself to go back to her room where she would have only the chessboards for company, Astra went down to the stables instead. She groomed Dannsair until her hands were too heavy to hold a brush. Then she curled up in the corner and pulled her coat around herself. The comforting sound of Dannsair chewing, the fragrant scent of straw beneath her, and the warmth of the stable was too much to resist. She was asleep within minutes.

The evening was cold, with wind whistling across the steppes and over the riverbanks. That was the only sound from among the thousands who had gathered. They stood silent, most bearing torches or candles to light Keeshiff's final journey. Astra could just catch the golden light playing off of his auburn hair ahead of her.

It was the knights who carried him forward in slow, careful steps. Behind walked Asher, taking on the processional role of a father. With his reddened eyes and tear-stained cheeks, he truly seemed to have lost his son. But with Keeshiff's brother captured and his sister at risk of harm, the only person left to walk in the stead of his family was Astra. She did not feel worthy of the role.

I'm so sorry, Louko. I'm so sorry. I should have kept him safe. The thought played endlessly through her mind, repeating with each step Astra took. *Do you even know? Have you had to take the news all alone?* He wouldn't even be given this chance to say goodbye. And Keeshiff had nothing to leave him besides memories. *You should have had the time to make so many more.*

The procession continued on, taking no notice of Astra's silent pleas for it all to be a dream. It was all so wrong. She wanted to stop, to scream, to make them put Keeshiff down and to shake him awake. Instead she followed, step by step. *I'm so sorry.*

The walls of the crowd on either side of them finally opened up into a wide expanse. Across the way, the entirety of the Merimeethian army stood watching. Like the Nythrilians, each man and woman held a light to stave off the darkness. Any who had helmets or hoods had removed them.

Two smaller parties stood at the fore of each army. Before the Nythrilians, Astra could pick out the shapes of Aelor Ven, her father, and Jahng. The Merimeethian generals were completely unfamiliar. In the field between them was a wide, dark outline with a small, lit brazier beside it: the procession's destination.

Astra and Asher stopped and stepped to the side as the knights set Keeshiff's litter on the pyre. A few adjustments were made so that his cloak and sword lay just right before they pulled back. Arrayed in his finery, with his sword resting beneath his folded hands, Keeshiff looked every inch a king. A king who would never reign. A leader who would never go home to the people he loved.

The skies were red now, colored with the last rays of daylight. It was as if they understood the grief that was gathered beneath them. Astra and Asher stepped forward, each receiving a torch from the soldier who stood at the brazier. As instructed, Astra walked around to the other side of the pyre and stood awaiting the signal. Her throat went tight—she wasn't ready. She didn't want to say goodbye. Not yet. *Please, just a few more moments….*

From the other side of Keeshiff's resting form, she saw Asher's torch rise. Astra did the same, and then in unison, they lowered the flames to the base of the pyre. The fire caught quickly, lapping up the dry kindling and spreading across the entire structure with a crackling sound. Astra stepped back as the pyre, and as her friend, were engulfed.

Her role now finished, Astra retreated to the Nythrilian side and fell in beside her father. Her whole face was wet with tears but she would not let herself make a sound.

A single voice split the air—Gavin—beginning what sounded like some ancient funeral dirge. Astra hadn't realized what a beautiful voice the knight had. It echoed, eerily accompanied by the roaring fire, words piercing Astra's very soul as it sung of returning home and reuniting with loved ones. Of the hope that waited on the other side and how those singing longed to one day follow into the sunlit hills of eternity.

And then, one by one, voices joined in with Gavin. The singing came from everywhere—even Ven joined in, many Nythrilians following in his footsteps. It spread up and down both sides of the frontline until the very ground beneath them seemed to echo it back.

Astra did not know the words to sing with them. Even if she did, she had no voice to offer. But as she watched the flames take what was left of her friend, she had a promise to give: *Go in peace, Keeshiff. I will bring your brother home—whatever it takes.*

CHAPTER XXI

<u>Mariah:</u>

Mariah had been allowed to watch the funeral from the back, where the knights would not notice her and where she wouldn't cause the attention to be taken away from what mattered.

And what mattered was that her brother was dead. The brother she'd started this whole mess to protect. The brother who'd rightfully hated her by the end. The brother Mariah had sworn to spend the rest of her life trying to prove herself to—to make up for her sins.

Now, Mariah sat back in her tent, alone and fiddling with the bandaging around her hand, trying to swallow tears once more. She did not deserve to mourn; and yet what else could she do? Her chest hurt from the constant reminder that she had wasted her chance. That this was something that was too broken to fix. No batting her eyes to fix the problem—no talking her way around people to calm things down. Keeshiff was gone and there was no changing that.

A muted conversation with her guard outside drew her attention and Mariah braced herself. But she got a little more warning before the person came in.

"May I enter?" The soft, raspy voice was undeniably Astra's.

"Yes," Mariah croaked in response, unsure why Astra was asking permission. She was, after all, still technically a prisoner, wasn't she?

The tent flap parted and Astra stepped in. The redhead's eyes were visibly puffy from crying and her whole face was flushed. But she still paused, bowing her head and saying, "I am sorry for all you have lost."

Mariah, unable hide her blatant confusion, said nothing, only waiting. Words were of little use, now. Her actions had spoken louder than any of her lies, and now Mariah knew her stupid lead tongue would do little to tell a truth sincerely.

Astra let out a long, shaky breath. She looked up, her unearthly blue eyes meeting Mariah's. "You know Merimeethian politics better than anyone here. What do you think happens next?"

Right. Mariah could be useful. She'd banked her survival on the ins and outs of politics. "I imagine one of the generals will try and seize control, if not the House of Allonbrais. I would be surprised if anyone still stood with Kaeden after this mishap." She struggled to keep her voice steady and calm, focusing her energy away from the image of Keeshiff's pyre and instead trying to recall the names of those she would think would be quickest to go for power. "General Baradeen is at odds with the House of Allonbrais, and both are afraid of the other advancing higher in politics than the other. I wouldn't be surprised if Baradeen makes a move. I also wouldn't be surprised if he was the one who suggested the truce for the…the funeral," she coughed the words out and tried to quickly continue, "He knows showing respect to Keeshiff's accident will gain support with the lesser nobles as well as the soldiers."

"Will the other nobles follow him?" Astra's gaze did not waver.

Mariah took a shallow breath. "Others will inevitably accuse him of arranging the accident. The House of Allonbrais controls most of

Merimeethia's foreign trade, and they'll use the excuse to cut off any funds going Baradeen's way." Mariah winced. This was going to be messy. But why wouldn't it? This was Merimeethia after all. This forsaken country did nothing but cannibalize itself. Mariah had picked that up all too quickly and mastered the skill for far too long.

Astra's voice dropped. "How many people know that you are not Omath's biological daughter?"

What was Astra getting at? "Fa—he kept it very quiet. I was a baby when he returned with my mother. I was born after their wedding. Many thought that was part of the reason for the hurried marriage, after all." Mariah thought of how many years she'd fought to quell the rumors. All the make-up and pretend, learning how to get into people's good graces so she could do damage control on the whispers that spread. So she could make people like her—the *her* she created to survive. *But you don't even know who you are, do you? You never have.*

"Then, as Omath's second-born, you are next in line for his throne, are you not?" Astra was watching her carefully.

Mariah's eyes widened. Astra couldn't be *serious*, could she? "I...I mean, yes, but Astra..." *I am the last person in the world you'd want to try and get on a throne.*

Astra went on. "Your claim would have precedence over all others. You would end the civil war before it could even begin and depose 'Kaeden' in the same move. Even if you do not feel that you have the capacity to lead, you need only get the country stable enough to appoint your replacement."

She was insane. She had to be. Mariah had no words. Where to begin? The list of reasons was so long it was impossible to know where to begin.

"There is no one else, Mariah." Astra's unnerving gaze finally dropped to the ground. "Your brother has left behind a legacy. There is no one else to carry it. If you do not bear it, it will all go to waste."

Mariah wanted to remind Astra of just how hated she was, and yet…she wasn't. The only people that hated her had been the people that had *mattered* to Mariah. The ones whose opinions she cared about. No one in the nobles' circle or even the general Merimeethian army knew what had transpired—except for Killyan, who at the time, had believed "Kaeden" like she had and that it had been to bring Louko to justice and clear Keeshiff's name. She was still well liked among those in power. Indeed, none knew the traitor and spineless coward she had found herself to be.

"But the choice is still yours. No one can force you to accept this task." Astra sounded…tired. Exhausted, really.

"I just…I can't. You don't want me ruling, Astra. You've seen the damage I…." Mariah swallowed, unable to finish the sentence.

"And I have also seen war. You have not seen that damage. It would destroy everything that your brother fought so hard for." Astra looked back up. "Louko is still in there." The statement was quiet, and yet there was no escaping it. "If Merimeethia falls apart, if Tyron becomes desperate, I do not know what will happen to him."

Mariah's blood chilled as she remembered Louko, still back at Melye. With…him. Astra was right, and she hated it. Keeshiff was the right person for this—but he was dead. Dead, and her actions had done nothing but help lead to it. If she had been a more faithful sister...then they would have trusted her when she'd tried to give him advice. Was this her penance? To be the ghost of her brother?

"I wish I could give you more time to think, but I am afraid I have none. The Merimeethians will likely announce their retreat by morning and withdraw by the next day. If you choose this path, you must take it before the opportunity is gone." Astra glanced back at the tent entrance as if already pressed for time.

"I will do whatever I can to get Louko back. If you all think this is how...then so be it," Mariah replied, hardly able to process what she was agreeing to. She didn't want this—all she'd wanted was her stupid brother.

Astra hesitated. "I do think so, but I also understand that this will reach far beyond Louko. If you agree to this, you agree to all of it. Are you certain you can do that?"

No. I am not. I don't want to sign my life away. But what choice did she have? What choice should she even be *allowed* to have? "Yes," she replied, taking a shaky breath. She wasn't the hero. No, she'd always been the villain, hadn't she? But now the real hero was dead, and she was all that was left.

Astra regarded her for a moment more. "Alright." The single word held the weight of what Mariah had just agreed to. "Then we have work to do. Follow me."

Keeshiff's funeral burning in her mind, Mariah got up and obeyed. She had spent her whole life trying to survive in the court of her father and the last thing she had ever wanted to do was lead it. That had been what Keeshiff was meant to do; to fix it…to make it safe. *Stop it, you coward. No more are you going to make others do the dirty work.* This couldn't be about her any longer.

"Have you ever met your uncle?" Astra asked as she led the way through the rows of tents. "I mean, truly met him?"

Mariah swallowed hard. "I have not." She remembered hearing how her uncle had been trying to get her and Louko back when they were young. For a while, she had wanted that—to be able to be safe and away from all the eyes; to belong and not have to hide the way she looked so different under layers of pretend. But then…then her father had made her publicly disavow him when she was young. He'd said it would help Merimeethians accept her—it would help her belong. He'd said Ven only had wanted her and Louko for his own political gain…and yes, while she had become accepted and even loved by the Merimeethian people, her uncle had since proven to be far above what her father had accused him of. He'd never given up on Louko. But he'd turned his back on her when she'd shown how little she cared for anything except self-preservation.

Astra stopped, now a stone's throw from what had to be the command tent. She turned towards Mariah and said, "Then brace yourself. He wants to hate you. He wants to blame you for much of the pain he currently feels. Before you can win anyone over from Merimeethia, you must first win over him."

"W-wait, I thought this was something everyone agreed to?" Mariah suddenly stopped in her tracks.

"I am afraid that no one agrees on anything anymore," Astra murmured. "Not without your brothers here to unite them."

This was going to be a disaster. But it was too late now. What was the worst that would happen? *Your uncle will demand an execution? You'll be laughed off and locked up forever?* Nothing she didn't deserve. Mariah didn't say a word, only forced herself to take another step, and then another.

As soon as Astra approached, one of the guards at the entrance to the command tent ducked inside. He returned quickly, nodding to Astra and holding the flap open for them.

Taking one last deep breath, Mariah entered the tent, hands clenched despite her injury as she prepared for the worst.

"This is…her?" A man's brittle tone almost immediately sounded as Mariah came inside, and she had little trouble understanding where it had come from: her uncle.

He stood next to Astra's father, both looking equally as sleep deprived but one looking more irritated and less forgiving than the other. Jahng stood silently across the way with arms folded.

"Mariah, this is the Ezai Ru Aelor Ven, your uncle." Astra angled back towards her, one hand gesturing for her to step forward.

Years of practice remaining outwardly calm and clueless had taught Mariah not to show just how much she wanted to scream as she made a perfect Nythrilian bow. "Ezai Ru."

Aelor Ven continued to stare at her with narrowed eyes. "Astra has convinced me that I should, for the sake of your brothers, give you a 'chance.'" His voice was deep and cold, each word sharpened to a point.

"Seeing your role in making the way for one's abduction and another's death, I don't see why I should. But," He held up his hands, palms facing upwards. "Here we are: Convince me."

Mariah shrugged in helplessness. "Honestly, I don't know how, because I can't convince myself. I don't want to try and rule anything and seeing as I have very little reason to be trusted with doing such, it seems the only thing that has Astra deciding I *should* is that I'm the only person left besides Tyron who won't just cause outright civil war and get Louko killed in the process by a madman. I would really love a better idea because I know exactly where I should be and that isn't leading a country."

If possible, Aelor Ven's gaze narrowed further. There was a delay before he sat down, folding his hands and resting them on the table between them. "Well, I'm glad we can agree on something, then. Because I'd much rather see you in a dungeon than on a throne. But," He tipped his head. "As you so *kindly* pointed out, I still have a nephew whose fate is tied to that of your wretched country. So if I do go along with this dreadful idea, how exactly are you going to make sure you don't end up as the next quickly deposed ruler?"

"Well, as it currently stands, General Baradeen is going to try and gain the support of the soldiers, but the house of Allonbrais is the one who controls trade and will oppose them. Those two factions going at it will end in Melye being stormed and one or the other possibly burning down the city to get to Kaeden. But I am good friends with the head lady of the House of Allonbrais and I am close with the son of General Baradeen. He is an officer under his father and has his father's ear without his pigheadedness. He also was a very avid sympathizer of Keeshiff and I had…um…I know he was willing to follow Keeshiff anywhere," Mariah stumbled a moment, still remembering how her brother had once been trying to overthrow their father. She'd used her influence as best as she could to discreetly help in the courts, knowing it had never been Keeshiff's strong suit. He'd done better in informal situations; he'd loved being among the people and the soldiers. He never knew it, but she'd always been trying to spread his influence through the nobility. How else had she believed Kaeden and her could easily absolve Keeshiff if they had brought back Louko instead? She'd been unsure at the time if Keeshiff had blown it and really murdered their father, or if Louko had finally snapped, but she'd hoped to either expose Louko or bury the truth if it had been Keeshiff. Turned out neither had been the case, and she'd ruined both their lives.

"You're betting an entire country on a few acquaintances?" Aelor Ven raised an eyebrow, somehow looking more unimpressed than before. "What are you going to do to win them over? Host a party? Invite them on an outing? Please, I doubt they'd accept you as anything more than the royal jester."

"With all due respect, Ezai Ru, I heard you overthrew the king in your own country on a few 'mere acquaintances.' Didn't you actually host a party?" Mariah's instinct made her mirror her uncle's tone and demeanor even before sense could remind her to tread more carefully. "Keeshiff had wanted to depose Omath for years. I'd merely been getting ready for it because I knew he was not good with those silly parties and mere acquaintances. I just hadn't expected it to be such a mess when it all happened." *And I'd panicked. Panicked and played the spy for Kaeden.*

Aelor Ven's expression remained unmoving. Then he sucked in his cheeks slightly. "Yes," he said bitterly. "A mess. One you played right into. Given that history, why *exactly* should I allow you the chance to go repeating it?"

"Because we both failed our families, didn't we? You didn't get Louko and I couldn't help Keeshiff." Mariah forced herself to look him straight in the eyes.

Her uncle looked straight back. For a moment, they were locked in that silent battle of wills, each evaluating the other and daring them to waiver. But to Mariah's surprise, it was Aelor Ven who broke away first…laughing, of all things.

"Well, Astra, I hope you're pleased with yourself." His humorless chuckle tapered off. "I will allow this insane plan of yours to proceed. However," His voice dropped as he looked back at Mariah. "I want to be clear: Should you cross me, should you ever pull anything even *remotely* suspicious, I will gladly inform the entire population of Merimeethia of your past and of your parentage. Knowing their penchant for killing their own kings and queens, I have no doubt they'll clean up your mess for me. Do we have an understanding?"

"Yes," Mariah replied, keeping eye contact. "We have an understanding, Ezai Ru. Even if you are resorting to blackmail." Wow. What in Eatris was she thinking?

With a scoff, Aelor Ven leaned back in his chair. "Fortunately for you, the only thing of any interest to me in your foul little country is my nephew.

And once I have gotten him back, he will never be returning; you can drive that place into the ground if you so please."

"Sounds good to me." Even as much as Mariah was screaming inwardly at herself to back off, she remained calm and assertive. She'd spent so long becoming what she had to in order to be loved or accepted that she realized she didn't even have a personality. Only minutes ago, she'd been sulking in the tent, and now somehow…somehow, she was facing off the uncle that rightfully hated her, telling him exactly why he should help her take back Merimeethia. She was nothing more than a shell, becoming whatever she needed to in the moment. A perfect princess for her father, an incompetent brat to hide that she was a spy, a repentant informant, and now the princess Merimeethia needed. Only, which one was her? Were any of them? She felt like a mirror, a reflection of those around her—a mere image without a soul.

"Well," Jahng cleared her throat. "If this is happening, it must happen soon. The Merimeethians will withdraw in a matter of days—they've likely already sent messengers ahead of them." She eyed Mariah now. "I can arrange a meeting with Baradeen, if that's where you want to start. But it may also be prudent to speak with your brother's knights. If any of them agree to back you, it could win you a lot of favor."

"I want to talk to both Baradeen and his son, Lieutanant Cederyc," Mariah clarified. "And if you somehow think talking to Ke-Keeshiff's knights would be beneficial after the last incident, I will do what is required." Mariah forced her reply.

"You need not fear a repeat." Astra's subdued voice came from behind her. "They have all been informed concerning the actual spy. They may or may not side with you, but none will harm you."

"Alright. Then I suppose best get on with it." Mariah squared her shoulders and prepared for what was to come, wishing she could feel as if Keeshiff was still with her in spirit but knowing she was very much alone in this, and deserved to be nothing other than that.

It was time to become her next identity. To be Keeshiff's replacement, no matter how insufficient.

Entrais:

Finally, Ent was back at Cithan, exhausted and on edge as he was let into his mother's house. The Miadoris was still in the little cage within his inner coat pocket, and he wouldn't be able to rest until it was safe in the vault they had prepared. Granted, he doubted he'd be able to rest easy even then.

"Ent! You're back!" Jade was the first to greet him, relief evident in every word.

He allowed himself to wrap his wife in a tight one-armed hug, though paranoia still kept the other hand by the pocket. "I need to get this to the vault. Everything went...mostly as planned," he said after giving Jade a gentle kiss and stepping out of their embrace.

He noticed both his mother and uncle waiting in the background, a shadow over their expressions as if he'd interrupted a serious conversation.

"You have it then," he heard his mother let out a deep breath. "Quick, the vault is ready for you. This way."

Ent immediately followed his mother as she made her way down the hall and to the cellar door. They'd agreed to transform the manor into the vault. One, it would be an unlikely choice—everyone would assume it would be kept in the armory building or somewhere more fortified. Secondly, the manor was one of the few completely finished buildings after the sacking of Cithan. Thirdly, his mother had been able to oversee the conversion of the cellar, and he knew she would never have agreed if she didn't think they could make it secure enough.

And sure enough, the doorway that led to the stairway held a few more locks than he remembered, two of which held no keyhole. After unlocking the few that did use a key, Ameri then used Gifting to manipulate the others. "The three keys will be distributed to Tallaman, the captain of the guard, and myself after we place it inside. I just assumed it would be better for me to have all of them first so that we could quickly get it inside. The last two keyholes require Gifting mastery that is quite high," Ameri explained as they stepped inside and went quickly down the stairs. "I will show you exactly how they work at a later time if you wish. But I thought it might be better to show…Astra." Why had she stumbled over her name?

Down in the cellar was a surprisingly empty room with a pedestal in the middle. On the pedestal sat a clear glass structure, orb-like and shining in the dim plight of blue torchlight.

"The lights are only ignited by Elvish blood entering through the door. It will be completely dark here otherwise, and the pedestal retracts into the floor."

This had been why Ent had trusted his mother. If nothing else, paranoia certainly ran in their family.

"The glass should hold the Miadoris with little issue, but I suggest keeping it in the cage all the same."

Ent nodded, walking forward and taking the small container that kept the Miadoris out of his pocket. It fit easily through the small hole at the top of the glass orb, but the moment it was inside the opening vanished, leaving the box suspended in air in the center of the glass.

A strangled sort of sigh of relief escaped Ent's lips as he stepped back to his mother's side.

But his mother said nothing, only touching his shoulder as she turned to lead them back out of the place. Why was he getting the feeling something was wrong? She had mentioned Astra being one of the ones who would be able to open the door, so Astra had to be alright, at least. But then why did his mother also stumble over her name? Why was she strangely silent when they had actually *succeeded* in something?

The door to the cellar shut and Ent was left in the hallway with his mother, waiting for the other shoe to drop. It was a feeling he lived with almost constantly, and yet somehow now it was unbearable.

"We were worried when you didn't arrive last night," she said, already leading the way back. "We feared Tirzah had turned on you."

"No. There were some unexpected obstacles, but she came through, surprisingly," Ent replied, brow furrowed as he surveyed his mother. Unable to take it any longer, he asked, "But what is the matter? Is everything alright?"

Ameri stopped, looking up and down the hallway before letting her shoulders drop. "Your sister arrived in the middle of the night two days ago. She went to Tallaman—someone needed healing, he said. She has not returned since." His mother paused; lips pursed. "The Merimeethian prince, Keeshiff...he's dead."

Ent stared at her for a long while. Then, finally, one word escaped his lips, harsh and unexpected. *"What?"* He hadn't known the prince very well, but Keeshiff had lent his aid during The War and had proven himself a good ally and a friend to Astra. Ent knew how Astra had to be taking this.

"Astra did not give any details as to how it happened, nor did she say anything about future plans, but your uncle said she was..." Ameri swallowed. "...distraught."

Of course she was. One of her close friends had just died—a horrible reality Ent had lived through too many times. "And she hasn't returned since?" he asked, trying to keep his tone controlled. Oh, but he was so worried now. Worried for what this would make Astra do; worried because he knew she would do anything to keep everyone safe...and that this had reminded her just how impossible that task was; worried because he knew this would make her reckless...reckless and closed off.

It would make her like him.

Ameri shook her head. "Even with the relay, any letter we try to send would take nearly two weeks to arrive. I don't think we'll have that much time. If Keeshiff is gone, everything in Nythril and Merimeethia is about to shift all over again."

Ent ran his hand over his face, despair as real as ever as he wondered which of his worst-case scenarios Astra was going to decide to do. He felt helpless—unable to stop the horrible conclusion to this equally horrible nightmare. He'd been where Astra was…too many times. And too many times he'd done exactly what she was about to do: something incredibly stupid.

"Your father is still with her. He won't let her do anything rash." His mother's demeanor shifted to a forced sort of optimism.

Ent forced calm. "Yes. Of course." He tried to relax, and yet logic and fear alike would not permit it. Fear screamed that Astra would try something stupid, and logic only agreed…because that is always what she had done in the past. "Let's go back to the sitting room so we can discuss with Jade," he suggested aloud.

Ameri seemed like she wanted to say something else, even shifting slightly as if about to speak, but instead put her hand on his shoulder again. All she said was a simple, "Alright."

Jade was standing in the room as they entered, eyes locking with Ent's as she asked, "She told you?"

He managed to nod. They shared a look that only proved Jade had the same worry Ent did. They both knew Destrin wouldn't be able to stop Astra if she decided to do something irrational. The power Ent's sister possessed made it so that if you couldn't make her see reason, there really wasn't any stopping her.

"I thought she'd come back the next day," Tallaman mumbled, eyes to the ground. Ent had somehow not realized his uncle was also in the room. Perhaps it was that he was sitting in a far chair, his entire form smaller than expected.

It gave Ent a small start, and he hoped he was able to hide it quickly as he replied, "She is unpredictable. I doubt there's anything anyone could have done to make her come back."

Tallaman looked up, eyes briefly meeting Ent's before averting once more. "That's what worries me."

Somehow Tallaman actually admitting he was worried about something and not making any sarcastic response only made Ent feel worse.

Jade came up alongside Ent then, putting a hand behind his back as she said, "Well, we can't stop her. We need to stop moping about it because it will not help. If Astra makes a bad decision...at the end of the day, it is hers to make. But we can put our trust in Destrin and we can hope those that are still around her will do their best to keep her from going off the deep end. In the meantime...I think it is better if we use our energy to make it safe *here* if she wants to ever be able to come home. Best not waste energy on the lost."

Ent wished he could put it all aside that easily, but he couldn't stop thinking how he'd hardly been a good example for Astra in this sort of situation. He knew exactly what was going through her head right now, and being unable to stop it only made it that much worse. Still, logically,

Jade was right. He couldn't get to her…she was out of reach. He needed to be as useful as possible *here* and hope his father would somehow be able to get through to Astra. And he needed to not think of his conversation with Tirzah, and how now, more than ever, he could so clearly see some of the consequences Astra might face should she act recklessly. Whatever happened, Ent could not allow her to ever be in Tyron's grasp again.

"You are right." Ameri took up the determined attitude. "The riots throughout Litash have not quieted. If anything, they've spread. With things changing in both Nythril and Merimeethia, who knows what effect it will have? We need to be ready to act."

The whole world was falling apart. Ent kept his shoulders square despite the sudden urge to collapse under the weight of failure. Everything he'd tried to accomplish during The War…the alliances he'd tried to form, the chaos he'd tried to stop, it was all in vain. "I am unsure if we will hear anything further from Tirzah, but I hope perhaps she will keep us informed of the state of the Court."

"Do you think she would be responsive if one of the Ethians remained in contact with her?" Jade asked.

"I'm unsure. She did prove herself, but I still don't understand her motivations." He did not so easily forget how Tirzah had paraded Astra in front of the Court for ridicule.

Jade frowned in thought. "Well, whether her motivations are good or not, I don't trust her. Nevertheless, she is one of our few ties to the Court: It would not be in our interest to cut her off just yet."

Ent agreed, though inwardly frustrated that it seemed once more they were sitting and waiting. The Miadoris was safe, and they were free of blame or suspicion. Meanwhile, Astra was still a country away, having just lost a friend and about to quite possibly make the stupidest decision of her life. What if she tried to save her friend on her own? More than anything, Ent was desperately afraid she would try and follow his example.

CHAPTER XXII

<u>Mariah:</u>

"You want us…to follow *you?*" Gavin's disgust was pretty much exactly what Mariah had expected.

"I am asking you to just pretend to in order to stop any other Merimeethians from dying. You can do whatever you want afterwards," Mariah replied simply, remaining as emotionless as possible. No fidgeting. No show of weakness or uncertainty. She needed them to believe she could do this—and they wouldn't believe her remorse or grief. The only way to them was through their countrymen.

"And how does following you help keep anyone from dying?" Coryn took up the questioning, folding his arms across his chest. "Last I checked, you're responsible for spilling more Merimeethian blood than any of us."

"Because as it is now, the Merimeethian army is about to withdraw and storm Melye. You tell me, how is that going to end?" She crossed her arms as she asked the question.

Gavin scoffed. "Kaeden has it coming."

"And all the people in the city do as well?" She bit back. "And when the House of Allonbrais and General Baradeen begin a countrywide feud for the throne, you think that will end well? Did you forget Louko is currently being held *in* Melye? What happens when it goes down in flames?" Mariah's heart pounded in her chest as she let the reasoning flow from her mouth. Part of her didn't feel like it was really her speaking—

the confidence felt like someone else. Maybe it was Keeshiff speaking through her. Maybe it was her trying to pretend she was him.

There were a few glances back and forth among the knights.

Lucian shifted, clearing his throat. "Even if we help you in the name of stopping a civil war, what's to say that having you for a queen won't be an even worse option?"

"You can't. I have a track record that would give you quite enough evidence to the contrary. If it helps, being queen is quite literally my worst nightmare. I have never in my life made any move for the throne and had been quite happy to let others have it. But Astra was right. I need to make this right as best as I can and she seems to think this is it." Her confidence wavered as she answered, but she tried to keep the facade. *You need to believe the words a little more, you drama queen.* Except soon she really was going to be stuck with the title of "queen." Maybe.

"Are you insinuating that this is *Astra's* idea?" Asher's voice was low, and yet somehow more hostile than all of the other knights put together.

Mariah sucked in a breath. "Yes, it was. I can have Commander Jahng confirm it. She made me talk to my uncle first, as well." She still remembered her uncle's threats.

The knights were looking to Asher now. The physician had gotten to his feet, hands clenched into fists. "I watched that girl jump off a cliff to save your miserable life. She *healed* you. And what did you do? Betrayed her to months of agony and almost to her death." Asher shook his head. "Maybe Astra can forgive you. But I have no intention of being part of your schemes ever again. For the sake of loved ones in Melye, I will not denounce you. But don't you dare ask me for support when you have been the undoing of every person around you."

Mariah could bear it no longer, her eyes falling to the ground. "And that is all I ask."

She could practically feel Asher staring her down. But the physician said nothing more before turning and stalking away from the group, leaving fraught silence in his wake.

"He...is tired," Ivinon spoke, quiet voice barely audible. "He has seen and lost too much in too short a time."

"He's still taking care of Rufio," his younger brother, Farian, added. "Although I guess we can be glad he's not treating Rhumir right next to him. That, uh," Farian looked at Mariah and then away. "That wasn't supposed to happen. We did have him under watch—we didn't even know he'd gotten out until the alarm was raised."

"I do not blame him. I'm only glad at least Rufio is alright." Even if Keeshiff wasn't. It was painful to think of.

There was another round of exchanged glances among the circle. And once more, it was Lucian who took the initiative.

"So what is your angle? You don't really have any reputation as a leader—much less a military one at that." Lucian let out a deep breath. "If Baradeen has anything, it's pride. He won't take kindly to someone without any experience telling him what to do."

"I spent years surviving in the court of Merimeethia. I knew Keeshiff was planning a coup to dethrone our father, so I started making as many friends as I could on his behalf. I knew he didn't like politics." Mariah recollected herself, trying to return to the charade of being ready for this.

"I am good friends with Lieutenant Cederyc and am well acquainted with General Baradeen, himself."

Coryn huffed quietly. "His son. Of course. I always heard he was better at attending parties than training sessions."

There were a few nods around the circle.

"Well, whatever we do, I think it best to stay together." Lucian now addressed the knights. "Let's put it to vote."

Resignation already began to form in Mariah's mind. She knew this would be split, and she did not expect it to be a majority, either. Part of her thought she would feel even worse if she *did* get a majority.

Her thoughts were confirmed when Gavin spoke up. "We already know Grandfather's vote. And to be honest, I'm with him. Keeshiff's been gone for just a few days and we're already putting *her* on his throne? Doesn't that seem messed up to anyone else?"

Exactly. It was just what Mariah was feeling. She didn't want to do this, and she didn't like how it made her look. Not that she deserved to be put in a flattering light.

"But letting Merimeethia sink itself into the mud wouldn't be what Keeshiff would want," Farian objected. "I say we back her." He elbowed his brother. "Ivinon?"

Ivinon sighed, looking at Gavin and letting out a long breath. "Look. I don't like it any more than anyone else, but what choice do we have? I agree with Farian."

Lucian turned to Bandon. The scout had been quiet for the entire conversation. Even now, Mariah could barely hear him when he said, "I'd rather stay in Nythril than follow her back to Merimeethia."

Coryn was next, shrugging broad shoulders. "I don't trust her. But I didn't trust Omath either. I think it's safe to say that Keeshiff was an exception and we won't see another like him in our lifetimes. Mariah will have to do."

Lucian frowned, turning his inspection on Mariah. She met his evaluation without flinching. It felt like minutes ticked away under his scrutiny before the knight shook his head and sat down.

"I say we go along for now. But we should be at this meeting with Baradeen. And if we don't like what you have to say, we're done."

Honestly, it would have been better if they had all reacted like Asher. It was what should have happened, and yet they didn't have the luxury of justice right now. They really didn't.

Gavin muttered something under his breath, but there was no other argument.

It seemed like she was really about to go through with this….

Mariah was sure she was going to sweat through all her clothes. This was by far the most nerve-wracking thing she had ever done, which was funny to think seeing as she had been a literal spy for a horrible person. *Yes, but that had been in your self-interest, hadn't it? You aren't very good at being brave for something that doesn't benefit you, are you, Mariah?* She once more adjusted the collar on her Merimeethian clothing, suddenly uncomfortable in it and the court cosmetics that she had once been so used to.

As they rode through the Merimeethian camp, following the assigned escort to the command tent, she only felt like more of an outsider. There would be no welcome if they knew what she'd done. It made it even worse to know that her brother's knights were riding right behind her, playing along in her latest game of pretend.

The procession came to an end in the center of camp. She could already recognize Baradeen and Cederyc as they stood in front of the command tent, flanked by several other officers.

"Princess Mariah," Baradeen began the formal greeting. "You are our guest. You have come in peace, and you shall be received in peace. Please, come sit in council with us."

"Thank you for your graciousness. May I repay it in kind," Mariah replied as was customary, waiting for one of the knights to dismount and aid her in doing so. They had gone over this before leaving; it was the easiest way to show she had the knights' support. Farian was the one that had agreed to do it, and in a moment, he was beside Mariah's horse, helping her down with all pretense of respect—respect she didn't deserve.

At Baradeen's signal, two guards held open the tent entrance. Baradeen and Cederyc entered first, then Mariah with Farian as a guard, before the rest of the officers and knights filed through.

"It is good to see you in good health, Princess," Baradeen began, waiting for Mariah to take her seat before taking his. Cederyc copied his father. "We were concerned for your well-being after hearing you were behind Nythrilian lines."

"They have treated me with respect," Mariah replied with a dip of her head.

Baradeen's mouth tightened at the corners, the change of expression nearly hidden beneath his beard. "Nonetheless, I am glad you have returned to us. It is already tragic enough that we have lost your brother. I speak for everyone present when I say that you have our deepest condolences."

Mariah knew soft words would get nowhere with the general. Besides an insufferable ego, he wasn't dumb. If Mariah buckled under this—if she didn't have the spine to assert her claim—then it would be Baradeen putting a price on her head. "Seeing as his death was entirely preventable if not for our Merimeethian pride, I find apologies emptier and action more acceptable," she replied, squaring her shoulders, making sure every word was deliberate and strong.

The knights behind her and the officers across the room all went still.

Cederyc raised both eyebrows, but remained silent as his father replied, "We are withdrawing from Nythrilian land with the intent of going home and ridding ourselves of that charlatan, Kaeden. What other action is there left to take?"

"And who is to lead you?" Mariah asked coldly. "Do you really think you alone are enough to stop the bloodbath? Has Cederyc informed you that the House of Allonbrais would not follow you? They are much closer to the coast—they'll be at the capital before you and then you'll have more than just Keeshiff's blood on your hands."

Baradeen leaned back in his chair, but the attempt at looking at ease was ruined by the stiffness in the motion. "I am quite used to taking factors such as travel and terrain into account. I am well aware of House Allonbrais's proximity, as well as their connections forged in trade. I see no reason why we cannot work together to pry Kaeden off his stolen throne."

"So *you* are leading them?" Mariah asked, giving a humorless, almost scornful smile.

Now Baradeen's discomfort was palpable. His tone dipped towards something more patronizing when he replied, "Given that I am the general of the Merimeethian army and the highest-ranking officer in the country, it is only right that I do so."

Mariah knew she had him, now. "Interesting that the one who had my brother murdered would be so quick to stake such a claim. What happens when Allonbrais leverages their trade and accuses you of being a power mongerer who killed the king on purpose?"

"Watch your words carefully, Princess." Baradeen was on the edge of his chair. "You are making very serious accusations for someone with no proof."

Cederyc cleared his throat. "Unfortunately, proof is not quite necessary in this case. You can blame the Nythrilians for what happened all you want, but as soon as the House of Allonbrais accuses you of being responsible—and they surely will—the whole country will turn on you." He shrugged slightly. "Even the army would have to choose whether to back you or to find a safer leader to bet on."

Mariah had been betting on Cederyc taking her side—but had been unsure if he would have the backbone. The flicker of resentment that played in his eyes, however, made her wonder if maybe he was tired of his father ignoring his words.

She quickly took up the conversation. "But if you offer the olive branch to me as penance—if you let me take the lead—I can talk to Allonbrais. I have made my fair share of mistakes, and I understand accidentally choosing the wrong thing. I will not fault you for my brother's death as long as you do not try and use it for your gain. But I have plenty of other friends, General Baradeen, and if you refuse me then I might begin to think you *did* have my brother killed on purpose."

Baradeen let out a laugh that sounded more like a scoff. "You? On the throne? Why would anyone follow you? I think you'll find your 'friends' won't be willing to risk their heads for your aspirations."

"Actually," Cederyc was nearly smiling. "The Princess Mariah has many powerful acquaintances along the coast, as well as with the northern lords—more than even Prince Keeshiff would have had. With just the right push, she'd have half of Merimeethia bowing down to welcome their lost princess."

Mariah, in truth, hadn't expected Cederyc to be *this* supportive. Perhaps her promise long ago to give him a high position in the Merimeethian court after Keeshiff took the throne had been taken to heart. Still, to go so publicly against his own father meant he had to have been very against them going for Keeshiff, if she were to guess. He was blaming his father, wasn't he? It worked in their favor, if nothing else.

"So, General. You have two choices. You withdraw without me, and face me on the other end before Melye. Or you let me withdraw back to Melye with you, and I can end this without any more Merimeethians being caught in your foolishness." She felt as if her heart might explode from the pressure, and yet all she could do is think of Keeshiff—think of his pyre burning, of the years she'd lost with him, and of how this could never make it right. But it could keep it from going to waste.

General Baradeen cast a disdainful glare at his son, but Cederyc's smirk remained unaffected. Baradeen looked back at Mariah with barely contained rage. "You have played your cards well, Princess, I will give you that." He stood up sharply, signaling the end of their meeting. "The army is at your service, and I with it. But do not think that your battles are over. Pick your friends wisely, or you may yet end up with a knife in your back."

Mariah knew better than to believe she had friends. It was allies she had to pick carefully, and she'd lived long enough expecting a knife in the back to be ready for one when it came.

Louko:

Tyron and Louko had spent the last few days formulating as many plans as possible for every scenario. How Tyron would redirect his thoughts—*where* he would redirect—and how, if he couldn't avoid harming Louko or Astra, he would instead go for a non-lethal area. In other words, Tyron could not guarantee that he would be able to *stop* himself, so the plan instead was to merely influence actions. They'd even gotten bold enough to try and force the Dragon out and test it—and by saying *they'd* been bold enough, it admittedly meant Louko had more or less done so...without Tyron's consent. Did Louko hate himself for it? Yeah, a little bit. But it had to be tested. They couldn't go in blind and Tyron had been too frightened of harming Louko to agree to it. But Tyron was, all in all, doing wonderfully. Perhaps it was because he'd been doing this already for years. Louko couldn't help but wonder how much worse it could have been if he *hadn't* been fighting the Dragon. He just hoped that having someone alongside to help was enough to defeat it.

But right now? Right now Louko was alone, bored of reading—if that were possible—and wondering exactly how many years might have passed. Somehow being dramatic amused Louko and helped him feel a little less like he was losing his mind.

"*You.*" The growl startled Louko nearly out of his skin. "Tell me something only Astra would know. *Now.*"

Louko jumped up from his spot to face none other than Tyron—or, well, the Dragon. Fists clenched, Louko immediately began running through reasons he could need such information, the most likely being he was going to prove to Astra that he was alive.

"I, uh...tell her I still want that cat," Louko grasped at the most idiotic thing he could—knowing that was the best bet, even if the very memory made Louko cringe. If Keeshiff heard about that, he was never going to let him live that down....

Tyron's eyes narrowed. "If you are trying to toy with me...." The threat trailed off, replaced by that slow, sinister chuckle that Louko had come to hate. "Months—*years* of planning, hundreds of backups, all this waiting...toppled by that pathetic prince of all people." The laugh twisted and broke into a roar as Tyron swiped at a stack of books, sending them flying into the nearby wall.

Wait. What had happened? Hope swelled in Louko even as he knew better than to ask for details right now.

"Don't look so happy," Tyron sneered. Then he was back to laughing. "You think he actually won his people back, don't you?" He shook his head, grinning. "Keeshiff? Leading a nation? Could you imagine?"

Louko's eyes narrowed. "Then what exactly has you all up in arms, eh?" What had happened? Keeshiff had to have done *something* crazy to get this level of reaction. But if not taking back the country, then what?

The shift was impossibly quick and yet impossible to miss: the real Tyron stood there, eyes wide in horror. "Louko, I-I…I'm so sorry." His voice was thick. "It wasn't supposed to happen. I didn't know. It wasn't—" The Dragon was back without warning, raging as he repeated, "This was not supposed to happen."

Wait. What…what had happened? "What are you *talking* about?" Louko growled. What was something *neither* Tyron nor the Dragon would want? What could Keeshiff have done to…. What had happened?

"And now the timing is all wrong—the moons are not yet fully aligned. But I'm not waiting. No more waiting." Tyron toppled another stack of books, almost seeming to have forgotten Louko was there. "She'll agree to a meeting. Of course she will. And if she doesn't, I'll take someone else—I'll kill them then and there."

The threat made Louko's body grow cold. What could Keeshiff—what could anyone have done to make the Dragon this angry? What in the world was going on? "What *happened?!*"

Tyron stopped, turning around. For several seconds, his expression wavered back and forth as two sides fought for control. The one who won looked utterly defeated. "Oh, Louko, I am so, so sorry. I didn't even know—I couldn't even try to stop it. I heard the news today a-and…." He swallowed. When he spoke again, it was nearly too soft to hear. "Louko, your brother is dead."

Louko laughed. He didn't know why he laughed, but perhaps it was that the words that came out of Tyron's mouth were so preposterous that there was no way on this planet they could be true. "What are you talking about?"

"He…he must have been trying to win the Merimeethians over. I knew he would assert his claim to the throne but," Tyron winced, one hand to his head. "I'm not even sure of how it all went down. He must have been trying a personal angle—meeting with someone he knew before he tried for a full engagement." He was back to pulling at his hair in distress. "I had told them—the whole front knew—he could be captured alive, but he was not be harmed under any circumstances. I had told them!"

"No…no." No, he couldn't be serious. Louko found himself repeating the word over and over until he could no longer tell if it was out loud or in his head. Another strangled laugh choked from his numb lips. No, Keeshiff wasn't…no, he couldn't be *dead*. There was some mistake. Probably only wounded, surely. Right? No way Keeshiff would let himself get killed. No.

"I am so sorry." It was a whisper, now. "I am so, so sorry."

"No! Stop lying, you can't be sure. Have you even *seen* a body?" Louko was shaking violently now, backing away.

NO.

Tyron looked away and closed his eyes. "Both sides called a truce for his funeral." He opened his eyes, staring down at the floor. "They gave him the ceremony of a king."

"Stop *lying!*" Louko screamed. A funeral? No. No, no, no. Keeshiff wasn't dead. He—no.

"I'm so sorry. I wish I was…I wish I was…." The hoarse words fell away.

That was the last straw. Louko broke down and sobbed, every moment with Keeshiff flashing before him. The hug in the Tower at Nythril. The joking in Litash. Him, Keeshiff, and Astra sitting around the fire trying to figure out a plan—just the three of them against the world. The "I love you" that Louko had been starved of for so long. The knowledge that his brother had his back, no matter what. The promise Keeshiff had given to stay safe.

There'd been a funeral. A funeral…and Louko hadn't been there.

"It was not in vain." The heavy statement was of little comfort. "The Merimeethians will follow 'Kaeden' no longer. Your brother united them in that end."

Louko couldn't breathe. He couldn't *breathe*. "He can't be gone." Louko didn't know who he was talking to anymore—he hardly registered Tyron was still even in the room. "I only just got him back; you can't take him away!"

"I'm so sorry…so sorry. You should have had more time."

"Get out! Leave me alone!" Louko screamed, all the pain thrust into the words.

Tyron vanished into thin air without even a word.

Head now buried in his hands, Louko cried for a long time. He cried until there wasn't anything left in him, and then even after that, he cried a little longer. But finally, a small voice inside him told him the crying wouldn't do anything—that it didn't change where he was or what had happened. Keeshiff wasn't here to see Louko's tears, and no amount of them would trick his brother into returning. So, taking a shuddering breath, Louko collected himself and sat up straighter. It wasn't easy. The constant whisper of: *Your brother's dead* echoed in his mind, bringing with it new waves of grief and agony. But Louko remained sitting up. Remained here. Remained strong.

For Keeshiff.

He awoke to what he hoped was the next day, the windowless room about as welcoming as the reminder that he had lost the only family who'd ever cared about him. Why should he be surprised though? It always seemed to happen that way…first his mother, now Keeshiff. Not even Ven seemed to have been able to stay in Louko's life successfully. It made it difficult to fight off that fear—that deep thought that had always tugged at Louko and claimed to be fact: *You will always end up alone. Everyone always leaves. If it's not because of you, it's despite you.*

"Shut up," he mumbled to himself, shocked at the broken sound of his own voice. His throat was still thick and sore from crying. Looking about the unforgiving cell, his eyes settled upon the tray of food and drink that was placed not far from the bed.

Tyron.

The name alone sparked a fiery mess of inner conflict. Another person that had left him. He was the source of all this mess, and somehow Louko's heart couldn't believe it. He couldn't lose Tyron as well—the one person left from his childhood. Not even the Dragon had wanted Keeshiff dead, making Louko's illogical state reason this couldn't be Tyron's fault. Keeshiff was dead because of the stupid Merimeethians. Those *idiots* and their uprisings and wishy-washy politics. The country was steeped in centuries of blood from their own people, and yet they continued to repeat it. Louko thought to the hall of portraits and all of the ones who had ended up dead by a fellow Merimeethian's hand. Of the king who had even created this castle out of paranoia—lacing it with endless mazes and inner tunnels.

"This whole country can go rot in its own mud for all I care!" Louko screamed, picking up a book by his cot and throwing it as hard as he could against the far end of the wall. The hollow thud as it struck its mark was like the hollow beating of Louko's own heart, just a little bit emptier now as he sat alone.

Almost predictably, Tyron appeared on the other side of the little cell. But unlike usual, he said nothing, green eyes scanning Louko from head to toe almost apprehensively.

After a while of silence, Louko's eyes wandered to the mug that sat atop the tray on the ground. "Is that tea?" he asked hoarsely.

Tyron hesitated, then nodded. He sat down cautiously against the wall. The mug between them glowed a faint blue and steam began to rise from its contents.

Louko hadn't realized how stiff he was until he tried to move. Everything was sore: his head, his back, his heart. But he still forced himself up, going over and gingerly picking up the mug before returning to his cot. He sat down slowly, and with his knees close to his chest, Louko maneuvered the mug around to his mouth, thankful for the warmth of the liquid even as he wished he could tuck further into himself and disappear altogether. Then maybe this nightmare would disappear, too.

That's when he noticed the satchel at Tyron's side, and the coat Tyron was wearing…and the swords he had strapped beneath it.

Tyron ran a hand through his hair. "Yes, we leave today," he murmured.

"L-leave?" Louko's grip tightened around his tea. Where were they going?

"The letter has been sent." Tyron's gaze went to some unseen, distant object. "It will all be over in a few days."

"W-what will? Where are we going?" Louko was sure the mug would shatter under his grip now, and he unfolded his legs, sitting rigidly straight on the bed.

Tyron's expression twitched, shifting too rapidly to catch before settling back into weariness. "Nythril. The site. To the end of The Game."

"We…we hadn't talked about this?" Louko said as he quickly put the mug on the floor and got up, fists now clenched at his sides. This wasn't part of the plan—they'd been going over things for days now. Tyron was still not in control of the Dragon!

The same fear that Louko felt was reflected in Tyron's shaking hands. "News of Keeshiff's death has already begun to spread. I'd hoped that

Kaeden could hold on a little longer amid the chaos, but Mariah has already won pledges of loyalty from the Merimeethian army—they will march right for Melye. The worlds are closer to the needed alignment than they will be for several more months." He looked up at Louko. "I...the Dragon already sent the note with all the instructions. I couldn't stop it in time, I-I'm sorry."

Wait, what? *Mariah?* What in the world...Louko didn't have time to process, however, the panic of their impending departure pushed the thought to the back of his mind. He focused on Tyron. "I-I see. Just...just stay strong. Stick to the plans—the strategies. We've talked about what to do, remember?" Louko stuttered, knowing this meant two things. This would either end in Tyron freeing Louko, or the Dragon killing him.

Tyron opened his mouth in reply, only to waiver and look away. It was a few seconds before he regained his composure well enough to nod. "Just.... I need you to promise me, if it comes to it—if you see an opportunity to kill him—you *must* take it. Please."

Louko's face twisted in horror. "*No,*" he said fiercely. "*No one* else is dying, do you hear me?"

Tyron was back to tugging at his hair, breathing ragged enough for Louko to hear. "You've seen all he's done; all he's willing to do. If I can't stop him, someone else must find a way. There has to be a way."

"There is—you *have* to beat him, Tyron! I can't lose you, too—I can't lose anyone else!" Louko hadn't meant to raise his voice, but right now he felt like he wasn't in control of anything.

Tyron's head fell into his hands, staying there for what felt like minutes as his breathing slowed and deepened. "My apologies," he said thickly, finally lowering his hands. "I should not speak out of fear." But the way he would not look up left the statement feeling hollow.

"Don't apologize. Just don't leave," Louko replied, voice dripping with emotion. Tyron *had* to win this—the Dragon wasn't stronger. He couldn't be.

Brow knotted; Tyron tried to nod. "I-I..." The raspy words faltered and he had to try again. "I never wanted to leave you. I..." He swallowed and closed his eyes. "You should eat. You will need your strength for the trip."

Louko didn't dare press the issue, knowing better than to push Tyron. Pushing only made the worst happen, and they needed Tyron on his best if they wanted to come out of this.

But all Louko could do was wonder if he was about to see Keeshiff soon, after all.

CHAPTER XXIII

<u>Astra:</u>

Astra followed her father up the front steps of the manor in Cithan, Tyron's final note in one hand.

Prince Keeshiff killed instead of captured—Black Bishop No. 3 takes White Knight No. 2

King Entrais steals the Miadoris—White Castle No. 3 right three

Mariah becomes queen—White Pawn No. 8 reaches the end of the bottom board, rises to the middle board

Black Queen blocks White Queen, White King is taken by Black Pawn No. 1

Or...

White Queen takes Black Pawn No. 1, Black Queen takes White Pawn No. 1

Two days after you receive this, go to the portal site after full dusk. Have Aelor Ven withdraw all his men to beyond the ridge, and do not bring anyone with you. Be careful that you do not make me take any more pieces than I already have.

Two days. Less than that, by now. Two days to figure out how to keep from losing any more of her family.

"Astra!" Ent had burst from the door even before they could knock, picking up Astra right off her feet and wrapping her in a fierce embrace. "Astra, I'm so glad you came," he whispered.

Tears pricked as Astra clung to him and buried her face in his coat. She wished she was just a little girl again, able to believe that her brother could keep any evil things away. But she was old enough to know better. Her throat was tight when she pulled away enough to say, "He left another note. We only have two days."

Ent's expression was grim as he let go and nodded. "Alright. Come inside." He put a hand around her shoulder as he opened the door for both her and their father to enter. Almost immediately in the entryway were Jade, Tallaman, and Astra's mother, all looking worried.

And all looking at her.

Astra opened her mouth, planning on saying the whole explanation she'd rehearsed in her head, only, nothing came out. She looked to her father in the silent hope that he could help.

"Tyron is bringing Louko to the portal site in two days. We either have to let him through this inter-world door, or...." Destrin trailed off, but the looks on everyone's faces made it clear they understood.

"So we need a plan, then," Ent stated, troubled, grey eyes meeting Astra's.

All Astra could think of was the last line of Tyron's note: *Be careful that you do not make me take any more pieces than I already have.* She felt herself nod. "Yes. M-Mitheau says that we cannot let him through—

that it would end in chaos. But if Tyron suspects that I will not let him through, he will kill Louko and take another hostage." She wished there was some other choice…some other way….

"But we have a rough idea for a plan already—we have no choice but to trap Tyron. We need a place we can have Astra transport into using this Doorway, but that does not allow external Gifting and is small enough to keep him from shifting," Destrin explained.

Astra watched her mother and uncle exchange a glance.

"When exactly is the trade supposed to take place?" Tallaman asked.

"Tomorrow night when the sky is dark," Astra answered, fear already rising until the cuff around her wrist ached. It wasn't enough time, was it? How could they possibly build such a thing in two days?

"How could we even make anything in time?" Jade rubbed her forehead as she leaned against a nearby wall, one hand resting on her stomach.

"Wait." It was Ent. He turned to Ameri, eyes alight. "The cellar. What if we used the cellar?"

…the cellar? Astra looked to her mother, bewildered.

But her mother looked just as excited as Ent. "Yes!" Ameri exclaimed, almost jumping in the air. "That is a brilliant idea—if it can hold the Miadoris it can certainly hold Tyron. We…we will only need to keep the Miadoris somewhere else for the time being, obviously."

"I can keep it with me," Ent was pacing now. "It seems stable enough in the box we made for it, and then we can keep Tyron in the cellar." He stopped abruptly, turning on his heel to again face Astra. Even before he opened his mouth, however, Astra knew what he was about to say. "We will need to figure out what to do with him after."

A chill ran down Astra's spine. She did not want to think of having to face him—of having their roles be reversed so that his life was in her hands. She did not want to know what she would do. "We won't know what state he is in until he is secure," she finally said. "If there is any of him left beneath the madness, then perhaps there is a way to cure it. It would be safer than killing him and risking him coming back in his remaining form, if he has one. Mitheau was unsure how that would work with a Human."

The quiet nod from Ent proved that was all he needed. The lack of argument from the rest of the room was enough for everyone else, for now.

"Alright. I can have it ready by morning. Ent—I will need you and your uncle's assistance." Ameri sprang to action. "We will have it ready, Astra. I swear it." She locked eyes with her daughter and her expression showed a steely determination. Or perhaps, a nearly desperate one.

Astra did not doubt her mother, but she could not say the same of herself. Already her thoughts raced through the endless ways this could go awry. What if she did not bring them precisely to the room? Or what if she brought herself and not Tyron? She had warned Ven against a trap weeks ago because she knew even then how risky it was.

"Perhaps this isn't such a good idea. I have failed so many times before. He'll kill Louko. We've already lost..." ...*Keeshiff.* She'd lost Keeshiff. *I'm sorry, I'm so sorry.*

"We have not lost, Astra." Ent's voice rang with unexpected force. "It will work, and it is our best shot. Trust us, please."

They were all looking at her again, various shades of concern across the room. And yet all Astra could think was that one of them could be the next to die for her failures. She made herself nod anyway, if only for her brother's sake.

His expression showed he didn't buy the ploy. He never did. All the same, he asked, "So what else needs to be prepared?"

"When the room is finished, Astra will need to see it and practice transporting back and forth a few times," Destrin replied. "We'll also need to keep Aelor Ven updated on the plan so that he can send official orders to the troops around the portal site. He'll have them withdraw so it appears that we are playing along."

What if Tyron didn't take the bait? What if he found out about the trap and tortured or killed Louko in vengeance? But what could she do that would not risk Louko's life?

The only way would be to let Tyron win The Game—to let him through. And Mitheau had already spelled out why that wasn't a real option.

Unless....

The room seemed to spin around her. *Unless she followed him through.* Then he would have no leverage, no way to hurt her family, nothing to use against her or stop her. Would she be able to overpower Tyron? Was the strength of her Gifting enough to overpower his skill? Astra wasn't sure. But even as the idea occurred to her, Astra knew her family would never allow it. She would have to lie and play along as if trusting their plan, then turn on it at the last second. Could she do that?

423

Could she afford not to, and risk losing one of them instead? Astra could not handle that again. She had to do whatever was required of her. If her family hated her for that, she could accept it—so long as they were still alive, it would be alright.

Suddenly feeling sick to her stomach, Astra turned back to the doors. She needed some air. "I will update Ven on the plan and return to help."

"Wait, Astra—" Ent crossed the room quickly. "Can I talk to you first? Privately?"

Astra's gaze darted around the room, but she could not bring herself to meet anyone's eyes. Could they tell her hands were shaking? She tried to take a deep breath as she nodded.

Leaving the buzz of activity behind them, Astra and Ent went into one of the adjacent rooms. Ent closed the door behind them. That sickly, spinning feeling grew until it was making her dizzy.

"Astra." His tone was low and gentle. "Please tell me you aren't thinking what I think you are?"

Astra wished he would be angry—she wished he had shouted or yelled or at least been stern. Maybe then she could have lied to him. But his gentleness made a sob bubble up and stick in her throat. "I…Ent, I…" She tried to swallow, to contain the grief that threatened to eat her alive. "I can't lose anyone else. I've a-already lost one brother; I can't lose you, too."

"When I sent you to Merimeethia—when I left you." Ent's voice cracked. "I thought you would be better without me. I thought it was the only decision to keep you safe. And what happened instead? He…got you…experimented on you…please learn from my mistake. I know it hurts. I know Keeshiff dying hurts a lot. But Astra…I need you. I need you to make it out of this." The words were stinted and a single tear slowly trickled down her brother's cheek. "And since when did we do everything alone?"

The last sentence, her own words from weeks ago now come back to haunt her, was the final blow to her already shattered resolve. She couldn't do this. Not to Ent. "I'm so sorry," she wept, wrapping her arms around herself. "I don't know what to do. I'm s-scared. I'm not enough to keep everyone safe. I can't lead like Ven or think like Louko or fight like you. I can't even control my own Gift. Even during The War, I was so *weak*. It was my fault we were caught. And then it was my fault Louko was taken, and that Keeshiff was killed, and now if this fails, someone else will fall because of me. I can't live through it all again."

Ent knelt down and put a hand on Astra's shoulder. "You are anything but weak. I know you're scared, Astra. I would be more worried if you weren't afraid. I just don't want you to make the same mistake I did. Because it didn't make anything better, and it only made me almost lose you, too."

"But how do I live with this?" The question was a plea. "How do I keep going if this Game takes someone else? Death has followed me for so long. I…I don't want to live if this is all life is."

"I don't know, Astra. I wish I did. But you really can't control other people's actions. Tyron tried to get you to believe it was a game with pieces you can control. But those pieces are still people, and we make our own decisions."

Astra covered her face with her hands, trying in vain to tame her ragged breathing. She couldn't think straight anymore. She knew she was being fearful, petulant, childish…and she could not seem to hold it back. "I wish it had been me. It should have been me."

Ent brought her in close, rubbing her back as he said, "I understand. I do."

Such simple words, yet they reached deeper than Astra could have ever predicted. Her brother *understood*. He had felt this all before. It was both a terrible grief and an immeasurable comfort to know that she was not alone in this pain. She did not know if either of them would be free of it, but knowing her brother was held captive by it, too, made her determined to hope.

"I'm sorry," she whispered, arms still wrapped around his neck. Exhaustion suddenly threatened to make her legs buckle. "I-I won't leave."

Ent's sigh was as if the weight of the world had been lifted from his shoulders, and his voice sounded choked as he replied, "Thank you, Astra."

Would he come to regret this? Would she? Astra didn't know. But she was not strong enough to go back on this anymore. Her only option was to win The Game before Tyron could take any other pieces.

I promised you, Keeshiff, and I still do: I will bring him home.

Louko:

Louko wanted to throw up, the stress of uncertainty straining at his every nerve. This was it—Tyron was either going to beat the Dragon, or the Dragon was going to kill him.

Or Astra was going to give Tyron what he wanted.... Louko didn't want to think of that as a possibility. But nothing but dark thoughts kept him company as he was chained and flown on the Dragon's back for days. They rarely stopped to sleep, and even when the opportunity was offered, Louko had found that only nightmares followed him there.

Finally, for better or for worse, they were there. Louko's sense of direction was muddled by so much time spent in the cover of clouds, but when they dipped down beneath them, he could see the wide ring of torches...enough to be an army. They had withdrawn from the dark valley in the center.

Tyron hovered a moment, beating massive, black wings. The lurching feeling of being transported came without warning and Louko had to clutch his stomach to keep from puking. He found himself sitting on a cold stone slab, the now Human Tyron wrapping his chains around the remnants of a pillar.

"Now what?" Louko asked the question to try and alleviate the bitter quiet more than anything. He didn't like the echoes it left him to hear in his mind.

Tyron did not seem to have heard him. He walked around the crumbling stone slab, keenly inspecting every detail. He would stop every few steps to look out towards the valley walls where the glow of torchlight emanated. When he finally crossed back to Louko, he seemed more preoccupied with the sky than anything else.

"Soon, soon," Louko could hear him murmuring under his breath.

Clearly, Tyron was not addressing him. Louko wondered what Astra was doing now—if she had a plan, and what it might be. If she was doing alright…if she…if she'd been alright after Keeshiff died. What if she was about to witness another funeral? Louko hated how much it made sense…his father's bloodline being completely cut off. Very Merimeethian. And yet, it hurt. It hurt so indescribably much to know Keeshiff wasn't one of the ones coming up with a plan to get him back…to know that he was just that much more alone, now.

Tyron's pacing came to a sudden stop. Then he began to chuckle, a deep, sinister sound that made Louko's hair stand on end. Light flared up around them to illuminate the single figure at the other end of the stone floor.

"So nice of you to join us, Astra. I'm glad to see you've been working on your punctuality."

Just like that, all the noise died away in Louko's head. The roaring in his ears, the throbbing of his heart and head…it was as if the world had grown noiseless. He had forgotten how long it had been since he'd seen Astra—since he'd seen *anyone* except for Tyron—and a deep pain exploded in his chest as he wanted nothing more than to run for her. But he was chained to a pillar, quite possibly about to be killed by the man he'd always wished was his father.

Astra was silent, unmoving, her blue eyes wide and fastened on Louko. "Enough games," she said, gaze snapping to Tyron. "Let's get this over with."

Tyron drew a dagger, swinging it idly. "Yes, let's. You are going to open the Door and walk towards me. When you get halfway, you will stop and I will transport towards the opening. I will drop the key to your friend's shackles as I exit. Do you understand the instructions?"

Louko was struggling to breathe. *Don't do it, Astra. Please don't.* He didn't think he could open his mouth and scream the words even if he tried.

"I understand." Astra drew a shaky breath, looking at Louko again as if she could hear his wordless plea. "But I refuse. How do I know this is not some illusion and you're going to drag him with you? Let me feel him, and then I'll do whatever you want."

That eerie chuckle came again. "Getting bold, are we? Fine, come speak to him—come feel for yourself." Tyron stepped behind Louko and he could feel the point of a dagger press against his ribs. "But do remember that illusions don't bleed; I am quite happy to demonstrate if you forget your place."

A chill ran through Louko's body, and it was difficult to swallow past his thick throat.

Tentatively, Astra stepped closer. Then again. Then she was close enough to reach out and lay her hand over Louko's.

Louko actually flinched, closing his eyes a moment and breathing in before whispering, "Hi." It took all his strength to manage the one word, and yet somehow, he added, "Been a while."

429

Astra's eyes welled up. "Are you alright? Did he hurt you?" Her whisper was gravelly.

"I-I'm fine. He didn't do anything—are you?" Louko found himself trying to hold back the emotion, his entire body almost shaking at the sound of her voice.

"I think you have your proof." Tyron's tone had shifted. Louko had heard it often enough to know he was right at the edge of snapping. "Step back."

Astra withdrew her hand, obeying.

"Now the Door, if you will."

Louko watched Astra swallow. "I cannot open it, but—"

"—I hope you didn't come here to toy with me, Astra." Tyron's dagger moved to Louko's throat, the cold edge of it pressing into his skin. "As delightful as our little Game has been, I have rather run out of patience."

"I will take you—I will." Astra's hands were up, palms open. "I can transport you into the Maze. I still cannot open a door, but I have found memories of the Maze that I have used to transport into it. Look, see?" She held up her wrist. "I'm still wearing red-bronze, but I transported myself here. It's all a function of the Maze: It will work."

"Astra—" The name came out strangled as Louko tried to interrupt, but was quickly silenced by a jerk of his chain. *Please. Come on, Tyron. Beat the Dragon. Please don't let this happen.* It was now or never. Louko took a deep breath, forcing every bit of emotion in the next words as he whispered, "Tyron, stop. You're—you're hurting me, stop." It had been the one thing that had always snapped Tyron back—the thing Louko had tested and found to be the truest way to get him back from the Dragon.

The knife pressed to his throat, even if it hadn't actually drawn blood yet, was hopefully enough with how Louko had played up the dramatics.

He saw Astra take half a stride forward only to freeze, terror on her face as she looked from him to Tyron.

Tyron, however, did not move. Louko could still feel the cold edge of steel against his skin, as well as the pressure from the chains around his wrists. Then the knife began to press. This would be a bad time for it to actually not work. Just as Louko considered trying to scream, his chains went slack and the dagger tumbled to the stone floor with a metallic clang.

The sound of shallow breathing behind him confirmed the switch. "Louko? What's…."

"Tyron, focus. We need you to let me go—Astra, please, he doesn't have much time before the Dragon is back!" Louko looked desperately between the both of them.

Astra was still frozen, her lips parted in shock.

Tyron was little better. "A-Astra?" Then he shook himself free of his horror. "The Maze—you said you could only transport me in. Please, is this a trap? Tell me it's a trap."

"Astra, do you have a plan?" Louko broke in. "Just tell me you have a plan and I'll trust you." He then turned to Tyron, whispering. "Please. Please hang on. Remember what we practiced. You don't want to get me hurt."

Astra stepped back slowly. "What is this? What kind of game is this?"

"It's not a game, Astra, trust me, please, we don't have time," Louko pleaded. "We found how to fight the Dragon, but it won't last long—Tyron is both kings; he's been them the whole time and you've been the queens. Please, there isn't time."

A nearly horrified understanding clicked in her expression as she stared at Tyron. "The white king…." Her focus drifted back to Louko. "I'm…I'm the…."

"Astra, *please*," Tyron begged. "I can't—" His voice twisted into something more taunting and he drew out each word: "He can't hold me for long."

Astra's gaze did not leave Louko's. "I will be right back," she whispered.

And then everything went black. It took several seconds for Louko to register that they were both gone, the Gifted light vanishing with them.

Moments passed, the thumping of Louko's heart like the ticking of a clock. Waiting. More time passed, and still no one. No one ever returned. What happened? Had the white queen taken the black king? Or had the black queen taken the white? Astra had said they would be right back…but now it was almost morning. As the dawn came, something else besides the light fell on Louko. A realization and deep sense of dread.

He was alone.

Entrais:

Ent had not slept in two weeks—despite Jade's constant pleading for him to try. He'd stopped sitting down in the cellar after three days, and had gone to pacing in his study, waiting until any word came. He couldn't talk—couldn't even open his mouth to explain the horrible scenarios running through his head. Worse was the knowledge that each and every scenario had played out before, and that awareness left his very skin to burn beneath the scars left behind. Why hadn't Astra come? She had promised—she had *promised*.

The instant the knock split the air; Ent stood motionless, unable to even breathe at the possibility that word on Astra had come at last.

"Entrais?" It was his father. "Can I come in?"

"What is it? Is there news?" Ent launched himself at the door and yanked it open to find not just his father but his mother and uncle as well.

All three faces looked drawn and downcast.

Something began to break deep inside of Ent. "What is it?" he repeated, desperate.

Slowly, his father held up the parchment with its broken seal. "It's...it's from Ven. Louko is alright—he's safe with them." He took a deep breath. "But—"

"Where is she?!" Ent ripped the letter from his father's grasp and poured over it himself to find exactly what his father was about to say. He stared a long time at the words, written so neatly on the page.

Astra and Tyron have completely disappeared. There has been no trace of either since.

He read it over and over again, each time breaking a little further until he felt more like shattered glass than anything else.

"It sounds, at least, like she did not try anything foolish like we feared." His father's voice sounded very distant despite him taking a step closer to Ent.

"As we feared?!" Ent snapped his head up and looked wide-eyed at his father. "This is *EXACTLY* what I feared! I—I—I need to check Melye. We need to find her we need to—" Ent prepared to Gift away, not caring how likely death was as long as he got to the Merimeethian capital.

Then something cold clicked against his wrist. Ent stared down to find a red-bronze cuff around his wrist, in perfect alignment with the scars that were etched in his skin. The whispering panic that had been echoing in his ears turned into a roar.

"Ent, you need to be here when she comes back. If she—"

Everything happened at once. The cuff, draining Ent's energy even as the memories, all too vivid, of Astra screaming for help—of steel piercing his own skin—bubbled to the surface in one tumultuous howl. "*I NEED TO LEAVE! LET ME GO!*" Ent clawed at the shackle on his wrist, uncaring if he was bleeding as he desperately fought even against its power to transport away. He needed to find Astra. He had to stop Tyron from…from…from…. The memories crashed down.

"Ent, please." He felt his uncle grab his arm. "Take a deep—"

Without thinking, Ent decked him square in the face.

"Tallaman!" His mother's voice joined the fray as she reached to catch her brother.

Turning and grabbing his father by both shoulders, Ent slammed him against the wall and growled like some animal. "Get this off me *now!*"

Destrin had tears in his eyes. He did not push back. "No. I will not lose any more of my children today."

"But she's the only one that matters!" Ent screamed.

"That is not true. That has *never* been true," his father whispered back. "And I am so sorry that you have ever been made to think that. You matter more to me than you will ever know."

"Please, please, just take it off. I can't do this. I can't let him have her—you don't understand. You weren't there—please I *can't!*" It became hard to yell, the words coming out between gasping sobs.

"They've already searched everywhere for her, Ent. Wherever she is, we cannot follow." Destrin was crying, too. "Killing yourself will not bring her home."

"*You don't know that!*" Ent dropped to his knees, weeping even as he screamed. "*Please let me go!*" Every night in that wretched cell stood in the front of his mind. Every day in that hellhole and even with no hope of escape there had been *something*. But not now. Now, Astra was likely off-world. There was no hope. He had to *try* to find her or else he would be left every day...every day knowing she was living a nightmare. He couldn't breathe. It would be better for her to have died.

His father knelt with him, one hand on Ent's shoulder. "I'm sorry. I'm so sorry."

"Just let me go! I am *begging* you." He choked on each word. "She's the one that mattered—she has to live, please, I need to go!"

"Ent, listen to me, *listen*." Now his father was gripping him by the shoulders, forcing him to look him in the eyes. "If there is any way to find her, it won't be this. We'll look. There has to be some door or relic or some way to reach her. But if you go—if you kill yourself trying to do this—there will be no getting her back. Do you hear me?"

"I don't care if I die!" Ent shouted, fingers curling into the wood floor as he made fists heedless of the splinters. "I have to try—I can't—I can't live with myself anymore. I can't—I can't sit here thinking about what he's doing to her. I can't keep watching it in my head!"

"I care—I care if you die. I need you." His father did not let go.

"Please, Ent." His mother was somehow kneeling to his right. "Please stay."

"I can't. I can't, I need to—I can't," Ent repeated hoarsely over and over again. "I can't keep her safe, I can't keep anyone safe. I'm no use. I need to at least *try* to find her. I can't. Please, I can't."

"We're going to look." His father said, more firmly now. "We're going to find her. We'll start with Tirzah—if anyone knows something, it's her."

They didn't understand. They didn't get it. In desperation Ent looked up at his uncle, standing just beyond them. "Uncle, *please*. Please get this off me—you *know* she's the only one that matters, *please*, I can make this right—I can fix it, please, just let me go."

Tallaman stared back at him, stricken. He opened his mouth as if trying to reply, but he didn't make a sound.

Ent threw his wrist in the air, holding it out in his uncle's direction as he gasped out one last, "Please."

Tallaman stepped forward, and for a moment, Ent's hopes rose. Then his uncle knelt with the rest of them.

"I am so sorry." Tallaman's voice cracked. "I am so sorry. I can't let you go."

Ent retracted his arm and covered his eyes, completely overcome and unable to fight the torrent of memories that were undoubtedly once more a reality for Astra.

"Why? I need to try," he whispered desperately, more to himself than anyone.

No one argued anymore. He felt his uncle's arm wrap around his shoulders. "I'm sorry. I'm sorry."

Weakened and unable to think, Ent found himself leaning in, crying into his uncle's shirt as he wondered what horrible fate he had let happen to Astra.

EPILOGUE

<u>Astra:</u>

"I will be right back," Astra whispered to Louko, barely able to hear herself over her own pulse drumming in her ears.

This had to work. What if it didn't work? What if this was just another trick and Tyron was going to turn on her before she could escape? Astra could barely breathe. She pulled at the world around her, willing it to wrap around both herself and Tyron, and thought of the containment room in Cithan.

Please, work.

The image of Louko chained to the pillar began to bend, warping into the night sky beyond. The familiar split second of weightlessness washed over her. But instead of the feeling of solid ground meeting her feet, Astra felt something grip her shoulder. *Hard.*

She tried to pull away, to push back, to scream. The weightless feeling crashed down around her and she lost her balance. She twisted away from her attacker as she fell, scrabbling away as soon she hit the ground.

"Do you have any idea what you almost just did?" A voice boomed from above her.

The one coherent thought that Astra could muster was that the voice was not Tyron's. The tall figure reached for her and Astra drew her dagger, brandishing it as she growled, "Stay away from me."

Movement to her right drew Astra's attention and she quickly tallied four people. The woman was armed, as was the girl with wings. But one of the men was so strikingly familiar that Astra couldn't help but stare.

"...Grenedil?"

Astra will return in Book 6

Next book in the *A Daughter's Ransom* series:

TO TAKE A WORLD: THE LAST ESMER

Ovok has The Living Stone…

And now all that's left to ensure the rebellion's defeat is for him to reopen the portal and escape to the other worlds. The problem? After Sven warped reality, the portal now resides in the center of the Underground, where the last of the free people of Baeno are hiding from Skayla and her MindHold.

Except Skayla has been nowhere to be found since the battle with her younger brother.

With enemies and allies changing at the blink of an eye, will Baey be able to trust her friends? And what of the redheaded stranger who shows up unexpectedly through the portal?

About the *A Daughter's Ransom* series:

The TetraWorlds live in ignorance of each other's existence...

One fallen behind in a Medieval time of fantastic and dangerous creatures, another fallen asleep in the comfort of their Victorian age, and the last torn apart by its own Modern innovation. When a dark threat rises up against them—one so quiet that none know to stop it, a Guard from each world must be called to protect their planet's source. But what will happen when these worlds entwine?

About the authors:

NIAMH SCHMID:

Born in Clifton Park New York, Niamh is (unfortunately) a human being. She would much rather be off in some pretend world battling an ogre or taming a rabid pegasus, but instead is currently engaging in completing a bachelor's in Piano Performance. In her spare time she cares for her two mini ponies (or monsters), Freddie and Taffie, as well as her Dorkie (dachshund/yorkie mix) Tobie. She also loves to compose, collect stamps, and dabble in being a very mediocre artist.

REBECCA SCHMID:

Though many seem to miss the fact, Rebecca is actually *not* Niamh. She is a separate human being, who just so happens to also be from upstate New York, also be a pianist, also love animals and literature and art, also have the last name Schmid.... Oh well. Perhaps she's a lot like Niamh. Rebecca lives with her husband and horde of dogs, and spends her time practicing piano, maintaining too many hobbies, and drinking way too much coffee.